THE SECRET JOURNAL

THE SECRET JOURNAL

God Stones Book 1

OTTO SCHAFER

Sound Eye Press

Copyright © 2019 by Otto Schafer

All rights reserved.

No part of this book may be reproduced in any form or by any electronic or mechanical means, including information storage and retrieval systems, without written permission from the author, except for the use of brief quotations in a book review.

All characters and events in this publication are fictitious and any resemblance to real persons, living or dead, is purely coincidental.

Published in 2019

ISBN: 978-0-578-57987-0 (paper)
ISBN: 978-1-7341154-9-9 (hardcover)
ISBN: 978-1-7341154-8-2 (e-book)
ISBN: 979-8-59422537-4 (large print, hardcover)

Cover design by Damonza
Editing by The Blue Garret

Sound Eye Press
www.ottoschafer.com

*For my mom.
I wish you could have read this –
I think you would have enjoyed it.*

Contents

1. Run	1
2. Discoveries Ruined	10
3. The King's Throne	33
4. Old Friend, New Plan	43
5. Subdue the Enemy	57
6. One Hundred Seventy-Eight Ghosts	73
7. The Book	87
8. Money Pit	93
9. Pete	98
10. Clearing Stones	104
11. The Date	115
12. The Cross	131
13. Lincoln's Secret	144
14. Hardheaded	149
15. Pete's Office	153
16. The Find	162
17. Eavesdropper	167
18. The Find	172
19. The Plan	180
20. Chardonnay, Scotch, and Nightmares	193
21. Keeper	201
22. You Must Search, Doctor	211
23. Wrong Number	221
24. Fourteen Seconds to Adventure	231
25. Dagrun	241
26. Down and Up	251
27. The Culvert	263
28. Tentacles	272
29. Abraham's Secret	277
30. This Must Be What It Feels Like to Die	287
31. Prime Focus	297

32. The Birthplace of Fire	316
33. That's Going to Leave a Mark	322
34. The Corner of Her Eye	329
35. Do You Accept?	342
36. The Flood	354
37. Focus	363
38. Trust and Protect	371
39. Feathers	377
40. Petersburg	384
41. Answers	393
42. The Past	404
Epilogue: Jack	431
Acknowledgments	435
About the Author	437
Sign Up to Read More	439

1

Run

Present day
Petersburg, Illinois

Garrett bombed down the narrow forest trail. Roots and rocks jutted out of the soil, threatening to grasp ahold of his foot and slam him to the ground. He begged time to just please let the sun hold fast to the sky a little while longer, but he knew it was a wasted wish. For soon the sun would set, the streetlights in town would be on, and if he wasn't home, he would be in deep shit. No, not even that – worse. Leather-whipped, that's what he'd be. Blistered for sure.

God, if time wasn't wicked, he didn't know what wicked was. Wicked in its unwillingness to speed up when you needed it to – when you wanted the bell to ring, chores to be over, or your stepfather's grueling bug-out training to end. But time was wicked the other way too. Refusing to slow down when you wanted it to, when you just needed a freaking break.

Garrett knew his only hope for avoiding the sting of his stepfather, Phillip's, razor strap wasn't going to be the universe granting him more time, but to beat back time itself, and so he ran recklessly. He wasn't even looking at his feet any longer. Risk was no matter now, as no risk outweighed the doom that awaited him if he couldn't get home before those damned streetlights fired.

It was still only March, but Garrett's odd-job work-history references had earned him a spot on the early cleanup crew at New Salem State Park, famously known as the place where Abraham Lincoln spent his early adulthood. The park sat nestled into the bluffs along the Sangamon River Valley right in the middle of central nowhere Illinois. Stepping into the village was like stepping back to a time one hundred and fifty years earlier. The village was full of beautiful cabins complete with all the furnishings of the era, a rail-splitter, and a fully equipped blacksmith's shop.

After an easy day of clearing an area of cigarette butts with a trash poker and hosing out the park garbage cans, Garrett had hastily stripped off his work clothes along with his steel-toed boots and stuffed them into his backpack, stashing it behind a small pile of brush near the trailhead. He had time then. He had the moments and the sun, and it was all fine.

Now, on the balls of his feet with arms pumping an urgent cadence, he wore a pair of school-issued cross-country shorts and an old tee shirt he had torn to be sleeveless. Even though his worn sneakers were in desperate need of replacement, as evidenced by the occasional rock biting sharply through his thinning soles, somehow they still managed to keep his toes contained.

Garrett had just wanted to go for a trail run after work. On the face it seemed a simple thing. He loved to run, but what boy didn't love to run? And he was on the cross-country team at Porta High. But he knew his love for the run went deeper. Sure, track running, street running, and even that little trail behind the school were all okay, but trails – true trails – that's what he loved, and New Salem had them. Besides, when was he closer to the trails than after work? Never. New Salem was near three miles from home. He was never closer, and so he'd thought, *Plenty of time for a loop through the upper trail section, even going easy – time for two if I fly.*

He questioned it now, as he ran, panicked. *What have I done?* But the trails had pulled at him, hadn't they? Calling to him to come run, *never mind the setting sun,* they beckoned… *You have time. Never mind the rules, you have a watch… plenty of time.* But he knew it was a lie. Time hid from him on the trail and he lost it – lost himself.

Garrett pressed hard for the trailhead as dim light filtered through the foliage, casting long rods of fading sun onto the forest floor. Evening was beginning to give way to darkness, and shadows moved as if alive.

Home before the streetlights. That was just one of many rules Phillip wouldn't budge on. Forget the fact that no other sixteen-year-old on earth had to be home by the time the streetlights came on. It didn't matter. "You will be in this house when the streetlights come on, or I'll blister your ass! You understand me?"

However bad Phillip seemed, Garrett's real father had been an alcoholic who beat both Garrett and his mother. When Garrett was five, his mother had summoned the courage to leave the drunk. After that, his father disappeared, never to be seen again. By the time Garrett was in sixth grade, he was told his biological father had died from a failed liver. One year after the divorce, his mother married Phillip, who was probably the grouchiest man alive. But most importantly, he had never beaten his mom, nor had he beaten him. Now though, Garrett was about to test his stepfather's resolve in the worst possible way. He was about to break the streetlight rule, and not for the first time.

Come on! Push, damn you!

Garrett had heard stories from his older stepbrother, James, about Phillip's razor strap. According to legend, when James was younger, around Garrett's age, Phillip began using the strap with extreme prejudice to issue otherworldly discipline. "You just wait, Garrett – you mess up, break the rules, and it will be the strap for sure. You're too old for him to use his hand. It will be the strap just like I got. Then you can forget sitting, not even on the toilet. You just better plan to hover." James seemed to relish seeing the blood draining from Garrett's face as he paled. For a long time, Garrett wasn't sure it hadn't all just been a bullshit story. An older brother messing with the younger.

Then one evening he arrived home late, after the streetlights were good and warm, and saw it for himself. The image was still burned deep in his mind. The razor strap sat coiled on the kitchen table. Its dark-brown leather was almost black from age, and it was twice the width of a regular belt, only shorter. Dull brass clasps adorned both ends. He remembered thinking there was no way he could survive it… no way. He knew then, despite James being a real dick, all those stories he told were arrow true.

What came next was the lecture of a lifetime. Even now, running to beat all hell, he could remember Phillip's hot breath washing over him as his chest lit with the sting of a poking finger. Then Phillip picked up the strap by one of the clasps, allowing the weight of it to uncoil with a rattle and a snap. Garrett hadn't heard much else after, shut in by the fear of it. But he didn't need to hear to be sure of the message. It would be the last time he broke the rules, or he would suffer the strap.

Now just look at what he had done. *Once just wasn't*

enough, was it? You got to go and push it again. He had finished work plenty early enough to get home before the streetlights lit, and he darn well knew it. Phillip would know it for sure.

He picked up the pace, pushing the limits even for him. He broke from the forest trail, snatched his backpack from its hiding place, and sprinted out onto the shoulder of the highway as if chased by an unseen pursuer. He was clear of the woods now but still had another two miles along the highway, then one mile across town before he would step onto his porch.

Twenty-one minutes. I can do it in twenty-one minutes – if I push. But would that be enough? He glanced down at his watch. *Dammit, this is going to be close.*

With the park behind him, he sprinted north down the shoulder of Route 97. Finally clear of the woods, he could feel the cool evening breeze, a welcome relief on skin fevered from blood pumping too fast.

He tried to control his breathing as he bounded into town, tried to slow his heart that now felt like a caged animal pounding wildly from inside his chest, threatening at any moment to burst from him. His muscles began to twinge ever so slightly, an unwelcome sign of oxygen-starved muscles, a foretelling of cramps to come. Cramping with a mile to go would spell complete and utter doom.

Water, he thought. *When was the last time I had a drink of water?* As he made his way into town, he passed the auto-repair garage on his left, then ran up and over a small hill. It wasn't much of a hill, but it felt huge now. Once he reached the summit, Petersburg opened up before him with its steep, tree-covered hills to his left, dotted with historic homes covered in slate roofs. To his right the Sangamon River twisted and bent like a powerful serpent, slithering its way along the hidden edge of town. Garrett paid no mind to either. He held his course to true north, not daring to allow his vision to stray as he barreled towards the heart of town. Quickly he descended, picking up speed as the National Bank flashed by on the right and then the Dairy Queen on the left. Nearing the center of town, he approached the county courthouse.

"Garrett! Oh, Garrett!"

Outside Double D's Dollar Store, elderly Ms. Pennington was holding a small bag of groceries. *Not now!* he thought. He knew instantly he couldn't ignore the woman. She was a friend of his mother's, and he simply wasn't raised to disrespect his elders. Besides, maybe she would offer him a ride.

"Be a dear and help an old woman with her groceries," she said as she pushed a paper sack of what might have been toiletries into his arms.

Garrett took the bag and quickly placed it in her trunk. Okay, it was going to be okay. That took, what, thirty seconds?

"My, my, you are sure sweating, Garrett. Are you out for a run?" she asked, adjusting her kerchief.

"Yes, ma'am." Garrett turned to leave.

"Oh, honey, I have three more bags inside. Be a dear and help me grab those too. I'm running late for bingo."

Garrett's eyes went wide as he screamed inside. "Yes, ma'am," he said with a forced smile. *So much for a ride*, he thought. Then he hastily crossed the sidewalk in three strides, shoving open the door to Double D's. The small bell clacked against the glass door.

"Easy with my door, Garrett!" a short, balding man growled as he looked up from a magazine and frowned from across the counter.

"Oh, sorry, Mr. Douglas," Garrett said, snatching the three bags from the counter.

Mr. Douglas shook his head with a smile as his eyes fell back to his magazine.

Garrett rushed back to Ms. Pennington's car and placed the bags in her trunk. Smiling politely, he said, "There you go, Ms. Pennington." Still out of breath, he tried again to make his escape.

"Now just hold on, young man! Let me give you something for your trouble." She began digging around in her purse.

Please, please just let me go. "It's okay, ma'am, really. I need to be getting home now."

"Oh, nonsense. Hard work deserves compensation!" she said matter-of-factly, continuing to dig, nearly elbow deep now, in the oversized purse.

All Garrett could do was stand there in quiet desperation, held hostage by an old woman and her purse the size of a duffel bag. Panicked thoughts flashed through his mind. *Razor strap. Why on earth would anyone need a purse that big? Oh, dear God! How much time have I lost now? Razor strap. What the hell does she keep in that thing, and how does she even carry it around? Razor strap. Is there such a thing as old-lady strength? Razor—*

"Here you go," Ms. Pennington said with the perfect smile of false teeth. "Garrett?"

"Oh! Thank you." Garrett held out his hand, willing her to just drop whatever she had dug out of that carryall of a suitcase she called a handbag into his hand.

Finally, Ms. Pennington dropped a single coin into his palm. "There! Now, you tell your mother I said hello. How is she doing? And your father, Phillip, how is he?"

Ahh! For the love of God! he screamed inside. "They are both good, Ms. Pennington. I will tell them you said hello. I hope you win at bingo tonight."

"Oh! My, yes. I'm going to be late."

Garrett took the opportunity to turn and run. As a final show of respect, he shouted back, "Thank you, Ms. Pennington!"

"Oh, what a lovely boy."

Moments later he was blowing out in short wheezing bursts between gasps of rapid inhalations. A dull stitch intensified into a sharp stabbing pain in his side, as if an ice pick pierced his ribs. *Hold on, Garrett, don't lose it,* he thought. Only a few more minutes and he would be home. But he didn't have a few more minutes.

Rushing past Petersburg's one and only stop light, his hope began fading with the last rays of sunlight. He stared at the streetlights lining the road and willed them not to come on. But all his hope was not enough, and just like that his worst fear became reality as – one after another, after another – the streetlights flickered to life. The bulbous bastards were dim at first, but as they warmed, they became bright beacons, like that of a great signal fire washing the night sky, the streets, and the neighborhoods in an artificial light for all to see – for Phillip to see. The soft hum of oversized lightbulbs pierced his mind like nails on a chalkboard. The signal had been sent, and he had failed the simplest of his father's rules – don't be late.

He turned onto Fourth Street, the street he lived on, and with four blocks to go, his hamstring began to cramp. *Nooooo!* He slowed his pace to a stiff-legged limp, the pain overwhelming him with nausea as he dry heaved, but he didn't stop. He continued to hobble as his stomach wrenched twice more before finally bringing himself under control during the final block home. He wasn't in a full-on Frankenstein, but he was damn close.

When he arrived, the old red Bronco was still parked in the drive, which meant his father would be waiting for him inside. The streetlights had been on for a full five minutes, fully warmed and shining at maximum illumination; he noted the light spreading across the front porch and all the way down the south side of the house, easily visible from the kitchen window. He stepped reluctantly onto the old concrete porch and grasped the handle of the dented aluminum screen door.

Sucking in a deep breath, he let out a long, exhausted sigh.

2

Discoveries Ruined

One year earlier
Mexico

"I'm telling you, baby girl, this mountain is beginning to piss me off. It doesn't make sense."

Breanne frowned, watching her father sliding haphazardly down the steep embankment. His hands were still strong from years of working the dirt, but he was no spring chicken. "Dad, please be careful. Maybe you should let me explore this gorge?" But she knew that, even with the sun well into its long arch high across the Mexican sky and the temperature rising just as fast, he wouldn't stop until he had explored to exhaustion.

Her father, the world-renowned archeologist Dr. Charles Moore, didn't know the meaning of the word *quit*. Apparently, he didn't know the meaning of the term *heat exhaustion* either. She worried about her father getting down into the gorge, but it was climbing back out in the heat that really concerned her.

"Okay, now we're talking. Look here, Bre." Struggling to

catch his breath, her father pointed towards the back of the ravine where it met the mountain wall. "This ravine has been washed out by Mexico's rainy season year in and year out. It's the one I was showing you on the map alright. If we're going to find that this mountain is truly a dirt-covered pyramid, this is the perfect place." Breanne's anxiety must have been visible, because he paused. "What? What's wrong?"

"Will you just sit down and rest for a minute, Daddy? Let me look around until you catch your breath," she said, her voice more commanding than even she intended. *Daddy* was reserved for when she wanted something, and right now she wanted him to just stop before he overheated… or worse.

Her father smiled. "Alright, alright. You win, baby girl. I'll radio your brothers and get Paul heading this way with some rope for the climb back up. Shout if you see anything."

Breanne cocked a skeptical eyebrow and nodded. "I will, and please… drink some water." She pushed the canteen towards him before turning her eyes to the back of the gorge. Drawing in a deep breath, she adjusted her favorite piece of archeologist attire, a wide-brimmed papyrus hat. Leaving the chinstrap loose and dangling below her neckline, she bounded off.

When she reached the back of the ravine, she scanned all along the steep mountain wall and the deep washout. Centuries of rainstorms had done a real number on the erosion of this gorge. It was just like her father had thought it would be, deep – the deepest she'd seen by far – but with nothing to indicate human activity. She searched up the sheer wall at the back of the ravine, along the bottom, and along the sides, but she saw nothing. There were no signs of ruins, Mayan or otherwise. As disappointing as it was, there was simply nothing here. It was hot, *so damn hot,* she thought. With a sigh, she turned to head back, but then a shadow caught her eye.

She approached the overhanging ledge of grey rock only a few feet off the ground. *A cave perhaps? Or maybe a den?* The last thing she wanted to do was stir up a mountain lion. Carefully she eased up to the small opening and pulled her flashlight from the pocket of her green cargo pants. As she shone the light down the dark shaft, it was apparent that the opening was a cave, and it went deep.

"Bre, what'd you find?"

Breanne lurched upward, dropping the flashlight and nearly cracking her head on the outcropping of rock. "Jesus, Dad! You scared the life out of me! I thought you were resting!"

Her father stood behind her, his chest heaving in laughter. "I'm sorry! I didn't mean to startle you."

Breanne held one hand over her chest and her other balled in a fist as she gave her father the stank eye. "What, are you practicing to be a burglar?"

"I'm sorry!" he said again, waving his hands in defense, his barrel chest shaking with laughter.

Breanne couldn't help smiling as she retrieved her flashlight. "Look at this, Dad." She sent a beam of light into the small opening. "I can't see all the way to the back, but it looks like it might open up."

"Oh! There we go! I've got a good feeling about this, baby girl." Charles rubbed his hands together in excited anticipation. "Alright, look out, I'm going in."

"Hold on a second! Did you call Paul? Maybe we could wait and send him in, let him see if it even goes anywhere."

"Nonsense. Your brother is like a bull in a china shop. Besides, at last check his ETA was twenty minutes. Daylight is burning, and we still have a long hike back to camp. I'll just check it out. By the time Paul gets here, we will know if this goes anywhere," her father said, already crawling into the opening.

The Secret Journal

"You're so stubborn," Breanne huffed.

"What's... that?" he said, grunting as he attempted to wriggle inside the opening.

She sighed. "I said be careful, Dad."

Breanne watched as her father sucked in his gut, doing his best to constrict his belly as he pulled himself into the narrow fissure. Little did he know she was right behind him.

Within moments, she was forced to her stomach as the space narrowed even further. Lying on her side, she stretched one arm out above her head, her hand grasping at an unseen hold and finding purchase. She pulled herself along, quietly wondering just how in the heck her father was managing to drag his sizable bulk through the dark void.

In the darkness of the crevasse, a flash of sudden memory halted Breanne in place. She found herself frozen, a sudden prisoner of the past. She tried to push it away, but it took hold, refusing to yield. Fighting back the urge to scream, she felt her pulse rise as panic set in. Her breaths came in short and ragged bursts. *No, no, no!* she thought. This had never happened before! In her nightmares, sure, but not while she was awake.

Then she was there, back in the car... back in the snow. Cold found her bones as the tight crevasse fell away, bending her mind to another place and another time. Twisted metal, snow, the sound of tires skidding and shattering glass. She was but a little girl. A flood of guilt raked across her soul. She squeezed her eyelids together until she was pressing them so tight that white spots replaced the dreaded reflections of her past. Slowly, her breathing calmed, and she heard the comforting sound of her father's voice somewhere in the darkness ahead.

"Shit, I've got to lose some weight," he said to no one as he reached out and snatched his leather fedora from the dry dirt floor. He stood, slapping his hat against his leg a few times to knock the dust off before placing it back on top of his head. "Bre? Honey, is that you?" Removing a chrome flashlight from the pocket of his khakis, he thumbed the switch, illuminating the space around him.

"It's me, Daddy," she croaked out, appearing from the small opening, squinting into the flashlight as she stood and began brushing herself off.

"I thought I told you to wait for me. There was no telling where this could have led."

She wiped a sleeve across her damp forehead. "Which is why I couldn't just let you go crawling off into the unknown."

He squinted, turning the flashlight on her, assessing her dubiously. "Baby girl, are you alright?"

"I'm fine, Dad," she said sharply, holding a hand up to shield her eyes.

"You can't worry about me all the time—"

"Well, someone needs to. You certainly aren't worried about yourself." She pulled a glow stick from her thigh pocket, bending it until it made an audible pop. A soft green glow illuminated her frown.

"Listen, baby girl, I know ever since the accident you worry, but you have to—"

"Look, over there," she said, pointing.

He didn't look. Not at first. Instead he held her gaze in the green glow a moment longer, his smile weak and wishing.

She knew what he was doing. Any time he brought up the accident, it ended with her changing the subject. Thankfully, he finally turned away from her to survey their surroundings. She watched as he flicked the flashlight beam to and fro, realizing disappointedly that he was not, in fact, in the man-made chamber of a Mayan temple – as he had hoped – but in a cave.

"Great, just a cave," Breanne said disappointedly, tossing

The Secret Journal

her glow stick down in front of the small crevasse to mark the entry point's location. Then she dug back into her thigh pocket and retrieved her own small flashlight.

From her current vantage point, the space seemed small and the floor uneven. Large rocks were scattered across the ground, having given up their grip on the ceiling no telling how long ago. As she panned her flashlight along the far wall, something caught her eye, and suddenly her disappointment waned. She squinted into the shadows, allowing her eyes to adjust to the darkness. Strange shapes several feet in the distance slowly came into focus. "Daddy! Do you see that?"

As they approached, the ghostly shapes took form, and they realized in unison what they were looking at. Her pulse quickened with excitement – they were *skulls!*

Arcing their lights back and forth, they cautiously made their way over to the skulls, batting down years of cobwebs as they maneuvered through a precarious rock garden. While Breanne navigated the obstacle course easily, Charles struggled.

Cursing at his flexibility, or rather lack thereof, he bent, pulling the cuff of his pants to assist his stubborn leg over a large boulder. "Did I mention I'm getting too old for this shit?" he grumbled.

Breanne scanned to her right. The reach of her flashlight would only allow her to see that the corridor continued on an upward incline to unknown heights. To her left, and much closer to her position, the tunnel seemed to make a sharp bend, disguising its intentions.

Directly in front of them, the ceiling of the cave descended, forcing Breanne and her father into an awkward stoop as they approached what appeared to be several skeletons.

"Watch your head, Dad, the ceiling drops even further

here," she said in a hushed voice, as if concerned she might wake the dead.

He grinned with excitement and pulled out his two-way radio.

"Paul, you copy? Over."

"I'm... here... Pops... Signal... breaking... Over."

"We entered a cave beneath an overhang at the back of the north gorge. Over."

"Cave? Did... cave? I should... Over."

"Cave at the back of the north gorge under a rock overhang. Over." He shouted louder this time.

"You know, Dad, it doesn't make him hear better just because you shout louder," Breanne said with a snort.

Her father shot her a disbelieving look.

"Copy... North... Twenty minutes... Wait for... Before you go... Over."

"Roger that. Over."

Bre looked up at her father and shook her head. "He isn't going to be happy we didn't wait."

He shrugged and smiled down at the bones. "Magnificent!"

Bre squatted down next to the bones, nodding. She studied one of skulls that sat canted and upside down. Over time, a portion of the cranium had settled into the floor. It reminded her of an apple being slowly dipped in a vat of caramel. Next to the sunken skull sat a fully intact jawbone, not yet consumed by the hungry floor. "They're beautiful."

Breanne payed close attention to her father now. She knew this moment well. The moment when he transformed from Daddy into the formidable Dr. Moore. She loved to watch him work.

Catching the attention of Dr. Moore first was the mandible, displaying perfect teeth that begged for a closer look.

Settling into the moment, Breanne grinned as Dr. Moore fell into the practiced analysis that could only come from decades of experience. "You have to let the bones speak to you, Bre. Let them slowly reveal their secrets like a heavy fog gently burning away under the morning sun."

He placed the small LED flashlight in his mouth to free both his hands. One he used to balance his awkwardly positioned body, the other to remove a small, round hand brush from the front-button pocket of his green safari shirt. Gently he began brushing away the loose sediment from the jawbone.

"There, you see this, Bre? What does it tell you?" he asked, removing the light from his mouth and training it on the jawbone.

She drew in a breath, pausing to gnaw at her lower lip. "These are the bones of young adults, possibly children. The second pair of molars is present, but the third have not grown in yet. I would guess this victim to be under the age of seventeen but older than thirteen."

"Good. Very good," he said, maneuvering his body around the bones as if engaged in a family game of Twister – right hand, red; left foot, blue.

"Careful, Dad," Bre said, trying not to laugh at her father's unnatural position. "It won't be much of a find if you collapse on top of it."

"I'm… good." He made a noise that was half grunt, half chuckle. From this awkward position, Dr. Moore began to examine a particularly well-preserved humerus lying under a crushed pelvic bone. "Dental work is great for identification, but don't discount what you can glean from the other bones. For instance, due to growth plates on either end, the humerus is a great bone for age identification." Dr. Moore swept the bone lightly with his brush. "Yes, see here, it is unfused."

Breanne nodded quizzically, giving her father her full attention.

"Now, what this quick and dirty investigation boils down to is this – these are indeed the remains of children, and at least one, probably all, were under the age of fifteen at the time of death," he said matter-of-factly while shifting awkwardly to his other knee.

"Now, tell me" – he grunted, then shifted again. "Oh, wait that's even worse. We had better move soon—"

"Because yoga poses don't seem to be your thing, Daddy?" she mused.

"Right. But you said 'victim.' How did you arrive at this hypothesis, young lady?" He shuffled back to find temporary comfort on his haunches and let out a relieved sigh.

"The damage to some of these skulls appears to be from bludgeoning."

"Good, but what else? There is more to see here, Bre. What else do the bones tell you?"

Her brows knitted in concentration as she began examining the bones with careful consideration.

Breanne felt her father's appraising eyes as she panned her flashlight beam over the entire area again, chewing her lower lip as she paid more attention to the positions of the bones than to the bones themselves. With a slow nod, she turned back to her father, a look of sudden revelation blossoming in her eyes. "They were not just victims, Dad, they were sacrifices. See here" – she pointed her beam at a group of bones – "based on the position of the pelvis over the humerus, and the two humeri crossing each other, it is possible – no, not just possible, almost certain – this victim's wrists were bound behind the back." She paused again, then whispered, "Dad, all these kids were tied up and beaten to death."

"Very good. The precise age of the bones will have to wait for a CT scan, and accurate dating of the bones can be further established with a carbon-14 analysis, but yes, I think we have seen all we can see with the naked eye."

"But how? How could they do something so awful?" Breanne's voice was quiet.

"Oh Bre, this was awful for certain, but in the Mayan culture, young sacrifices, even children, were a common practice, believed to be a plea for rain from Chaack, a god who lived on the fringe of the underworld. Most theories on the Mayans' disappearance hold that their pleas went unanswered and those who survived the drought were forced to flee, abandoning their massive cities, which were then slowly consumed by the jungle, lost to history."

"Well, thanks for the textbook answer, Dr. Moore. You realize my question went completely over your head, right?"

Her father blinked.

"It's different seeing it for real, you know? I asked *how* could they do it? How could they kill their own kids so violently? Look at this one," she said, pointing at the pile of bones. "This could have been a young girl. She could have been sixteen like me, maybe even younger."

"You're right, that went straight over my head," he admitted. After a pause, he continued, "They thought this would save everyone, Bre. Thousands were suffering – no, dying – from drought, many of them kids. I think it came down to the sacrifice of a few for the many."

"Yeah, well, guess it's good not to be a kid in the days of the ancient Mayan, huh?"

Dr. Moore gave a forced smile and placed a hand on his daughter's shoulder. "I think we've seen enough here – let's move on."

Bre nodded her agreement, and they moved cautiously towards the bend. Once clear of the nook they could stand upright, and in fact, the ceiling opened up well beyond their reach.

Her father took a moment to stretch his back, and they moved on.

As they rounded the bend, Breanne froze with a gasp at the sight of a perfectly symmetrical archway of stacked stones. Her pulse quickened as they stepped forward.

Completing the archway was a huge lintel with a carving of a winged beast. She had seen carvings of both the Mayan and Aztec versions of the feathered-serpent deity before, but this carving seemed to fit neither. Adorning both sides of the archway were several giant orange pieces of pottery. The lid of each piece was in the shape of the same winged creature on the lintel, with two tails curving gracefully out from the sides to form handles. Breanne could see the pottery still showed faint, once-artful images, but there was too much sediment to make out anything other than shapes. Amazingly, most of the pots were still whole and in remarkable condition.

"Holy Mother Mary, baby girl, this is it! These have to be Mayan offerings, left here for Chaack. These are offerings for rain!"

They were now close enough to cautiously peer through the archway. The floor of the cave dropped away to stone stairs that appeared, under the glow of their flashlights, to be meticulously cut into the floor on a precision curve descending downward into the unknown.

Dr. Moore furrowed his brow. "Wait a second. This is odd."

"What is?"

"Bre, I have never heard of a Mayan cave having an archway like this or, for that matter, curved stairs cut into the floors. I mean, I can't be sure without a little research, but I think this is something truly special."

"I know what you're thinking, Daddy, but maybe we

should go back and get Paul before we go further." Breanne's voice was heavy with concern.

He looked at her for a long moment, his face failing to hide the battle raging in his mind, and before he even spoke, she knew she had lost.

"Wait here, and I will be right back," he said reassuringly.

"Dad, please wait, or at least let me go with you."

Her father started to object, but she quickly cut him off for fear of an answer she couldn't reverse. "I'm not a little girl, Daddy."

"Alright, baby girl. We quickly, and carefully, go to the bottom of these stairs and take a brief look around, but no matter what we find we come right back up. Most likely this will lead to a cenote, and we won't be able to explore further without dive equipment anyway."

Breanne nodded, sighing in relief. In truth, as excited as she was to see what was at the bottom of the stairs, she also didn't want to be left alone. Not in the dark. Not even for a minute.

A few dozen steps later, they reached the end of the spiraling staircase. Eagerly, they began arcing their flashlights back and forth like lightsabers, taking in the scene.

Breanne's breath caught in her throat, and for a long moment she forgot to breathe.

"This is no cenote," her father said as they gazed into a perfectly round chamber.

The chamber was approximately thirty feet across by fifty feet high. In the center of the room stood a giant stone statue that reached almost to the ceiling. The statue looked like that of a Mayan king or god, and as Breanne aimed her flashlight up at the god king's face, she flinched at its facial expression and the menacing lips turned upward in a snarl. The giant's head was adorned with a flying-serpent headdress bejeweled with precious stones. The statue's arms were extended forward, his palms facing outward as if pushing something. *No, not pushing,* she thought, *warning someone to stop?* Freezing in place, Breanne swallowed hard.

"Not a very friendly fella, are ya," her father muttered, continuing to scan his surroundings from the bottom step of the stone staircase.

Pulling her gaze from the statue, she took note of several beautiful ancient torches placed around the chamber. The torches stood tall, taller than her father, and lifeless, having not been licked by flame for centuries. Positioned between each torch stood a rack of human skulls, which had been formed by shoving wooden rods through severed heads and connecting the rods with vertical shafts.

"Bre! Do you know what these are?" he asked in an excited whisper.

"I... I don't remember the name, but I know I've seen photos before."

"These are known as *tzompantli*. Traditionally these would have been placed at the entrance to a city or at the top of a pyramid, not hidden in a cave. I can't believe this, Bre, there are so many! And still whole!"

Breanne shook her head. "Dad, I don't remember this from my Mayan research."

"No, not Mayan, Bre. Aztec."

"Aztecs? Here?"

"Aztecs sacrificed their enemies and severed their heads, creating racks like these as a show of their might. Aztecs were known to do this, but no Mayan skull racks have ever been found. Jesus Christ! Not even Aztec skull racks have ever been found complete, or on this scale, and never in a cave!" Hundreds of skulls lined the walls all around them. "This will be the greatest collection of *tzompantli* ever discovered. But what I don't understand is why they are here. This makes absolutely no sense," he muttered, pulling off his fedora to run his hand through his hair. "We may have found something much older than we could have imagined."

"Is the great Charles Moore stumped?" Breanne asked, taking complete joy in watching her father struggle with an explanation.

"Yes," he smiled. "By God, yes I am! But the answers are here, Bre, right in front of us. We just need to see them."

"Maybe the answer is on the walls?" Breanne aimed the beam of light towards scenes of colorful cave drawings depicting what appeared to be some kind of battle scene.

"Notice no other tunnels exit this chamber. This appears to be the only room."

"Dad, do you think there is any significance to the skulls facing inward towards the center of the room – towards the statue?"

"Perhaps." He scratched at his chin in thought.

Then Breanne noticed it. On the floor in the center of the room was a circular shadow as dark as night, even when she shined her flashlight right on it. The shadow was directly between the legs of the giant statue. "Do you see that?"

"See what?" her father said, his focus still drawn to the painted scenes.

"Under the statue. There," she said, pointing. "Don't you see?" Then, against the warning of a nagging inner voice and a menacing giant, excitement took hold of Breanne as she stepped off the bottom step and onto the chamber floor.

"Bre! Wait!" Her father lunged for her arm but was too late.

Her foot landed on the hard stone and... nothing happened. "What was that about?" she said, walking towards the giant statue.

Gingerly extending his toes to the floor and tapping a few times, he decided it was safe and allowed the full weight of his own right foot to land on the floor. He paused there, listening to stillness.

"Dad, what are you doing?" Breanne asked with a chuckle.

"The last thing I want to do is trip some sort of ancient booby trap. I am too damn old to be dodging any Indiana Jones rolling-boulder bullshit."

"You realize how that sounds, right?" she asked, laughing openly now. "Traps?"

Her father frowned. "Logically, yes I realize how it sounds. But when you are in a chamber with a pissed-off giant statue seemingly motioning you to stop, a little precaution seems common sense, don't you think?"

"Fair point. Sorry, Dad."

They approached the shadow between the giant's legs and could see it was actually a hole. In fact, it was a perfectly round hole, positioned dead center in a perfectly circular room, a perfectly circular room surrounded by spiraling stairs – this place was feeling less like a cave every minute. Breanne knew she had to see what was in that hole. Easing forward, she prepared to take another tentative step. Whether it was because of her father's words or the statue's demeanor she paused then, suddenly suspicious, a prickle wriggling up her spine like a nightcrawler trying to avoid the hook. Her hesitation left an opening for her father's curiosity, though. Suddenly, his foot clapped down against the cold stone as he maneuvered between the giant's straddled legs.

Instantly, they both realized his mistake as the stone sank beneath his foot before stopping with an audible *click*.

Her father's eyes grew wide. "Shit," he huffed. "Not good."

Breanne gasped, her heart knotting up in her chest, unable to beat. She held her breath as the echo of the click reverberated off the chamber walls.

The Secret Journal

After a long moment… nothing happened.

"Jeee-suss!" her father exhaled.

Breanne nodded. Then, taking in a shaky breath, she slid in alongside of him and leaned over the opening in the floor. Shining her light down the shaft, she strained to see the bottom of the abyss but had no luck. Abandoning her attempt to pierce the depths, she turned her attention to the shaft walls. "Look at the walls, Dad. They are perfectly smooth."

"Impossibly smooth."

"What in the hell are we looking at?"

"I don't know," he said. "Maybe this is a cenote of some kind?"

"It would be weird, though, for the statue and skulls to be part of a cenote."

Her father frowned. "It would, wouldn't it?"

Suddenly they heard Paul's voice echoing from the entrance of the cave. "Pops, Sis, where are you guys?"

"That's it. Let's get out of here," her father said. "We are going to need to get the team in here and all the gear!"

"You two okay?" came the voice again.

"Yeah, we're great, but stay out. We have a hell of a find here."

"I'm coming down!" Paul shouted back.

"No! Don't come down, we're coming up." He turned to Bre. "Jesus, your brother is like a bull in a china shop – better he stays up there."

Paul responded, "Listen, you need to come out anyway. You have a call on the satellite phone, it's Jerry. He says it's important he speak to you right away."

He frowned. "That doesn't sound like Jerry. Is he okay?"

"Everything is fine, but Jerry said he has to speak to you now – something about changing history forever."

With a long sigh, he called out, "On my way!" Turning

25

back to Breanne, he said, "You first, baby girl. I'll be right behind you."

Breanne and her father quickly made their way back to the stairs.

"Dad, did you hear something?" Breanne asked, pausing abruptly.

Her father paused, turning an ear upward. "What kind of something am I listening for?"

"I… I'm not sure."

"I don't hear anything."

"Me either. I… I guess I imagined it." As much as she dreaded squeezing back through the tiny tunnel, she was ready to go. "Never mind."

"There you two are." Paul waved his flashlight in one hand and Breanne's glow stick in the other as they appeared from around the bend. "Over here. I knew I was in the right spot when I found your little clue. Nice." he said, dropping down to his knees, then disappearing headfirst into the crevasse.

"Okay, Bre, I'm right behind you," her father said, placing a hand on her shoulder. "You got this."

Breanne drew in a deep breath and got down on her hands and knees. She pointed her light into the void, illuminating several feet of the tunnel as it sloped gently upward. Ahead she noticed ancient dust streaming from the ceiling like sand poring through an hourglass. *Was it doing that before?*

Drawing a long, slow breath, she exhaled, pressed her lips into a determined line, and began crawling. The loose earth felt cool between her fingers and against her knees, even through her cargo pants. She shivered as a chill passed through her, raising goosebumps on her ebony skin. The only comfort Breanne found in the tight crevasse was the musty fragrance of earth. That and the solace she took in knowing her father was right behind her.

As she approached the tightest spot of the crevasse, her anxiety rose. *Just breathe,* she thought, *breathe and move.* Stretching herself out onto her belly, she shuffled forward and began to pull herself through. She was acutely aware of her father's presence by the sound of constant grunts, muffled cursing, and the occasional flashes of light coming from behind her. She couldn't see her brother up ahead and figured he had already cleared the crevasse.

Suddenly, a soft grinding filled the silence of the cave. It was the sound she thought she had heard earlier, but there was no doubt now. Breanne paused and frowned. "What is that?" she managed.

Her father didn't answer, and for an impossibly long second, no one breathed.

As the grinding hushed, a decisive *click* echoed from deep within the bowels of the chamber, and a single stone tile finished its slow rise back to its rightful position. The earth began to rumble, the ground started shaking, and all around the Moores, dirt and rock began to fall.

"Bre! Get out! Get out! Get out!" her father shouted frantically as he scrambled forward.

Breanne couldn't move. Unconsciously, she clapped her hands over her ears. She heard the shouts of her father and the rumble of the angry mountain as it shook and fell all around them. But Breanne was no longer in the tunnel. She was in a place worse than death, hanging upside down, deep within a memory of terror, a seatbelt suspending her. The rumble she heard now was an engine, and the shouts were from a stranger. She forced open her eyes and looked down at the ceiling of the car. *No! Please!* Blood pooled below her. *Not her blood. Dear God, it was not her blood!*

Music played from the radio. "Rudolph the red-nosed

reindeer…" Not that song! Not that song! Shattered glass covered the roof. Blood-red crystals of glass. The smell of iron filled her nostrils. *God, please!*

Something was shaking her, shaking her foot. Someone was shaking her foot!

"Bre! She isn't responding, Pops!" her brother shouted frantically.

"Bre! Baby girl! Listen to me now. You are not in that car! You are *not* in that car! You are here! I am here, but you have to move! You have to move now!" Charles shouted with urgency. "We triggered a goddamned Indiana Jones fucking trap! We got to move! It's coming down!"

Paul grabbed her by the wrists, yanking her hands off her ears, and began to pull her forward.

Breanne felt herself fall as someone pulled her out of the car. "This one is unconscious, but she has a pulse."

"The driver is deceased." The voice echoed in her mind. "The driver is deceased. The driver is deceased. The driver is deceased."

All of the other reindeer…

"Bre! It isn't your fault! Jesus Christ, Bre!" her father shouted. He tried to push her feet, but her legs buckled.

"It's too tight! I can't drag her! I have no goddamn room, Pops!" Paul shouted in panicked frustration as small pieces of rock and dust fell from the ceiling only inches overhead.

Breanne's eyes shot open. *I'm… I'm not in the car? I'm in the tunnel. Paul?* Paul was facing her now. *How did he do that? How did he turn around?* Dirt and tiny rocks were spilling from the ceiling, and she felt like she was going to fall off the ground… fall off the world! The tunnel became choked as the ground continued to quake. Breanne blinked tears away from her eyes as she finally began scrambling her way forward.

"That's it, Bre! Crawl to me! Crawl to me!" her brother said, working his way backwards.

Seconds later she could see light through the dirt-laden air. As she was about to clear the opening, she heard the sound of a pained cry coming from behind her, and her heart leapt to her throat. As her hand broke the plane of the crevasse, Paul grabbed it and yanked, pulling so hard it felt like her arm would rip from its socket. Then he was gone, headfirst back into the hole.

Breanne lay on the ground gasping, choking, her mouth full of dirt. Even clear of the crevasse she could feel the rumbling coming from inside. *What have I done!* Tears streamed down her face, leaving wet, muddy trails. *What have I done!*

Breanne sobbed as she listened to her father and brother's shouts.

"My ankle is pinned! I can't move!"

"Can you yank it loose?" Paul shouted back.

"No! It's no use! I… can't even bend my leg in here! It's too… damn… tight!"

"I'm coming, Pops!" he shouted, with a soldier's no-man-left-behind determination.

"Go back, boy! You're going to get yourself killed! Leave me and go!"

A massive gush of dirt-filled wind washed past them with a *wumpf* as the large upper chamber gushed shut in a complete collapse.

Breanne let out a terrified scream as the cloud of dust and debris belched forth from the mouth of the crevasse. It was as if a hand grenade had just gone off inside the hole. She thought for sure her father and brother were done for. Then she heard her brother's voice, and a breath she had no idea she was holding escaped her.

"Not a chance I'm leaving you in here, Pops – now push!"

Breanne could see her brother's feet now! Grunts and shouts continued to spew forth from the crevasse as they pushed and pulled together to escape the madness of the mountain.

Just as the two men launched themselves free from the mouth of the tunnel, the mountain let out one final dirt-choked groan, as the rest of the tunnel imploded in on itself, gasping shut with finality.

The Moores lay on the ground in the hot Mexican sun, gasping for air. No one spoke for a long moment.

"What the hell happened?" Paul asked.

"It was a trap. Whoever built this actually had it rigged with a trap!" Her father winced as he pushed himself up on one elbow.

"Are you okay? How bad is your ankle?"

"I don't think it's broke."

"Why didn't you wait for me? You took Bre in there, and you didn't have any gear. No helmets. Nothing. What if that had happened before I got here? Jesus, what if I couldn't have found you?" Paul said, sitting up. "It is my job to ensure safety, and I can't do that if you are going to go all cowboy."

"We're okay. We just wanted to check it out, and daylight was burning. Don't overreact," Charles said, turning to Breanne. "Bre? Baby girl, are you okay?"

"Overreact!" Paul said, surprised at his own violence.

"You... you almost died," Bre said, barely above a whisper. "And it's my fault... It's my fault!"

"Hold on a second. This was not your fault, Bre," her father said with concern.

She shook her head. "I shouldn't have let us go in. It is my fault." A horrible thought filled her mind. One that left her sitting in that gorge, trying to figure out how to get help for her father and brother, who were trapped under a collapse. *What if I had lost them? What if I had killed them?* She couldn't bear it… not again.

"This was not your fault," Paul said, narrowing his eyes at his father, then looking back to his sister. "Not your fault."

Silence once again overtook them. After they lay there for mere minutes, the all-consuming Mexican sun began to extract moisture from their skin, saturating their clothes and threatening to turn them into part of the surrounding scrubland.

As the two men stood, brushing themselves off, Breanne wiped her eyes on her dirt-covered sleeves and walked back towards the mouth of the crevasse. Thoughts and emotions spun asunder through her mind, bits and pieces, broken and panicked. She worried, *did I scream out loud? What did I say?* Best to push all of it away, she knew. Push it as far as possible.

She searched near the mouth of the now-collapsed opening, quickly locating the satellite phone. When she returned, she caught the tail end of the conversation.

"She should talk to someone, Pops. It might help," Paul said.

"You think I don't know that? But you know she wo—"

Paul suddenly noticed his sister holding the sat phone and cleared his throat.

"Found the phone," Bre said. "What are you two talking about?"

"I was telling your brother what he did for us back there, I'm not going to forget that."

Paul smiled easily. "You're my family – getting you two out was never a choice."

"Listen, I am an old man, and if something ever happened to either of you, well, I… I just don't know. God, I just couldn't..." He threw his arms around them, pulling them both close and hugging them for all he had.

"Alright, Pops!" Paul chuckled, patting his father's back.

Breanne croaked, "You're squishing me! Remember Jerry?"

Her father laughed and let go. "Oh, shit! We forgot about Jerry. I think I owe him a thank-you. If it hadn't been for his insistence, we might all be buried under that mountain."

3

The King's Throne

Present day
Petersburg, Illinois

Garrett crossed the threshold from the front porch into the living room with all the vigor of a death row inmate stepping out of his cell to make the final walk to the electric chair. Pausing just inside the door, he kicked his shoes into the pile near the edge of the linoleum entryway. The smell of his mother's cooking triggered an immediate response from his stomach in the form of a deep growl. He had not realized how hungry he was.

His older brother, James, sat on the floor with his legs outstretched and crossed at the ankles, his back leaning against the couch. He flipped the lid of the Zippo lighter open then shut, open then shut, over and over. Garrett never understood his obsession with the lighter, especially since he had caught himself on fire when he was three years old playing with a lighter. The event had nearly killed him, leaving him badly scarred.

"Where's Mom and Dad?" Garrett asked, dripping with sweat as he rubbed at the cramp in the back of his leg.

Breaking his focus from the television, James grinned widely. "Well, that's a stupid question. They're where they always are."

"C'mon, James, quit being a jerk. Have they said anything?" he asked, tossing his head towards the kitchen.

"You're late, asshat. Not sure what you were thinking, but I'd say you're screwed. Now shut up, I'm trying to catch the end of this before dinner." James turned back to the television.

Nearing the kitchen doorway, he could hear his parents' voices, but the sounds of dinner cooking, dishes clanging as his mother set the table, and the nightly news on the TV prevented him from hearing the conversation.

Garrett peeked around the doorframe into the kitchen. He didn't see the razor strap, but he did see Phillip. The tall, stout man was there alright, with his midnight hair cut high and tight. His dark complexion and high cheekbones displayed his Native American Blackfoot heritage. He was sitting right where Garrett knew he would be sitting, in the chair they called the King's Throne when Phillip was out of earshot. The throne was just a normal dining chair, nothing fancy, with the addition of a cheap seat cushion and a pleather supportive backrest to help Phillip sit comfortably with his bad hip. The kitchen was the hub of the house because Phillip spent the majority of his time on the throne.

Garrett couldn't see the table from this risky angle; he couldn't see Phillip's hands either. He could only imagine them clasped, his giant fingers interlaced, two slabs of steel covered in flesh intertwined, resting atop the table – no, not resting, covering something underneath. Hiding the razor strap under freakish mitten hands.

He wondered for half a beat, if Phillip pulled the strap, could he run? After all, Phillip also had an artificial hip, the result of years of hard labor. But according to legend, Phillip could move, and move fast. James said he'd put it to the test once but only once. If James was telling the truth about the strap, then why not about how fast Phillip could move? It didn't matter – he knew no matter what happened he wouldn't run.

Garrett shook himself and swallowed hard. Not wanting to appear any later than he already was, he stepped reluctantly into the kitchen.

The kitchen was not large, but it had enough room for a table with four chairs, five if they had company. Yellow, square-patterned linoleum covered the floor, nearly worn through, its thin factory gloss long gone, along with the luster of its original bright lemon-yellow color, faded now to the color of dull butter.

Once over the threshold, Garrett froze in place, transfixed by fear, completely incapable of taking in the wonderful aromas, the sound of sizzling meat, or the rattle of a boiling pot of potatoes, its steam permeating the air. The only smell his mind would register was the whiff of death.

The stove buzzed as Elaine, Garrett's mom, dashed over and silenced the timer with one hand while snatching her oven mitt with the other. Effortlessly, she retrieved the large pan of baked bread and spun like a ballerina towards the table, having grabbed the pot of potatoes from atop the stove with her free hand. The smell of baked bread wafted past Garrett as his mom rushed to place the bread on the bread rack before finally spinning back in the opposite direction to the sink, where she flipped the pot of potatoes upside down into a strainer to drain. Then, as if speaking of top-secret Christmas present locations, both parents stopped their conversation mid-sentence, noticing Garrett had entered the room.

"Just when did you get home?" Phillip asked.

"A few minutes ago," Garrett said, looking at the floor.

"Well, haven't the streetlights been on for a while?" Phillip asked, his eyes flicking towards the soft glow illuminating the street beyond the window.

Garett didn't respond; his father knew exactly how long the streetlights had been on. His gut told him this was going to be bad.

"Answer me," his father said, aggravation seeping into his voice.

"I… I…" he said, daring to look up and glimpse the table. *Dear God, no razor strap.* He dared a second glance to find Phillip's hands weren't clasped. They weren't hiding anything.

His mother sighed. "Relax, Phillip. I heard the screen door slam a few minutes ago. Now stop with this."

"Bull… shit," Phillip responded. "I have an easy way to deal with a boy who can't follow the rules." Suddenly the razor strap appeared from below the table! Phillip slowly panned his eyes from the strap to Garrett. "How many times have I told you, Garrett? How many times have we discussed the importance of following the rules? How many times should I allow you to disobey?"

Garrett's guts twisted and his heart caught, refusing to beat. His eyes betrayed him, fear-filled and obvious, as they ballooned, fixed on the coiled razor strap. It was really going to happen. He was going to get the strap. Suddenly his gut rolled, and he thought he might be sick. Then he found words. He didn't know how they came, but they came. "I don't understand why I have to be home when the streetlights come on. I'm sixteen. How does this help me with my training?" His tone was passionate, and instantly he knew he had made a mistake.

It was Phillip's turn to look as though his eyes might pop from his head. "Martial arts training, sword training, cross-country, your additional studies, your side jobs – these disciplines take great dedication. I need to know – no, I have to know – you're disciplined enough to follow the rules even when no one is looking. You are so close, Garrett…"

Garrett could tell his mind was somewhere else. He wanted to ask what he meant, but he was too afraid to speak.

Elaine shot Phillip a sharp look. "What your father is saying is—"

"What I am saying is you have to be disciplined, and when you fail there must be consequences!" Phillip said, his voice louder now. He placed his palms on the table and stood to his full height. "The rules are not to be questioned, boy! How they matter is not for you to ask or even imagine. Your sole, singular, solitary, and only purpose is to obey them unconditionally!" Phillip's height seemed to rise along with the volume of his voice.

Garrett's cheeks flushed as he began to sweat. Helplessly, he watched as the razor strap uncoiled in Phillip's hand.

Suddenly, Elaine reached over to the kitchen counter and snatched up her flyswatter. "Mr. Man, you are damn close to a strapping and a grounding, you understand me? Your curfew is set for a reason, and if you're to learn responsibility, you need to manage your time better and ensure you are in this house by the time the streetlights are on… Period. This is not negotiable and will not be tolerated. If it happens again, you will be whipped. No more excuses." She leveled the flyswatter even with Garrett's nose. "Do you understand me?" She slapped the flyswatter down hard on the counter – *whack!*

Garrett blinked, startled out of the trance the strap held over him.

"No exceptions!" She struck the flyswatter on the counter a second time to emphasize her point – *whack!*

Yes, ma'am," Garrett responded, looking down at his socked feet. He knew she was really mad, because she had called him Mr. Man. But he also heard something else. *If this happens again, you will be whipped.* Which meant he wasn't going to get whipped this time? He dared to glance back over toward his stepfather still holding the uncoiled razor strap.

Phillip screwed up his face, then shook his head in disgust. "Go get cleaned up. You're a sweaty mess, and you smell. If you're late again, I'm beating your ass and I really don't give two shits what your mother has to say about it."

Garrett blinked in disbelief but wasted no time taking advantage of the opportunity to flee the kitchen. Once beyond the threshold, he leaned heavily against the wall, his legs weak. He quickly realized he was still within earshot of his parents.

"Phillip, please tell me you were not really going to beat him with that razor strap?"

There was no response. Then Garrett heard his mother's voice again. "I love you, Phillip, and I am grateful you're here, but surely you understand that would break our deal, effectively voiding this arrangement... permanently."

"Not here, Elaine," Phillip responded in an oddly deadpan tone.

"He is getting older, you know. He is going to start to questio—"

"Not... here," he said again, absolute. Then he lowered his voice.

Garrett leaned in, straining to hear.

"All things in time."

Arrangement? Garrett thought. She sounded strange too

The Secret Journal

– they both did – but he couldn't put his finger on it. The sound of footsteps coming towards him from the kitchen broke his trance, and he moved away from the door. *Don't be stupid now, Garrett. You're lucky to be alive,* he thought. *Holy shit, am I really in the clear?* All he knew for sure was that he owed his mom big time for this one.

After washing up, Garrett headed back toward the kitchen but was intercepted by James. "You know, when I was your age, I would have been slaughtered for showing up one second after the streetlights came on, and you show up like ten minutes late and somehow you manage to skate out of there without a scratch."

Garrett was no longer in the mood for his older brother's crap. "Oh yeah, and when I'm your age, I'm going to have a car, a girl, *and* a house, and not be living at home with my mommy and daddy till I'm like thirty." He attempted to push his way past to get to the kitchen. James blocked his brother's move, placed a hand on top of his shoulder, and pinched ahold of the neck muscle with a ridiculous grip, dropping Garrett to his knees instantly.

"I'm not thirty, asswipe," James said between clenched teeth.

"Ahhh… uncle, uncle!" Garrett pleaded, trying to break his grip but failing miserably.

"What in the Sam Hill are you guys doing in there?" their father yelled. "It's time to eat."

Over dinner, Garrett's father yelled at him twice for chewing his food too loudly, and yelled at James once for being too finicky and not allowing any of the food on his plate to touch. The round steak could not touch the potatoes, and the potatoes could not touch the green beans. Frustrated, his father asked, "What the hell does it matter if your food touches or doesn't touch? It's all going to the same place anyway. And I got news for you, son, it's all going to touch when it gets there."

"Oh, Phillip, leave him alone if he doesn't want his food to touch," Elaine said, turning her attention to Garrett. "Eugene called today and asked if you would be available to help him with some yard work this Saturday. I told him you would and that you would bring some friends, maybe Peter and Lenny?"

"Yeah, Mom, that sounds great! What does he need us to do?" Garrett was not one to turn down any opportunity for extra work, and his cleanup job at the park was only after school. Besides, he really liked Eugene.

"Well, he can give you the details Saturday, but I think you will be digging up a stump in the backyard. He mentioned using the hole to put in a goldfish pond." Elaine passed the mashed potatoes to James, who carefully segregated the potatoes from the other food on his plate.

Phillip sighed, shaking his head.

Taking a bite of his round steak, Garrett said, "Okay, I'll get a couple buddies together, and we'll knock it out for him."

Through clenched teeth, Phillip stabbed at the air with his fork in Garrett's direction. "For the third time, stop smacking your lips while you eat, and chew with your mouth closed. After dinner help your mother clear the table, feed the rabbits, and do the rest of your chores, then practice your sword for one hour. Study geography and plant foraging for thirty minutes each. I want you to focus locally. Seeing as how you like to ignore the rules by staying out late to run, tomorrow night you will be practicing emergency bug-out techniques. I want you to map three separate routes that will take you ten miles out from the house with no human contact. If I deem one of your routes acceptable, then you will navigate it tomorrow night. This land navigation will require the use of stars. No compass this time, so you better pay special attention to the topography maps as you plan."

Garrett frowned. *No compass and in the dark?*

His father paused, frowning back across the table as if he could read Garrett's mind. "That's right. No compass. James won't know your route, and he will track you. I will pick you up at the end of the route at a designated time. If you miss the cutoff or if James is successful in tracking you, you will get to hike back home, getting even less sleep. This exercise will also double as sleep-deprivation training."

"Yes, sir," Garrett said. He knew James would be able to track him no matter how careful he was – somehow, he always could. What Garrett didn't know was how Phillip knew he was late because he had been running. For the remainder of dinner, the family sat eating in silence, and Garrett was careful to chew his food with his mouth shut.

As Garrett and his mother cleared the table, Garrett made use of the private moment to ask one of many questions that had been bothering him. "Do you think other kids are practicing bug-out techniques?"

"Why do you ask?"

"Well, I think between James and me, we pick some of the best routes for a bug-out, and I have never seen anyone else on them. I've never seen tracks from anyone either. Also… well…" Garrett paused.

"Well, what?"

"I've never heard other kids talk about their bug-out practice," he said carefully.

"Garrett, you know the answers to these questions. You know the rules say we don't talk of these things outside the family. Don't you think their rules say the same?"

"I suppose so," Garrett said, wringing out a rag. He did suppose, but he wasn't convinced.

"Listen to me," his mother said softly. "All kids have their own trainings and practice. Yours may be different, that's all." She turned from the table, hands full of silverware. As she placed the silverware in the sink, she glanced back at him with a look of serious appraisal and asked, "Have you been asking your friends about their training?"

"No! No, ma'am. Of course not. I was just curious."

"Careful with curiosity – it can be a dangerous thing," she said, placing the last dish in the sink. "Now run along, feed the rabbits, and get to your training."

4

Old Friend, New Plan

One year earlier
Mexico

Breanne handed her father the satellite phone, and he accepted it with a pained grunt.

"Jerry, is everything okay?" he asked anxiously, placing a hand on his lower back and twisting.

He nodded. "Oh yeah, we're okay here, but you are part of the reason for that. If you hadn't called when you did, we wouldn't have been on our way out. What's happening on your end?"

Her father listened for a moment. "Oak Island in Nova Scotia? Jerry, there's nothing on Oak Island except wishful thinking – please tell me you're not asking me to participate in the next Oak Island reality show."

Breanne arched an eyebrow.

Her father returned her look with a shrug and continued to listen to Jerry. "So you're telling me there was a legit team there doing *real* archeology?"

Breanne watched as an incredulous look spread across her father's face. "Daddy, what is he saying?"

"My God," was all he could get out. "My God, my God. On Oak Island? And have they performed carbon dating?" Dr. Moore asked with all the seriousness of a priest taking confession.

As her father began to pace, Breanne began to pace with him.

"So, what, they just disposed of them? And then buried—"

Breanne shot Paul a frustrated look. "Daddy? What is it? What did they find?"

"But I don't understand. You're telling me the Knights Templar…" He looked over his shoulder as if expecting to see someone there spying, then he spoke in a lowered voice. "Who is funding this thing anyway?"

Breanne had positioned herself so close to her father she could almost hear what Jerry was saying… almost.

Paul laughed, shaking his head at her tenacity.

"What do you mean you can't tell me who he is? You expect me to just drop what I got going here, come to Oak Island, and lead an expedition for some secret funder I know nothing about?" Her father spun in a circle, nearly running into her, the phone pulling away from his ear as he flailed for balance.

That was the opening she was waiting for. Breanne dodged with precision timing, reached around her father, and pressed the speaker button on the satellite phone.

He blinked at her, unamused, as Jerry's voice filled the gorge with his regal British accent. "There are some rules to this, some things you will need to agree to in order to lead this. There is a plane waiting for you at the airport – how soon can you get there?"

"Wait a minute! I can't leave here now! I just made a huge

discovery – I almost died. This might be one of the greatest discoveries of my career—"

"Charles, you know I wouldn't be feeding you codswallop. *This* will be the greatest bloody discovery of your career. We already pulled the team out. It will only be you and your sons. Completely secret, and you will be able to publish anything you find on the island, including the recent discoveries. And dammit, man, you said it yourself – *you owe me!* For what I've no idea, but nevertheless! You'll have full funding, Charles, anything you need – now get your arse here."

"But Breanne. She's here now. She graduated high school two years early. She's planning to spend a year with me before college. I can't just—"

"Breanne, yes. Brilliant girl. Well, bring her with you."

Breanne's chin jutted upward at the compliment as she nodded in agreement.

"This site, Jerry, I can't just leave it. We made a hell of a discovery." He quickly brought Jerry up to speed.

Breanne observed her father as he stared back at the newly collapsed entrance. His face dropped like a brick as his emotions flipped from elation at being alive to gut-wrenching disappointment.

"Charles, listen to me, old chap, if I am understanding you correctly, your remarkable find is buried under God only knows how much rubble, and will take God only knows how long to dig out. I have all your travel arrangements made. Put a team in place there to handle your affairs, stop faffing about, and get to Oak Island," Jerry begged. "Have you talked to Sarah? She would be perfect to lead a team there – you should call her."

Breanne smiled again and nodded.

An awkward silence filled the line, bouncing off some unassuming satellite before finding its way back to earth.

Jerry was right, and she knew it. Her dad should call Sarah. Why did adults have to be so difficult?

"Listen, chum. Despite how things were left between you two, can you think of anyone better to lead a team on this specific site? After all, she is a bloody speleologist – the best in her field. You need the expertise of someone who specializes in cave archeology, someone like Sarah."

Paul and Breanne shared a look that said, *You tell him, Jerry!*

"Charles?" Jerry said. "Are you there?"

Dr. Moore pulled off his fedora and ran his hands up his face and through his hair. "I'll do it. I'll come to Oak Island."

∼

In the airport terminal Breanne sat across from her father, journaling her harrowing Mexico expedition on her laptop. She had another motive for sitting as close as she could to her father, though – to eavesdrop on his conversation with Sarah. Her father had refused to elaborate any further on the Oak Island finds. Instead he told her a little patience would be good for her. It was a load of crap. To make matters worse, she knew almost nothing about Oak Island. Ask her about Egypt, Mexico, South America, or any number of archeological hot spots, and she was practically an expert... but Oak freaking Island?

Paul and her other brother, Edward, returned from a coffee run, bringing her a raspberry iced tea. She paused, the plastic cup cold in her hand, careful not to let the condensation drip on her computer keys, thinking about Sarah and her father. Sarah was one of the reasons she wanted to become an archeologist. Sure, her father was a powerful influence, but Sarah – Sarah was a vision of independence and strength. She traveled the world leading digs, and she was brilliant too. Breanne thought about the summers she got to work alongside Sarah when she would visit her father's digs. She had learned so much from Sarah, and not just about archeology. They talked, really talked.

Breanne was so disappointed when her father had blown it. She just didn't understand why. She watched him now; he looked like he was going to be sick. *Serves him right,* she thought. He had left Sarah on a site in Egypt. Walked off and didn't even tell her he was going.

That he loved Sarah was plain, but something had held him back when he had the chance. She knew what it was, but her mother had been gone for over six years. A woman like Sarah wouldn't wait forever. Since her mother passed, he had never shown interest in anyone else, only Sarah.

As the conversation continued, she saw him relax. Soon enough, as they got onto the business of the site, his voice was eager and filled with enthusiasm. From what she gathered, Sarah would have her own team in place inside of a week.

Breanne looked to her left and saw she wasn't the only one watching. Paul and Edward were watching too; both nodded toward their father as they all shared a smile that needed no explanation.

∼

The jet engine droned a soft hum as Breanne slept, her head leaning against the oval window. To anyone watching, she would seem deep in a state of peaceful rest, but peace seldom visited her in her dreams. Today was no different.

The tan leather of the oversized passenger seat looked warm but felt cold on her bare legs. As she looked to the left, her mother smiled and said something. Not talking… singing. All around her, snow-covered cornfields. Blacktop.

Tires screeching. Her mother screamed. Breanne felt her body go upside down. Glass rained over her. She screamed. A hand on her shoulder, shaking her.

"Baby girl. Bre. Wake up. It's okay. It's okay – you're on a plane."

Breanne gasped, "Daddy?" She sat up, orienting herself.

"Nightmare again?" he asked.

She didn't answer.

"Are you okay? You want to talk about it?"

"No, Dad. I'm fine, really."

He gave her a skeptical look.

Shaking off the all too familiar nightmare, she stretched her arms and let out a long yawn.

"Bre, you can talk to me," her father said, searching her eyes.

She turned away towards the window and peered onto the checkered fields of the Midwest.

At barely sixteen Breanne had graduated high school. Even with a year off after graduation to spend working in the field with her father, she was on course to earn her PhD before her twenty-third birthday. In one year, she would be reporting to Columbia University, his alma mater. Once there, she would begin studying for a career that would no doubt bring her a fulfilling future full of mystery, travel, and adventure. Her mother's death had been difficult on them all, but for Breanne… there were just no words. Rather than the horrible tragedy extinguishing the drive within her, it fed it, manifesting in an insatiable determination to not only learn but master academia in the field of archeology. Breanne pushed herself beyond what was ordinary, perhaps even beyond what was healthy.

Despite her father abandoning the Mexico site, there was nowhere else she would rather be. Okay, well, not abandoning it, but opting to hand it off to peruse Oak Island. *But*

Oak Island?! How did that even make sense? Well, regardless, she was happy to be with him, but she would have researched the crap out of this place if she had known. She'd tried to do some research at the airport, but the internet refused to cooperate. She hated not being in the know. "Well, since you won't tell me why you're dragging us to this Oak Island place instead of staying in Mexico, on a *real* site, will you at least tell me something about where we're going?" she asked in an effort to change the subject from her nightmares.

He smiled. "I want to surprise you, and like I said, consider it payback for when I was on the phone with Jerry."

"The plane won't land for another hour... Please, Daddy," she whined. Resorting to the whine always worked on Charles.

Her father's shoulders bounced as he chuckled. "Yes, dear. Yes, of course. How could I say no to such a persuasive request?"

She smiled – she had him. *Works every time.*

"It's quite the story, actually. Legend has it that in 1795 a young man in a small fishing boat noticed lights coming from the island and decided to investigate. Searching, he did not find the source of the lights, but instead found a clearing where he suspected the lights had originated. In the clearing, he discovered a depression under an old oak tree. He also noticed scarring on one of the old oak's thick branches, directly above the depression. It was as if something had been lowered from the branch, possibly using a block-and-tackle rope system. Deducing he may have stumbled onto a pirate's secret treasure stash, he left, returning the next day with two friends, pickaxes, and shovels. And so began the first dig in what would later become known as the legendary Money Pit."

Breanne frowned skeptically. "Well, did they find anything?"

"Indeed," he nodded.

"Well!" she said, shifting in her seat to face him fully.

Again, her father's shoulders began to bounce as his barrel chest rumbled with laughter. "I think you might be the most impatient person I have ever met. Do you know that?" he asked between breaths as he took full enjoyment in her misery.

"And you must be the *slowest* storyteller I have ever met!" Breanne said, slapping her father on the shoulder in mock annoyance.

Her father threw a hand over his shoulder and winced, feigning injury. "My dear child, someone… Oh, who was it?" He paused again, pretending to consider.

Breanne rolled her eyes dramatically.

"Well, I forget who, but someone," he continued, "once said, if history were only taught in the form of stories, it would never be forgotten."

Breanne batted at the air. "I have a saying too. If my dad was the only guy on earth in charge of teaching history and chose to do it with stories… well, the world wouldn't have many stories. Will you please just get on with it?" she begged.

"Alright, alright," he said, holding his hands up in surrender. "Well, as the young men began to dig, they quickly realized they were onto something, as evident by the pick marks scarring the walls of the pit. At ten feet, they hit a layer of flagstone, sparking immediate excitement, followed by the discovery of a layer of wood logs directly below the stones. They knew they were about to discover something wonderful! After all, why in the hell would you put logs so deep in the ground if not to hide something? After much effort, the logs were removed, but to the disappointment of the men, they only discovered more dirt below."

"That's it?" Breanne interrupted.

"No, that's not it." He smiled. "They kept digging, and around twenty feet, they found that another layer of wooden logs was blocking their way. Finally, at around thirty feet, the men uncovered a *third* platform of logs. When the men found only dirt beneath the third platform of logs, they recognized they were not equipped to continue their quest. Now convinced more than ever that a pirate's ill-gotten gains must lie somewhere below, the men vowed to one day return and continue the hunt when they were better prepared."

"You're kidding me! They just gave up?"

"Bre, I know you have been on digs with me, but honestly, have you ever tried digging down to thirty feet with nothing but a shovel? I know I haven't."

"Well, no, but they couldn't have just given up."

"It took the men nine years to return, but when they did, they did so with a partner and financial backing. They began digging again, and this time they were better equipped and able to dig much deeper. As the men pressed on, they continued to encounter the strange wood platforms around every ten feet. In addition, the men discovered bizarre layers of material at various depths, such as coconut fiber, some sort of putty, and charcoal. Finally, at a depth of almost ninety feet, they found a remarkable stone with markings unlike anything they had ever seen sitting on top of yet another wood platform. Legend has it that the stone inscription, translated years later, read, 'Forty feet below, two million pounds of gold.'"

Breanne's eyes widened.

"The men were excited, wanting so badly to continue, feeling they must be within reach of the treasure, but the sun had begun to set, plunging the pit into complete darkness. The escalated risk of working in the pit after dark was just too dangerous, so they decided to abandon the dig for the evening. They would get a fresh start the next morning at sunup and claim the prize they had worked so hard to retrieve. But the following morning they returned to the pit to find it had flooded, filling all but the first thirty feet with water."

"Oh, no!" Breanne said.

"Oh, yes, and after several desperate attempts, the men realized that no matter how hard they tried, they could not remove the water fast enough, and the pit continued to fill. Ultimately, the men admitted defeat and were forced to abandon the dig."

"That's awful! All that work and for nothing," she said, throwing herself back in her seat in disappointment.

"For these men, I'm afraid it was, but that was to be only the beginning of the story. Over the next couple hundred years, many more attempts to reach the bottom of the pit took place, but all ended in disappointment. In addition to the Money Pit, treasure seekers expanded their search of the island, making many discoveries, which all seemed to lead to more questions and ever-changing theories, but never to the treasure itself. Excavations continued from the mid-1800s all the way through to the present day, but all were unsuccessful. In total, six lives were lost over the years."

Breanne leaned forward again. "Six lives? That's horrible."

Her father nodded. "The biggest obstacle thwarting treasure seekers' attempts to get to the bottom of the mystery was *water*. Every time they exceeded ninety feet, water flooded the pit at an estimated rate of one thousand gallons a minute – too fast for a pump to keep up with. An attempt to dig a second shaft adjacent to the original pit also failed, ending in collapse."

Breanne shook her head in disbelief. "How crazy is it people are willing to spend so much money and even die for a rumored treasure based on hearsay from three hundred years ago! All with no facts to support such an investment."

Charles nodded, smiling. "You're my daughter alright. You see things through the logic of a scientist. But humans are curious beings by nature, and thus have a primitive need to discover – to understand. Now, while the island has been stubborn about yielding its secrets over the years, it has slowly given up tiny nibbles, just enough to keep treasure-hungry hunters foraging for another bite."

Breanne laughed. "Like what kind of tiny nibbles?"

"Now, this is all legend, and I don't put much weight in legend. Allegedly, in the mid-1800s treasure hunters discovered coconut fiber under the rocky sands of a beach located on the north side of Oak Island, in an area known as Smith's Cove. Further investigation led to the discovery of five separate tunnels that all connected to one main tunnel leading away from the beach west towards the Money Pit. Later, theorists speculated that the man-made tunnels were filled with stone, covered in coconut fiber, and hidden beneath the sands of Smith's Cove. It was likely that these small tunnels fed water from the ocean all the way to the Money Pit, connecting at a depth of around ninety feet—"

"A trap!" Breanne exclaimed, putting it together before he could finish explaining. "That's why they couldn't get past ninety feet – why they couldn't bail the water fast enough. It was designed to flood!"

"Precisely! The tunnel flood system was the perfect booby trap for would-be treasure hunters. The discoveries at Smith's Cove led to theories that more flood tunnels may exist."

Breanne's interest was growing as she allowed herself to be drawn into the mystery.

"Other examples included interesting material allegedly pulled from impossible depths on the end of drill bits or sample plugs. These strange items included gold chain links, pieces of parchment with some kind of writing on it, mysterious metal pieces, and pieces of wood. Then there were the stones with strange markings arranged in all sorts of shapes, from a giant cross to strange triangles, positioned in various locations all over the island. No one knew for sure what any of the markings or arrangements meant, but everyone had theories."

A moment of stillness passed between them as her mind raced; the only sound was the even drone of the plane's engines. Something wasn't adding up. She opened her mouth to ask the nagging question, but her father continued before she could articulate it.

"Finally, there's the swamp."

"Swamp?" she asked with a shrug.

"Yes, the swamp. Similar to Smith's Cove, it's just out of place and oddly shaped – like a perfect triangle. It sits in a low spot, nearly splitting the island in two. It's only around eight feet deep, but all attempts to drain it have been unsuccessful. Treasure hunters have always theorized the swamp to be a large part of the mystery. People have said it symbolizes a woman's womb or that it hides the Holy Grail, Templar treasures, Freemason connections, possibly a pirate ship. One theory even claimed the swamp to be the secret hiding place for Shakespeare's lost works."

Breanne blurted out a chortle of laughter. "Shakespeare's lost works! Daddy, that's ridiculous!"

"Indeed. But ridiculous or not, this island has captivated many treasure hunters to the point of losing not only their life's savings, but their own lives to the quest."

Breanne raised a skeptical eyebrow. "Okay, fine, but my father, the great Dr. Charles Moore, world-renowned archeologist, the best in his field, would not for one minute believe that there was *anything* more than fabricated legend and clever hoax associated with a story like this. So please, tell me, Dr. Moore, why are you buying into this? What do you really know that you're not saying?"

The Secret Journal

He smirked. "You know, sometimes your cleverness scares me. Not only do you detect there must be something more, but then you try and flatter me. And you're right, associating myself with a wild treasure hunt on the scale of Captain Kidd's treasure or the Lost Dutchman Mine is a good way to ruin my reputation as a credible archeologist. In fact, I would be smart to have run the other way. Most everything that had supposedly been found has either disappeared over the years or become nothing more than a combination of legend and hearsay."

"So why? Why risk your reputation? Why waste our season on something you couldn't possibly be interested in?" There was no more laughter in her voice, only concern.

He hesitated and drew in a long breath. She was serious, and he knew it. "You're right, Bre. I've never had any interest in having an association with this island, and for good reason. Up until a year ago, there was no proof of physical evidence – if it ever *really* existed in the first place."

"Until a year ago?" she asked, the words not escaping her sharp ears. "Then what? What is it?" she begged.

He leaned in close and whispered in her ear. "I am not going to tell you."

"Daddy!" she said, pulling away.

"Don't *Daddy* me. I think a little adventure will be good for you before you head off to college. A little treasure hunting will be good for the soul."

He laughed as she crossed her arms and frowned.

"Alright, here is your one clue. I am specifically interested in discoveries Jerry's team made in the swamp over the last year."

"The swamp?"

"The swamp."

She stared at him in stunned disbelief. The man who taught her respect for the craft, respect for the process, respect for the skill required. Those words had come from *her* father, a man who had never had anything nice to say about the reckless methods of treasure hunters, their careless tactics, or their lack of process. *A little treasure hunting* – she wanted to check him for a fever.

He had continued to hold her in suspense as the plane descended into Halifax. He had said nothing more as they transitioned to the helicopter. In fact, it wasn't until the helicopter finally touched down on Oak Island and she stood staring out over the swamp that he finally divulged the reason he had brought her here. It was the reason he himself had agreed to come in the first place. It was the bones.

5

Subdue the Enemy

Present day
Petersburg, Illinois

Garrett pulled the bottom of his shirt up to his brow and wiped the stinging sweat from his eyes. Turning his face to the late-morning sky, he squinted into the sun appraisingly. They had been at it for three hours now, and the sun was stretching higher into the sky with each passing minute, turning the breezeless hole into a hotbox of static air.

It was way too warm for this time of year, wasn't it? Gosh, it had to be. Garrett swallowed, feeling grit in his teeth. It was all up in his nose too. His stomach growled as he scanned the small canvas of green leading to the back door of Eugene's old Victorian house, perched atop a steep, wildflower-covered bluff overlooking a rustic cobblestone street. Usually you would get a breeze up on the bluffs, but if there was one, he sure couldn't feel it today.

It was already nearing noon, but only now were Garrett and his pals Pete and Lenny beginning to get under the roots of the old gnarly stump. Feeling the time trickle away, they attacked with spade and shovel, removing scoop after scoop of dirt. Hard-packed and full of rocks, the ground around the old stump had proven a challenge. The stump's roots stretched down deep into the earth, as if in search of the center. Even after a long life perched high on the bluff witness to the birth of Petersburg, providing shade to the old Victorian for nearly a century – even now, in death, the old stump stubbornly refused to give up its decades-old purchase.

Eugene, an accountant by trade, had agreed to pay the boys ninety-nine dollars and ninety-six cents for the project, each boy receiving thirty-three dollars and thirty-two cents along with one additional penny to throw into the pond upon completion of the project. This put Eugene at a total project cost of ninety-nine dollars and ninety-nine cents – one cent under budget, leaving Eugene one penny to throw into the pond along with the three boys.

The back door sprung open as a slight middle-aged man, clean-shaven, with just a horseshoe of manicured hair rimming his bald head, appeared, a wide grin on his face. "Once we get this stubborn oak octopus to let go of the earth, the rest of this project will be a breeze! We'll turn this wooden grave into a goldfish pond in a flash!" Eugene declared, crossing the yard with purpose. He began circling the hole, his hand on the rim of his khaki slacks, which rode too high on his hips. "Then we'll have the best part." A wry smile broke across his face.

"What's that, Eugene?" Garrett asked with a grunt, his gloved hands prying back the shovel handle.

Lenny leaned into Garrett's ear. "Um, getting paid and getting the hell out of here."

Garrett cleared his throat loudly, frowned, and shot him a look.

Lenny shrugged and shot the look back, accented with a mischievous grin.

"Throwing a penny into the pond to make a wish, of course. It's just a good-luck thing to do," Eugene said gleefully. His distinct voice sounded as though it belonged to someone much older, even though at forty-something he was plenty old. Eugene's voice might sound elderly, but it was always full of jolliness and childlike laughter.

"You know, boys, when Lilith and I first found this old Victorian a couple years back, we just fell in love with it. I remember when I first saw this little backyard. The first thing I said was, 'Lilith, this old unsightly stump will make the perfect place for a fish pond.' I have just been so busy remodeling I haven't been able to get to it."

Garrett nodded. "This place sure has come a long way, Eugene."

Eugene turned from the hole back toward the house. "Well, I'm just lucky to have some good boys around to help me with this hard labor! I'm not quite built for this, I'm afraid. Maybe once, in another time," he said, gazing into the distance. He made a fist and thrust it into the air. "But don't let these shoestring arms fool you. I may have spent years counting beans, but I'm stronger than I look." He headed back toward the house, calling back to them, "Let me check on lunch. In the meantime, keep at it, boys – embrace the struggle. Accept that it is – only then you *will* overcome!"

The eccentric man vanished through the door as they jumped on their shovels, bent, and wrenched.

"Strange dude," Lenny said, his head shaking.

"Aww, he isn't bad," Pete said, working the spade between two roots with little success.

With his odd interests and wonderful collections, Eugene was strange alright, but it didn't bother Garrett. Actually, that was the best part about Eugene. He knew a whole lot about everything, and he absolutely loved to talk about the stuff he knew. What he talked about most were the many things he collected. He collected old things, antique things, and even a few ancient things, all of them adorning his home from top to bottom. He had collections of old coffee grinders, giant pieces of pottery, oil lamps, and the list just went on. Even their furniture was antique. Heck, even his house was an antique.

Eugene would be content to sit and talk about the history of washboards and moonshine jugs for hours on end. Most kids would say the best of all the things he had amassed was his incredible coin collection. He had coin book upon coin book, each in its own protective sleeve. But for Garrett, it was Eugene's collection of Native American artifacts that rose supreme. The items were fascinating – small arrowheads, large arrowheads, pieces of pottery, a piece of hematite shaped for the sole purpose of weighing down a fishing net, even two stone tomahawk heads – but it was the story about how each stone artifact was pulled from the earth by Eugene's own hands that brought them to life. The stories only Eugene could tell.

Minutes later, Eugene appeared suddenly alongside the hole once again. He stooped into a half squat, his hands on his knees and his butt pushed out behind him, peering down into the hole. "You boys getting hungry yet?" he asked, patting sweat from his balding head with a folded handkerchief.

All three of the boys nodded in unison. Pete and Lenny were over waist-deep in the pit, sweating and grunting with exertion, positioned on the opposite side of the stump from Garrett, as they fell back into a rhythm of push, pull, dig, and repeat. Eugene appeared to be assessing the state of the hole. Standing back upright, he pursed his lips thoughtfully. "You boys ever hear of a fella named Sun Tzu?"

The boys paused, looking at each other in shared confusion, and shrugged, shaking their heads.

Jumping off the ground and landing with both feet hard atop the shoulders of the shovel, Garrett muttered, "Never heard of him," as the shovel bit reluctantly into the earth.

"Well, take my word for it, he was a great general about five hundred years before our Lord Jesus Christ was born," he said, now circling around the hole with one hand atop his hip. "He wrote a whole book on military strategy called *The Art of War*."

The boys stopped working altogether, giving Eugene their full attention as he continued to pace.

"Something he said in that book comes to mind now. 'The supreme art of war is to subdue the enemy without fighting.' Yes, that's it," he said, stopping abruptly. Spinning on his heels, he pointed at the stump. "You boys are at war with that stump, and I would say you are in one heck of fight." He snapped his fingers thoughtfully. "I think after lunch we need to change to Sun Tzu's strategy." Turning towards the house excitedly, Eugene said, "Lilith is making up some sandwiches and sweet tea for you – shouldn't be long." Then, just before entering the house, he shouted back at the boys. "After lunch, we subdue the enemy!"

The boys stood in the pit, looking at each other like they had just witnessed a one-legged man sign up for an ass-kicking contest – it made no sense. Lenny was the first to speak. "Dude… what the hell was that?"

"I've no idea, but evidently we will be subduing this thing after lunch," Pete said.

"Fellas, I'm having a little trouble picturing Eugene subduing anyone, let alone a tree stump," Garrett said.

"I know, right? What is he, like fifty?" Lenny laughed.

A few minutes later, Eugene called out the back door, "Lunchtime, boys."

The boys stood around the long dining table with heads bowed in silence. The only sounds were Eugene's kind voice leading them in prayer and the creaking of the old hardwood floor as restless boys shifted in anticipation of food to come. Finally, the boys ate.

"Eugene, what's the plan after lunch to – what did you call it? Subdue the tree stump with the Sun guy's strategy?" Garrett asked, tearing a bite off his fistful of sandwich.

Eugene chuckled. "Sun Tzu. Yes, he was a great general." Then, with an ornery wink, he gave Garrett one more clue to the mystery. "After lunch, we'll go to the basement, and I will show you."

To the basement? We are going to subdue the stump from the basement? He waited for Eugene to elaborate, but he seemed to be taking immense joy in Garrett's curiosity and was obviously not willing to give up his secret so soon. He made a mental note to find this *Art of War* book. Heck, his stepfather might even let him read it as part of his training.

Eugene turned to Lenny. "Lennard, how have you been? Are you still playing that electronic guitar of yours? You know, that invitation to come play a hymn or two is still open. The youth group would love to have you. I bet Lilith would be happy to play the piano with you," he said, turning back to Lilith. "Wouldn't you, dear?"

"Oh, yes, how wonderful that would be," she said, smiling fondly at Lenny.

Lenny nearly choked. "Um, I'm really not very good yet, but maybe if I keep practicing, someday we can... ah... do that."

Garrett made a poor attempt to hide his grin. "Lenny, buddy, everyone knows you shred on the guitar. Stop being so modest. Shoot, I bet there's nothing you couldn't play."

Lenny blinked in disbelief, then fixed Garrett with a death stare.

Peter couldn't resist piling on. "Bro? You don't want to play the Lord's music?"

Garrett smiled back at Lenny innocently. "Lenny?"

Lenny gave a forced smile as he tried to find Garrett's shin under the table. "Oh, of course, I mean, I'm just so busy – school, chores – but… I mean…"

"Oh, lovely!" Lilith said.

It was true: even without an axe in his hands, one look told you Lenny was a musician. Even in his work clothes – blue jeans with a dozen frayed holes, a ratty Korn shirt, and a blue bandana tied across his forehead, supporting an impressive Afro – his inner rocker simply couldn't be denied. But put a guitar in Lenny's hands, and it became a part of him, an extension of his soul. Take it away and you might as well be taking Mjolnir right from the hand of Thor.

Eugene nodded at Lenny and said, "Well, if you change your mind, you're always welcome. Hey, by the way, I see your shirt says *Korn* on it. Is that referring to sweet corn? Reason I ask is we blanched some and froze it last season – I can get some out for you if you want." He grinned and jabbed his thumb back towards the kitchen.

"Eugene, that's a band the kids are listening to nowadays. You're so silly," Lilith said, shaking her head and laughing.

"Ah, a band, you say? Well, I was wondering why you spelled it with a *K*, thought maybe I had it wrong all these years." Eugene gave Lilith a wink. "Peter, how about you?"

"Oh, I'm a… really, not a very good guitar player, sir," Pete said in a sentence laden with *r*'s he couldn't pronounce.

Pete was already very tall, lanky, and uncoordinated, and as if that were not enough, he had been born with the pièce de résistance of dork in the form of a severe speech impediment, which caused him to mispronounce the letter *r*. Garrett couldn't remember the technical term, but Pete's speech issue led to kids calling him Elmer Fudd and mimicking his speech impediment with ongoing baby talk. Garrett couldn't count how many times he had stepped between Pete and the hornets' nest. He'd narrowly avoided getting himself suspended more than once. Guess he figured if he was going to take a whipping, he'd take one for Pete.

"No need to call me sir, Peter. Call me Eugene. I meant how have you been, and how is your mother doing?"

"Oh, uh... good, sir, I mean Eugene. Mom is good too, working a lot." Pete took a gulp from his sweet tea before pushing his thick, brown, too-large-for-his-face rimmed glasses further up the bridge of his nose.

The conversation continued, but Garrett zoned out, his mind drifting to the work awaiting him and the conundrum of the stump.

"Earth to Garrett, anyone home in there? You look a little flushed, dear. I hope talking about sex doesn't embarrass you," Ms. Lilith said with a concerned smile.

Pulling himself back to the present, Garrett responded, "Huh?" His mind flashed, *What? Sex? Why?* He had obviously missed part of a conversation that he was about to wish wasn't taking place.

"We were just discussing that you boys are at that age where you might be thinking about having girlfriends. What I was saying was, you don't have to have sex to be cool. I know many kids your age are starting to experiment with sex, but the Bible clearly states in Corinthians 6:18 that sex is to be saved for marriage, and to be shared between two people who love each other. Just look at Eugene – he waited until we were married," Lilith said, looking to Eugene for support.

"That's right, boys. Forty-two years old before I had sex, and let me tell you, it was worth the wait." Lilith blushed as Eugene threw her a toothy grin, stood, and carried his plate towards the sink.

The Secret Journal

Lenny shot Garrett a look of pure disgust, forcing him to quickly look away to keep from belting out a laugh.

"Oh, now, I'll get that," Ms. Lilith said, moving to intercept Eugene. "You boys go play with your tree stump."

"Play," scoffed Eugene. "This is serious business!" He slapped his hands together, rubbing them vigorously. "Boys! To the basement!"

The boys followed Eugene down a rickety set of stairs to the basement of the old Victorian, which was in complete contrast to the beautiful main floor. The main floor featured refinished hardwood floors, a completely remodeled kitchen with all-new, stainless-steel appliances, and vaulted ceilings framed in decorative crown moldings. The basement, however, was dark and dank, smelled of mildew, and felt confined in the low light and dark brick.

As the boys followed Eugene, the deep-reaching bowels of the basement seemed to twist on and on through one tiny room after the next. After the boys navigated a few more turns, they reached the furnace room, where a single workbench sat next to a massive antique furnace. The Goliath furnace looked as though it might be asleep. At any moment it might open its eyes to spy them passing. Lenny eyed the old furnace suspiciously, giving it a wide berth as he walked past, similar to how one might keep a wary eye on a stranger's unleashed dog.

With his hands fisted at his hips, Eugene sighed at a pile of old, busted-up drywall in the opposite corner of the room. "The previous owners had drywalled most of the rooms down here, covering up the beautiful original brick." He pointed at the drywall pile, shaking his head disappointedly. "Now that most of the upper levels have been gutted and remodeled, I figured it was time to bring this basement back to the nineteenth century. Garrett, I'll probably need some help one of these days hauling this drywall out of here."

Garrett nodded, serious, assessing the pile of drywall.

"That's really awesome, sir," Pete said, admiring the recently exposed brick walls.

"I think so too, Peter, and just call me Eugene."

"What's with the big square hole at the top of the wall, Eugene?"

Eugene smiled. "That's a very good question, young man. That was originally left open to allow access to different parts of the house that don't have a basement under them. For example, if a pipe were to break you need to have a way to crawl under there to make a repair. The funny thing is, previous owners had covered up that access hole with drywall," he said, shaking his head disapprovingly. "The first thing I thought was, how in the world are you supposed to make a repair if you cover your only access?"

Garrett's eyes settled on the hole in the brick wall, drawn to it like a bug to a light. He didn't want to go in, but to see in. He squinted his eyes, as if this would give him some superhuman ability to see into the pitch black. The darkness looked so deep, so thick it might have gravity to it. Despite his will, the darkness beyond refused to abate. He thought it might, if he stared long enough, pull him in.

Suddenly whatever spell the curious crawl space had over him was broken as Eugene turned towards the workbench and announced, "Alright, boys, to subdue the beast, we're going to need three things, one for each of you." He reached above the workbench to the wall and unhooked a pair of loppers. "Garrett, you take these." He grinned as he passed the loppers over to the boy. Then, picking up a hatchet from atop the bench, he turned to Lenny. "Lennard, this is for you, but please be careful with this – it has a darn sharp edge on it." Finally, he focused his attention on Pete. "Peter, this one's for you," he announced, giving the boy a wink as he handed him a small handheld pruning saw. "This thing

The Secret Journal

will chew through wood like a rat through a piece of cheese."

Then, raising his hand in the air and clenching it into a fist, he pointed back in the direction they had come. "Bring your weapons, boys! Now we subdue the beast!"

Back in the hole, the boys quickly went to work on the stump. If a root was too big to use the loppers, they attacked with the pruning saw, and if it was too big for the saw, they chopped with the hatchet. Relentlessly, they severed root after root with their new weapons in hand. It took but a mere fifteen minutes to topple the great oak beast, and when the mighty stump fell, all the boys, even Eugene, cheered in unison. Victory was theirs.

The rest of the work went quickly, and by sunset, the boys were wrapping up.

"Boys, if you wouldn't mind, please return those tools to the basement for me."

The boys each grabbed their tools and headed down the old stairs. As Lenny reached to hang up the hatchet, he paused thoughtfully, turning to Garrett. "Hey, do me a favor, bro. If I can't close the deal with a chick by the time I'm forty-two, kick me in the balls 'cause I ain't using them anyway, and I ain't trying to be an old crusty dude before I get laid!"

Pete turned to Lenny without missing a beat. "With a face like that, you may not have a choice."

"Ooooh, damn!" Garrett said, high fiving Pete.

"Oh, it's on now." Lenny threw his hatchet onto the bench and assumed a fighting stance.

Pete held out his pruning saw in one hand while extending his empty hand behind him, arm bent at the elbow in an en garde position, as if preparing to carve the letter *z* in Lenny's chest. "Bring it on," he said, peering over the rim of his glasses with confidence.

"Okay, Zorro, you asked for it." Lenny front snap kicked the pruning saw out of Pete's hand, sending it flying through the air. All smiles faded as the tool sailed across the room right through the square hole atop the brick wall, vanishing into the crawl space.

"Oh, shit," Pete said.

"Dude." Garrett blinked.

Lenny shrugged. "Uh, sorry."

Garrett closed his eyes as he pinched the bridge of his nose. "Okay, who's going in?"

Both Lenny and Pete pointed at each other.

Lenny waved his hands. "No way I'm going in there."

"You're the one who kicked it out of my hand, bro."

"Guys, we got no time for this. I don't want to make Eugene mad for losing his tools. I do a lot of work for him. He pays better than anyone." Garrett looked back over his shoulder, sensing the need for urgent action. "Rock, paper, scissors now," he ordered frantically, and at his count, the two boys quickly threw out their signs. "Rock. Paper. Scissor. Shoot!"

Lenny threw rock, and Pete threw scissors.

"Yes!" Lenny clenched his fist in victory. "You're smashed, bitch!"

"Dammit." Pete sighed as he positioned himself below the hole in the wall. He jumped up and grabbed the ledge of the opening. Then, with the boys pushing him from underneath, he pulled himself up and shimmied through the hole into the crawl space and into the darkness beyond.

"Do you see them?" Garrett asked desperately.

"It's so dark in here I can't see shit. Wait, I bet they fell down in this gap between the wall and the dirt. Dude, I kinda don't want to stick my hand down there and feel around."

"Dammit, Pete, just do it."

The Secret Journal

"I don't even know if I can reach the bottom because I can't see."

Again, Garrett pleaded, "Pete, just try. I don't want to tell Eugene we were horse-assing around and lost his saw."

"Fine, but if I lose my hand, I will never forgive you!" He reached down and swept his arm back and forth, finding the bottom of the void at nearly the extent of his reach. "It feels like there's a lot of accumulated crap at the bottom," he said.

He pulled out an old can and chucked it through the hole at Garrett.

"Hey, watch it!" Garrett said, throwing it back through the hole.

Next, he found what looked like an old glass bottle. He tossed it out of the hole, too, sending it bouncing and clanging across the floor.

"Hey, I found it! Hold on... I can't reach..." Pete stretched down a little deeper. "I feel... something else. It feels like... paper or cardboard... It's stiffer, though."

"Who cares, just find the saw!" Lenny said.

"Fine. Just chill, I can feel the saw now."

"Hurry up, Pete!" Garrett urged.

"I got it!" Pete shouted in relief as he passed the saw over the wall to Garrett, who quickly put it back on the workbench.

"Boys, what are you doing down there?" came Eugene's voice from the top of the stairs.

"Nothing, we're on our way up now," Garrett shouted back, but the creaking told them Eugene was already on his way down the stairs. "Crap, Pete, get outta there!" Garrett begged desperately.

"Hold on," Pete said, as he reached back down into the void.

"Are you kidding me, Pete? He's coming! Lenny, go."

69

Garrett motioned Lenny toward the door as he moved into position to help Pete down from the hole.

"What are you boys up to down there?" came Eugene's voice quizzically, but as he reached the bottom of the stairs, Lenny intercepted him.

"Hey, sir, they're coming… just hanging up the tools." He threw his hand back in their direction as if to say, *Forget those guys.*

However, Eugene wasn't biting on Lenny's ruse. "Call me Eugene," he said, easily sidestepping the boy as he continued to proceed towards the furnace room without missing a beat.

Straining his shoulder to the point of pain, Pete swept his fingers along the bottom of the void, but this time he found only small pieces of brick where he thought he had touched the object before. Shimmying further to the right, he moved along the wall and swept his fingers across the bottom again – and there it was. "That's weird, I was sure I hadn't gone that far over when I touched it the first time. Maybe I knocked it further across the void when I was trying to grab for the saw."

"Pete, I don't know what the hell you are talking about, but you better get the hell out here now or we're all busted," Garrett warned through gritted teeth.

With the tips of his fingers, Pete strained just a little more and grabbed hold of the thin object, pulling it from the void. Quickly scrambling back into position, he prepared to climb back down the wall, but there was no time left. A shadow approached through the doorway as Eugene's voice called again, "Boys, just what are you up to?"

Out of options and time, Pete dove headfirst out of the hole, landing hard on his side. Quickly, he took the object and stuffed it down the back of his pants, frantically rolling onto his back just as Eugene entered the room.

"What on earth is going on in here?" he asked, confusion

The Secret Journal

blossoming uncharacteristically across his normally jovial face.

Pete sat up, coated in a thick layer of drywall dust, thankfully disguising the fact he had just army crawled around inside a hundred-and-fifty-year-old crawl space. His eyes were as big as saucers as he peered up at the man with a pained expression on his face, unable to answer.

Garrett looked at Pete, unsure if he couldn't answer because he didn't know what to say, or if he had had the wind knocked out of him from the fall. Thinking fast, Garrett stepped forward. "Sorry, Eugene, Pete was just so impressed with the work you've done here with the old wall and crawl space, he wanted to climb up and take a look, and, well, he couldn't hold himself up there and fell. But he's alright – aren't you, Pete?"

Eugene stood there for a long moment, as the boys' hearts paused in the silence, waiting for the man to respond, until finally, he unknotted his brow. "Well, jeez, boys, we could have gotten a ladder and looked together. Pete, that's a dangerous business climbing up there with no ladder – are you alright?" Eugene reached down to offer the boy a hand.

Pete let out a relieved breath. "I'm okay, sir."

"Hey, did you see anything interesting in there?" Eugene asked with interest. "Any treasures or old bones? This house has been here a long time. You never know what you might find."

Pete gulped hard. "I really didn't get a good look, sir."

"Peter, call me Eugene." He reached out to brush the boy's back off, but Pete turned away quickly. Eugene frowned, then placed a hand on his shoulder. "Well, as long as you're alright, why don't you boys head on upstairs and I'll get the lights."

After Eugene ushered the boys out, he turned and walked to the center of the room, where a single source of light shone brightly from overhead. He reached up to tug the pull-chain hanging a few inches below the bulb. He hesitated. Something reflected from under a piece of the drywall pile, catching his eye. Curious, he walked over to the object and knelt down beside it. It was a very small, very old glass medicine jar. Pursing his lips, he picked up the bottle, stood, and walked across the room, placing it on the bench. Then, fixing his eyes on the opening to the crawl space, he hesitated for a long moment before gently pulling the chain, flooding the room with darkness.

6

One Hundred Seventy-Eight Ghosts

One year earlier
Oak Island, Nova Scotia

Breanne found herself on Oak Island standing next to Jerry and her father on the dam that separated the ocean from the legendary swamp. She gazed out over the football-field-sized swamp, her mind unable to form words for what she was seeing.

"Charles, listen, I know it looks bad and I know what you're feeling – I felt the same way," Jerry said. The robust man looked completely out of place in his dress slacks, Italian shoes, and blazer with a notch lapel.

"Are you kidding me, Jerry?" her father said, pointing at the mammoth tractor. "There is a goddamn bulldozer sitting in the middle of my dig site!" His eyes bulged. "Is that a fucking ripper attachment on the back? Jerry, those things are designed specifically for ripping through arctic permafrost!" He turned to look at her. "Did you know that, Bre? Permafrost! Not archeological sites!"

Breanne's eyes were wide. She wasn't used to seeing her father this upset.

His mouth opened then closed, his disgusted visage saying plenty. He turned away from her, shaking his finger at the ridiculous monster still sitting in the deepest part of the drained swamp bottom. Giant heaps of dirt were pushed into mounds at the far end of the swamp.

"Now, Charles—"

Charles swung his finger around to point it in Jerry's face. "This is how you found the bones, with a bulldozer? The archeological sequence is *completely* destroyed – I can't accurately… I can't tell anything from this! Jesus, Jerry, you've destroyed the entire site." He was really shouting now. "The context! The strata! What the hell am I working with?"

Charles's hands were flailing everywhere, and if she were not so worried his head might pop, she would have started laughing at the spectacle.

"Never have I wanted to punch you in the face so bad, Jerry."

"Daddy! He's your best friend! You will do no such thing," she commanded with a confidence that surprised even her. Suddenly the thought of her mother flashed through her mind. She sounded just like her.

Her father paused his finger wagging and lowered his voice. "Yeah, well, my best friend chose not to tell his best friend about the site contamination. I know why you did it, Jerry, but it doesn't make it right."

"I'm sorry, old chum, but honestly, would I have been right? Would you have left Mexico to come here if I had dropped a clanger like this on you?"

"Well, maybe I wouldn't have come, but that's not the goddamned point! You should have told me."

"Charles, you still have the bones."

The Secret Journal

Her father sighed, rubbing a hand over his face. "Bones you drove a bulldozer through."

"We bloody well can't go back and change the way this was uncovered. It is your mystery to solve now, so you will just have to work with what you have."

"So, what do I have?" her father asked, his hands collapsing to his sides in reluctant surrender.

"You have a lab analyzing some of the bones, and so far, we have already been able to date the bones to the early 1300s via carbon-14 testing, and we can say with some degree of certainty the bones are consistent with Asian ancestry."

Asian ancestry, Bre thought. "Wait, what do you mean Asian?"

"That's what I wanted to surprise you with." Her father shook his head as he shot Jerry a contemptuous glare. "The swamp is littered with human remains. Native American, to be specific."

"How many?" she asked.

"We don't know yet – dozens, maybe hundreds," Jerry said.

"Hundreds?" she whispered.

Jerry nodded absently. His focus was on her father's disposition.

Bre's brow crinkled tightly. "I thought there was a Templar connection."

"Ah, yes," Jerry said, wringing his hands. "Dear girl, that's the wonky part and precisely what I need you and your flustered father to figure out. You see, we have not proven Templar presence yet, but the time period from the carbon-14 testing fits a Templar connection perfectly." Jerry shot a tentative glance to his friend.

Charles huffed. "The time period fits, but that doesn't prove squat."

"Come now, Charles, someone had to sacrifice all these people, and they must have done it to hide something brilliant."

"And now it is my mess to sort, and again I ask you, Jerry, old pal, what do I have to work with?"

Jerry pushed a hand into his pants pocket. "Well, you have the aforementioned bone data. You also have the swamp, excavated down to twenty feet below its original base level." He swept an open palm across the swamp as if he were selling the Moores a beautiful oceanfront property. "In the center of the triangle, the excavation went even deeper, down to thirty feet. We were sure something would be found in its center, but as you can see nothing was."

"Jerry, *please* do me one favor, huh? Do not refer to what has taken place in this swamp as an excavation – this is a shit-show, a goddamn shitshow."

"Charles, it will all—"

"And Jerry, get that goddamn bulldozer off my dig site."

∾

It didn't take long for her father to develop a strategy and order the special equipment they would need to execute his new plan. Per this new plan, and much to her dismay, they began working in the nasty bug-infested swamp, where they would end up spending their entire summer. Even though it was drained, the swamp was still gooey from seepage, and it smelled faintly of rotting vegetation, like a job-site porta-potty. The total devastation of the swamp gave a new meaning to 'overcutting,' one of the first terms Breanne had learned in archeology. To overcut meant to remove too much material – *what an understatement.*

Next, they did what they could with the bones, setting up grids, sieving with large mesh screens, and then meticulously cataloging each and every piece they found. Finally, they determined at a minimum 178 bodies were in the pit, with a potential for more. Unfortunately, other than a tally of skeletal remains, they could not learn much more from the bones that they did not already know. The bones had been soaked in a swamp for some seven hundred years and then bulldozed into a heap. What little additional information her dad could gather only told them they were dealing with young men, completely stripped of all clothing and other possessions before ending up under the floor of the swamp.

As the summer wore on, everything got worse, including the heat, the bugs, and the stench. By late summer, her work cataloging the bones began to wind down. Just in the nick of time too. Her father's equipment had arrived.

"Pops, check this out. Top-of-the-line GS5000 ground-penetrating radar. It's got your onboard operating system with a state-of-the-art processor for real-time results, multi antenna with triple frequency, and this baby is tough too. Dirt resistant, mud resistant, moisture resistant—"

"Okay, Ed. You're not selling me the thing," Charles interrupted with a chuckle.

"Maybe you have a future on the shopping network… selling purses." Paul tossed his brother an unruly smile.

"Watch it, little bro," Edward grinned, pulling the GS5000 instruction manual from its waterproof plastic jacket. "I'm in charge of site management, and I will throw your ass off this site."

"You think just because you've been through BUD/S training and you have an MBA that you're either smart enough or physically capable of tossing me? You better bring a packed lunch because kicking my ass is going be an all-day event." Paul snatched the instruction book from his brother's hand. "Besides, who would operate the equipment and pilot your ass around?"

"Oh no! The big bad Army Ranger wannabe isn't going to chauffeur me around in his helicopter. In case you haven't noticed, we're on an island surrounded by water. I've never been more at home."

Here we go, Breanne thought. *The Navy SEAL versus Army Ranger argument.* She didn't get it, especially since neither was a SEAL or ranger. Paul had applied to become a warrant officer right out of high school and from there attended Army Aviation School. During his active military duty, he specialized in medical evacuations and search-and-rescue missions. Now a reservist, when not training or activated for a mission, he handled all the construction needs, heavy-equipment operation, and transportation on their father's dig sites.

"I never wanted to be an Army Ranger, but if you're asking, yeah, I still think a ranger is more badass than a SEAL. Oh, and by the way, I fly a UH-60 Black Hawk – I'm elite, bro. You should count yourself lucky to have a pilot like me fly you around."

"Rangers more badass than SEALs? Not a chance," Edward scoffed.

Edward had made it through hell week in BUD/S and was on course to becoming SEAL until he tore his ACL doing boat lifts. He had said it was the worst pain he'd ever felt. She was proud of him, though. Despite having to give up his dream, Edward went on to earn an MBA and now worked for their father handling all site management, including taking care of all the red tape so Charles could focus on his work.

Breanne shook her head. So much testosterone. What this island needed was another woman… like Sarah.

"Listen, Ed, I don't even know why you argue this with me. Rangers and SEALs are designed for different applications," Paul argued.

"Agreed, but I am talking a straight-up, one-on-one ass-kick—"

"Knock it off, you two," her father said, rubbing his hands together eagerly. "Alright, it's time to put the next part of my plan into motion."

He set both Paul and Edward to work scanning the edges of the swamp site. As the data was collected, her father began analyzing it. Breanne shadowed him closely, learning all she could about GPR and how to decipher the data.

That's when things got weird. The equipment experienced constant malfunctions, like false readings and interference. It was so screwy Charles assumed the GPR was faulty, so he ordered a replacement unit, but even the new equipment continued to malfunction.

Honestly, the whole damn place gave her the creeps. All those bodies in the swamp – she couldn't stop thinking about it. Why were they there? Who put them there? Why were they naked? Then, at night, her normal nightmares had taken on a strange twist. They started the same, with her in the car with her mom, but then she was in the swamp and the bodies were climbing out of the muddy swamp bottom. Her nightmares were bad enough without the addition of zombies. There was more to the dreams, but her memory seemed to be covered in a layer of hazy fog during the waking hours.

She hated going to sleep, but what she really hated was this damned swamp. Her father was no help; he seemed fascinated by the swamp in all its sloppy, bug-ridden, stinky glory, content to spend eternity here. Of course, Mr. Logical had a theory for the equipment issues, too, concluding the malfunctions must have to do with electromagnetic fields in the area. *Yeah, right… or maybe it's the 178 ghosts of the swamp!*

As frustrating as all this was, somehow her father still

managed to find a pattern in the data. Even with the mixed signals, false readings, and interference, they continued to detect a strange anomaly near the east wall, beneath the floor of the excavated swamp bottom. So he gave the go-ahead to dig by hand, and dig they did. At right around twenty-five feet, five feet deeper than the previously excavated swamp floor, thanks to Mr. Bulldozer, they found something.

"My God. There is a structure here!" her father said, pushing the long probe several inches into the ground. He pulled it out, moved over, pushed it in again, and again he struck something.

"This better not be a big rock," Breanne said.

"No, listen." He pulled the probe up and dropped it again: *thunk*, then twice more, *thunk... thunk*. "That's the sound of wood!"

Breanne was so excited she wanted to just dig the whole thing up right then and there. Not her father, though – years in the field had taught him patience.

"The ground that gives up the best secrets gives them up slowly, Bre. Patience is the key to profound discovery. Bulldozers wreck dreams and ruin discovery."

"Really, Dad? Bulldozers wreck dreams. That's a new one," she said, smiling.

"Well, I'm still pissed about the bulldozer, what can I say?" He shrugged. "But truly, Breanne, we have found something here! Something that shouldn't be here!"

Over the next several days, using nothing more than a trowel and a radio with a cassette deck playing her father's favorite Motown, blues, and jazz mixtapes, she and her father methodically worked the object, peeling back the layers of earth like an onion. They worked long hours, only stopping occasionally to swat a mosquito or grab a drink or snack. Meanwhile, BB King coaxed the blues from Lucille like a snake charmer coaxing a fanged serpent from a basket. They worked with all the patience and care of surgeons delicately performing a triple bypass. She loved to watch her father work and admired the great care he put into it… even if the suspense was killing her.

It soon became apparent that what they had discovered was a wooden structure about three feet wide. Could this be *the* wooden vault? The one that many Oak Island legends claimed held the site's treasures? Once they uncovered the top, they carefully began excavating down the sides of the structure. It was unadorned, bearing no markings whatsoever, made solely of rough-cut timbers. Simple wooden dowels bound the timbers together, creating a uniform box framework.

After they exposed the top and two of the sides, they worked to expose the end of the box. Since one end seemed to go back under the undisturbed wall of the swamp, and therefore was under some thirty feet of soil, they chose to work the structure carefully back toward the center of the swamp. Using this strategy, they hoped to find at least one end of the wood box with less digging needed. Their strategy paid off as they reached the end only a few yards away.

Excavating down into the front of the framework, using only a spade and mattock, they discovered it was open on the end. Breanne's heart pounded with anticipation of a treasure to come.

Instead of treasure, what they found was more daunting work. The open end was sealed with stones piled from top to bottom. *Okay, no big deal. They must have just sealed it with a wall of stone,* she thought. With help from her brothers, Breanne excavated a five-foot-deep trench in front of the structure's open end, complete with steps to allow them to climb in and out of the trench. They would need these stairs and the room to work for removing the stones obstructing the entrance.

The stacked stones filling the opening were large, most weighing between fifty and a hundred pounds. To compound the difficulty, stinking seepage was pooling at the bottom of the dirt steps, requiring the use of a pump to constantly pull the liquid stank from the hole. While Breanne had never had an issue working in the dirt in the past, this was something different. It was God-awful gross, plus it drew bugs in clouds. As interesting as the wood structure was, she just wanted to be done with it.

Unfortunately, the stones seemed to just keep going. Behind each stack of stones were more stones, and behind those were even more stones. The stones didn't seem to just be blocking the entrance; they seemed to be filling the structure entirely.

"Dad, I don't think this is a treasure vault at all," Breanne said, her pants covered in stinky swamp mud.

"No. It isn't." Her father looked up from the map he had been studying and gazed off into the distance. "Based on angle and direction, we're dealing with a tunnel, and if my calculations are correct, it appears to lead towards the Money Pit."

"*The* Money Pit?" she asked in surprise.

"What's the big deal with the Money Pit?" Paul asked.

"Well, for starters," Charles said, "the Money Pit is probably one of the most dug-up places on earth. However, since it has been dug up so much over the years, the original location was lost. We know the general area, but treasure hunters have been trying to find the true location since it was first discovered a few hundred years ago. Interestingly, the general location is about a couple hundred yards to the east."

"Then what is this?" Paul asked, tossing a large rock into the pile.

"Perhaps an additional flood tunnel designed to usher water from the swamp into the Money Pit. Legend says the

The Secret Journal

Money Pit is booby-trapped to flood whenever someone tries to dig in it, and historically the area has flooded right around ninety feet each and every time. Think about it. This swamp could have provided plenty of water to get the job done before it was drained." He pointed at the rock pile. "The rocks were likely to keep the tunnel from collapsing or filling with debris while still allowing water to flow through. Other tunnels supposedly came from Smith's Cove, but why not pull from various places? It's ingenious, really – a design to prevent would-be treasure hunters from ever reaching the bottom of the Money Pit."

"You don't sound convinced, Dad," Breanne said.

Her father pursed his lips and nodded. "I don't know, something doesn't quite fit. I'm missing something."

"Maybe it was more than a flood tunnel," she said slowly.

"What do you mean?" he asked with interest.

"Well, we have already concluded through soil samples in combination with examination of the strata from both sides of the swamp that it is a complete fake, right? We know this island was once two separate islands with a channel running between them. It seems like an awful lot of work to hide a flood tunnel."

Paul and Edward tossed their stones into the pile, then paused to listen.

With a captive audience, Breanne started to pace back and forth, looking down onto the wood structure. "It's too big, and so deep in the ground – it just seems like so much work for nothing more than a flood tunnel. Why make a flood tunnel this big?"

Her father twisted at his whiskers thoughtfully. "You're right, Bre. I think you are really on to something!" It was like a veil had been lifted as it dawned on him. "This tunnel may be a *treasure tunnel* – the one that leads directly to a treasure chamber. Hah, it is too big. Much bigger than the flood tunnels of legend, even big enough to transport a treasure through." He pointed into the distance. "At this trajectory I would bet money it will end up far deeper than needed for a simple flood tunnel. And the placement. It is too well hidden, like you said… too deep. There has to be a connection with the bodies. They must have dammed off both sides, moved the treasure in, and sacrificed the builders right here so they could never tell anyone. Then they construct this artificial swamp right over the top to hide the evidence."

"Pops, you really think someone killed all these people and just dumped 'em at the bottom of the swamp, all so they wouldn't talk?" Paul asked.

"Well, we need only look at history to answer that. Qin Shi Huang, the first emperor of China, ordered the killing of an unknown number of people, maybe thousands involved in the building of his great tomb and terracotta army, all to protect the location from discovery. The same goes for Genghis Khan. He allegedly ordered the death of one thousand foot soldiers to protect the location of his tomb from ever being found."

"That's messed up," Edward said, twisting his face in disgust.

"Indeed," his father replied. "You know, before coming here, if you were to ask me about this island, I would have laughed and said it was nothing more than a wild goose chase – heck, I would even have been willing to put substantial money on nothing ever being found here. But just look at this! Undeniable proof that something is hidden here, something even bigger than a mass grave!" He paused, shaking his head. "The treasure hunters of the past spent their lives searching this island, knowing in their hearts something's buried here, and you know what? They've been right all along… I was the one who was wrong."

The Secret Journal

"The question is who would do this, and what were they hiding?" Edward asked.

The boys worked for several days removing stone after stone, climbing up and down the carved dirt steps. Breanne helped with any rocks that were light enough for her to manage them, but after a few days, it became apparent this was not going to work. The problem was that the wood was so old and waterlogged with centuries of swamp water that, as the boys removed the heavy stones, the tunnel began to slowly collapse. The final straw came when they arrived one morning to find the tunnel had completely collapsed overnight.

"I sure hope we don't plan to give up like those guys did when they found their Money Pit had flooded overnight," Breanne said.

"Not a chance, baby girl. We need a new plan, and it just so happens I have one." He smiled at her. "Did you know that a television show filmed in the Money Pit, as one of the last great mysteries, intent on capturing the big find on network TV? The hardened treasure hunters spent season after season drilling, digging, and pulling back the earth, but – like Geraldo opening Al Capone's safe – the big find never came. But do you know what we have that they didn't?"

They all stopped and looked to him expectantly.

Their father pointed at the tunnel. "We have a big fat arrow." He quickly measured the drop of the tunnel over the twenty yards of length they had uncovered and plotted its trajectory. With his calculations complete, he deduced at what depth and location the tunnel would intersect in the area of the old Money Pit. This was assuming, of course, that the tunnel stayed true to course over the next one hundred yards. "Time to go."

Everyone, especially Breanne, was elated to be leaving the

swamp. With their new coordinates in hand, they packed up their equipment.

By now, summer was nearing an end and soon the ground would freeze. Rather than risk partial excavation and unknown complications, like more hidden flood tunnels, Dr. Moore decided to mark the location and wait until spring thaw to start again.

Breanne's year was up, and she was supposed to report to university for the fall semester. As much as she wanted to throw herself into her studies, she was too invested in this mystery. She had to see it through. Besides that, her father needed her. Who else would keep him safe? Not her brothers. They were liable to let him do something stupid. No, she needed to stay, to see it through. She just had to somehow convince her father to let her postpone school. Finally, she cornered him and went for it. "I've already spent a whole summer doing the worst of it in that nasty swamp, and you know I can be an asset in the research, preparation, and planning for spring. I'm way ahead in my studies anyway. School can wait just a little longer." She stood up straighter and looked her father directly in the eye. "This could be a major discovery, one of the biggest of all time."

He smiled softly and, just like that, she was back in. She hadn't even needed the sad puppy dog face and "Please, Daddy?" she had kept in reserve. There was one condition, though. After this upcoming dig season, she would have to report to university, no matter what the condition of the site. She thought she would be happy, but she didn't feel happy – she felt something else, something... ominous.

7

The Book

Present day
Petersburg, Illinois

With the final rays of the day's light fading, shadows came out of hiding to impose their will, slowly devouring everything into darkness. Garrett, Lenny, and Pete made their way down the steep driveway of the old Victorian. "You boys come back tomorrow. The pond will be filled, and we can throw those pennies in and make a wish!" Eugene shouted after them.

"We will, Eugene. See you tomorrow," Garrett yelled back up the driveway.

"Hey, speak for yourself – I'll be okay if I don't get to throw my penny in the pond. What does he think, we're twelve?" Lenny said.

"We don't want to hurt his feelings, man, c'mon. It won't hurt you to swing by, Lenny," Garrett said before turning to Pete. "Oh, and you, dude," he said, pointing a finger. "What the hell was that? Not cool. Work is difficult enough to come by – the last thing I need is to lose a repeat customer like

Eugene, who also just so happened to mention he had even more work for me to do in the basement. So out with it. What did you steal?"

"I think saying I stole it is a bit of a stretch," Pete said.

"Just because he didn't know it was behind the wall doesn't make it cool to take it, asshole," Lenny said.

Pete pointed a finger at Lenny. "Okay, dickhead, just for that—"

"Guys, knock it off!" Garrett interrupted. "Dammit, Pete! It wasn't yours, and you almost got us caught!"

"Jeez, I'm sorry," Pete said.

"Yeah, well, that was a real bonehead move, asshat," Garrett said with a scowl.

"Well, what do you want me to do – give it back? He doesn't even know he had it."

"What the hell is it anyway?" Lenny asked.

"I don't know, some kind of old book or something. I didn't get a good chance to check it out."

"When we get around the corner, let's see it," Garrett said.

The boys quickly made their way down the driveway and turned onto Snake Hollow, a winding road that led past one of the largest mansions in Petersburg. Once they were certain they were out of sight of Eugene's house, Pete reached behind his back and produced the object from his waistline.

"It looks like part of a busted book," Lenny said.

"It looks old. Well, nice going, Pete, you stole old trash," Garrett said.

"I didn't steal it! And if it's just old trash who cares? It is old, though, very old," said Pete, turning the book over. The front cover was missing, but the back appeared to be made of black leather that was brittle and peeling, sucked dry of all moisture over countless years of sitting behind Eugene's basement wall.

Flipping it back and forth, Pete continued to appraise the find. "It looks like a good chunk of it is missing – at least several pages along with the front cover – but it's hard to say how much without knowing how thick it was in the first place." Pete frowned critically at the book, observing that the remaining pages were crisp, water stained, and yellowed with age.

"Open it and see what you can tell already," Lenny said, growing impatient. "I have to get home."

"You guys called and said you'd be home a little late. Stop freaking," Pete said.

"Yeah, but my parents know how long it takes, and they know I am on my way, so just hurry the hell up, would you?"

Pete turned his attention back to the book. The front of the first page was completely faded, and nothing was legible in the dim glow of the streetlight. As he started to turn the page, it cracked and a corner broke off, brittle with age. "Man, this thing must be really old. I'm afraid if I force it open, I'll destroy it. Let me take it home and figure out what I can do with it. Then tomorrow after church we can see it in the light."

"Whatever," Garrett said. "But if it's worth anything, we better give it back to Eugene somehow – I don't know, tell him we found it or something. He likes antiques – he would probably dig it." Taking a step closer to Pete, he slugged him in the shoulder.

Pete yelped, raising his free hand to rub his shoulder. "What the hell was that for?"

"You almost got us caught. Be more careful," Garrett said. "Oh, and guys, whatever you do, don't tell anyone about it. I don't want people thinking we're thieves and it getting back to Eugene or my parents – God only knows what they would do to me." But Garrett knew all too well what his father would do and what he would use to do it.

"All right. Deal," Pete said.

"Sounds good to me," Lenny said.

Their pact sealed, the boys parted. Garrett and Lenny headed down the sidewalk towards the north side of town. Pete quickly crossed the street to make his way across town in the opposite direction towards the dilapidated apartment building he called home.

"Hey man, you down to run home?" Lenny asked.

Garrett smiled. "I know we got permission to be a little late, but these streetlights are making me nervous."

"Race you!" Lenny said, taking off.

"Oh, it's on!"

The boys were the epitome of best friends. They had a lot in common, sure, but fate played a part too. To deny that would be to deny fish swam. In a town the size of Petersburg, didn't fate have to play a part in bringing together two people with so many similarities? Both boys were adopted. Lenny was fully adopted, with white stepparents, while Garrett still had his biological mom. Both boys loved music, and both boys were on the cross-country team. Also, both boys loved everything related to martial arts, including Bruce Lee, ninjas, and Kung Fu theater. Both boys took taekwondo from a local dojo up on the square. Since neither of the boys had much money, Grand Master Brockridge had worked out a deal with the boys back when the dojo first opened. They had taken every belt test together and achieved their black belts in only a few short years.

However, the kinship Garrett felt with Lenny went beyond friendship. He had always felt they were more like brothers. On the surface, it was plain enough – they did everything together. But Garrett knew it was more. To Garrett, Lenny was what free looked like. Lenny was free with his thoughts – freer still with his tongue. God, he wanted that. He wished he didn't have the damned rules, the training, the secrets, and the questions he was finding harder to ignore. He wished he could be more like Lenny. It was like Lenny didn't worry, not about nothing, while he worried about it all.

Feet slapping pavement, the two boys reached their neighborhood a few minutes later. "Dude, are you getting slower?" Garrett grinned.

Lenny was hunched over, gasping, with both hands on his knees. "No, bro, you're getting faster. I haven't lost any speed. What the heck are you doing? Taking protein shakes?" He spit between his feet, then rubbed it into the gravel with the sole of his shoe. "I could barely hold you in sight. If we were running much further, you would have dropped me for sure."

"Like I could buy protein," Garrett said, holding one side of his nostril closed with a thumb while clearing the other side with a sharp exhalation. "I know cross-country practice doesn't start until August, but I can't help it, I'm just feeling it, so I run a lot more – like to and from work and school."

"Well, it's working, man. See you tomorrow," Lenny said, as he turned to head down the alley to his place.

"Hey, Lenny, can I ask you something?"

He turned back towards Garrett. "What's up?"

Garrett stepped close, glanced over both shoulders, and in a lowered voice asked, "Do your parents make you do extra training in the evening or at night?"

Lenny raised an eyebrow and for an uncomfortably long moment just looked at him. Then in a deadpan voice he said, "You know we aren't supposed to talk about the 'chores' we do at home. You know the rules."

Garrett blinked in disbelief. He wasn't the only one! "Yeah, but I just didn't know if… if anyone else had to do this stuff or if—"

"Or if it was what? Only you? Well, it isn't. It started

when I came to Petersburg. Ever since I was adopted, there has been a training regimen, and I have to follow very specific rules. As I got older, I asked, and they told me all kids in Petersburg train and all have the same rules. They said I could never talk about it… ever."

That's something, Garrett thought. Lenny was told only kids in Petersburg while his mom told him all kids. "So, you think there are others? You think it is all the kids in town?"

"I guess. I mean, I wondered, sure – thought maybe I had been adopted by some crazy foster parents, but now… Listen, how in the hell should I know? I sure as shit ain't going to go around asking. The consequences for disobeying and breaking the rules are harsh." Lenny glanced back, lowering his voice even more. "Listen, we shouldn't be talking about this at all and certainly not here."

Garrett nodded. "Okay, Lenny. But do you know why? Why we have to train?"

"Shit, Garrett. Did you hear anything I just said? If you really want to talk about it, let's not do it here. See you tomorrow."

"Yeah, man, see you tomorrow." For the first time, Garrett felt like Lenny might not be as worry-free as he thought. Ashamedly, he knew something about that made him feel better. Not that his friend wasn't as carefree, but that he was more like him after all. Maybe Lenny just hid it better.

Garrett cut through a neighbor's backyard and was home. His mind raced. He wanted to ask more questions. He wanted answers, but that would have to wait. As he approached his back door, he knew this was only the beginning of his night. Now it was time to train. As exhausted as he felt, he took some solace in knowing that he wasn't alone.

8

Money Pit

Present day
Oak Island, Nova Scotia

By spring, Jerry was chomping at the bit to get to the bottom of the tunnel mystery. Anything the Moores required was provided without question. By late February, they were back preparing the site to dig. Breanne and her father had spent the winter researching every scrap of information they could find on Oak Island, Native Americans from the region, and even the Knights Templar, even though the connection was yet to be proven. Paul and Edward made equipment arrangements and upgraded mobile living arrangements with Jerry, ensuring they would have everything they needed, including a monster of a crane. Since frequent travel was necessary to properly prepare the site and Paul had been a pilot in the military, Jerry was able to acquire a helicopter for supply runs. Apparently, money really was no object for the mysterious stakeholder.

By early March, the Moores were in the Money Pit, utilizing the cable crane with a clamshell bucket. By late

March, they had already reached a depth of close to 125 feet. Unlike treasure seekers of the past, they didn't have the same issue with water. Her dad assumed it was because the swamp was drained, cutting off the water from the last of the undiscovered flood tunnels.

All Breanne knew for sure was no seeping sewage water was a good thing. It meant less muck and fewer bugs, and that was fine by her.

They were nearing the last days of March. The Nova Scotia chill would soon be giving way to warmer temperatures, and the sporadic freezing rain would be nothing more than a bad memory. Those days made Breanne miss the warmth of Mexico and all it could have been. Today, though, was not one of those days. Today the sky was clear and blue, from what little she could see anyway. Today, like most days, Breanne found herself nearly 150 feet below the surface, deep inside a damp pit, her exposed skin clammy from the cool wet earth surrounding her. She wore dozens of small jet-black braids pulled back into a loose ponytail that stretched down the center of her back, ending near her waistline. The cuffs of her green Carhartts were crusted in semi-dry mud, as were her well-worn leather work boots. Even in the cool temperatures of March, she found her grey hoodie too warm in the noonday sun, opting instead to tie it snugly around her waist, there if she needed it. On her head, she wore her wide-brimmed papyrus hat, the chin strap loose and dangling below her neckline.

Breanne's father passed her the trench shovel. "Careful, Bre. Go easy… easy."

"I know, Dad, just give me a second," she said, her tone that of a teenager pushing forty. She guided the shovel into the earth with surgical precision. The shovel, having not penetrated more than a few inches, made a soft but audible *thunk*, then halted abruptly. Breanne's eyes widened expectantly. "Please don't let it be another piece of leftover junk from past digs."

Her father locked eyes with her and allowed himself a rare moment of expressed hope. "Baby girl, years of working archeological sites have taught me hope can be a dangerous thing, more often than not ending in disappointment. But I don't think that's what this is. We're too deep into the Money Pit for that now, and we've definitely moved outside the old dig radius." Spinning on his heels, he pointed to an orange flag placed in the loose soil some feet behind them. "This is virgin material. I think… Yes, we've got something, Bre!"

Breanne smiled at her father, allowing herself to fully appreciate his sense of joy and wonder. Noticing her expression, he went still, allowing a broad smile to stretch across his bewhiskered face, as if also sensing this was a moment to cherish, to hold on to, to stretch out for just those extra few heartbeats until the suspense was too much to bear. And when it was too much, they both knew it at the same moment. Grinning from ear to ear, they dropped to their knees in unison and began frantically brushing the dirt away, dragging their cupped hands across the earth, eager to reveal the mystery below.

They had been so careful using the soil probes and shovels, but their diligence sweeping the pit floor with ground-penetrating radar had only continued to yield confusing images that made no sense.

The crane, outfitted with a clamshell bucket, had cautiously skimmed the earth bit by painstaking bit, shallow scoop after shallow scoop. The progress had been slow, and at a depth of 150 feet, repeated hand probing in two-foot increments began to take its toll. Up until now, however, all they had pulled from the hole were chunks of debris from past digs, a constant reminder of history's failures and lost hope.

As Breanne frantically pulled her hands across the loose

soil, her mind reeled at the implications. In a mere fraction of a second, the story her father had told her of Oak Island and all the events leading here, to this very moment, flashed through her mind like a near-death experience.

A chunk of old wooden timber came into view beneath her hands.

"This is it! We've found the tunnel, baby girl!" her father said. "Alright, it's getting late, and we have put in a long day. Let's probe the edges, flag them, and we will expose the entire structure at first light. We can breach the wooden structure first thing in the morning when we are fresh and can hopefully see this through."

Breanne looked grave.

"What is it?"

"Dad, should we really risk leaving this? I mean, I just keep thinking of that story of how the treasure hunters came back to find the pit flooded."

"Ah, yes, I understand your concern, Bre, but that's precisely why I don't want to continue."

"I don't follow."

"If we continue on, we need to get artificial lighting down here because we are losing the sun quick. That means working in the dark and probably well into the morning hours. Even then we don't know how long we will be clearing stones once we breach the tunnel. What if we can't finish? What if we pop the top, and we somehow trigger a trap? I just don't want to risk it. This is a good point to stop. A safe point," he said, removing his fedora and scratching his head.

She couldn't argue with that – wouldn't, not after Mexico. Shit, this was part of the reason she insisted to herself she needed to be here, to keep him from doing something risky. Yet her curiosity tugged her on. Who was she fooling? Who was really the fool? Maybe she should have gone on to school after all.

"Besides, you look really tired." Worry lines were etched deep across his forehead. "Your eyes, they seem sunken? And you look thin. Are you sleeping okay, baby girl?"

"Of course," she lied, punching his arm. "But thanks for telling me I look like crap!"

"That's not what I said." He rubbed his arm, one corner of his mouth turning up.

She knew her father was right, but that didn't mean she had to like it. Long days in the pit were grueling, and she always hit the sack consumed with fatigue. But fatigue didn't equate to sleep… not for her. Only today was different. Despite her apparent sickly appearance – *thanks for that, Dad* – she was invigorated with a sheer excitement. Today marked the end of painstaking days working their way down to the wooden tunnel. No more worrying they may have missed it – they had finally found it. Still, she hated the thought of leaving without knowing. Damn his patience, and thank God for it.

"It will be here waiting for us tomorrow, Bre," he said with a consoling smile.

Reluctantly she nodded. "I will call Paul and let him know we're ready to come up."

With the promise of a new adventure tomorrow, it would be hours before sleep would find her.

She would do her best to push it away as long as she could, but finally, when she slipped away into unconsciousness, she knew she wouldn't be alone – she never was.

9

Pete

Present day
Petersburg, Illinois

Across town, Pete walked with a sense of purpose, eager to get home with his mysterious find. As he shuffled down the sidewalk approaching the square, he noticed two figures coming towards him. When Pete recognized them, his pulse quickened.

"What's up, Fudd!" Jack called out.

"Not much, just trying to get home. Been working at Eugene's all day."

"What you got there?" Albert asked, pointing at the book.

Shit, I should have hidden the book when I saw them coming. "Nothing, just some old book I found – probably trash," he said nervously.

Albert laughed. "Pwobabwee trawsh?" he mocked.

"Let me see it." Jack held out his hand.

"It's really fragile, Jack. I want to take it home and see if I can open it," he said, not even considering his word choice.

The Secret Journal

"Weawwy fwagile, is it, Pete?" Jack laughed. "Well, that doesn't sound like 'twash' then, does it?"

No matter how many times someone made fun of his speech, the embarrassment never lessened. Pete felt his face erupt in red heat. "I have to go, Jack. I'm rea—" He stopped himself, choosing different words. "It's getting late, and I have to get home."

"So where did you say you found it, Pete, at Eugene's? You said you were working there?" Jack asked accusingly.

"Yeah… I mean, no… I mean, yeah. We were… I mean, had been… work—" *Shit, new word.* "At Eugene's, I mean, but I just found it on the way home. I got to go, guys." Pete moved to step around the boys.

Jack lunged forward, snatching Pete by the arm, squeezing too tight, as an adult might snatch up a child who was misbehaving. "You're acting 'weiwd,' Petey. Go on home and maybe tomorrow you can show me that book," Jack said, pointing at the book clutched in Pete's hand. "Maybe on your way, you think about this. Your mom's been dating my dad for almost two years now. She ends up marrying my dad, and we'll be brothers, Petey – can you imagine that? You and me, brothers? Well, imagine this, you little shit, what's yours is mine. So, yeah, you run on home, and I'll see you tomorrow, little bro!"

Pete yanked his arm away and turned quickly to make his escape down the sidewalk. "Asshole," he muttered under his breath.

The two boys remained for a few moments longer to laugh and shout after Pete. "What's that, Pete? Did you say something? Kinda hard to understand you when you don't speak so cweawy!"

"Yeah, see you tomowwow, Petey." Albert chortled, high fiving Jack.

Pete shuffled across the apartment building's parking lot and ascended the stairs to the entrance of the old brick building. Once inside, he climbed yet another set of stairs, making his way past the doors to apartments ten, eleven, and twelve – their paint chipped and faded – finally arriving at apartment thirteen. Jamming the key into the worn deadbolt, he cranked it to the left and threw his hip into the door.

"Peter, you're home. Let me guess, you were at the library again?" his mother asked.

"Uh-uh," Pete said, grabbing a cold grilled cheese off the kitchen counter and jamming half of it into his mouth. "At... Eugene's... working... Garrett," he said with effort as he struggled to manage the mouthful of cheesy goodness.

"Okay, I think you said you were working at Eugene's with Garrett?"

"Yup, I got to go study."

"Okay, boy, wait just a minute. Now, I know you don't study. So what are you up to?" she asked.

She was right that he didn't study. He didn't need to. School wasn't even a challenge for Pete. It just came easy.

"Research, I mean. I have some research I want to do before bed."

"Now that I believe. What's the topic tonight?"

Pete thought about that for a moment. "History." Then, grabbing another grilled cheese for the road, he turned to leave the kitchen. "Love you, Mom."

"I love you too. Hey, make sure you shower before bed, Peter," she called after him.

"I will, Mom."

Once in his room he carefully turned the book back and forth, searching his mind for a solution. Then he remembered reading somewhere that if the pH level in old paper fell below a certain number, it could only be preserved, not restored. Where had he read that? He also remembered that for less valuable documents, one could mist the paper, being careful not to get it too wet, which would result in smudging the ink. Well, that seemed risky since he couldn't even open it without breaking it. Contemplating what to do, he came up with two options. He needed to get the paper moist without ruining it, or he needed to remove the binding. Freeing the pages would allow him to lay them out individually. The former was the scenario he preferred, as he wanted to at least try and keep it intact; after all, it could be quite valuable.

He went to work, creating a humidity chamber from a garbage bag, his desk chair, a couple hangers, and the humidifier his mom had purchased for his asthma attacks. He was careful to leave the chamber open on one end to allow moisture to escape, ensuring he did not inadvertently create a wet environment; he wanted humidity, not moisture. With the humidifier placed on the floor, spout pointed up, the book placed on the seat of the chair, and the newly fashioned plastic tent over the chair, his design was complete.

Pete checked the book's progress after he showered, and then a few more times before getting ready to turn in for the night. Just before he hit the sack, he decided to give it a try and see if he could turn a page in the book. He remembered having seen curators use white gloves to handle fragile scrolls and documents. He didn't have white gloves, but he had some old brown jersey gloves, so he donned those and slowly attempted to turn the first page.

Pete grimaced as if in pain as he applied the slightest amount of pressure. The page slowly yielded, folding over without breaking. "Yes!" Pete exclaimed. Remembering his mother was in the next room, he added in a lowered voice, "Victory is mine."

Carefully placing the book on his desk, he examined the newly visible pages. The page on the left side was completely ruined. He could see only the remnants of writing in the form of an inky smudge. But the next page was covered with old-fashioned cursive handwriting, legible though difficult to read. Here and there, old water stains blotted out bits of the text. Grabbing his notebook, he began transferring the text, putting *x*'s in the place of words he couldn't make out.

*Now you know the story **xxx xxx** is to believe. When that young man, the Potawatomi boy, found me that warm day, July 10th of 1832, my life changed forever. Now **xxx** I **xxx** **xxx xxx** great danger and my urgent desire to pass this information on to someone I can trust. My conscience has been **xxx** much despair holding this deep secret. My **xxx** **xxx** heavy and must be unburdened before it is too late, which it may be already, as I am afraid I have hinted too often at the truth I so wish to speak.*

*Oh **xxx** you **xxx xxx xxx** a good friend to me, but I must caution **xxx xxx** on the information I bestow upon **xxx** as I unburden my conscious from **xxx** secret I have held for so long. You must **xxx xxx xxx** the journey shall lead you. If **xxx** happens to me, you must decide whether you tell the world or if your heart can stand to hold this truth. I bring you this heavy load because I believe you will do the right thing. However, you must be cautioned of the peril you will face should you decide to make this a public affair.*

That was the end of the page. *What the hell is this?* thought Pete. *Eighteen thirty-two? Native Americans? July tenth? Dammit, why do I know that date?* He was sure he knew the date, but from where? *Crap, that date is important.* He couldn't place it, but he was sure he knew it.

The Secret Journal

Pete returned the book to the humidifying chamber and climbed into bed. He slept restlessly, pulling his blankets off, then on. Then off again. That date from the book and mention of the Potawatomi boy played out in his dreams. He could see *1832* written somewhere else… in another book? In a book he had read. The next morning, he woke with a start. He had had an epiphany, and it had come to him in his dreams.

"I do know that date!" Pete said, jumping out of bed.

He needed to see Garrett and Lenny right away.

10

Clearing Stones

Present day
Oak Island, Nova Scotia

Breanne's body jolted into consciousness as she sucked in a startled gasp. She looked from side to side, trying to understand where she was. The fire cracked loudly, throwing sparkling embers into the air like miniature fireworks. When she recognized this as the sound from her sleep, her pulse slowed and she settled back into the camp chair, pulling her throw blanket tightly to her chest. Her back ached from the chair, or maybe from the day's work with the shovel – probably both. She was too exhausted to make the trip from fireside to the camper, despite her protesting lower back, and decided instead to stay in the chair, at least for a little longer. Besides, the campfire saturated her in warmth, too difficult to abandon on this chilly night. In the background, she recognized one of her father's favorites, Coltrane's "My One and Only Love," playing softly. Softer still, somewhere under the carpet of melody, she could just barely make out voices from inside the camper, where her brothers were engaged in what must have been an intense game of spades. Focusing on the dancing flames, she felt her eyelids sag as she allowed Coltrane to softly lull her back to sleep with his sax.

The next time Breanne woke, it was to the whisper of her father's voice as he tapped her shoulder. "Bre, baby girl, it's time to turn in. We've another early day tomorrow."

She was reluctant to move, her body having found *just* the right position, so she moaned disapprovingly instead.

Her father responded with a sigh. "Baby girl, you can't sleep in the chair. You need a good night's rest – in a bed."

With some effort, she cracked open an eye and surveyed her surroundings. Where once a crackling campfire had washed the campsite in dancing firelight, now only a dull amber glow remained. She could no longer hear her brothers' voices, and even Coltrane had put away his saxophone for the evening. "What time is it, Daddy?" she rasped before clearing her dry throat.

"Bre, it's not even late anymore, it's early," he said, smiling lovingly as he held out his hand.

Stretching, she forced herself to open both eyes, then took his hand and stood reluctantly, smiling back at her father. "What are you still doing up? I'm not the only one with an early day coming."

"I was on a conference call with Sarah. We had a lot to go over. It seems her team finally finished clearing the tunnel, along with most of the cave containing the sacrificial children. But it sounds like they won't be able to get to the skeletons – apparently, a giant chunk of the mountain crushed them." He guided Breanne gently by the arm, back towards the camper entrance. "Any day they should be at the huge archway and lintel. Sarah said they have been able to make good progress in that direction. I'm not holding my breath, but I'm really hoping some of the pottery and lintel survived the collapse. As far as the other direction goes, they were only able to…" He paused at the metal steps leading into the camper. "You're not hearing any of this, are you?"

"No, I am… really," she said, trying desperately to show she was paying attention, but her heavy eyes betrayed her. A great struggle was being waged between her interest and her eyelids, and her eyelids were winning.

"This can wait till morning. Now off to bed with you," he said with a chuckle.

∼

How could you do it? How could you kill your own mother, Breanne!

Breanne gasped, lurched, and choked back a sob. She gasped again. Fire, and her mother's voice clear as death. She threw her head side to side, squeezing her eyes shut, willing it away. She sucked in deep and smelled fire. Her eyes popped open in wide-eyed panic. She expected to see flames, feel heat, but there was nothing, just her bed and the camper. Her brows pinched. There was no fire in the crash that had taken her mother. Yet she could smell it, sooty and black. It was there, real and fresh, as if the room were filled with ash.

She calmed, and breathed steady. Slowly the echo of her mother's voice was replaced by the sounds of laughter. The soot in her nostrils faded, too, replaced by the smell of bacon, eggs, and grits. She sat back, realizing she didn't even remember when or how she had gotten to bed.

The voices outside told her that her brothers were already up, and the camp was a bustle of activity. She was used to her father's dig sites resembling an ant colony as students, fellow archeologists, and excavation teams scurried around camp all throughout the day. But that wasn't the case on Oak Island. This site was different. There was no team other than her, her brothers, and her dad. Oh, and of course, the weekly visit

The Secret Journal

from Jerry. Usually, she beat them all out of bed, but not today.

She pushed herself up onto her elbows and could see the faint early morning glow coming through the small camper window. She still felt tired but she knew one thing for sure: she had no intention of closing her eyes. She lay there a moment longer, shaking off the nightmare. Then she remembered what today was, and excitement quickly replaced sleepiness. She threw back her blanket, the promise of a new mystery to solve propelling her out of bed.

A few minutes later there was a rapping sound on the camper door followed by Edward's voice. "Sis, you decent?"

"Yep."

The door popped open. "Well, it's about time you get up. Sleeping in, today of all days?"

"No freaking way, I just stayed up too late last night. Too excited, I guess."

"Yeah, I guess, if you call sawing logs in a camp chair staying up late," he said with a laugh.

"Whatever! I was not snoring!" Bre found one of her socks and slid it on. "You know what sucks about this place? The dig site is so secret I can't even tell my friends about this place when I write them. I mean, what's the point of being on a really cool secret dig when you can't even tell anyone?"

"You know Pops is going to let you publish with him, right? Think about it – you will be a published archeologist before you even finish college. Picture this, you get to college right around the time this story breaks and boom, you become famous!"

Breanne laughed. "You're crazy! And I think you're getting a little ahead of yourself." But the thought was exciting. The possibility of co-publishing with her dad. *That would be epic.* "Do you see my other sock?"

He pointed under the kitchen table. "Over there."

She took the sock and pulled it on. "Hey, you know what I find odd about the site? How come this mystery stakeholder guy never comes around? Why all the secrecy? Why can't we meet this guy?" She pulled her braids back to bind them with a stretchy hair band. "I know Dad presses Jerry about it. Even he knows this arrangement is weird."

"Have you been listening to Pops's calls with Jerry again?"

"Well, yeah, but it's not like I'm eavesdropping."

"Maybe the guy is famous or something. Some rich celebrity who doesn't want to be associated with this publicly."

"Maybe."

"Oh, I know! Maybe it's Bill Gates! He's loaded," Edward teased. "Or maybe it isn't a guy at all. Maybe it's Oprah! I mean, the person funding this has a money-is-no-problem-the-sky's-the-limit attitude."

Breanne laughed. "You're stupid, you know that?"

Edward feigned hurt feelings.

"Seriously, Ed, you have to admit it is weird."

"Sure, it is. But the guy is just private, that's all," Edward said assuredly. "No more worry talk. This is a celebration. Yesterday was a big deal, Bre – we found it. Finally, we found it."

She knew her brother was right. They had been digging that damn hole so deep, for so long, that she honestly had begun to wonder whether her father's calculations were correct or if they would keep going until they hit bedrock. Of course, he was correct on the location of where to dig within a few feet of his calculation. The depth, however, was so much deeper than anyone could have imagined.

"Well, at least this ought to settle Jerry down for a while. Have you noticed how worn down he looks?" she asked.

"Yeah, I think the pressure from his boss must be getting to him."

"I think the strain between him and Dad isn't helping either. The arguing during their conference calls is getting even worse."

Edward furrowed his brow in disapproval as he turned towards the camper door.

"What? Camper walls are thin," she said before shoving her toothbrush into her mouth.

Turning back, he grinned. "Let me guess – it went something like, 'By the *queen's knickers*, don't get all *wonky* on me, Charles. You *bloody hell know* that's not what I want!'"

She spit her toothpaste in the sink in a fit of laughter. Her brother had flawlessly mastered Jerry's British accent. "Ha! Yep! And you know Dad was like, 'I won't be rushed into making foolish mistakes *further compromising* this site, Jerry! You'd better not rush me, Jerry – I'll be off this site so fast it'll make your head spin, Jerry!'" she said, summoning her deepest voice.

Edward laughed. "Listen, when you're finished primping for your date with the dirt pit, breakfast is ready."

Hastily, she ate breakfast as she packed her daypack. Then, quickly pulling on her steel-toed boots, she grabbed the last of her gear and was ready to go. Her brothers and father had already made their way over to the pit area and were doing pre-workday safety equipment checks on the crane, including the cables, bucket, and basket.

Today Breanne was surprised to find Jerry was at the site and manning the controls to the crane – a job that usually belonged to Paul, heavy-equipment-operator extraordinaire.

"Jerry, you will be fine," Paul said. "It isn't like you will be digging with it. You are simply lowering us down and pulling us out, and that is only if the remote system fails, which is highly unlikely. Really, it's just an added precaution so we can all be in the pit today."

"I bloody hope you realize I have never used heavy equipment in my life," Jerry said with concern.

"Jerry, stand out there on the viewing platform where you have a good visual of the bottom and simply press this one for up." Paul pointed at the control.

"My dear boy, I am not a huge fan of heights." Jerry said uneasily.

"There's a guard rail, Jerry. You will be perfectly safe," Paul said, giving Jerry's shoulder a slap.

Breanne leaned in close to her father. "Dad, you sure about having Jerry run the controls?"

"It was this, or I was going to make you stay up top and do it," he said seriously.

She drew back.

"Look, I need your brothers' muscle for moving these stones, but I knew you would *Daddy* the hell out of me. And besides, we should all be down there for this."

Breanne kissed her father's cheek. "Thanks, Dad. Like I was saying, Jerry is a good choice." She winked.

"Uh-huh," he grumbled.

Paul pointed towards the pit. "Pops, I took a load of tools and a pile of four-by-fours down. We have plenty of room on the pit floor to spend the entire day pulling stones and stacking them if we have to. But if the pile gets too big and we start to run out of room, I'll switch the basket out with the clamshell, and we'll have to spend a day hauling them up."

Her father smiled. "Hopefully we aren't pulling rocks that long. Now let's get started!"

Her father allowed less finesse in the excavation of the tunnel this time. Since he knew what it was and that they were going to have to cut through the wood structure to gain access, there was really no need to be overly careful. As they cleared the dirt off the top of the wood, they noted it looked the same as it did over in the swamp. A solid wooden structure held together by wood pegs. Then as they uncovered the tunnel to the furthest eastward section nearest to the pit wall, they noticed that gaps started to appear between the timbers, maybe a couple inches wide. Between the gaps, they could see a fibrous material.

"Pops, what is this?" Edward asked, shoving his fingers into the crack between the timbers and pulling out some of the fiber pinched between two fingers.

Breanne had spent her whole winter immersing herself in Oak Island's history. She had even watched all the reality shows and researched every theory she could find on the internet. She recognized right away what her brother was holding. "Dad! Come look at this!" she called.

"What you got there?" he asked, laying a handsaw down on a pile of boards.

"That's coconut fiber, isn't it?"

"I'll be damned if it isn't!"

"So, what's the big deal?" Edward asked.

"They put it there to act as a filter between the dirt and rocks. This fiber keeps the cracks from filling with dirt and sealing," Breanne said excitedly.

Edward shook his head, puzzled, as he inspected the fiber. "But I don't understand. Why would they need to prevent the cracks from filling a tunnel they buried anyway?"

Her father smiled a great big smile. "Because they wanted water from the swamp to be able to pass through this tunnel, then come out through these cracks and flood the area. And do you know *why* they wanted the water to flood this specific area?"

Edward smiled.

Paul snapped his fingers. "We're close!"

"Indeed, we are," her father said. "The only reason for them to construct these gaps in the wood is to allow water to run through, and the only reason for the builders to do that is to flood *this* particular area. They are protecting something, and we're damn close! Bre, let's bag some of this fiber. I want to get it off to the lab for analysis." Motioning to his son, he said, "Ed, let's pop the top."

Breanne nodded and began collecting samples.

Edward positioned himself onto his knees next to the tunnel and as close to the wall as he could. Using a cordless reciprocating saw, he began cutting through each timber one by one, stopping occasionally to remove any chunks of coconut fiber threatening to bind in the saw blade. Within a few minutes, he had opened a hole big enough to climb through, and one by one, they began removing stones until Paul was fully inside the tunnel.

They spent the rest of the morning pulling rocks out of the hole to the sounds of Motown on cassette. Paul lifted each stone up and over the side of the hole before plopping it onto the pit floor with a *thud*. Breanne helped with the ones she could handle. Edward, who looked like he spent his spare time in the gym doing squats and dead lifts and who had grown into a beast of a man at six two and 230 pounds, effortlessly plucked each large stone from the ground and carried it across the pit, idly tossing them into a pile. A few times, Charles offered to give him a break and carry rocks, but Edward wasn't about to let his pops carry the large rocks. "I got this, Pops – I like the workout." By the time lunch rolled around, they had a pretty good pile going.

"How are we looking in there, Paul?" Charles shouted through the opening.

Paul shouted back from a few feet down the tunnel. "Muddy as all hell, and I think I need to put in a brace, Pops. I'm not trusting this structure."

"Okay, well, I have the four-by-fours cut to the measurements you asked for – but after lunch. Let's get you out and head topside to eat."

Breanne lay down on her belly next to the hole and poked her head inside.

"Don't even think about going in there, Bre," her father said.

"I'm just looking," she said innocently. She was surprised at just how much of the tunnel Paul had cleared. She clicked her flashlight on and pointed it towards her brother, illuminating his back as he squatted in front of the stacked stones, preparing to grab another one.

"For real, I am starving," Paul said. He hefted a small boulder free and froze.

"What is it, Paul?" she asked.

"There is no stone behind this one." He placed the stone on the soggy floor of the tunnel behind him, then turned back and grabbed another.

Breanne's pulse quickened.

He repeated this twice more. He looked back at her with disappointment. "I think we hit a dead end."

"What did he say?" her father asked.

"A dead end," she said, her face dropping.

"From what I can tell, there is a wooden wall with gaps just like there are on the top of the tunnel. Wait… wait just a second." He pulled another large stone from in front of the newly discovered wall.

"Daddy, you better get over here." Breanne couldn't tell what had her brother so excited, but he was frantic now as he slapped palm to stone again and again, heaving, tugging, and tossing until he had cleared away enough to see whatever had caught his eye.

"What did you find?" Charles asked, rushing over to the hole and dropping to his knees next Breanne.

"Um, Pops! Sis! I think lunch is going to have to wait!"

Edward, hearing the commotion, tossed a stone into the pile and hurried over. "What did he find?"

Paul popped his head up through the access hole in the wood tunnel. "The stones stop, and it's just a wall with the same gaps like in the top and sides, but there's something else, Pops!" Paul swallowed.

"Well, what is it?"

"Mounted to the wall from top to bottom and side to side... it's... it's a giant cross!"

Her father's eyes went wide. "A cross!"

"But it looks weird."

Breanne stuck her head back into the hole and shone her light past her brother, illuminating the end of the tunnel and... the cross.

"Weird – what do you mean weird?" he asked.

"Well, it flares out on the ends and gets really wide, but narrower towards the center. I don't know, Pops, it just looks weird," Paul said, shrugging with excitement.

"My God, son, it sounds like you're describing a cross pattée."

"A cross pat what?" Edward asked.

But before he could answer, Bre shouted, "A medieval cross! I see it, Daddy! It's really there! It's huge!" She yanked her head from the opening. "It's really there!"

"What's that mean, Pops?" Paul asked.

Charles sprawled out onto his stomach next to her as she handed him her flashlight. "It means a hell of a lot! You know who else used a medieval cross?"

If it were somehow possible, Breanne's smile widened even further. "The Knights Templar!"

11

The Date

Present day
Petersburg, Illinois

When church finally let out, Garrett saw Pete heading towards him with wild in his eyes. He slapped Lenny on the shoulder. "What's with him?"

"Hell if I know, but I think we're about to find out."

"Christ, Lenny, you swearing in church?"

"Doubt God cares any more about me saying hell or you saying his name like that, seeing how they threaten us with going there all the time," he said with a shrug.

"Fair point."

Eugene appeared from around a row of pews, also heading right towards them and just about as excited as old Pete was. "Boys, did you bring those pennies for the pond? I believe I owe you a wish," Eugene said, stopping Pete mid-stride. "Why don't you come on by the house. I'll make good on my promise, and while you're there we'll get you a glass of Lilith's fresh-squeezed lemonade."

"Okay, Eugene, that'll be swell – we'll head right over," Garrett said.

"Garrett, we need to talk about the book," Pete said, whispering into Garrett's ear.

Garrett yanked his head back. "Easy, man, I'm not your girlfriend. Just wait till we get away from the church."

Lenny raised an eyebrow.

The boys made their way out of the church parking lot and onto the street where Eugene and Lilith lived. The old Victorian was a short walk.

"What are you two whispering about?" Lenny asked. "Wait, let me guess – hmm, I would say Pete is probably giving you crap about using the word 'swell' in a sentence," he said, laughing at his friend. "That'd be swell, Eugene," he mocked with a wink, as he hooked a punch into the air with exaggeration. "Either you been watching too much Nick at Nite or we suddenly stepped through a time portal to the 1950s."

"I don't know, he's freaking old! Old people like that stuff. Tell you what, Lenny, how swell would it be if I kicked your ass?"

"You wish," Lenny replied.

When they were sure they were out of earshot from Eugene or any other potential prying ears, Garrett nodded to Pete. "So, what's up, Pete?"

Abruptly Pete stopped, then reached out and caught their arms, pulling them close. "Guys, get serious for a minute. Some stuff happened last night after I left," he whispered. He looked over both shoulders as if he expected someone to be following them. Seemingly satisfied, he proceeded to peer at them over the rim of his glasses, all schoolteacher serious.

"Dude, what the hell is wrong with you? Have you lost your shit or are you trying to get your hand broke?" Lenny asked, shaking Pete's hand off his arm.

"What stuff?" Garrett asked.

"I was able to read the first pages, and it's very weird. At first, I couldn't make sense of it, but then when I woke up this morning, I knew the date. I know the date!" he said excitedly.

"Hold on, Pete, back up a second. What date? What are you talking about?" Garrett asked.

Pete launched into a quick explanation, then read his transcription of the journal passage in a deep, formal voice. "At first the date didn't click, but I figured it out in my sleep—"

"Number one, why did you read the note in that creepy voice?" Before Pete could offer any sort of explanation, Lenny said, "Never mind, I don't even want to know. Second, in your sleep? What do you mean in your sleep?" He turned to Garrett and, pointing a finger at his head as he spun it in circles, sang out, "Craaazy!"

"It doesn't matter – the important thing is that I figured out the date, well, at least the year. Eighteen thirty-two was the year of the Black Hawk War!" Pete exclaimed.

"There is something seriously wrong with you, Pete," Garrett said. "I mean, who knows this kind of shit? I knew you practically lived in the library, but is that all you do? Sit around reading historical books? I would accuse you of being dropped on your head as a baby, but that doesn't usually turn someone into a nerd."

"Screw you, Garrett." Pete flipped him the bird. "I tell you this old book references the date of an historical event, and you want to give me crap," he said, thrusting a thumb towards his chest.

Lenny and Garrett just stared at each other. "Okay... so what? What does all this have to do with the book?" Garrett asked.

Pete launched into a frenzy of explanation. "*Potawatomi*

boy. Don't you see? Whoever wrote this met up with a Native American that changed his life forever – gave him information that for some reason he, or maybe she, kept secret for what sounds like a long time, long enough to really bother this person. And the date, July tenth – I need to figure out what in history happened on July tenth. After we do this penny thing, we should go to my place and see what the next page says."

"Alright, Pete, I'll go with you," Garrett said, despite the fact he had gotten a total of three hours' sleep thanks to his father's bug-out and sleep-deprivation training. "Lenny, you in?"

"No can do, fellas. If I don't get home and get my chores done, I'm dead – meaning I won't get to go to taekwondo class tonight, and no way am I missing class. You guys will just have to fill me in on what you find out. Garrett, you making class tonight?"

"Yeah, man, wouldn't miss it," he said, giving Lenny a fist bump.

"Cool, bro, I need a good sparring partner. Mr. B is so big, and he hits like a mule," Lenny said, before turning to address Pete. "Seriously, you're the smartest guy I know, but I got to tell you, man, that whole Native American thing sounds like a pretty far-fetched theory to me."

Pete looked at Lenny over the top of his thick glasses, sighed, and shook his head.

They arrived at the driveway of the old Victorian, and Pete stopped abruptly. "Guys, wait, there is one more thing you need to know. Don't be pissed... but..."

Both the boys stopped and stared expectantly because a statement like "don't be pissed" meant they were going to be pissed.

"Jack and Albert know about the book," he mumbled.

Garrett's eyes morphed to twice their normal size. "Pete! Why would they know?"

"They cornered me on the way home last night! I thought they were going to try and take it but—"

"Shit, man. Why didn't you hide it or run or something?" Lenny asked, shaking his head.

"You weren't there, man. I did the best I could. Besides, they didn't get it, and I didn't tell them where I got it. Well… they might have guessed… since they knew where I had come from."

"Pete? Why would you tell them where you'd been?" Garrett asked, slapping a hand to his head.

"You weren't there," he repeated. "They didn't get the book! Maybe they suspect, but they don't *know* where I got it. Now, lay off me. You have no idea how close I came to getting my ass kicked."

"Smooth, man," Lenny said.

"Whatever!" Pete shot back.

"Let's get this over with and get to your house," Garrett said, idly kicking at the loose gravel in frustration. Jack was a problem he didn't need.

"Sorry, Garrett," Pete said earnestly.

Garrett patted Pete's shoulder. "Don't worry about it, Pete."

They arrived at Eugene's pond, where they were treated to glasses of fresh-squeezed lemonade. "Now, boys," Eugene said, squatting slightly, like a wrestler preparing to shoot in on his opponent, "when you throw your pennies, make a wish, but for Pete's sake—" He paused, glancing over at Pete. "No pun intended, Peter."

Pete raised an eyebrow.

Eugene smiled and continued, "For Pete's sake, don't tell anyone your wish. If you tell it to anyone, it won't come true." Then, still holding his awkward squat, he began retreating a few cautious steps, as if he were carefully backing away from a grizzly bear he had just stumbled upon. Satisfied, he motioned the boys to proceed.

The boys tossed their pennies into the pond.

"Great job, boys!" Eugene announced, applauding. "Alright, now I know you boys are in a hurry, but Garrett, if I could have just a moment to talk business?"

"Sure, Eugene," Garrett replied, then turned to Pete and Lenny. "I'll hurry."

Eugene put his hand on Garrett's shoulder as they walked over towards the house. "I still have all that drywall that I need to get removed from the basement. Would you be interested in taking care of that for me this week?"

"I sure would, but I am working early cleanup at the park a few days a week, and I take and teach martial arts a couple times a week. Can we do it this coming weekend?"

"Martial arts, you say? What sort of martial arts?" Eugene asked with interest.

"I teach advanced taekwondo, hapkido, and advanced sword fighting."

"Oh, my. I should say you're a busy young man. Well, this coming weekend would be fine, Garrett, just fine." He chuckled as he attempted a poorly executed karate chop. "Just don't be using any of those karate moves on me. Now you better run along – your friends are getting antsy."

"See ya later, Eugene. Thanks again."

The boys sped down the driveway of the old Victorian and back out onto the road.

"I got to split, fellas," Lenny said, as he broke off from the two and began sprinting down the sidewalk on the opposite side of the street.

"Later, man," Garrett shouted after him, then turned to Pete. "Let's get to your place and figure out this book."

On the way to Pete's, Garrett convinced him to jog. Pete

was definitely not a runner, any more than Garrett was a walker, so a light jog seemed a good compromise.

"Pete, can I ask you something?" Garrett asked.

"Shoot," Pete said.

After Lenny's reaction, Garrett knew he needed to be careful with how he asked. "Does your mom make you do night-time chores?"

Pete hesitated, then said, "What, like take out the trash, clean my room type stuff? I mean, yeah, hell, I got to clean the whole apartment on Saturdays. Before you ask, I don't get much allowance either. Why you asking – you need to borrow money or something?"

"What! No, I don't need to borrow money," Garrett said. "I mean, do you, like, have to do training in the evenings?"

Pete slowed his jog to a walk. "Training for what?" Pete asked.

Garrett stopped altogether.

Pete stopped, too, and the two boys faced each other.

Garrett looked over his shoulders, then back to Pete, searching his eyes. "You know, training?"

Pete frowned. "No, Garrett, I don't know. I spend most of my time at the library. I don't participate in sports. You know that. What kind of training are you talking about?"

Garrett searched his eyes again. "Never mind."

"Never mind? You ask me a weird question like that, and then you say never mind?"

"Let's just get back to your place and check out this book. Can you jog?"

"Crap, do I have to?" Pete moaned.

When the boys arrived at Pete's twenty minutes later, their excitement turned to dread as they saw who sat on the front stoop of the apartment building, waiting for them.

"What's up, boys," Jack said, standing up to greet them. "I figured you'd be showing up soon, Pete, but I been waiting a while." He turned his head and spit a long stream of brown tobacco juice into a shrub, then nodded at Garrett. "What's up, Garrett?"

Garrett shrugged indifferently, doing his best to look casual. *Nothing to see here, dickhead, now go away,* he thought. He couldn't stand Jack. No one could, yet somehow, he was tolerated. The somehow really wasn't a secret – it was just something Pete preferred never be mentioned. It seemed only a matter of time before Pete would be calling Jack stepbrother.

Jack stood with his arms crossed, leaning against the door of the apartment building, blocking their path. "Yeah, probably going up to check out Pete's little find, I figure. Hell, I think I'd like to check it out, too, seeing how Pete was acting all secret about it last night."

"You going to just stand there in the way or what?" Garrett asked in annoyance.

"Riiight," Jack said, grinning at Garrett. "Why? You going to make me move?"

Garrett locked eyes with Jack for a long, silent moment.

It was Jack who broke the silence first. "Or maybe I will move. Maybe Pete's ready to show me why he was acting all secret last night." Jack shifted his glare to Pete.

"Maybe, or maybe it isn't any of your business, Jack," Garrett said.

Garrett watched the switch flip behind Jack's eyes. They went suddenly darker, colder, and they hardened to frozen right there in front of him. Frozen by the mean streak in Jack that ran as deep as the Sangamon. The reaction was as obvious as striking a hornet's nest with a stick. Jack's face flushed then, as he unfolded his arms and balled his fists. His lips curled back and he spoke, but his jaw was set tight as stone, unmoving. "Watch it, man – I will knock the fucking

The Secret Journal

shit out of you." He growled the words, biting down so hard his jaw muscles flexed.

Garrett's heart quickened, warning him he was on the cusp. He had pushed Jack into the red. Push any further, and he would be forced to fight him.

Pete pressed his lips in a tight line, shot Garrett a look, and nodded towards Jack.

Garrett understood. Pete wanted him to make Jack leave, whatever it took. With a single nod, his friend had given him permission to do what needed to be done. Garrett would not admit it to himself in the privacy of his own mind, let alone to his friends, but he was afraid of Jack. It didn't make any logical sense, but despite his denial, deep down he knew it was true. Maybe it was because Jack was plain fearless, because when it came to fighting, Jack wasn't even very good at it. But it didn't matter, because Jack never lost. Garrett had seen a bigger kid give him the beating of his life and Jack just kept getting up, smiling through broken teeth and a mouth full of blood as he threw haymaker after haymaker until he caught the older boy with one and dropped him like a wet towel.

"Well, Garrett, is it my business?" Jack asked as he dropped his balled fist low to his side, haymaker cocked and loaded.

Playing it off, Garrett gave the boy a wry smile and held up his hands in mock surrender. "Just saying, man."

"Alright, guys, c'mon, let's just go in and check it out," Pete said, clearly disappointed.

"Yeah, maybe that's a good idea, before Garrett gets his clock cleaned," Jack said, not breaking eye contact with the boy.

Pete rolled his eyes and motioned Jack out of the way. Jack stepped aside, then followed Pete in. Garrett followed after, letting out a long sigh of relief. He had only now realized he had been holding his breath.

The three boys entered the apartment building single file. As they crowded around Pete's apartment door, Garrett made sure to catch Pete's eye as he fumbled for the key. Summoning all his focus, he did his best to convey a look that said, *only tell him what you must.* Yet despite all of Garrett's telepathic effort, Pete returned a look containing a scrunched brow.

"So, where did you get the book?" Jack asked as they entered Pete's bedroom.

"Like I already said, I found it on the way home."

"Found it where, Fud?" Jack asked.

Garrett frowned.

"In a box of old books sitting next to someone's trash cans," Pete lied.

"Hmm. In a box of old books?" Jack questioned.

Pete shifted uncomfortably.

"Alright, well, now you know," Garrett said. "Pete, turn the page already and let's see what it says."

"Right," Pete said, rubbing his hands together excitedly. "So, I created this humidity chamber to moisturize the pages in a controlled environment. What you want is for the moisture to be just right. Too much and the book could get soggy, destroying all the writing. The way it works is by pumping steam up through here and—"

"Looks like a humidifier stuffed under a trash bag stretched over a chair to me," Jack interrupted.

"That's because you're an idiot," Pete mumbled under his breath.

"What did you—"

"Alright already, Pete, we get it. Let's go," Garrett urged.

"Fine. Now this will take a minute. I need my notepad to transfer the words from the book." Pete gathered a notebook

The Secret Journal

and pencil from his desk drawer, then, like a surgeon preparing to operate, he carefully tugged on the old jersey gloves. Ever so gingerly he persuaded the page to bend, and reluctantly the page obeyed, folding over without breaking.

The boys stared over Pete's shoulders.

"Mmmhmmm," he hummed.

"What, Pete?" What is it?" Garrett asked, leaning against the boy as he tried to see if anything legible remained on the page.

Pete shrugged Garrett back. "A little room, please," he said. "Well, there's text here, now I just need to copy it over."

The boys continued to watch over Pete's shoulders as he carefully copied over the letters from the page to his notepad. "Most of this left page is legible, unlike the last page."

*Finding what lies in hiding is only part of the journey. The Masons are everywhere and while I cannot say how many are in this elite sect; I can say with certainty they will stop at nothing to find the location of this secret. They have watched me closely for all **xxx** years and they **xxx** know my conscious grows heavy.*

"Why are you writing those *x*'s?" Jack asked.

"Because it's illegible, but I want to know there was a word there, so I write *x*'s where the word should be. Maybe later we can figure out what words fit if we need to."

"Makes sense," Garrett said. "Keep going, Pete."

"That's all that was written on the left page. The last half was blank, or at least I don't see any writing, or maybe there was a picture or drawing, but no way to tell now – it's just a water stain." Pete turned his attention to the right page and began the letter transfer.

*Bowling Green and I carefully concealed the entry **xxx xxx xxx** through meticulous means. I spent many a fortnight working in the dark by no more than the light of my lantern, taking careful measures to ensure no one unearths this secret – a secret I deeply regret allowing to ever burden my ears.*

I now have reason to believe our dear friend Bowling Green, who was like a father to me, was murdered nearly twenty-three years ago to this day by the Masons' most secret inner sect, the Keepers of the Light. Sorrowfully, I believe this to be true as they have learned that I confided in him, a Mason himself, the forbidden knowledge I have now confided in you.

Garrett looked curiously at Pete. "Bowling Green? That's an odd name. I feel like I should know that name."

"Well, that's a pretty damn stupid name, if you ask me. Who in the hell ever heard of naming someone Bowling?" Jack said, shaking his head. "Do you recognize the name, Pete?"

Garrett looked at Pete expectantly, but Pete said nothing as he just stared at the page. His eyes were searching back and forth across the page as he began to chew his lower lip. He knew something. *Don't you say it, Pete!* Suddenly Pete began bouncing on the balls of his feet, his knees practically hitting the top of his desk. *For Christ's sake, whatever it is, don't you freaking say it.*

"Fud! You home in there, dipshit? I asked you a question. You ever heard of this guy Bowling Green?" Jack said, in an annoyed tone.

"I... I... No... I don't think so. I mean, like Garrett said, the name sounds familiar, but I need to do some research to see if I can figure out who he was. I'll go to the library

The Secret Journal

tomorrow after school and research the name." Pete stood shakily from his desk and closed his notebook.

"Hey, what the hell! Turn the next page and see what it says. Maybe it will give us another name or something." Jack frowned, pointing at the book.

"I need to let the next page moisten before we turn it, otherwise it will just break or – even worse – crumble. Plus, my mom will be home soon, and I have to have my chores and homework done. I have two tests tomorrow, and I still need to study for those. If you want to stay and help me clean while I do my homework, I might have time later to try and turn the next page and transfer some more text – if it is moist enough."

Garrett didn't say a word as he listened to Pete ramble on like he was trying to ask a girl out on a date. The explanation of why they couldn't turn the page now was coming in a long burst of gibberish. *Not gibberish,* Garrett thought. *Bullshit.* Pete was bullshitting Jack – but why? If he knew anything about Pete, it was that he didn't have homework to finish. He never had homework, because he finished it all at school. Also, in all the years Garrett had known Pete, he had never seen him study – ever. He never needed to.

"Yeah, right, I'm not sticking around this place to babysit you, your chores, or your homework. So how about this, Fud, I'll just take the book home with me and figure it out myself," Jack said, reaching over to the desk and snatching up the book before anyone could react.

Pete's eyes went wide. "Careful, Jack!"

"Wait a minute, Jack, what are you getting all worked up about? The kid said he has stuff to do. If you go and take the book, you're probably going to mess it up and we'll never find out what it says. I say we listen to Pete," Garrett said.

Jack paused and locked eyes with Garrett in an awkward moment that lasted just a little too long.

"Come on, look at it – it's already breaking apart," Garrett said, pointing at the floor where a piece of the leather lay at the boy's feet, having chipped off the corner, no doubt a result of Jack's aggressive grab for the book.

"Please, Jack, put the book down – please." The blood had drained from Pete's face.

"You're already in, man. You know what's up. We'll figure it out tomorrow after it has had more time to get soft or whatever," Garrett said.

"Fine, but if you little shits try and screw me over, I'm kicking the crap out of both of you." Jack pointed both his pinky and index fingers, one at each of them.

"Screw you out of what? It's just an old book. An old book that *I* found, not you!" Pete said.

Jack's face filled with angry blood. "Yeah, right. I'm not stupid. Really old crap like this can be worth a lot of money. I want to know what it says by tomorrow, then I want to figure out which antique store will give us the most money for it, and we will split it three ways. You understand me, Petey?" Jack said, pointing a finger in Pete's face. "If you two double-cross me and that book disappears, I will decide myself what it was worth and that's what you'll pay me."

Garrett seethed internally, but he said nothing. As bad as he wanted to stand up to the kid, he didn't. In his mind, he told himself to just let it go. Jack was leaving and wasn't taking the book – *just leave it alone.*

Jack made his way from Pete's room across the small apartment and into the kitchen. "See you shits tomorrow," he said as he slammed the door.

"What the hell was that, Pete? Are you trying to start crap?" Garrett asked.

"Can I ask you something, Garrett? Why don't you just beat his ass, man?"

"He's not worth my time, Pete," he said, knowing the

The Secret Journal

answer was lame. "Why don't you tell me why you lied to him to get him out of here?"

"How do you know I was lying?" Pete grinned, cocking an eyebrow.

"Really, man, homework? Study? We've been friends since grade school."

"Well, it's good to know you can pick up on my codes when I need you to."

"Okay, so what is it, man?"

"Right, you're never going to believe this. It was bothering me all day even before this. July 10th, 1832 – I know what the date is! It's the date he was mustered out of service at the end of the Black Hawk War!"

"He who?" Garrett tried, but Pete babbled on excitedly.

"Holy shit! My God, oh my God, oh my freaking God! Do I know the name? Hell yes! I know the name. Why wouldn't I know the name? Shit! And I know who thought of Bowling Green as their father too – holy shit! Can this be real? This can't be real! But it has to be, right? I mean, shit! It has to be real!"

"Pete! Slow down and tell me what are you talking about." Garrett laughed – he had never seen his friend this flustered.

"I know who Bowling Green is, dude!" Pete said excitedly. "But more important than that, I know who looked at Bowling Green as a father." Pete began pacing back and forth. "At first, I couldn't believe it, man, but yeah, I think I know who wrote this book!"

"Who? Jesus, Pete! Who wrote it?" Garrett pressed.

"Abraham frickin' Lincoln!"

"What! No way! That's not possible!" Garrett said.

"I'm telling you, Garrett, it has to be. It's the only logical explanation!"

Both boys looked back toward Pete's room, wide-eyed.

Without a word, both broke into a run, coming to a halt in front of the book. They froze, staring at it anew. Could this really be Abraham Lincoln's journal?

"How long before we can turn to the next page, Pete?" Garrett asked, grabbing Pete by the shoulders. "How long!"

"I lied about that too." Pete smiled, snatching the jersey gloves off the desk. "We can try and turn it now!"

"Turn the page, Pete! Turn the freaking page!"

12

The Cross

Present day
Oak Island, Nova Scotia

The sky was a deep blue with the afternoon sun high overhead. Outside the Money Pit, the air actually moved. Breanne sat at the picnic table, her face turned to the sky and her eyes closed to feel the breath of the breeze on her face, not wanting to take the moment for granted. She could almost enjoy it... almost. She popped one eye open and scrutinized Paul with disgust as he sat at the picnic table across from her, shoveling handfuls of potato chips into his mouth between bites – no, chomps – of his third sandwich. Both eyes were open now as she fixed her gaze on her apparently starved sibling. A deep crease formed across her brow, and she crinkled her nose. "Do you even chew your food or do you just inhale it like a ravenous dog?"

Paul paused, smiling through stuffed cheeks. "You wrestle those heavy stones out of the tunnel for a few hours and see how starved you are," he said, taking a gulp of water.

"You look like a chipmunk, and not a cute one either. Stop trying to talk and just chew your food."

"You asked me, remember?" he mumbled, stuffing more sandwich in.

"Pops, who are the Knights Templar, and what's the big deal?" Edward asked, between bites of his own sandwich.

"Yes, Charles, do tell us the significance of the Templar connection," Jerry said, dabbing a napkin at the corner of his mouth.

Charles looked up from his plate, delighted at an opportunity to launch into a historical lesson. "What's the big deal, you ask? Well," he said, swallowing as he wiped his mouth, "up until now we had to assume this was the work of Native Americans or, less likely, Mayans, Aztecs, or some other known or unknown society. But now, we have Christian implications, plus the timing is correct for the Knights Templar. Now, why is the Templar connection so important? Well, what has always been thought – to me, at least – to be a far-fetched conspiracy theory, is that when the Knights Templar occupied the Solomon ruins on the Temple Mount in Jerusalem, they excavated the ruins and found the Holy Grail and the Ark of the Covenant." He paused and frowned. "I guess I should tell you who these guys were first. The Templars were basically a Christian army formed around 1120 AD, after the occupation of Jerusalem took place during the First Crusade. They were religious badasses during medieval times, put in place to protect pilgrims visiting the holy site. So, like I was saying, the theory is that they found the Holy Grail in the ruins of Solomon's temple."

"And the Holy Grail is the cup Jesus drank out of at the Last Supper, right?" Edward asked.

"Biblically, yes, the Holy Grail is the cup that Jesus drank from during the Last Supper, but there is also a conspiracy theory that the Holy Grail is really Jesus's bloodline. Regardless, cup or bloodline, the conspiracy scenarios hold the Knights Templar obtained it and hid it here on the island. The same theory pertains to the Ark of the Covenant, a wooden chest dressed with gold, containing two stone tablets recording the Ten Commandments, along with Aaron's rod and a pot of manna. This is all Old Testament, Moses stuff." He waved his hands as if to wipe away any further need of explanation on the subject. "Anyway, back to the Templars. They disappeared around 1312, give or take. This was after Pope Clement V, under the orders of King Philip IV of France, disbanded them, wrongfully accusing them of crimes, leading to their cruel torture, including burning many of them at the stake."

Dumping a pile of chips onto his plate, Edward shook his head with disgust. "That's messed up."

His father nodded. "Indeed, but they weren't all killed, and the conspiracy nuts…" He paused, considering. "Well, it isn't really fair to call them nuts, not after today. Not after what we've found. The conspiracists say that the Templars have always been here, protecting a secret, and that all this time they have been in hiding. One thing is for sure – something is down there, it's a big damn deal, and we are going to find it!"

Jerry lifted his plastic cup. "Like I have said all along, Charles, my dear man. What you find down there will change history forever!"

"Hooah!" Paul shouted, raising his own cup.

Breanne raised her cup, too, alongside the others, and they cheered.

After lunch, they completed their safety checks, secured their rigging, and descended into the pit, where Paul quickly went to work bracing the tunnel and Edward continued to remove the remaining rocks from the tunnel. The mood was high as Dr. Moore slapped the tape deck closed and got the

Four Tops singing about how there "Ain't no woman like the one I've got."

Taking Breanne's hand in his, her father pulled her towards him, then twirled her away. He smiled warmly, singing along with the lyrics. With his free hand, he snapped his fingers and began alternately kicking each foot out in front of him to the tempo of the music. "The dance floor is ours, baby girl," he said, smiling.

Breanne quickly fell into the rhythm, matching his movements, giggling at her father's strange timing for a father-daughter dance. Her father masterfully spun her to and fro, twirling her with his one hand only to retrieve her with the other. As she spun back, he spun himself, too, crossing one foot over the other and dipping his hips low before falling back into the step rhythm with perfect timing.

The two laughed as she spun in slow circles, her bound braids flipping from one shoulder to the other as the Four Tops faded away, replaced by another of her father's favorites.

"Bre, do you know who this is?" he asked.

She shook her head.

"Me and Mrs. Jones," her father sang. "That" – he pointed at the radio – "is the satiny smooth voice of Billy Paul."

Paul's head poked up from the tunnel. "Well, you're no Billy Paul, Pops – better not quit your day job," he said with a laugh.

Dr. Moore turned to Paul with a frown. "My voice is smooth as a warm glass of brandy."

Bre raised a skeptical eyebrow towards her brother.

"Ha, well, whatever – that magical voice of yours had me thinking someone was hurt, so I thought I'd better check on you two."

"Boy, don't make me come down there."

Paul laughed.

"How is the progress?"

"Almost done. Can you pass me a couple more boards?"

Her father passed the boards to Paul, and he disappeared back down the hole.

"Daddy, can I ask you something that's been bothering me?"

"Of course, what's on your mind?"

"How do you think all those people in the swamp died?"

He cocked his head, concerned. "Well, we don't know, baby girl – we just don't know. The lab didn't find any blunt-force trauma, so maybe they were sacrificed through some sort of ritual bloodletting."

"But, Dad, that was before we found the cross. I mean, does it even make sense that the Templars would sacrifice them in a way that didn't break any bones? Or, for that matter, does it make sense Templars would sacrifice the Native Americans at all?"

He paused, clearly stunned by her revelation.

"What?" she asked.

"The depth of your intelligence never ceases to amaze me. Honestly, I don't know if I will ever get used to it."

Her face flushed with embarrassment.

He placed his hands on his daughter's shoulders, his eyebrows raised in keen anticipation. "Baby girl, you have a theory of what happened to those people in the swamp? How they ended up there?"

Breanne hesitated, knowing how what she was about say would sound. But it wasn't only the cross that had led her to this idea. She had another clue, though it was so ridiculous she wouldn't admit to it. Something in her nightmares... Native Americans, walking into the bottom of the swamp one after the other. The nightmares always started the same, in the car, upside down, but then she was here on the island. Except it wasn't now; it was then. That didn't mean what she dreamt about Oak Island was true. That was ridiculous... crazy. It was just her brain working to solve it, that's all.

"Bre?"

Pulling herself back to the moment, she looked at her father and narrowed her eyes, nodding slowly. "I think they walked into that pit on their own, and I think they killed themselves." There, it was out. She'd said it, and it was out.

Suddenly Paul shouted from inside the tunnel opening, causing both of them to jump. "Hey, can one of you hand me down that pouch of nails? It's hanging on the sawhorse."

Her father passed the nail pouch through the hole to Paul, then turned to Bre. "Go on."

"When you think about it, it makes sense. The Templars were not enslavers, and if they wanted to force a people into slavery to hide religious artifacts, they would have been ill-equipped to do it. If the Templars were here, then they were fleeing with these religious treasures after the majority of their order had been tortured and killed at the order of King Philip. I just find it hard to believe they were in any condition to pull this off. There were simply too few to overthrow and murder hundreds of Native Americans."

"So, if you have come to this conclusion, do you have a hypothesis as to why they would kill themselves?"

"No, I don't, but I think we will get our answer behind that cross, Dad. The question is what would make a group of Native Americans willingly help Christians hide something and then freely sacrifice themselves? I just can't wrap my head around it. Maybe they were tricked into it somehow? I... I just don't know." Breanne shook her head in frustration.

"I have this thing braced up solid as a brick shithouse," Paul said, his voice echoing from inside the tunnel.

"We will find the answers," her father assured her with a tight smile as he removed his fedora to loop a leather camera strap over his head. Replacing his fedora, he turned to the

The Secret Journal

hole. "Alright, I'm coming in! Bre, wait here till I say it is safe for you." He stepped onto a short stepladder and made his way down into the tunnel.

Stepping off the last rung and into the mucky bottom of the tunnel, Dr. Moore's senses were assaulted with the pungent odor of rotting swamp and decomposing wood. "Good God, man, this place smells worse than a truck stop toilet." He pulled his bandana up to rest atop his nose. "Grab your helmet and come on down, Bre."

Breanne hesitated for a moment. It was one thing to work the pit with its open sky, but to go down there into the tunnel made her pulse quicken and her hands sweat. *Please, not like Mexico,* she thought.

She drew up her courage, pulled her cave helmet on over her braids, cinched up the strap, and began descending the ladder into the muck. As soon as her boots touched down, they were sucked into the spongy floor, and her breath caught as she drew in the odorous air. God, it was so pungent. She wasn't ready. She gagged and heaved, nearly losing her lunch. Somehow, she kept it down.

"Yeah, it's gross, but you get used to it," her brother said, backing up in the other direction to allow her room to move ahead. The tunnel was tight. "Watch your step, guys, the floor is really soft." He pointed his flashlight down the tunnel to illuminate the strangely shaped cross. "Check this baby out!" he said with pride, as if showing off his freshly waxed car.

The roof of the tunnel was low, forcing Breanne to hunch awkwardly as she followed her father to the cross.

"My God, my God, my God," her father whispered. With shaking hands he attempted to steady his camera as he began photographing the wooden cross. Finally, he said, "Bre, take this and photograph it all – remember how I've shown you?"

She took the camera eagerly. "I remember," she said, the camera already clicking and flashing.

He pulled a sample bag from his shirt pocket and carefully removed a small piece of the cross, gingerly placing it inside the bag. The cross had been preserved in the swamp water for centuries, but now that the swamp, and therefore the tunnel, was drained, the air had dried it out.

"I was afraid of this. This is a typical concern when trying to preserve archeological finds that include submerged organic specimens. Sometimes specimens can slowly devitrify into useless slivers or powder within hours of removal from water. This looks to be the case here. The cross has devitrified and might very well be destroyed if we try to remove it."

"What do we do? How do we remove it without damaging it further?" Paul asked.

"We'll have to try and get it out of the tunnel carefully. From there we can submerge it in preservation solution." Charles pulled a small notepad from his shirt pocket and began scribbling. As he wrote he shouted back through the hole. "Ed, radio Jerry and tell him you're heading topside. Then get these supplies pulled together." He tore loose the piece of paper and passed it through the hole.

"Roger that," Edward said.

In the background, "War" played on the radio.

Her father set to work taking measurements, sketching the position of the cross and its orientation in the tunnel, as she continued photographing from every angle possible.

After close examination they concluded that the cross was simply hanging on the wall rather than set into it. Breanne exited the tunnel to stand ready to help maneuver the cross through the tunnel opening and out into the pit. From above she listened nervously, biting at a fingernail as her father and brother struggled to free the cross.

The Secret Journal

"Careful, Paul, damn it, I can't see what's holding this thing – it should come loose," her father said.

"I don't understand what's… holding it," Paul grunted.

Then she heard it. A gut-wrenching crack from inside the hole. Her father's colorful choice of words told her the priceless artifact might have come free, but not without a cost.

"Shit – that's fine… it's – shit! Motherfu— It's fine. Just very, very carefully set your side down and help me with this side, then we will get your half—"

Then she heard more confused shouting. She threw herself onto her belly and looked into the hole. Her father's half had broken into three more pieces right there in his hands.

"Okay, well, it's okay, hold still, Paul – don't move a muscle."

Her father carefully handed the three pieces out of the hole one by one as she accepted each piece with reverence.

In the meantime, Paul stayed frozen in place, as unmoving as the cross had been for centuries. She had never seen him like this. He was never one to get invested in the find. His idea of fun wasn't the artifacts; it was the adventure. It was flying the chopper, operating a massive crane. She smiled. She liked seeing this side of her brother.

As they worked to remove Paul's half from the tunnel and get it to the pit floor, it too broke, but only into two pieces rather than three like his father's half. Paul was very quiet as Breanne and her father packed the large chunks into the tub of solution and prepared them for extraction from the pit.

"Son, this could have been much worse – the whole thing could have disintegrated right before our eyes. We're actually pretty damn lucky the moisture inside the tunnel floor has kept the humidity high enough that it didn't completely dry out. With the right conservation techniques applied, this cross can be preserved and pieced back together." He placed a hand on Paul's shoulder. "You did a good job, son. There is nothing more you could have done. Now let's get back in there and see what is behind that wall!"

Her brother nodded, the corner of his mouth curling into a slight smile. "Right, the wall." He hurriedly climbed back into the tunnel.

Once back inside, Charles began examining the tunnel where the cross had hung. "I don't see any latches or hidden levers, and the corners are laced together like the interlocking logs of a cabin."

"Can you see anything behind the wall, Dad?" she asked.

He pressed the flashlight up to the gaps, trying to see between. "There's indeed a void behind this tunnel, but how far it goes or to what end, I can't tell. Go get the Sawzall, Paul – we're cutting our way through."

The wood beams cut very easily, and in minutes they were through.

"Here we go," her father said, cautiously stepping forward to poke his head through the newly cut opening as he flashed his light into the darkness.

"The good news is there's no more of those cursed stones to move, nor is it made of wood. But the bad news is that this tunnel drops away at a steep angle."

"How steep is it?" Breanne asked.

"Well, steep enough I don't want to step inside. Christ, I can't even see the bottom. I swear, nothing wants to come easy on this island, does it?" he said, running his hand over his face.

"What now, Pops?"

"This tunnel appears to go down right into the bedrock. How in the hell is that even possible?"

"I think we're going to need to rig up some rappelling gear – I'll be back in a few minutes," Paul said, rubbing his hands together.

The Secret Journal

Stooped awkwardly, she and her father waited at the edge of the sloping tunnel, staring in quiet awe down into the darkness.

It was Breanne who broke the silence. "Dad, how are things going with you and Sarah?"

"Good. Great, actually. My first order of business after we finish here is to get back to Mexico and join her on the site. Phone conferences are one thing, and she has done a fine job keeping me posted on the progress, but I will be ready to get back in there for sure."

"Uh-huh." She arched her eyebrows. "Let me try this again. How are *you* and *Sarah* doing?" She wished she could see his face, but she didn't need light to recognize the sound of uncomfortable shuffling. She knew he didn't want to talk about this.

"Ah, fine. We are fine. Listen, I know, you must wonder why I did what I did."

She blinked. *Well, that was unexpected.* "Why did you, Dad? Why did you leave her?"

She heard him swallow.

"I wasn't ready. I thought I was but I just wasn't, or at least that's what I told myself. But I miss her."

Her heart broke a little as he sighed heavily there in the darkness. She was suddenly glad she couldn't see his face as she felt the weight of it. Maybe talking here in the darkness made it easier somehow. "Daddy, was it because of me that you weren't ready?"

"What? What do you mean because of you?"

Now she shuffled. "Because of Mom, what happened, or maybe because you worried about me?"

"God, no. It had nothing to do with you and everything to do with me. I was the one who messed it up. I am the one who thought I wasn't ready and blew it. It had nothing to do with you or what happened. It was all me."

"Yeah," she said.

"Okay, now I was honest. I want you to be honest. I know you don't want to talk about this, but you need to—"

"Dad, I don't want to talk—"

"Yeah, well, dammit, I didn't want to talk about Sarah, but you asked me and I was honest. Now I am asking you, are you okay? What's going on with your sleep and the nightmares? I know you're not sleeping."

"Dad…" Now it was her turn to shuffle her feet. "Fine. The dreams about Mom and what I did… they're bad, really bad. It's this place, and the bodies and the swamp." She shook her head as if to shake away the thoughts. "But I just need to stay busy, and it will all be fi—"

"Wait, what do you mean what you did? Bre, you didn't do anything. It was an accident. You know that. I want you to talk to me or to someone."

"Another shrink? To tell me what? No. I just need to work."

"You can't bury this forever, baby girl. What happened was an accident."

"You know it wasn't!" Her hands began to shake. "I forgot! Me! And we had to go back because of me! God! She shouldn't have been driving so fast. She wouldn't have been rushing!" She began to cry. "She wouldn't have been driving so fast on the snow. Goddammit, it was my fault!" she choked.

"Oh, Bre, it was not—"

"Back!" Paul said from just behind them, a length of coiled rope in hand.

Her father flinched, smacking his head on the roof of the tunnel. "Christ! You scared the crap out me, kid!" he said, removing his fedora and rubbing the top of his head.

Breanne turned her face, allowing the darkness to hide her tears as she tried to pull herself together.

Her father situated his fedora back atop his head. "Bre, I want to finish this conversation later," he said, reaching for her hand and squeezing.

She squeezed his in return. "I need to get some air," she said quietly. "I'll be right back." She slid past her brother.

"I miss something?" Paul asked.

"No, she'll be okay," she heard her father say. "Alright now, you have the rope secured?"

"Yep, and I am ready to rappel in."

She climbed up through the hole and onto the floor of the pit, pulling in a shaky breath. Despite being at the bottom of a deep pit, the air seemed fresh and crisp. Turning her face upward, she gazed out beyond the dirt walls, past the crane cables, and into the circle of blue sky above it all. No sun. No clouds. Only pale-blue nothingness. She thought about her mom – her mom's smile, her laugh, and even her voice and the way it sounded when she sang. That was the hardest, and she felt her chest ache with shame. She couldn't remember the sound of her mother's voice. For a few minutes she sat and cried. *More salt – cake it in, and rub it deep. Feel it burn. You deserve every bit. You deserve every single bit.* An unmeasured moment of time went by. Finally, she pressed her lips into a tight line and climbed back into the tunnel.

13

Lincoln's Secret

Present day
Petersburg, Illinois

Garrett watched with wide eyes as Pete pulled on his jersey gloves and ever so gingerly worked to finesse the page over to reveal the next part of what just could be a long-dead president's secret journal. Pete had been careful with the journal from the start, but now that he had established and spoken his theory aloud, Garrett could see clearly the newfound level of reverence with which his friend handled the journal. Garrett couldn't blame him; after all, if Pete was correct, this was no longer just some really old book. This was Abraham Lincoln's journal. He felt his own palms growing damp and his mouth dry, suddenly glad he wasn't the one trying to turn the page.

Neither dared gamble a breath as they watched the page fold over without incident.

"Okay," Pete said in a loud exhale, "I will start transferring the text."

Garrett swallowed dryly, staring over Pete's shoulder as he began to write.

> *Let this journal be your guide in gaining access to the temple entrance, but understand, dear friend, I cannot tell you what traps lie beyond the final path. I only looked onto the chamber within from the temple entrance and never **xxx xxx xxx xxx xxx xxx** place. Thus, I can only offer assistance to get you past the traps Bowling Green and I put into place to ensure no man casts eyes upon it or what foulness it holds. Bowling and I worked meticulously to set traps that, without this account, will surely put end to any man seeking entry. Should you choose to gain entry to this most unholy place, you must follow the direction here told within.*
>
> *I began my survey for the town of Petersburg in 1835, and in doing so, I ensured the tunnel entrance was concealed but still accessible through clever brickwork hidden inside of a drainage duct. You can find this duct spills into the Sangamon River.*

"Holy shit, Garrett! Holy shit!" Pete exclaimed.

"What? What is it?"

"Don't you see!"

Garrett shrugged pleadingly.

"*I began my survey of Petersburg in 1835*! Seriously? Come on, Garrett. I know you know this. You don't even have to be smart to know this one!" Pete said hopefully. "Who surveyed Petersburg?"

Too excited to be offended, Garrett slowly sat down on the edge of Pete's bed. "Oh my God, Pete," he said, his eyes wide. "It can't be. It just can't. God, Pete what have we found? What the hell have we found?!" He shouted the words and leapt back to his feet. *Hell, if you lived in Petersburg, you damn sure should know who surveyed the historic city.* Garrett cupped his face with both hands, "Abraham Lincoln! It's Abraham Lincoln's journal. You're right, Pete. I… I didn't believe it, but this is proof that this was written by him, right?"

"Well, it was either written by Lincoln – and yes, I believe it was – or it was written by someone from the time period pretending to be him, because I think this thing is definitely old enough!"

"Transfer the other side," Garrett said, feeling the excitement build inside of him.

> *Begin at my survey marker and walk directly east until you reach the river. At the end of the street head due **xxx xxx xxx** paces. Look carefully over the side, and you will see a drainage opening large enough for a man to enter upright.*

"Drainage pipe." Garrett pressed his fingertips into his pursed lips.

"What are you thinking?" Pete asked.

"I don't know yet – keep going."

Pete eagerly continued to write.

> *Once inside, look for the archway, which holds a **xxx xxx xxx**. When you find **xxx xxx** remove **xxx** beloved **xxx** and, once removed, reach inside and pull the lever. This will allow the way to open, showing you the path.*

"Okay, there's some kind of roughly drawn map on the bottom part of the page, but it's all smudged up. I can't make much out of it." Pete turned the book towards Garrett. "These two squiggly lines here" – he pointed – "see how they run horizontal, then they bend? These could be the river?"

"Yeah, that makes sense. Pete, if this leads to a temple, it must be underground. What do you think is in it?" Garrett cocked his head to one side as he studied the smudged lines.

"I don't know, man. He talks about a temple and booby traps. What's in the temple is anybody's guess, but it has to be something of great value or importance."

"Jesus! This is some *Goonies* shit, Pete!" Garrett said. "Can you turn to the next page?"

Pete bit his lower lip, considering. "Let me try." Carefully, he slid one gloved finger under the page, almost as if trying to will it to just bend over. But this time the page didn't bend; it began to crack.

For a heart-stopping second, Garrett thought it would break in half.

Pete froze, slowly extracting his finger. "We really need to put this back in the humidity chamber before we go further. The pages need to moisten up a bit."

"You mean, back under the garbage bag?" Garrett asked, smiling.

"The *humidity chamber*," Pete stressed, correcting his friend.

"Okay, genius, we know the beginning of this thing starts at the river… somewhere." Garrett began to pace. "We need to figure this out and decide how we're going to deal with Jack." Garrett stopped pacing, abruptly turning to Pete. "What the hell could be in this temple?"

"Like I said, it's anybody's guess. We're missing the first section of the book, plus we're missing words so I don't even understand which way to go once we get to the river, but I do know one thing."

"Yeah?"

"I know exactly where to start." Pete carefully placed the journal back under the bag before grabbing his notebook and stuffing it into his backpack. "We need a meeting. Let's go to my office."

Garrett smiled. "I'll call Lenny."

14

Hardheaded

Present day
Oak Island, Nova Scotia

When Breanne approached the opening cut into the back of the tunnel wall and peered down the slope, her headlamp fractured the darkness, revealing a taut rope vanishing around a bend. She was not happy. "You let my daddy go down there by himself? Why didn't you go?"

Paul held out his hands helplessly. "He insisted. I argued, but he wouldn't listen to me. Almost as soon as he started down, he vanished." He pointed his light. "Right there, you see? He must have... I think he went around a corner. Damn old man is going to get himself killed."

"Jesus Christ, Paul!" Breanne glared at him.

"Don't do that, and don't stand there and act like you're surprised he insisted on going."

"That's not the point. He isn't fit to be rappelling, Paul."

"Tell me about it. He's bullheaded and stubborn just like you."

She began to panic. "I can't see him. How long has he

been down there? Do you know how deep it goes? What's at the bottom? What if he just drops off? How much rope does he even have? What if he runs out of rope? Did you two even think about that?"

"Jesus, Bre, knock it off!" Paul turned back to the corridor and shouted down into the void. "Pops! Can you hear me down there?"

A distant voice echoed up from below. "I can hear you. I think I'm almost at the bottom. It seems to go maybe forty yards down, in a sort of bend."

Breanne let out a relieved sigh.

"I'm down. I passed under an arched opening that seems to be cut right into the bedrock. This is magnificent."

"Pops, you ready for me?" Paul shouted.

"Yes, both of you get down here, but be careful – it's a bit slick."

Adjusting her helmet and snatching up the rope without a second thought, Breanne started to back towards the edge.

"Hold on!" her brother said. "We're going to do this right. You're going to gear up."

But it was too late. She wrapped the rope around the back of her waist and descended into the darkness.

"Who has the hard head now, Bre!" Paul shouted after her.

The slope was slippery as hell, and she fell to her knees twice before reaching bottom. She wondered how she was going to make that climb back up – or how her father would make it.

"I'm down," she shouted back up the slope before turning to find her father waiting.

"On my way down," Paul's voice echoed from above.

"You know what, Dad? You used to say a hard head makes for a sore ass. Maybe you should take your own advice."

"Watch it… young… lady," he grunted, stretching his back. Mud was smeared on the front of his clothes, hands, and face.

"Daddy, are you okay?"

Her father smiled weakly. "I'm okay – the slope was a little slippery, that's all." Quickly changing the subject, he said, "Look at the size of this place, Bre."

"How big is it?" She spun in a slow circle, several inches of watery muck sloshing over her boots as her flashlight illuminated the space before her. She was in an expansive cavern. The ceiling was high and natural, stalactites plunging downward like menacing teeth. The floor appeared to have a combination of either muddy muck or standing water, extending as far as she could see.

Paul arrived a moment later. "Holy shit. This place is huge."

"Okay, listen, as we look around, stay close and don't walk through any standing water. Could be hidden holes," her father said.

"Roger that," Paul said, starting forward.

They started to venture around the cavern, moving further from the slope. As they approached a rock formation at the center of the cavern, Breanne first thought it was just a random stalagmite. She had already maneuvered around several throughout the cavern. But as she drew closer, she could see the top was perfectly flat. Unnaturally flat. *Strange,* she thought. Either this was a trick of the shadows or… *Wait a minute, there is something atop the stone.* Breanne's heart caught in her throat. Her pulse quickening, she tentatively approached the structure, each step sinking deep into the muck. Then she saw it clearly. She wanted to rub her eyes to clear them of the mirage she could not be seeing. Atop the stone stood a man.

"Daddy!" she yelled. "You better get over here!"

Her father's boots squished towards her. "My God, Bre! My God, you've found it!"

Paul quickly trudged his way over and then froze. "What in the world?"

Atop the flat stone, a skeleton knelt on one knee. In the skeleton's right hand was a medieval-looking sword, its tip touching the rock, almost as if the skeleton figure were about to drop it. Held in the skeleton's left hand and strapped to its forearm was a shield, held out in front of the skeleton in a defensive position, as if it were about to deflect a strike. The skeleton wore a very brittle, very faded, but very familiar Knights Templar robe, complete with a red cross on the chest. Over the skeleton's head, neck, and shoulders was draped a rusted chainmail coif. As amazing as the sight of the skeleton was, all their eyes fell to what sat below the shield at the bent knee of the ancient knight.

A treasure chest trimmed in shimmering gold.

For a long moment, no one spoke.

"Don't touch anything," their father finally rasped. Then, turning to his children, he threw an arm around each of their shoulders. Pulling them in close, he whispered in a quiet voice, as if speaking too loud could somehow undo what they had discovered, "We've found it. Something that should not be, oh my God. We've actually found it!"

She smiled wide. Finally, after hundreds of years of failed searching by generations of seekers, she and her family had found the Templar treasure.

15

Pete's Office

Present day
Petersburg, Illinois

"Step into my office and have a seat, Lenny," Pete called quietly from across the vast room.

"Your office smells like moldy books, bro. You should really do something about that." Lenny stepped into the basement with his face crinkled.

"Greatest smell in the world." Pete stretched out his arms as if the entire place belonged to him and him alone.

Looking around, Garrett figured the library basement might as well be Pete's, as he suspected it didn't get much use. Most kids probably just did what he did and used the school library.

The library basement was large, and from what Garrett could tell it contained a lot of middle-grade and younger books. The floors were a bland time-worn tile that seemed to match the water-stained drop ceiling. Both were a complete contrast to the colorful block walls, which provided a canvas for local art students and were covered with murals matching each section's genre. A row of old computers with dial-up modems sat lonely on a long table below a painted mural of Tom Sawyer and Huck Finn navigating a raft through unruly waters. The caption read ADVENTURE. Garrett's eyes hovered over the word.

"So, what's the big emergency?" Lenny asked.

"Adventure, Lenny," Garrett said with a nod. He and Pete sat at a round table on the far side of the library by the historical section, with the whole place to themselves.

Pete waggled his eyebrows and leaned back in his chair.

"Adventure? Are you both high?" Lenny asked accusingly.

"Alright, let's get serious," Garrett said. "We don't have much time before martial arts class, and we have a lot to figure out, like our next move."

The boys quickly brought Lenny up to speed on the afternoon's events, including Jack's involvement and their discovery that they were holding Lincoln's journal, complete with directions to a secret temple.

"Again, I ask, are you two smoking something? That or you're yanking my chain." Lenny stood up and spun his plastic chair around, casually straddling the chair and resting his arms across the back.

"I wouldn't shit you, Lenny – you're my favorite turd," Pete said.

Lenny shook his head disappointedly. "That's a lame joke, bro. Anyway, assuming what you're saying is legit, then that's crazy! Hey, you know, guys, Jack is a real dick, but he did say one intelligent thing."

"Do tell, Lenny, because I didn't hear anything intelligent from that nutsack." Garrett gave Lenny a sideways look.

"Like he said, this journal has to be worth some cash, and he didn't even know it was Lincoln's. What does that little fact make this worth, Pete?"

"You can't seriously be suggesting we sell this to an

antique store? That's not happening." Pete threw himself back in his chair and crossed his arms.

Lenny held out his hands defensively. "I'm just saying the thing really could be worth a lot, right?"

"Yeah, sure it *could* be – once authenticated – but I think you're missing the bigger picture, Lenny!" Pete said too loudly.

"Chill, man, you are going to get us in trouble, and we don't want to get kicked out of here. We have some research to do, right?" Garrett said, attempting to calm his friend.

"Yes, we do, actually. Which brings me to the big picture, Lenny." Pete stood and began to pace. "Abraham Lincoln – if we're to believe the journal was his, and I think we do – was keeping a secret that was bothering him really bad. According to the journal, it has to do with a hidden temple that a Native American boy told him about. I have read the text multiple times, and I think the Masons must have known about the temple and wanted it to stay hidden. Perhaps it was their temple? Abraham obviously felt like he was in life-threatening danger from the Masons. I don't know – maybe because he was starting to talk about whatever he had seen, and the Masons caught wind of it. Obviously, he wanted to unburden his conscience but was sworn to secrecy."

"Wait a second. Who in the hell were the Masons?" Lenny asked.

"Yeah, I mean, I know they still exist today, right? But what are they, Pete?" Garrett asked.

"Riiight," Pete said slowly, then sighed. "Okay, guys, pay attention. The Freemasons go all the way back to, like, the fourteenth century. They are a secret fraternity, a brotherhood that have a lot of secret rituals and mysterious crap. And yes, Garrett, they're still around today. There are tons of conspiracy theories linking them to everything from the Illuminati, to the dollar bill, to the Egyptian pyramids. Heck, they're even linked to the bloodline of Jesus Christ and to the Holy Grail. There are tons more, but I won't go into all of them because I have no idea how any of this is relevant right now."

Lenny leaned forward, pressing his chest against the back of his chair and bringing the front legs off the ground. "You know, I remember seeing Uncle Frank wearing this weird ring, and when I asked my mom about it, she said he was a Mason. I asked her what that was, and she explained that he belonged to a secret club of sorts. She said he mostly hung out at a lodge that didn't allow girls, and she suspected the guys played lots of cards and drank. Sounds like there might be a little more to it than that." Clanging the chair back down onto all four legs, Lenny turned to Pete. "So, does this mean there is some giant conspiracy going on, and all these Masons know about this hidden-temple thing?"

"Look, there is definitely a lot of secrecy with the Masons, but I don't know at what level it starts," Pete said. "At your uncle's level maybe they do just sit around playing cards, but per Lincoln's journal there was a secret sect within the secret society, and it was this inner circle either threatening or trying to kill him. Since we are dealing with a temple, according to Lincoln, maybe it has something to do with God. Maybe it is a secret Freemason temple. I don't know, but we need to learn all we can about these Keepers of the Light."

Garrett nodded slowly.

Pete uncrossed his arms and placed his palms down on the table. "Here's a little history lesson, you guys. Abraham Lincoln was not a Freemason, but most of his friends were. No one knows for sure why he never joined up. It would have made perfect sense for him to join too. The Masons were very powerful, and it could certainly have made his political career even easier. But for some unknown reason, he never did. Another theory that I have read is that the man who killed Lincoln, John Wilkes Booth, was also a Mason."

Garrett shook his head. "Seriously, so the guy who ends up killing Lincoln is actually a Freemason?"

Pete nodded. "Yep, and that's legit history." Straightening, he began pacing again. "Further, Lincoln was killed in 1865 and Bowling Green was killed in 1842, and that, my friends, is a major clue that I nearly overlooked." He snatched up his notebook off the table.

"Question," Lenny said, making a show of raising his hand. "Pete, man, how could anyone know this much useless shit?"

Pete frowned, pushing his glasses up his nose.

"Don't pay attention to him. Keep going," Garrett said, motioning to Pete to continue with one hand, while flipping Lenny the bird with his other.

"Listen to this," Pete said, and started reading from his transferred notes. *"I now have reason to believe our dear friend Bowling Green, who was like a father to me, was murdered nearly twenty-three years ago to this day by the Masons' most secret inner sect, the Keepers of the Light. Sorrowfully, I believe this to be true as they have learned that I confided in him, a Mason himself, the forbidden knowledge I have now confided in you."*

Both boys just stared at Pete, neither of them understanding.

Pete smiled. "Subtract 1842 from 1865, guys."

"Twenty-three!" they both said at the same time.

"That's right! Congratulations, you can both do math at a second-grade level." Pete rewarded them with a slow, mocking clap.

Both Garrett and Lenny rewarded Pete with the finger.

"Anyway," Pete continued, "Lincoln said he was in

danger. He writes this journal to his friend, then he dies shortly after."

Garrett traded glances with Lenny. Good, he wasn't the only one not getting it.

Pete rolled his eyes and shook his head in disgust. "Let me spell it out for you two. Lincoln died precisely twenty-three years after Bowling Green gets murdered by the Masons. Lincoln had to have died right after he wrote this, because he writes that it has been twenty-three years since Bowling Green was murdered.

"Ah! Well, why didn't you just say that?" Garrett said.

Pete sighed. "The question is, what the hell were the Masons hiding that they would kill a president of the United States for?"

"And what the hell did Abraham Lincoln see in that temple that he felt the need to keep secret for so many years?" Garrett asked.

"And if all this is true, why was this book hidden in a basement behind a wall? What happened to the mystery friend? I mean, how do we know he didn't already go to the temple thing and take whatever was there?" Lenny asked.

Garrett gazed across the vast expanse of books, his expression serious. "I don't think so, guys. If a temple had ever been found in Petersburg dating back to that time, I think we would know. Christ, I think the world would know. I mean, maybe it's possible Lincoln's friend lived in that house, and that the Keepers of the Light killed him too."

"Or maybe the journal never made it to the friend, and Lincoln stashed it in the wall?" Lenny suggested.

"More likely it did make it to the friend, and the friend stashed it behind the wall," Garrett said.

"Maybe, but it is just as likely Lincoln was in that house and hid it there himself," Lenny countered.

Pete waved his hands. "Stop, you're both as likely to be

The Secret Journal

right or as likely to be wrong. It could be some other explanation altogether. There are just so many variables that unless Lincoln tells us somewhere in the text why the journal ended up behind the wall, we will probably never know." Pete shrugged.

"We can sure as hell find out where it leads, though," Garrett said, his eyes flashing with excitement at the possibility of adventure.

"Yeah, but it would be nice to have the whole journal. Then we could understand what we're dealing with," Lenny said.

The three boys sat in silence for a brief moment. "Guys, I just had a thought. I'm pretty sure the other half of the book is still behind the wall," Pete said, sitting back down at the table.

"What? How do you know?" Garrett asked in surprise.

"Well, when I was fishing around for the pruning saw, I grabbed the journal but then dropped it when I found the saw. When I reached back in to grab it again, I couldn't find it, so I kept searching. I eventually found it, but way down, much further into the gap than where I originally found it. I figured since I was scrambling to find the stupid saw, I must have somehow hit the journal and knocked it further down. Once I found it again, I didn't really think much of it. But now I think it was two different pieces."

"It makes sense, right? Why would only half of it be there to begin with?" Lenny asked.

Garrett laced his fingers together and gazed at his thumbs, knowing exactly what they needed to do. "Guys, we have to get the other half of that journal."

"But how?" Lenny asked.

"Just so happens I will be working in Eugene's basement removing that pile of drywall this Saturday," Garrett replied, glancing up, his eyes sharp.

"That's going to be risky, bro. He watched us like a hawk last time," Lenny said. "How about you take me with you, and I somehow distract him?"

"That might work," Pete said.

"I don't know... I saw how well your distraction worked last time, Lenny. He sidestepped you like you weren't even there," Garrett said with a chuckle.

"Yeah, well, that was off the cuff – I wasn't ready."

"Okay, I agree. We give it a shot," Garrett said.

Pete looked around and lowered his voice even further, as if someone had just walked into the room, though no one had. "Perfect, you two have a mission and so do I. I need to research what this secret sect, the Keepers of the Light, is. Plus, we need to know how to find this tunnel. I already know where Lincoln's survey stone is—"

"What?" Garrett said, holding out his arms. "You already know? Why didn't you say so?"

"I did say so," Pete responded, confused.

"When did you say so? I don't remember you saying crap about knowing where Lincoln's survey stone is."

For no reason Garrett could identify, Pete let loose a good hearty laugh. He continued to laugh until it became infectious, and the three boys laughed together, none knowing why. Garrett only knew something inside him craved this, needed it like a desert needed rain. True laughter with true friends.

Lenny, catching his breath, finally spoke. "So where is it, Pete?"

"The survey marker? My God, man, do you two even go school? It's right on the square on Jackson Street. Actually, one street over from where we are now." He looked at each of them in disappointment. "Across from the old middle school? You guys probably walked over it a hundred times."

"Well, how would we know?" Lenny asked.

The Secret Journal

"I don't know, Lenny, maybe the metal plate embedded in the sidewalk or, wait, maybe the big-ass sign next to it that says THE SURVEY OF PETERSBURG on it," Pete said, shaking his head.

"You know what, Pete, just because I don't spend my time sitting around a basement studying the history of—"

Achoo, came a muffled sneeze from across the room.

The boys froze.

"What the hell was that?" Lenny whispered.

Garrett stood slowly. "Guys, we're not alone."

16

The Find

Present day
Oak Island, Nova Scotia

"Paul, go up to the pit and radio your brother and get him down here! Tell him we made the greatest discovery of all time!"

Breanne wanted to open the chest so badly that the next hour of careful photography and measurements seemed like a dozen hours. "Dad, what do you think is in it? The Holy Grail? The Ark of the Covenant?"

Smiling, her father said, "Could be." Then, pulling a deep breath of the cool, damp air, he nonchalantly placed a hand on the chest. "You know, Bre, I don't think we will ever fully understand how this place was designed to conceal whatever is in that chest, but you have to appreciate what we can see. Think about it, these Templars somehow created a tunnel that led down to the bedrock. Then they carved through it to gain entry to this natural cavern. They create this elaborate way to ensure the cavern stays flooded, and that if anyone digs down to this place, the man-made swamp, acting as a giant reservoir, floods their hole, making it impossible for anyone to discover it. Now, add to that, they somehow knew if they chiseled into the bedrock they would hit an empty cavern in which to hide their treasure. All these years, people dig and drill and search, and each time they hit floodwater or bedrock – never knowing the treasure lay beneath the bedrock and that the entrance was almost impossible to find. Even with modern technology, we couldn't pinpoint a hidden cavern over 150 feet underground and below bedrock. Everything they did was so precise, so purposeful in design. How? How could they know?"

Her father looked at her expectantly as if she might enlighten him, but she was as baffled as he was. Finally, she said, "And we can't forget, nearly two hundred people helped to construct this, then died to keep secret whatever is in that chest."

Her father nodded his agreement and stared at the knight, scratching at his beard.

Breanne followed her father's gaze, saying what her father was probably thinking. "If only you could speak… the secrets you could tell."

Over the next ungodly long hour – during which, much to Breanne's dismay, they still didn't open the chest – they performed a perimeter search of the cavern. The search, conducted only with flashlights and helmet lights, yielded no other points of egress in or out of the cavern. Additionally, no other pieces of evidence or items were discovered in the room. Finally, after all the photography, measurements, and surveying were completed to their father's satisfaction, he announced he was finally ready to remove the chest.

The Moores would be using a portable winch system to pull the chest up the slope. "I'm not as worried about the slope as I am about getting the chest off the pillar and onto the pallet," their father announced.

"Pops, I am sure whatever is inside this chest, Ed and I can handle." Paul looked at his brother, who nodded in agreement.

"It isn't that. Remember Mexico? I set off the booby trap."

Paul and Edward instinctively stepped back from the chest while their father inspected it.

"How can we be sure?" Edward asked.

"We can't be one hundred until we pick it up," Paul said.

"The altar appears to be a giant piece of stalagmite that they repurposed by chiseling it down flat to about three feet tall to allow enough room for the Templar Knight and chest to sit on. I don't see how they could have booby-trapped a piece of existing stalagmite formed right from the floor," their father said, closely inspecting the stalagmite altar.

As her brothers prepared to lift the chest, Breanne was directed to go back up the slope and wait in the tunnel, just in case. She tried to convince her father to at least wait by the slope with her in case the whole place came down like in Mexico. She knew that her athletic brothers stood a decent chance if forced to run, but her dad didn't. Of course, hard-headed Dr. Charles Moore was not leaving their side, insisting he be present when the chest was lifted. So she went to the slope, waiting and watching, and when her father was engrossed, she crept back over to a smaller piece of stalagmite and crouched, staying just inside the shadow's edge with her helmet light off.

Her brothers did some light stretching, and Paul slapped each thigh a few times. The two acted as if about to square off against each other in a wrestling match. *Posturing,* she thought. *Just pick it up already!* Finally finished with their macho-boy ritual, they were ready. They carefully positioned themselves on either side of the altar and began cautiously sliding the chest towards the edge. As they all held their breaths, the sound of scraping metal on stone echoed throughout the cave as they reached the edge of the altar and paused. The brothers looked apprehensively into the empty eye sockets of the Templar Knight. The knight stared back vacantly.

Nothing happened.

"Pops, do you think he was alive when they sealed and flooded this place?" Paul asked in a whisper, nodding up at the knight.

The three men paused.

His father answered in a low whisper. "No. He was placed here after death, after his body had somehow been prepared to stay rigid. I can't tell through the robe. I still don't know how they got his bones to stay fixed like this. Some type of wire maybe?"

"Why would they do that?" Edward asked, also speaking softly, as if trying to be careful not to wake the sleeping Templar Knight as they attempted to steal his chest right from under his nose.

Breanne rubbed the back of her arms, hugging herself. *No different than the tomb of a pharaoh,* she thought.

"Maybe he is here as a warning or as a guardian of this chest, or maybe this was his treasure and this is his tomb. When you think about it, this place really isn't much different than how you would expect to find an ancient Egyptian pharaoh or a Mayan king entombed. The application may be different, but we could be looking at something very similar here," their father said.

She grinned to herself.

"Alright now, let's do this." Grinning with uneasy excitement, Charles raised his voice back to its normal volume. "Alright, boys, on my count – one, two, three… lift!" They lifted the chest off the altar, straining with every muscle fiber to keep from dropping it. Realizing they could not hold the heavy load long, they quickly squatted down, plonking the chest onto the skid with a loud *thud.*

"Easy, easy," their father said, checking for damage. The brothers froze, their eyes darting all around, waiting for something and prepared for anything. They expected at any moment to hear a low rumble and to feel the earth beneath them begin to shake. As the moments passed, the men dared to exhale and venture a look into the vacant eyes of the Templar Knight. The hollow black sockets stared back, expressionless, as nothing happened.

Once Breanne was sure her family was safe, she let out a relieved breath and retreated back to the base of the slope and shouted, "Everything okay?" as if she had been there the whole time. Then she flipped on her headlamp and crossed the distance back to her family.

"Yep! We're good. Okay, let's get her out and get her open!" her father said, climbing onto the pallet with the chest. "Bre, take her away!"

Her brother tossed her the winch controller, and she toggled the up button. "Engaged!" she announced as the skid jerked, then slowly began to slide across the cavern floor with one Templar treasure and one archeologist father.

"What?" her father smiled. "I need to make sure this baby stays secure until we get to the top of the slope. We can't risk any errors with a priceless treasure now, can we?"

"Sure, Pops, right. You hold the hundreds of pounds of treasure secure. Wouldn't want the one-mile-an-hour winch to throw it off the pallet it's strapped to," Paul teased.

Edward laughed. "At least we solved the mystery of how Pops planned to get back up the slope."

17

Eavesdropper

Present day
Petersburg, Illinois

"That came from behind the middle row in the fantasy section," Pete whispered with assurance.

Lenny rose from his chair silently.

"Who's back there?" Garrett demanded as he and Lenny slowly worked their way around the bookcase from either direction.

Silence.

Pete hung back at the table, quickly gathering his notebook and other supplies and hastily packing them into his backpack in case he needed to make a run for it.

The boys' apprehension grew as they crept closer and closer. Garrett and Lenny locked eyes with each other in one final confirmation before springing around the corner from both sides.

A petite girl with black-rimmed glasses and brown hair cut in a bob sat on the floor, leaning back on the bookcase. Her knees were pulled to her chest, and the heels of her

Chuck Taylor tennis shoes were pulled up to her butt. She wore a V-neck sweater and a long plaid skirt covering her knees. She looked up from a book. "Heya, fellas."

"Janis? What are you doing back here?" Garrett asked, recognizing the girl from one of his classes.

"Well, what most people do here, I suppose. It should be kind of obvious from the book I'm holding, right?"

"Why didn't you say something? I'm sure you heard us, right?" Lenny asked, narrowing his eyes at the girl.

"Um, I was kinda back here already when you guys came down and then, well, um, yeah, I kinda overheard your secret thing. And I admit, as you guys kept talking I kinda became interested, and then, well, it kinda of felt too late to get up and be like, 'hey I'm here,' so basically, I was kinda waiting you out... but, yeah... then I sneezed," Janis said, scrunching her nose.

Just what he needed. He already had Jack to worry about, and now this. "Listen, Janis, you need to just forget what you heard, okay? Can you do that? Can you keep a secret?" Garrett asked.

"Um, sure, I guess so. But it might be better if I could help. I'm really good at research, and maybe if I can look at the journal with you guys, I can help you solve it?"

"Garrett, can I talk to you for a minute in private?" Lenny asked.

"Sure." Garrett turned to Janis. "Be right back."

As the two boys stepped across the library, Janis looked at Pete, who up until this very moment had stood mesmerized by the realization this mystery person behind the bookshelf was Janis.

"Hold up, Lenny, look," Garrett whispered, pointing carefully back towards Pete and Janis.

"Oh, this is going to be good," Lenny said in a low voice.

"Hi, Pete," Janis said.

The Secret Journal

"Hell-hi-o, Janis," Pete said, flapping his hand back and forth in the kind of wave a toddler gives a stranger at the grocery store.

Janis laughed and gave Pete a kind smile. "You're funny. I have you in a few classes, right?"

Pete nodded, using his opposite hand to pull the other unruly appendage back down to his side.

Janis stood, holding her book to her chest as if giving it a long, tight hug. "Yeah, you're smart... for-real smart. I just overheard you explaining your theory of that journal you found. You figured all this out by yourself? That's so cool – you could be some kind of detective or investigator or something."

Pete smiled dumbly, his face reddening by the second.

"Jesus, he looks like he is going to burst into flames," Lenny whispered with a smirk.

"Why is he staring at her chest?" Garrett asked, wishing he could elbow his friend.

"Probably wishes he could be that book." Lenny laughed. "If he doesn't find her eyes quick, he's going to blow it."

"Thanks," Pete managed finally. "I see... you, um... read."

"Yeah, I read." She giggled, then glanced down at her book. "Oh, this? It's *Quantum Sorcery, Druids, and Earth Magic: A Complete Guide*."

"Interesting," Pete blurted.

"Hah, well, it's interesting. Not my normal jam, but I am researching for a book report. Now, the Keepers of the Light. That sounds important and far more interesting. I can help you research that if you want?"

"I'll, um... don't go back, uh... in just a sec. I mean, um, don't go. Stay here. I mean wait here... I mean I'll be back."

Janis giggled.

Pete hurried over to where Garrett and Lenny were pretending to not be paying attention.

"Here he comes," Garrett said, tapping Lenny with the back of his hand. "Pretend like we've been talking."

Lenny nodded. "Like I said, just get rid of her. She doesn't know where the tunnel even is."

Garrett rubbed a hand over his face. "But she knows way too much, man. She knows where we got the journal and everything. She heard us explain the whole thing to you, and then she heard Pete's theories on everything. Crap, man, she even knows about Jack. This thing is getting out of hand. We need—"

"I'm keeping her," Pete interjected.

The two boys turned to Pete.

"I mean we're keeping her… I mean she's in." He stole a shy glance back towards Janis.

"What? What the hell are you talking about?" Lenny asked.

Garrett's lips twisted into a smirk.

Pete stepped closer to the two boys and whispered with an uncharacteristic authority, "We are keeping her. She is going to help me research. She's in. I'm bringing her in. I need her for my research."

"Garrett, are you sure this is such a good idea?" Lenny asked with a skeptical glance towards Janis.

"Lenny, man, I'm not sure any of this is a good idea, but we're in it now. And you heard him. He needs her for his research. Decision made." Garrett slapped Pete on the shoulder.

Pete let out a relieved sigh.

"Janis, can you come over here for a second?" Garrett asked.

"Sure, you fellas done deciding my fate?"

"Listen, Janis, Pete here convinced us to bring you in,

The Secret Journal

and because we trust him, we're going to trust you too. But you have to pinky swear with all of us right now that you won't tell a soul about this. Agreed?" Garrett held out his pinky.

"Well, of course." Janis locked her pinky into his, then, holding a piece of her skirt in the other hand, she promptly curtsied. "I swear. I won't tell a soul." She repeated the process with Lenny, then finally Pete.

Garrett watched Pete hold her pinky as if it was the first pinky he'd ever held, the first girl he'd ever touched, and knew it just might have been. His friend didn't let go and, oddly, Janis made no attempt to let go either, so the two stood there, pinkies locked.

Garrett looked to Lenny and grinned. "And then we were four."

18

The Find

Present day
Oak Island, Nova Scotia

The sun descended off the western coast of Oak Island little by little, as if being softly quenched into the ocean. In its wake remained only a faint auburn glow on the horizon; soon it too faded, like a fleeting afterthought, chasing the setting sun into the evening-blue abyss. Darkness followed as clouds crept across the late-evening sky, the harbinger of a moonless night.

The Money Pit lay vacant, cast into dark anonymity. Its only occupant still knelt on one knee atop a stone altar where it had been for hundreds of years, surrounded by absolute darkness and deafening silence.

Topside, however, was a bustle of excitement and energy. The chest sat under the field tent, washed in artificial light from a tripod work light. The entire family and Jerry gathered round for the reveal. It was time to open the chest.

"Even after all these years covered in stagnant swamp

water, the chest is still in phenomenal condition. It's almost like the water preserved it," Dr. Moore said.

"I don't understand why it wasn't like that for my cross?" Paul asked, having taken to calling it *his* cross.

Breanne snapped a photo, then let the camera fall back into place around her neck. She pulled her folded field journal from the pocket of her cargo pants and began scratching notes, an excited smile stretching across her face.

"Yes, good question," her father said, kneeling and examining it closely. "The wood is not the same. This is some species of rare wood, probably acacia. It's bound together with—"

"Acacia?" Breanne asked in disbelief. "You know what you are saying, Dad?"

"Yes. I know," he said with a smile.

"Well, I don't bloody know! Care to enlighten me?" Jerry asked.

"I'm not sure, but look at it. An adornment of golden bands, and through the bands are staves of wood. It's similar to the biblical account of the Ark of the Covenant."

"*The* Ark of the Covenant? Charles... I... Bloody hell, man!" Jerry said, slapping both hands against his face.

"Settle down, Jerry. I said similar. According to the Old Testament, the Ark of the Covenant was built by Moses to hold the Ten Commandments handed down to him by God. Could this be the Ark of the Covenant? I'm not certain."

Breanne walked around it, snapping more photos. "I don't see some of the features I would expect to see based on the Bible's description of the Ark. For example, the mercy seat was supposed to be a solid golden lid, complete with the two golden statues of cherubs on either side, but this lid doesn't seem to fit the description. The size measures a little larger than the biblical account at approximately three feet wide by two feet tall and two feet deep."

Jerry looked at Bre, then at her father. "Smart, this one, Charles, very smart. Well, I don't know the biblical accounts verbatim, but I know there is only one way to find out. Pop the top, flip the lid, and Bob's your uncle, we'll know if this is tosh or the bee's knees," Jerry said, motioning wildly with his hands.

Her father stared at him. "I've no idea what you just said, Jerry."

Breanne laughed.

"Alright, everyone, let's open it!" her father said excitedly. He motioned for Breanne to join him, and slowly they removed the staves.

Just as they prepared to lift the lid, Breanne paused. "Daddy, there is supposed to be a curse that goes along with lifting the lid off the Ark, right?"

"Actually, it's when you touch it. If you aren't a priest, you supposedly die," he said.

Paul and Edward looked at each other and then to their father.

"What the hell, Pops? You had us lift that thing off the slab!" Paul said.

"What if it had killed us?" Edward asked.

"I made sure I touched it first," Charles responded with an easy smile. "Now can we get on with it?"

"You touched it knowing what could have happened?" Breanne asked.

"Bre, you are a scientist. You are rational. Surely I don't need to convince you how ridiculous the Old Testament accounts are? Now please, can we do this?"

Bre and her father gave each other a final nod and lifted the lid off the chest.

No one spoke as they stood transfixed by the contents of the chest. Golden coins, rubies, jewels, and other precious items were instantly visible. A bejeweled crown, a gold-hilted

The Secret Journal

dagger, and an unthinkably large emerald necklace could all be seen intermixed with the vast coin hoard.

Edward was the first to find his voice. "Wow, unbelievable. That's the real deal, Pops. We've found a legit treasure!"

The statement pulled everyone from their stunned paralysis, and instantly the site became abuzz once again. Breanne and her father gently placed the lid onto the table.

"We need to start cataloging this, Dad. There's so much, my God. So much!" Breanne threw her arms around her father in a huge hug. She pulled out her field journal and began jotting notes.

"I'll start taking photos, sis," Paul said, smiling and slapping his father on the shoulder.

Breanne lifted the camera strap from around her neck and passed it to her brother. "Unreal, right!"

"Crazy!" he responded, donning the camera.

"What can I do to help?" Edward asked.

"Grab some packing crates from the storage container, Ed. We'll need to carefully pack everything once we're finished," his father said.

"On it." Edward darted off.

Breanne laid out a tarp and then, on top of it, a white cloth. Donning a pair of white gloves, she began placing the objects one by one onto the cloth as Paul photographed each piece. "Look at this gold bullion! And all these coins! Do you know what these are?" She didn't wait for an answer. "These are silver *gros tournois*. These were minted during the reign of King Philip IV. There's so much!" she said, pulling several pieces from the chest before freeing a more substantial golden cuff bracelet embedded with large, blood-red rubies. "Are you seeing this, Daddy?"

Paul snapped photo after photo as Breanne took measurements and logged them into her journal.

Jerry stood next to her father, both of them lost in

thought as Breanne continued to empty the chest of invaluable riches. She worked with a careful urgency, ever eager for what came next as the entire wealth of the Templars spilled forth, piece by piece, in organized rows across the white cloth.

Finally tearing her eyes away, she found her father, hoping to share a knowing smile at the ridiculousness of it, but his expression said something else. "What's wrong, Dad?" He looked unsure – or was it disappointment?

"I… I don't know." He smiled. "This is amazing, isn't it?"

He asked as if he didn't know that it was more than amazing. It was unbelievable. She waited a moment, studying him, then said, "Of course it is. It is a career find in and of itself. Dad, this rewrites history."

He sighed. "You're right, of course, but there is no golden pot of manna, no stone tablets, no Aaron's rod." He paused and shook his head. "No Holy Grail."

"We haven't even pulled everything out yet – maybe it's buried beneath the treasure."

"No. You won't find it because it simply isn't there," he said flatly.

"Okay," she said. "So we didn't find mythological artifacts. But come on, Dad, we found the real deal – a real Templar treasure – and you're pouting? Jeez, Dr. Moore, what's it take to satisfy an archeologist of your caliber?"

"Baby girl, you're absolutely right. Of course, this is magnificent." But his tone lacked conviction.

Jerry turned away, pulled out his satellite phone, and began to dial.

Her father cocked his head curiously at his friend.

Jerry approached, holding out the phone. "Charles, old chum. My boss would like a word with you."

"Well, put him on speaker. I want everyone to hear his excitement," he said.

Jerry clicked the speaker button and handed him the phone.

"This is Charles Moore. To whom am I speaking?"

"Ah, Dr. Moore, it is a pleasure to finally speak to you," came the stranger's voice.

"Well, I have been here working for about a year now. You could have had the pleasure a long time back, Mr....?"

"You were fully aware of the agreement, were you not?"

"Yes, of course, but I don't understand the need to keep your identity secret from me. I can assure you that you have my—"

"Repeat it to me, Dr. Moore," the caller demanded.

"Repeat... what?"

"The agreement. Repeat it to me."

Breanne frowned, confused, as Edward and Paul traded looks and walked over to listen.

Her father drew in a breath, and she could see he was vexed by the stranger's tone.

"The agreement, right. I agreed I would not know the identity of the person funding the operation. The dig is to remain secret and only my family and Jerry can be in the know. I will be allowed to publish my findings after the conclusion of the dig. Jerry assured me you agreed that all artifacts would be donated to the museum of my choice. I never understood what's in it for you, but Jerry said your only interest is proving the island is not a fraud and that it truly holds a secret—"

"That's enough," the man said impatiently. "This was and is the agreement, Dr. Moore, so I suggest you honor it. Now, Jerry tells me you have found treasure and a Knight Templar skeleton kneeling atop an altar?"

"Yes, a Templar Knight was found robed with shield and sword, and the treasure is... well, it's astonishing. It fills a giant chest that—"

"Right, very clever. The chest, you have removed the lid. What is the chest made of?" he asked.

Charles pulled an irritated face and looked at Bre. "Gold and wood. I have not analyzed it closely enough to see what kind of wood yet but—"

The man gave a loud sigh. "You're not finished here, Dr. Moore."

"Of course not, we still have months of work to do to try and understand what we've found here and why it was hidden in the first—"

"That's not what I mean, Dr. Moore. I mean *you* have not finished *looking*."

Breanne held her palms up and mouthed a single word. "What?"

Dr. Moore furrowed his brow in confusion. "I searched the cavern for hours – there is nothing else there. We found the treasure of the Templars, we found the knight, we reached the end and found the prize. For God's sake, we've changed history! You, whoever in the hell you are, have been proven right. This place is a legitimate Knights Templar treasure hold – *the* Knights Templar treasure hold!"

The voice on the other end of the phone struck out sharply. "Dr. Moore, I hired you because you are supposed to be the best! Use your intelligence – or was I mistaken in my assumption that you possess any?"

Completely caught off guard by the man's insult, her father began to get the look she had seen very few times. It was the look of rage. She had seen it once when Paul borrowed the car and wrecked it, and another time when Edward snuck a girlfriend in the house. Being the respectful girl she was, she'd removed her shoes but then left them sitting at the back door, where Charles found them the following morning. "Just who in the hell are you?" he shouted into the phone.

The Secret Journal

"Who I am does… not… matter!" bellowed the voice. "Ask yourself, doctor, does this feel like the end to you? When you can answer that question, then tell me if I have made the wrong choice or if you are ready get back to work and finish this. You must search, Dr. Moore – search until you have left *nothing* unexplored and no stone unturned!"

Before her father could say another word, the line clicked dead. The voice on the other end was gone.

Her father stood motionless for a long moment, his hands shaking.

No one spoke. Perhaps they were all as stunned as she was by the bizarre conversation. Finally, her father's face transformed back into his normal visage, and he spoke.

"You know what bothers me?" he said.

"I know what bothers me. That guy needs an ass-kicking," Paul said.

"Maybe – but, no, that's not it. What bothers me is what he said. He said, 'Does this feel like the end to you?' In a strange way, that very question has been pulling at me since we opened that chest."

"Dad, what are you saying?" Breanne asked.

"I don't know, baby girl, but tomorrow at first light… we're going back into that cavern."

19

The Plan

Present day
Petersburg, Illinois

The four teenagers made their way back across the library to the circular table on the far side and sat down in the plastic chairs. "Now listen, guys, Lenny and I have to get to taekwondo class, and we still haven't formed a plan yet," Garrett said.

Lenny turned to Garrett. "What are we going do about Jack?"

"Good question. Pete, I think you should start getting whatever is left in that journal transferred over."

"You're not suggesting we give him the journal, are you?" Pete asked disapprovingly.

"Yeah, screw that! And screw Jack! You guys could kick his ass anyway, so just tell him to go pound sand," Janis said, making a fist.

Pete smiled.

"Yeah, I don't think we should give it to him either, Garrett – what if there is no temple or we can't find it? At least then we have the old journal, which might at least be worth something," Lenny said.

"Worth something! Are you an idiot? Of course it's worth something. It's priceless. We're not selling it. It isn't some paycheck, Lenny. It's a priceless artifact – an artifact I found, by the way." Pete leaned forward and peered over the frames of his glasses like an irritated schoolteacher.

Lenny held up his hands and laughed. "Easy, Petey, it was just a suggestion. Look, we won't sell it, just settle down."

Pete sat back in his chair.

"I kind of like this side of you, Pete, all taking command and stuff," Lenny said with a smile.

"Look, guys," Garrett said, "I'm not saying we give it to him. I mean the last thing we want is Jack shopping this thing around town and people asking questions, but let's face some facts that will help us be prepared, okay? Pete needs to keep the journal to transfer it, and neither Lenny nor I can be there to protect you all the time. So just get it done, then we can figure out how to hide it. But right now that journal has a huge target on it. Agreed?" Garrett asked.

They nodded in agreement.

"Now we need to figure out when and where to start. I want to get to Eugene's house and try to find the other half, but I scheduled the work for Saturday and that's almost a week away," Garrett said.

"Can you move it up?" Pete asked.

"Maybe, but I need some help. Lenny, can you teach the beginner class on Tuesday?"

Lenny made a sour face like he had just smelled something bad. "Oh, bro, you know I hate teaching beginners. Besides, I thought you needed a distraction at Eugene's?"

"I do. That's why Pete is going to be my distraction," Garrett announced.

Pete raised an eyebrow.

"Think about it, Pete – it's perfect. You just have to keep Eugene busy talking about history and get him to show you some of his stuff. He has an awesome coin collection, and even better, he has a killer Native American artifact collection. In the meantime, I will search behind the wall."

"I'm in," Pete said without further hesitation.

"Okay, then, Tuesday it is," Garrett said.

"Between now and then, Janis and I will try and figure out who in the hell the 'Keepers of the Light' were." Pete looked hopefully to Janis.

"Yep, and I'm available for a couple more hours tonight, Pete, if you are? I don't have anything going on tomorrow after school either," Janis said.

"So, what about me, man – how can I help?" Lenny asked.

"Right. Hey, Pete, read that part again about the tunnel and the arch," Garrett said.

"Okay, hold on a sec." Pete retrieved his notebook from his backpack. He scanned his notes and, finding the passage, began to read in his deep Lincoln voice.

"*Look carefully over the side, and you will see a drainage opening large enough for a man to enter upright.*"

"Keep going," Garrett said, spinning his finger in a circle.

"*Once inside, look for the archway, which holds a **xxx xxx xxx**. When you find **xxx xxx** remove **xxx** beloved **xxx** and, once removed, reach inside and pull the lever. This will allow the way to open, showing you the path.*"

"Okay, now back up and read the one before that. The part about the marker."

"The journal says to go to the west side of the river, and then it's smudged out – here it is," Pete said.

"*Begin at my survey marker and walk directly east until you reach the river. At the end of the street head due **xxx xxx***"

xxx paces. Look carefully over the side, and you will see a drainage opening large enough for a man to enter upright."

"See, the problem is we don't know how many paces or in which direction to go once we reach the river. This is an old drainage tunnel – it may not even be there anymore," Pete said.

"Look, if it's there it can't be far either way, right? I mean, we're talking paces," Lenny said.

"That could be anywhere. There are at least a half-dozen drainage pipes emptying into the river, and that's just off the top of my head. And none of them sound like the text describes. All the ones I know of are round and concrete, not arched and brick, and not really tall enough for a man to stand upright. Even in the biggest ones, you would have to hunch down," Lenny said.

"Lenny has a point," said Pete. "Petersburg was built along giant bluffs with the entire downtown area and a few lower-income areas built in the river valley below, between the bluffs and the river. The bluffs are very steep and stretch all the way across the town's east side. Thus, every time it rains, large quantities of water flow off the bluffs and right through town. Well, not exactly through town, but underneath it. The only way to ensure the river valley doesn't flood each time it rains is to have large drainage pipes under each street running east to west. This large drainage system ensures the water is carried beneath the town and safely deposited into the river."

Garrett stared at Pete. "I'm not even going to ask."

"I read." Pete shrugged. "Now, all the pipes I have seen draining into the river are round and look fairly modern. I think an arched tunnel from that era would have been noticed by now."

"It could be hidden somehow, I guess – maybe something's covering it?" Janis said, tapping her pencil eraser on the table. "I don't know, a big stone or something? There are all kinds of chunks of old concrete littering the sides of the river. Or maybe it could have caved in dozens of years ago."

Rapping his fingers on the table in thought, Lenny said, "I have been up and down this river running bank poles with my dad, all the way between here and New Salem, going south and almost all the way out to Altig Bridge Road going north. I've never seen anything like he described in the journal. But I've never searched for something hidden or signs of a caved-in tunnel either. Going by the journal, at least we know it has to be on the west bank of the river, so that narrows it to one side."

"Good point, Lenny – that should make the search a little more manageable," Pete said.

"You want me to start searching the riverbanks for something hidden?" Lenny asked uncertainly.

Garrett had sat back in his chair, quietly lost in thought. Suddenly, he realized everyone at the table was looking to him for direction. A smile stretched slowly across his face. "Lenny, I don't think you'll have to search at all."

Now it was Garrett's turn to stand and pace.

"Think about it," he said, tapping a finger to his head. "Lincoln said start at his marker, which we know, thanks to Pete, is uptown on the square. So we can say with some certainty where, at the Sangamon River, we need to start—"

"Yes, but we still don't know which direction to go in," Pete interjected.

"I know, but hear me out," Garrett said. "Ask yourself, do you really see him pacing off thousands of steps? I don't – in fact, I see him pacing off in the low hundreds, tops. I think most people would lose track of steps if you tried to go too far into the hundreds. Besides, wouldn't you just pace from one point to the next?"

The Secret Journal

"What do you mean, one point to the next?" Lenny asked.

Janis excitedly chimed in with the answer. "Of course! Okay, for example if I had something hidden miles from here, wouldn't it be easier to say, 'Start at the river and go one hundred paces to X.' X can be anything – a tree, a rock, a bend in the river… anything. Then say, 'From X go another one hundred paces to Y.'"

"Exactly!" Garrett said. "So, since he didn't do that, it leads me to believe it isn't that far! And that has me thinking." He paused for effect. "I know where the arched tunnel is!"

Everyone looked at Garrett, stunned.

"Are you freaking serious?" Lenny said.

"Where? Let's go now!" Pete said.

"Well, hold on. Here's what I am thinking, but I could be wrong. You guys remember a couple years back when we were all into exploring every drainage pipe we could fit into? Remember we found that old mine entrance behind the concrete company, but it had caved in and didn't go anywhere. We also built that fort in the Z tunnel under the highway?"

"Yeah, yeah, but what's that got to do with this?" Lenny pressed.

"I'm getting to it. We also explored a few of the drainage pipes that dump into the river. Not far from here is a large one – it empties at the river bend right before you head out of town, just past the bank."

Pete frowned. "The one behind the lodge."

"I've fished below that pipe. It just juts out the side of a steep embankment," Lenny said.

"Yep, that's the one. It's really tricky to get to," Garrett said.

"But, Garrett, that pipe is circular, around maybe five

feet in diameter tops, not old enough, definitely not arched, and not tall enough for a man to stand upright in," Lenny said, turning his hands palms up in confusion.

Garrett continued to pace in front of the group. "Exactly, but as I was saying, we were exploring pipes all over town. Lenny, I think you were grounded or something, I can't remember, but I wasn't with either of you that day," he said, motioning to Pete and Lenny. "So anyway, Jack, Albert, and David explored it with me. I remember we went back into the pipe a good sixty feet before we reached the end of the concrete section." He turned to Janis. "Normally the pipes we explore get smaller and smaller until you have to belly crawl. Usually, when they'd start getting pretty tight, we'd chicken out, afraid of getting stuck. Sometimes we even had to shimmy out backwards because the tunnels would get too tight to even turn around."

"Right… why wouldn't you spend your spare time crawling around drainage pipes? Makes total sense," Janis said, her face failing to hide her disgust.

"That's right! I remember this, you were really pissed at Jack after that," Pete said, recollection lighting up his face. "Didn't he kill a bat or something?"

"Exactly, I was super pissed at him for that. The bat was cool, and just hanging there minding its own business, and for no reason Jack takes a stick and whacks the thing, knocking it down, before going psycho on it and beating it to death." Garrett shook his head. "I can still see the thing, squirming under the beam of the flashlight, screeching in pain. Jack just laughs at it and hits it again and again," Garrett said.

"There is something wrong with that kid," Janis said bluntly.

"Right," Lenny said, his brow pinched earnestly. "Now that you mention it, I remember you telling me about that.

The Secret Journal

But I don't get what this has to do with the old brick-archway drainage tunnel we're looking for."

Garrett continued to walk back and forth, slowly wearing a hole into the tile floor. "Guys, the concrete tunnel was sixty feet or so, but then it ended and, instead of getting smaller, it got bigger. It opened up. You actually had to step off and out of the concrete tunnel down into a larger area that was both wider and taller. I remember it was like a transition area maybe thirty feet across to the other side, where it stepped up, connecting to a much smaller drainage tunnel. Oh yeah, and to get across you had to walk through nasty stink water that was pooled almost knee-deep." Garrett crinkled his nose as if he could still smell the stagnant water.

"Can you remember what the – what did you call it, the 'transition area'? What it was made of?" Pete asked.

Garrett stopped pacing and turned to face his friends. "Oh, believe me, I wish I could forget Jack, the bat, and that whole damn day. Yeah, I remember exactly what the transition area was made of. The whole distance across to the smaller section of tunnel was made of very old brick, bigger and more squarish than the normal bricks that we use today. And you know what shape it was in?"

The three exchanged glances.

"It was a long brick arch from end to end," Garrett said.

"No way! Are you sure?" Lenny asked.

"Now that sounds like the description in Lincoln's journal! Listen to this," Pete said, dragging his finger down the page of his notebook. Clearing his throat, he began to read in his deep Abraham Lincoln voice. "*I began my survey for the town of Petersburg in 1835, and in doing so, I ensured the tunnel entrance was concealed but still accessible through clever brickwork hidden inside of a drainage duct. You can find this duct spills into the Sangamon River.*"

Pete flipped his notebook shut. "And it makes perfect

sense. Of course no one has noticed it! It's sixty feet back behind a modern-day drainage pipe."

"But, suppose that is the same tunnel, isn't it a bad sign that there is a newer section of tunnel added on? What if the city workers who installed the new pipe destroyed the part of the arch we need to find?" Janis asked.

"I don't think so. The journal said, *once inside, look for the archway.* I mean I don't think the whole thing was probably ever an archway, or you wouldn't have to look for it once inside," Pete said.

"Plus, if the city had destroyed the entrance to install the new pipe, surely they would have discovered the opening," Lenny said.

"Okay, Lenny, you wanted a job – tomorrow get in that pipe and check it out. You will need a flashlight. What exactly should he be looking for, Pete?" Garrett asked, sitting back down.

"Well, I think we are looking for some markings on the bricks, like a year or something – probably a specific brick. So just check the arch top to bottom for any markings or strange shapes of some kind – anything that doesn't belong. You probably want to take a notepad and write down anything you find. If you don't find anything, I guess we just—"

Lenny busted in. "Wait a minute. Are you actually serious? Garrett, are you for real with this?"

Everyone looked at Lenny in confusion. "What's up, man?" he asked.

Lenny leaned forward in his chair. "So, let me run this back. You guys" – he looked at each of them in turn – "are sending me into the spooky-ass mystery tunnel, with stank-ass water – and bats! Have you not *seen* any scary movies? I know Garrett has because we've watched them together. So how in the hell are you going to send the one who always dies first into the scary-ass mystery tunnel! Why don't you just send me in with a blaster and a red shirt while you're at it!"

Pete and Garrett laughed.

Janis did not.

"Oh, yeah, real funny, huh? I'm still not going in the creepy tunnel alone. You can forget it," Lenny said, sitting back in his chair and crossing his arms.

Garrett shook his head. "When you put it that way, Lenny, I don't want you to go in the creepy-ass tunnel alone! I guess I didn't think about it like that," Garrett said, still laughing. "But listen, we need to figure this out. I can ride my bike to school and to work tomorrow, then skip my run and just hurry to the tunnel to meet up with you." *Then get home before the streetlights come on and do whatever training Phillip has planned for me.* Exhaustion washed over him at the thought.

"Hey, wait a sec, why don't I just take David with?" Lenny asked, snapping his fingers.

"Whoa, wait a minute. Are you suggesting we bring David in on this?" Pete asked, not pleased by Lenny's suggestion.

"Well, I don't see why not. Just because he doesn't get to hang out as much doesn't mean he's not still part of the gang, right? I trust him and don't see what it would hurt to bring him in. Are you saying you don't trust him, Pete?" Lenny asked.

"That's not what I'm saying at all. I'm just concerned that this is getting too big, and I don't like the idea of bringing in more people, that's all," Pete said.

"Look, I didn't like the idea of you telling Jack about the book. I didn't like the idea of you bringing in Janis—"

"Hey! I am sitting right here, Lenny!" Janis said with a hint of hurt in her voice.

"Sorry, Janis, I'm good with it now. I'm just saying, I don't think it'll hurt to have David. He is one of us. Besides I've got some selfish interest in this. David's built like a brick shithouse, but he's slow. If any craziness goes down in that tunnel – like rats, bats, or some Friday the thirteenth shit – I can just push David in between me and whatever the hell is trying to kill or eat me and make my escape." Lenny brushed his hands together as if to say, *Problem solved.*

"Nice, Lenny!" Garrett said, laughing.

"Shit. Somebody's got to live to tell the story, and I'm okay if that somebody is me," he said.

They all laughed.

"Alright. We all agree that we can trust David?" Garrett asked.

They all nodded, but Garrett thought Lenny still seemed uneasy.

"Okay, tomorrow bring David up to speed, swear him to secrecy, and then take him with you to explore the tunnel. And you two" – he turned his attention to Janis and Pete – "try and see what you can find out about the 'Keepers of the Light.' I guess going forward, since you two will be here anyway, this place can be our base of operations. Plus, our parents are more likely to let us all stay out a little later if we're at the library working on a school project. If that works for you guys, we can just meet here starting tomorrow. I'll come by here on my way home from work, and we can discuss what you guys found. Sound good?" Garrett asked.

Everyone agreed.

"Okay, we got to split – Mr. B won't be happy if we're late," Lenny said, as the two boys made their way toward the library stairs.

"See you guys tomorrow," Garrett called back to Pete and Janis, who looked like they were locked in a staring contest. He slapped Lenny on the arm. "Check it out."

The Secret Journal

Lenny glanced back. "Well, good for old Petey – it's about time. I just hope they spend a little time looking at books rather than each other."

⁓

Pete suddenly realized he and Janis were alone, making him instantly uncomfortable. He fidgeted in his chair, looking around the library, trying to focus on anything other than Janis.

Thankfully, Janis didn't seem to be having the same issue. "Pete, thanks for speaking up for me with your pals. I'm really excited to be part of this."

Swallowing hard, Pete found his courage and attempted to reply, praying to himself that the words wouldn't come out a jumbled mess. "Yeah, I was really lucky to find you behind the bookcase." *What! Why did I say that? That sounded stupid!*

Janis smiled. "Lucky, huh? Well, good. I'm glad you feel that way."

A moment ago, the large round table had four of them sitting around it, but now that it was just the two of them sitting side by side, neither moved to take advantage of the extra space. "Janis, if you don't mind me asking, what were you doing down here anyway? I'm here almost every day and have never seen you here before."

"Well, I normally hang out at the school library, but it's closed on Sundays, so I thought I might as well give this old place a try. I have a book report due in a little over a week."

"I'll have you know this old place is hands down the better choice."

"That is yet to be seen," Janis said, looking around the old library doubtfully.

"You spend a little time with me, and I'll be happy to prove it to you!"

"Looks like you will get your chance, Pete," Janis said, smiling again. "Can I read through the notes that you transferred from the journal?"

Janis slid her chair even closer to Pete as he positioned the journal between them and opened his notebook. She was close enough that he could smell her hair now. As she focused on the journal, he leaned in and discreetly drew in a deep breath through his nose. Her hair smelled of orange and… and something else. What was it? He drew in a second breath. Orange and… ginger. He smiled.

"You okay?" she asked.

"Uh… yeah. Why?" he said.

"I don't know, I just heard you sighing a couple times and thought maybe you were becoming impatient with me. I'm sure you've probably memorized all this stuff by now."

"No!" he said too loudly, causing Janis to jump. "Oh crap, sorry. I mean, no, you're fine. I am not impatient with you at all, please take your time. I was just working through a few questions in my head." *Like how in the hell it's possible for you to smell so, so good.*

Janis giggled before changing her focus back to the journal.

Wow, she thinks I'm funny, and not in the way other people think I'm funny. Not once so far has she mentioned my speech impediment, and she overheard my entire explanation earlier from behind the shelves. "Okay, well, I am thinking the best place for us to start looking for these Keepers of the Light is in anything we can find on Freemasons. Take your time with this, and I will see what books I can find," he said, adjusting his glasses.

Janis smiled, watching Pete walk away, and pulled the journal a little closer.

20

Chardonnay, Scotch, and Nightmares

Present day
Oak Island, Nova Scotia

It was approaching the midnight hour before the family finally finished cataloging the contents of the giant treasure chest. Edward, Paul, and Breanne had all turned in for the night.

Despite her excitement, Breanne had no trouble finding sleep. As soon as she felt the soft down pillow caress her cheek, she slipped easily into unconsciousness. But sleep could never just be easy for Breanne – not for years, not since the accident.

Her mother's voice. Cold leather on her legs. Snowing. A Christmas song playing on the radio. The window was fogged. She pressed her finger against the cold glass, drawing a circle. Barren cornfields passed. Snow fell. Her mother screamed. *Oh God, the scream.* The foggy glass exploding inward. Metal twisting.

Suddenly she was thrown into fathoms of black so vast she instinctively knew she was no longer in her bed – nor was she in the camper, or the island. She felt nothing pulling her, and she thought it possible she was no longer in the world. The familiar nightmare had changed. She couldn't see her mom, or the blood. The song was gone, too – only infinite measures of darkness remained. Then the silence cracked with a single scream. Her mother's scream – but soon joined by many screams. Flashes pricked the dark. Small glimpses whirred through her consciousness. *Where am I? In a city?* The stench of smoke and burning flesh was palpable. Screaming pierced her mind, not fuzzy but fatal. She was thinking. In her own mind, she was questioning. *You don't think and question during nightmares, do you?* So many people screaming, and running, and burning. Her vision returned fully as a horse galloped towards her, its hooves beating the pavement louder and louder. Smoke pushed in all around her, so thick she couldn't breathe. She could only see the swirling smoke, thick and promising to swallow her. A voice from somewhere within the smoke. A man's voice. *No, not a man,* she thought, *a boy's voice.* He was speaking to her. "Hey? Can you hear me?" the voice asked. She tried to speak, tried to answer, but she was choked silent by dirty black smoke. "Can you hear me?!" the voice begged.

Breanne jolted up, gasping for air. She coughed violently, tasting the soot. She sat still, trying to catch her breath and sort it out. For years, nightmares of the accident had been her normal, but as long as she stayed busy, immersed in her studies, the nightmares remained, for the most part, mild and fuzzy. A startled gasp followed by a few fragments was the norm. When she wasn't busy all the time, guilt felt overwhelming and the nightmares got worse. But not until she had come to Oak Island had she experienced anything like this. The closer to the secret they came, the more bizarre, more detailed, and less fragmented were her nightmares. Fuzzy had given way to vivid, and not just in memory but in all her senses. *What's happening to me?* Her mouth salivated as a wave of nausea overcame her.

She got up. It was late or early – she wasn't sure which, but it was still dark outside. Flipping on the bathroom light, she went to the small camper sink, turned on the faucet, and splashed water on her face. *Hey, can you hear me?* The young man's voice echoed in her mind. She could still smell the burning bodies in her nostrils and those screams. *God, those screams.* She splashed another handful of water on her face, coughed, and spit black into the sink. She frowned. *Can't be. Don't even think it. Yeah, but there it is. Don't think it, girl, because that would be ridiculous and impossible. You were in a tunnel full of swamp mud, that's all. Surround yourself with dirt and you're bound to breathe it in, get it in your sinuses. What about the burnt taste? You sit next to the campfire every night, don't you? That's what you taste and that's what you smell. That's all.*

Walking back towards her bed, she heard voices coming through the camper window. She peeked out the window to see Jerry and her dad were still awake, relaxing by the fire. Jerry palmed a scotch while her father sipped from a glass of chardonnay.

"Who is he, Jerry?" her father demanded. "I know, I know I agreed not to ask, and for a year now, I haven't, but I want to know. Because, let me tell you, there is something not right about him. He knows more about this place than he possibly could or should know. Who the hell is he?"

Jerry took a slow sip from his glass of scotch, then sucked air through his teeth. "Charles, I don't know who he is."

"What? Come on, I get it if you won't tell me, but how do you expect me to bel—"

"I don't know who he is, Charles! I have never seen him, and all the money is handled through electronic wire transfers. I've never met the man."

Her father sat back in the camp chair, removed his fedora, and ran a hand through his hair. "Dammit, what the hell have we gotten ourselves into?"

"Don't worry, old chap," Jerry said, waving off the concern. "He has kept his end of the bargain up to this point."

"You realize nothing about this makes sense. Look, you're my friend and, man, we go way back, but if you know something and you're holding out, you owe it to me to tell me."

"For God's sake, don't you go all barmy. We have come too far." Jerry's voice betrayed a hint of offence.

"I'll tell you, Jerry, this does not make sense. Just hear me out. We have this mysterious anonymous billionaire taking an interest in Oak Island. By the way, the Oak Island myth has not been considered credible by anyone in ages. Obviously, before I came on board, mystery man had done some serious research, because he decides to spend millions draining and excavating the swamp, which turns out to have nearly two hundred skeletons buried under it. Now take—"

"Of course, you're right," Jerry interrupted. "It is bloody strange that he wants to keep himself anonymous, and yes, he followed the history and believed there was something here. He has the means and wants to prove it, and thanks to you, he has indeed."

Finishing off his wine, Charles stood and walked to the picnic table, pouring the rest of the bottle into his glass. "That's fine, but it doesn't make sense. It has been too perfect. This tunnel we found in the swamp led to a natural cavern in the bedrock. Now, they didn't stumble into this cavern from the top by chance – they tunneled into the side." He pointed his finger horizontally at the palm of his hand. "They also must have known that within several feet they would be able to carve a doorway through the bedrock, gaining access to the cavern. Jerry, come on, *how* in the hell could anyone possibly know how to do that? How could they predict it?"

"Bollocks! There's a logical explanation, Charles. I'm quite sure of it." Jerry straightened in his camp chair before standing to refill his glass.

"I would have topped you off."

"Nonsense, I need to stretch the old back anyway. I'm afraid we're not getting any younger."

Breanne pressed herself closer to the window, careful not to be discovered. She knew her dad was right – something wasn't adding up.

Her father swirled his wine in the glass, the creamy liquid catching the firelight just right, giving the chardonnay a golden glow. "That's just part of what's bothering me, though. The phone call was strange too. When I described for him what was in the chest, he acted like he didn't even care. No, wait a minute – now that I think about it, I didn't even get a chance to describe what was in the chest. He only asked questions about the chest itself. Has he told you anything over the last year about what he thought would be here?"

Jerry paced back and forth in front of the fire, allowing the blood to flow to his back and legs as he stretched. "In the last year we have spoken very little, and when we did it was mostly me who did the speaking, and always in regards to your progress. He usually spends the majority of our conversations giving me the what for and demanding speedier results. He has never shared with me his thoughts, and I have never asked." Jerry stopped pacing and turned to face Charles. "My friend, I am earnest with you when I tell you he came to me with a proposal and has paid me the agreed-upon fees for my services. Tonight, when we spoke, I told him of the treasure, but all his questions centered around the chest. He became irritated with my answers and asked to speak to you."

Dr. Moore studied his friend for a long moment. "We go way back, and we've been through a hell of a lot. I want you to know, I'm damn glad you're in this with me. You're a good friend."

Jerry gave Dr. Moore a tight smile and nodded. "As am I, Charles – as am I."

"Well, tomorrow morning I'm going back in the cavern for a more thorough examination, plus we need to process the knight as soon as possible since we have exposed the chamber to fresh air."

Jerry paused his pacing long enough to tip his glass, drawing a sip of scotch between his teeth before looking inquiringly to his friend. "What do your instincts tell you?"

"I don't know, but something isn't giving me a warm, fuzzy feeling."

Finally calmed down enough to give sleep another try, Breanne crawled back into bed. As she drifted off, all she could think was, *I haven't had the warm and fuzzies about this place since day one.*

Waking before the sun, she found herself once again engrossed in darkness. Throwing back the covers, she quickly dressed and began preparing breakfast for the family. She wanted to earn some points with her father. After inadvertently – okay, maybe purposely – eavesdropping on last night's conversation between Jerry and her dad, there was no way she wasn't going with him into that cavern.

Dr. Moore appeared from the camper, hastily pulling on his overshirt. "Bre, you're up early this morning, and I see you've made quite the breakfast!" He navigated the camper stairs and made a beeline for the picnic table.

"Well, Daddy, I figured we'd want to get an early start

and you would need a full tank for the work ahead." She smiled as she set a loaded plate in front of him.

"I see, so you thought maybe you would bribe me with food to ensure your place on the cavern expedition this morning?"

Breanne's eyes gave nothing away as she skillfully maintained the ruse.

"But I don't understand. The treasure is here – don't you want to stay topside and finish cataloging?" he asked, digging into the pancakes with purpose.

Jerry was up now and moving towards the picnic table. "Ah, lovely! Thank you, dear girl," he said, heaving a leg over the bench.

"Daddy, most of the basic categorizations have already been completed. Now we need to start running the items through the database so we can actually start identifying where these pieces fit in history." She nodded towards Jerry, placing a plate in front of him. "Since Jerry specializes in antiquities and you asked him to lead that effort, I thought I would assist you in the cavern with our Templar Knight. At least for today. If Jerry needs help tomorrow, I will stay with him to assist." She gave a shrug, then put on her best innocent smile and handed him a glass of orange juice.

Her father turned towards Jerry. "And there it is. First she starts off with 'Daddy,' usually a dead giveaway she wants something. Next, she makes her argument, but does so while I sit here, cramming my face with the delicious breakfast she made me."

"Nice touch," Jerry said, stuffing a forkful in his mouth.

"Then finally, she closes with the innocent smile you see plastered on her face right now," he said, a knowing smile creeping across his face.

Breanne's own smile faded as she realized she wasn't fooling her father in the slightest.

"You're too clever for your own good, baby girl. How much did you overhear last night?"

"Well, I don't know what you're talking about," she said unconvincingly.

Dr. Moore set his fork down on the table and sighed. "Bre, you're smart as a whip, but you're a horrible liar."

Breanne's shoulders slumped as she accepted her fate. "Fine. But come on! I've known something was wrong with this place since the beginning. Your feeling is right, Dad! We are missing something. I just want to help you figure out what it is!"

"So you listened in on my conversation with Jerry?" he asked.

"Not on purpose," she said softly.

Dr. Moore cocked an eyebrow.

She sat down next to her father. "Not at first?" Her eyes began to well up.

Her father glanced to Jerry.

"I think she has a point, Charles."

"Alright, baby girl, you're with me," he said, smiling a knowing smile.

"Really! I can go?" Tears fell freely now, but they weren't sad tears. She flung her arms around her father's neck and squeezed, kissing him on the cheek. "I love you!"

Her father's barrel chest bounced as he chuckled. "I love you too, baby girl, now stop crying. All I wanted was for you to be honest with me. Besides, how can I tell you no after a breakfast like this!"

21

Keeper

Present day
Petersburg, Illinois

Garrett and Lenny arrived at the dojo just in time for class. They donned their doboks and knotted their belts. Tonight's class was only for the most advanced students, black belts and above. Since Lenny and Garrett were the only black belts, class would only include the two of them and their master, Mr. B.

Since the first day the boys met, they had watched, studied, and discussed every martial arts movie they could get their hands on. But back then, to take lessons, real lessons, would have required going to Springfield, and that simply wasn't going to happen. There was no way their parents had the means to transport the boys to or pay for classes. Then one day they had heard whispers that a real martial arts academy was opening up town.

That day, a few years back, it seemed fate had brought them an impossible opportunity. Hell, after their watching, wishing, and praying, it was nothing short of a dream realized. A taekwondo academy had opened uptown, right on the square. They ran to beat hell as soon as the rumor got to them, and sure enough there was a sign out front that read COMING SOON TO PETERSBURG, THE ACADEMY OF TAEKWONDO.

When the boys stepped inside the dojo, eager to introduce themselves and determined to find a way to attend, they were shocked by the mess. Last Garrett knew, the place had housed a failed restaurant. A construction worker was precariously balanced high on a ladder near the center of the large room, messing with some light-fixture wiring. The sweaty man was wearing painters' pants, a tool belt, and a flannel shirt. The worker was quite portly, probably pushing three hundred pounds, and looked completely out of place high up on the ladder.

"Excuse me, sir – can you tell us where to find the owner?" Garrett had asked.

"Hello, boys, I am Mr. Brockridge. How can I be of service?"

"You're... the instructor?" Garrett asked, making no effort to hide his confusion.

"I am," Mr. Brockridge said, smiling down at them.

"Oh, wow... well, yeah, we saw the sign out front," Lenny said.

Mr. Brockridge chuckled as he descended the ladder, unfastened his tool belt, and draped it over one of the ladder's rungs. "I'll tell you what, boys, I need a break anyway. How would you like a demonstration?"

"Heck, yeah! We sure would. If it's not too much trouble. I mean... *yes, sir*, we sure would." Garrett straightened up, knowing enough from the martial arts films that you always addressed the teacher as *sir*.

"No problem at all – come with me."

The boys followed him across the dojo, carefully stepping

over piles of building materials and skirting stacks of drywall before finally reaching the back door of the building. "This should be good," Lenny whispered with a giggle.

Garrett elbowed Lenny, shooting him a silencing glare.

In the alley behind the building, Mr. Brockridge gathered four patio blocks from a pallet stacked full. He stood each patio block on end, one after the other, on top an old cabinet, creating what looked like an oversized domino line.

"First, I will demonstrate mind over matter in the form of raw power. This row of blocks equals about eight inches of solid concrete."

"No way," whispered Lenny.

Again, Garrett elbowed him.

As the boys watched with saucer eyes, Mr. Brockridge assumed a fighting stance, positioning both feet about a shoulder's width apart. He drew his right fist all the way back by his rib cage. In one fluid motion, he stepped forward, launched his fist out, and opened his palm towards the sky before striking the first of the patio blocks.

The boys gasped as the man's hand blasted through the block with stunning force. But the momentum did not stop with the first block; it carried through block after block with lightning speed, creating a magnificent explosion that rained small pieces of concrete all over the alley. It was as if a wrecking ball moving at full speed had collided with the patio blocks, which had never stood a chance.

"Wow! No way!" the boys shouted out in unison.

Mr. Brockridge smiled. "The key is in the focus of the mind. You look beyond the blocks, through the blocks, and then you simply go there." The large man then walked to the center of the alley. "Now, I will demonstrate form." He bowed to the boys and began a complex, high-ranking form, which included front kicking above his head and head-high sidekicks to both the left and the right, followed by a fast succession of various strikes. With perfect technique, he performed roundhouse kicks, jump kicks, and finally a jump back kick, before ending his form in the exact same place he had started. Once again, he bowed to the boys. The display would have been impressive if performed by a physically fit person, but to see it performed by a man of his girth seemed to defy the laws of physics.

The boys stood with mouths agape, unable to speak for a long moment. Finally, they picked up their jaws and found their words, eagerly inquiring about the cost of lessons. But when the boys found out it would cost fifty-five dollars a month, plus the cost of the required dobok, they were crushed with disappointment. They knew neither they nor their parents could afford the lessons.

Garrett could hear his mother now. "Now, honey, you know that would be a nice-to-have, but we can barely afford the have-to-haves right now."

The teacher noted the disappointment on the faces of the boys and pursed his lips in thought. After a moment, he asked the boys one question. "Why do you want to take martial arts?"

Something about the tone, the look, or the question itself made Garrett realize his answer was critical. He felt like the universe was listening, holding its breath waiting for him to speak, so that he could be weighed and measured. His and Lenny's dream could live or die on this answer.

"Well, sir, we don't want to fight or anything like that, but we are best friends in a small town where people aren't so friendly to people who are different, and we want to be able to defend ourselves."

"And I think chicks would dig it," Lenny said, eliciting another elbow from Garrett.

Mr. Brockridge chuckled deeply, smiled, and said, "Okay, boys, one final question."

"Shoot," Lenny said.

Garrett nodded expectantly.

"What do you boys know about drywall?"

The rest was history, and the boys had been taking classes for a few years and now were the highest-ranking students in the school.

Tonight, the boys started their routine as normal, warming up on the heavy bag, followed by running the outside edges of the large blue-matted dojo. Once sufficiently warm, they practiced drills with each other – kicking, blocking, punching, blocking, kicking. Then on to hapkido throw drills and grappling. After donning their sparring equipment – including head gear, gloves, shin guards, and chest protector – they practiced their fighting skills with contact sparring. Lastly, they practiced their forms.

Mr. B watched on, commenting occasionally as he corrected their technique.

On his third form, Garrett removed a practice sword from a rack on the far side of the dojo, bowed, and began to move the sword in a complex series of strikes and blocks.

Suddenly, Mr. B called them to attention. "Garrett, I need to see you in my office. Lenny, please stay here. I will return momentarily."

Garrett and Lenny traded confused glances as Garrett handed Lenny the sword and followed Mr. B towards his office.

Mr. B closed the door and motioned Garrett to take a seat on the opposite side of his desk. The office, located in the front of the school, was small; tonight, with the shades of the window facing out onto the town square drawn closed, it felt even smaller.

"Garrett, how have you been doing?"

Mr. B had never asked Garrett about his life outside the

dojo, and Garrett was taken slightly aback by the question. "Good, Grand Master."

"Sir," Mr. B corrected, waving a hand. "You know how I hate that pomp and circumstance. Are you sure you're good?"

"Yes, sir, I am sure. Why do you ask?"

Mr. B looked at Garrett for a long moment. "I want you to know you can trust me. You can tell me if something is bothering you or if something is going on."

Garrett scrunched his forehead in confusion. "Yes, sir."

"And you are sure nothing is bothering you? There is nothing that you want to tell me?"

"Yes, I am sure." *What the hell is this about?*

"You have been running a lot. Yes?" he asked.

"Yes, sir." *Is this because I was slacking during practice?*

Another awkward moment passed as Mr. B studied Garrett. Finally, leaning forward in his chair and looking intensely at the boy, he said, "Well, you have been acting strange – distracted – and you lack focus. I need your assurance you are ready to test."

Holy shit, is that what this is about? Mr. B was calling a test? Students never knew when a test would be called, and at his and Lenny's level it could take years to earn even one degree. "If I am selected to test, I will give it everything I have, sir."

Another long moment of silence passed between them. "You will test Wednesday after school. You will be getting home late. I will call your parents and inform them. Garrett, this is a closed testing session. No one will be allowed here but the three of us."

The three of us? Perfect, Lenny must be testing too. He could not imagine Lenny not testing with him. They had tested for every single belt together. *Crap.* He was supposed to work Wednesday, but he would have to get out of it. This was considered an honor, not an option.

The Secret Journal

"Garrett? Do you understand?"

"Yes, sir."

A soft knock came at the door.

"Yes?" Mr. B said.

Lenny popped his head in. "Sir, sorry to interrupt, but there is a lady here inquiring about the cost of classes."

"Alright. Thank you, Lenny. Tell her I will be right with her. Excuse me, Garrett, I will be right back."

"Yes, sir."

Mr. B left the office, closing the door behind him. This was the first time Garrett had ever been alone in his instructor's office. As he sat, he replayed the conversation in his mind. It seemed strange for Mr. B to tell them separately. But even stranger was that the testing was to be a closed event. This meant no one, not even his parents, would be allowed to watch. In the past, his mom had always watched his tests, along with anyone else he wanted to invite. Heck, students of the academy were usually required to watch. Why was this test closed? He resolved to ask Mr. B when he returned – there must be a good reason.

Garrett looked around the office as he waited. Among the many items on the office walls were photos of both Lenny and Garrett receiving their black belts and, hanging directly behind his desk, a certificate awarded to Grand Master Brockridge for his ninth-degree black belt. An ornate wooden box sitting on Mr. B's desk caught his attention. It was open but with the hinged side facing him, and he was unable to see inside. The box was not large – about the size of a cigar box. Garrett wondered what his master would keep in a box like that. *Surely, he doesn't smoke cigars.*

It felt like several minutes had passed since Mr. B closed the door. He listened for any sound indicating his teacher might be approaching, but heard nothing. Sliding forward to the front of his chair, he reached over to the wooden box carefully, turning it ever so slightly to allow him to peer inside. Much to Garrett's relief, there were no cigars in the box, only a few pieces of jewelry and a watch.

This must be where Mr. B kept items he did not wear while training, which made perfect sense. He felt a pang of guilt wash over him. He had no business going through Mr. B's stuff. *What am I doing?* He started to push the box back into place, but something caught his eye.

Coiled among the items lay a plain silver necklace threaded through an unassuming silver ring. Something was etched on the inside of the ring. Garrett squinted, trying to figure out what it was, but he couldn't tell – words maybe. Glancing back at the door, then back to the box, he reached in and rolled the ring over. In the center of the ring was a symbol he did not recognize with the letter *G* in the middle. Another symbol was etched on the inside of the ring. It looked like it might be the sun, except that the rays emerged only from the bottom half of the circle. He heard a voice from beyond the office door. *Shit.* He glanced quickly at the silver band and was only able to make out one word, but it made his heart quicken as he whispered it aloud. "Keeper."

The knob rattled and turned.

Garrett let go of the ring and thrust himself back into the chair. The door opened and Mr. B stepped through, followed closely by Lenny. "Alright, I will see you boys Wednesday after school – come prepared, come focused. I wish you good luck."

Oh no! Garrett screamed inside as he stared at the box. It was cocked slightly sideways from where it had been. His heart hammering in his throat, panic took him and he stood abruptly, wanting nothing more than to get out of the small office. He stumbled as he stepped away from the desk, light-headed from standing so suddenly.

"Are you alright, Garrett?" Mr. B asked in surprise, as he reached out to steady him.

"Yes, my... leg just... fell asleep," Garrett said, shuffling around the imposing man.

A moment later, the boys were walking home.

"Can you believe it, Garrett? Second-degree black belt!"

"Yeah, it's awesome," Garrett said in a monotone.

"What's wrong with you? Aren't you excited?"

They stopped to wait on a car passing by before crossing the street. "Lenny, can I ask you something?"

Lenny looked over his shoulder. "I know what you want to ask."

"You do?" Garrett said in surprise.

"You want to ask about chores. About the training and rules, right? Well, listen, I don't know much more than I already said."

That was definitely something Garrett wanted to talk about, but it wasn't what he was going to ask. "Okay, Lenny, since you bring it up, yeah, I want to know whatever you can tell me."

"Well, like I said, it all started when I was adopted. My adoptive parents started making me study, sometimes late into the night. The material had nothing to do with what was being taught in school."

"What do you study?"

"All kinds of stuff. Astronomy, history, a lot of extra studying on topography and mapping, navigation by stars – oh, and the currencies and languages of other countries too. As time went on, they added hands-on survival training and primitive survival training, like how to build shelters, trap food, make a fire from two sticks. When we started the taekwondo, they added weapons training. They make me spend hours a week practicing with the bo staff."

"You never wondered why?"

Lenny looked at him like he was an idiot. "Of course I wondered why. I asked once or twice. The first time they said, 'This is Petersburg, and in Petersburg we train, we prepare. We never, ever talk about it – not to anyone.' I pressed and asked why, what is the purpose."

"What did they say?"

"I was told I would need these skills when things went bad and never to ask again. They said if I so much as questioned the rules, let alone broke them, I would be sent back to foster care. I knew they meant it too. God, it was plain in their eyes they meant it."

Garrett only nodded in answer as they continued to walk.

"Look, I like it here, Garrett. I like you and my family. Sure, the secret chores and rules suck, and I don't understand them any better than you do. Hell, sometimes the people here suck, too, but despite all that I wouldn't trade it. It's hard to explain, but I feel like I am supposed to be here." He looked back over his shoulder again. "Honestly, I am nervous as hell even talking about this."

Garrett sighed, having hoped for more. "Okay, Lenny. Hey, you remember you said you had an uncle or something that was a Freemason?"

"Yeah."

"You said you have seen his ring. What did it look like?"

"Umm, well, it had like a square and a compass kind of laid over each other with a letter in the middle. It was a *C* I think, or wait, maybe it was a *G*. I can't remember for sure, but I know it had a letter on it too."

Garrett felt his stomach twist into a tight knot.

22

You Must Search, Doctor

Present day
Oak Island, Nova Scotia

After breakfast, Paul lowered himself, Breanne, Edward, and their father into the pit. Jerry was up top working with the items from the chest and acting as their point of safety via the two-way radio. Charles prepared himself to rappel down the forty-yard slope for a second day in a row. But Paul stopped him, cleverly persuading him to ride down on the skid by telling him someone had to keep the tripod lighting and other supplies secure. Her father said he would do it, but only for the good of the equipment.

Once inside, Breanne went to work setting up the tripods. Soon the cavern, along with the Templar Knight, was showered in artificial light, giving the whole place an ominous glow. Ominous or not, the additional lighting allowed for a more thorough search.

Although the cavern wasn't large – around 150 feet long and at least 50 feet wide – the uneven walls, jagged outcroppings of rocks, and stalagmite columns slowed the search. In addition, there was the issue of the mucky floor and areas of standing water, some of them almost knee-deep, which required extra caution to avoid stepping into a submerged hole in the floor. Edward and Paul used long poles to feel their way tediously, back and forth, across the deeper areas. When they would strike something with the pole, they would investigate and rule out any possible hidden artifacts. Their father also had them flag every rock, even the submerged ones, in order to create a layout of all the rock locations. He would later analyze the layout to ensure he was not missing any hidden messages.

In the meantime, Charles decided he and Breanne would focus their efforts on the Templar Knight. "Bre, what is he looking at?" her father asked, following the gaze of the eyeless knight.

"It seems like he's looking down at the floor to me."

"You know, between the muck and the water, I don't think yesterday's search of the cavern was as detailed as I thought. Let's shovel out the area in front of the altar and see what he's looking at," Charles said, clapping his hands.

Breanne nodded and they went to work.

Twenty minutes later, they had cleared a six-foot-square area right down to the bedrock floor. But they found nothing obvious. Her father rinsed away any remaining dirt and, using a stiff-bristled brush, brushed the whole area and found nothing: no clues, no seams, no symbol – nothing.

Breanne studied the Templar, then the ground. "Well, it is possible his head has changed position over time, Dad. Maybe he was looking further out. I doubt his head could have lifted, but it could have sagged lower, right?"

"Huh, you're absolutely right. Very good. We are going to have to clear the entire distance between us and the wall to be sure we don't miss anything."

"Great, so I'm glad I made that point. Now my reward is

The Secret Journal

digging out another twenty-five or thirty square feet," she said, smiling.

"I believe you wanted to be down here with *Daddy*, right? You could have been sitting topside with the warm sun on your face and a breeze in your hair, but, oh no, you wanted to be down here – in the mud." He handed her a shovel with an ornery grin.

Breanne rolled her eyes dramatically as she stomped a foot down on the shovel.

Shortly after they went back to work digging, her brothers finished with their detailed search of the cavern and joined in to help.

"Well?" her father asked. "Anything?"

"Nothing," Edward said. "Nothing in the nooks, nothing in the crannies, nothing in the water."

They continued clearing the muddy area for the next two hours, reaching the far wall but finding no new clues.

Ready to throw in the towel, their father mumbled something under his breath, turned, and idly splashed the remaining water from the pitcher he had been using to clear the muck off the floor. The channel the team had dug between the altar and the wall was now several inches deep, reaching down to the stone floor. This newly created channel was now steadily pooling with water.

"Guys, it's no use. We need to start planning the removal of the knight. Maybe that will give me time to think of something we missed," Charles said, fatigue and frustration beginning to show.

"What about the tunnel?" Breanne said suddenly, new excitement in her voice.

"What do you mean?" her father asked.

"Well, we assume the tunnel leads back to the swamp, but what if there is another cavern, or a passage leading to another chamber somewhere between here and the swamp?"

As the thought developed, excitement began to build. "Yes, we have to clear the tunnel in the other direction to know for sure – we could have missed something huge!"

"Maybe," her father said, rubbing his chin in thought.

Her brothers rolled their eyes at each other, obviously not in favor of clearing more of the heavy stones from the tunnel.

While his three kids stood staring at him, waiting for their fates to be decided, Charles stared past them, back towards the altar, lost in thought. Breanne knew the look: he was pondering her suggestion. But then she noticed his gaze found focus and he stared in puzzlement. "Do you see that?" he said.

They all craned their heads to try to see what he was seeing.

"See what, Pops?" Edward asked, looking at the knight atop the altar.

"Look down!"

They all looked down, then at each other, then at their father, and then back at each other. No one was seeing whatever it was he was seeing.

"That's it, dear God above. Of course!"

Breanne raised an eyebrow. "What's it, Dad?"

"Ha! You all really don't see it!" he shouted with a laugh.

They tried again to follow his gaze, staring under the knight, then at the altar itself, then back to their father.

"Look at the floor, dammit!" he said, pointing at the base of the altar.

Breanne was the first to see it, and her eyes blossomed in understanding. "Bubbles!" she said excitedly.

At the base of the altar, water had pooled in the newly created channel, and it was now bubbling ever so slightly.

"That's right, baby girl! Air from underneath must be exiting, which can only mean water must be draining through!"

Paul looked dubious. "Maybe there is a low spot or washout underneath?"

Dr. Moore began hastily clearing all the muck from around the altar. "No, I don't think so. I assumed this altar had been chiseled from a natural stalagmite, but that would mean it was part of the floor. However, bubbles can't be here if this is one piece of stalagmite developed over time. I think this structure was placed here! I think this altar is hiding something underneath and I just bet, if we remove all the muck and water from this entire cavern, we could find the spot they cut and moved this giant stone from."

"How would they have moved it? It has to weigh tons!" Breanne said.

"Well, there were at least one hundred seventy-eight people here to move it," Edward said.

"One hundred seventy-nine, if you count this guy," replied Paul, hooking his thumb back towards the Templar Knight.

"Pops, you're not going to make us clear all this water and sludge from this entire place to find out if your theory's right, are you?" Edward asked, already dreading the daunting task.

Paul smiled at his father. "We don't need to do that to find out if he's right," he said, turning to his brother. "We just need to move this big rock."

"Exactly," Charles said.

Goose bumps blossomed on Breanne's arms as the back of her hair sprang up. "Hey, Dad? Do you remember what Jerry's creepy boss said?"

The three men looked at her.

"You must search, doctor… until you have left nothing unexplored and—"

"No stone unturned," her father interrupted quietly.

They stared at the giant stone for several seconds.

"Come on, guys... I'm sure it was just a coincidence," Paul said in a voice that implied otherwise. "What we need to do now is move this rock."

"And just how in the hell are we going to do that when there's only four of us? Actually, only about three and a half." Edward looked at Breanne, who promptly punched him in the arm.

Paul walked around the stone, held his thumb out sideways, closed one eye, and gauged the slope of the tunnel off in the distance. "I have a plan."

"Right, I think I already know where you're going with this – the winch?" his father asked.

"No, I don't think so. Even if we all push and use the winch, I don't think it'll give us the power we need to pull it. I'd be concerned the cable would snap or the rigging in the tunnel would fail. Any of those scenarios play out and someone could end up hurt," Paul said, still studying the stone and the archway leading out to the ramp.

Edward walked around the giant stone and stopped next to his brother. "This stone has to weigh several tons – several times more than the treasure chest weighed, even with Pops sitting on it."

The comment elicited a glare from his father. "Watch it, boy!" he said, wagging his finger up and down in Edward's direction.

"So what are you thinking, little bro?" Edward asked.

"Well, guys, we just so happen to have a big-ass crane, with giant cables."

"The crane is at the top of the pit, Paul. I don't see how that can help," Dr. Moore said.

"Right, we need to get to work. We have to build better rigging in the tunnel, and I need to add a rig to that doorway." Paul pointed to the archway entrance to the room. "I think I can anchor a pulley into the bedrock easy enough."

"This sounds sketchy," his father said.

"Well, I can't promise this will work, but as far as safety goes, I'm not worried. My biggest fear is damaging the wood tunnel, causing a cave-in. But we don't need to be down here when we pull the stone with the crane. You guys can go up and I can make the final connection, then evacuate to the pit. If the tunnel caves in, no one gets trapped down here."

Breanne and Charles walked around the stone and stood in a small huddle with Paul and Edward. Everyone stared at their father as he pondered his son's plan. He removed his fedora, ran his hand through his hair, then placed it back atop his head. "Well, I don't like it. You still have to be in the pit. Is there another way we can move this?"

"Well, I could drill some holes in it, set explosives, and try a controlled blast. There is more risk in this chamber caving in, though, and if that happens, I don't know that we could ever get back here," Paul said.

"No explosives," he said, waving off the suggestion immediately. Then with the deep-chested chuckle Breanne had come to love, he turned to his sons. "You military guys and your damn explosives. What's with you boys wanting to blow shit up all the time?"

"Just giving you the options as I see 'em, Pops." Paul turned to Edward, adding, "Besides, blowing shit up is what we do."

"Hooyah!" Edward said, fist-bumping his brother.

"Alright, let's get started on this rigging of yours," Charles said, exhaling a long, wary sigh, as if he had just been told he would have to walk ten miles back to the car after a long day's work. "Nothing comes easy on this goddamn island," he muttered.

The Moores spent the rest of the afternoon and hours of the evening bringing down the equipment, building materials, pulleys, and tools needed to create a rigging system that would allow the stone to be pulled without destroying the fragile wooden tunnel leading to the slope.

With all the material safely transported to the bottom of the pit, the Moores cranked up the tunes and set to work cutting four-by-fours that would be used to create, for all intents and purposes, a box within the box shape of the tunnel. Paul's theory was that the newly built structure would give the cable a solid place to find purchase, rather than ripping through the centuries-old wood of the tunnel, possibly resulting in a collapse.

Breanne measured and marked out the boards, her father made the cuts, and Edward and Paul constructed the reinforcement.

"Pops, I think we're good here," echoed Paul's voice from the tunnel. A moment later his head appeared from the hole in the floor of the pit. "Bre, hand me that hammer drill and box of concrete anchors – oh, and a hammer. Time to install this pulley, and we'll be ready to rock."

"On it," Bre said.

By the time the rigging was complete, it was getting late and the family had put in a long day. They gathered around the giant stone altar one last time as Paul double-checked the cable connection that now wrapped completely around the stone.

Exhausted, Breanne leaned against the stone altar. Immediately she noticed something strange – felt something strange. She turned to face the stone and placed both hands flat against it. The others took notice.

"What is it, Bre?" Edward asked.

She didn't know how to explain it. "Put your hands on the stone and feel this," she said.

Everyone followed her lead, spreading out in a circle around the altar, laying their palms flat on the stone.

Her father spoke first. "That is the strangest sensation. It feels like, I don't know, like electricity is running through this stone. Lots of it!"

"It's like some sort of energy," Edward said.

"I feel like at any second I'm going to get electrocuted," Paul said, yanking his hands away. "That's some creepy shit, man."

It didn't feel creepy at all to Breanne. It just felt odd. She felt the sensation all the way up her arms and radiating into her chest. "It feels kind of like if you put your hands on a car while the engine is running, but without the sound."

"What could this mean?" Edward asked.

"Honestly, Ed, I... I just don't know." Dr. Moore rubbed his face. "Well, it is unlikely, but perhaps below this stone is a powerful current of water. Rushing water may account for the vibration transferring through the stone."

The Moores looked at each other gravely. They all knew what that would mean – the end of further exploration.

"Is that what you think it is? Water-flow vibration?" Paul asked.

Her father paused for a long moment, seeming to search the vast archeological archives of his mind. He slowly placed both hands back on the altar. "No... no, I don't think it is water flow."

"Then what?" Breanne asked, her voice barely above a whisper. She thought it, knew everyone else was thinking it, and for some reason none of them wanted to say it. The Ark of the Covenant? The Holy Grail? Aaron's rod? The Ten Commandments?

He looked to each of them, allowing his eyes to finally settle on Breanne. "I don't know. I can't think of a single logical explanation."

"Only one way to find out, I guess," Paul said.

Her father let out a long sigh. And she knew before he spoke, she would not get to look under that stone tonight.

"As tempting as it is to push on, we are tired, hungry, and plain worn out. It wouldn't be safe to do this tonight. We can't afford a mistake. It will be much easier to monitor the cables and operation in the pit with the sun up, when we're fresh. I know none of you want to hear this, but let's call it a day."

23

Wrong Number

Present day
Petersburg, Illinois

As soon as they entered Garrett's house, the boys were enveloped with the aromas of sweet Italian sausage, oregano, and garlic bread. After their taekwondo class, the boys were starved.

"What's for dinner tonight? It smells awesome," Lenny said.

"Spaghetti, I think."

Lenny nodded excitedly.

His mother's voice came from the kitchen. "Boys, you home? It's time to eat."

"Yeah," Garrett called back to the kitchen as he kicked off his shoes.

"Did you boys wash your hands?" Elaine asked.

Both boys raced to the bathroom.

"Settle down!" Phillip yelled after them from his throne.

They quickly washed their hands and returned to find

Elaine placing a giant serving bowl filled with goulash on the table.

"Lenny. Don't you have a home?" Phillip asked, provoking an instant glare from Elaine.

"Yes, sir, I do," Lenny said, laughing.

"Then why in the hell are you in mine? Why don't you go to your own home?" Then, turning his attention to Garrett, he said, "Jesus Christ, I'm not trying to feed the whole godforsaken neighborhood."

"Alright, mister, that's about enough of that," Elaine said, pointing her finger at Phillip before turning to Lenny. "Now, Lenny, you know you are welcome here anytime. Don't pay any attention to Phillip." She threw Phillip a stabbing glare.

"Thank you, Mrs. Turek," Lenny said.

Reaching for the garlic bread, Elaine said, "Boys, tell me about your day."

Lenny perked up. "Garrett and I get to test for our second-degree black belts on Wednesday! We just found out at class today."

"Oh, good, I will plan to come watch!" Elaine said.

"I absolutely hate goulash," James said. "Everything is mixed together, and mushrooms? Ugh."

Phillip glared at James. "You know what, James? You are going to eat that goulash or so help you Go—"

The phone rang.

"Well, that's just it, Mom, you can't. It's a closed test, so no spectators – not even students or family can be there," Garrett said.

Phillip drew in a breath, reached over, and picked up the phone. "Tureks… Yes. Yes, I understand. How long? I see." Phillip looked directly at Garrett. "He has to be. Thank you." He hung up the phone and looked at Elaine.

Garrett watched as his mother's eyes searched Phillip's. "Who was that?"

Phillip broke eye contact with Elaine and turned to Garrett. "Wrong number."

"Wrong number?" Elaine blinked, the blood draining from her face to leave behind a wide-eyed ghost. "Did you hear Garrett? He said the test is closed. No spectators. No family." Her voice cracked.

"Lenny, why don't you stay here tonight?" Phillip asked.

Lenny blinked. "On a school night?"

"Yes. Just this one time," Phillip said.

James dropped his fork into his bowl and froze.

It was like their whole world stopped. Everyone gaped at Phillip in shocked silence. Never had Phillip personally invited Lenny to spend the night, and never had he allowed it on a school night.

"I… I don't know, sir. It's a school night, and I have chores," Lenny managed.

"It will be fine, Lenny, and you can both take the night off training," Phillip said.

Garrett's mind literally blew. *Did he just say* training *in front of Lenny?*

Lenny blinked. "I… I don't…"

Garrett looked from side to side. Dumbstruck faces stared back.

"Listen, instead of training tonight, why don't you spend some time talking about where you are in your training and what you have learned?" Phillip said.

Garrett heard the words, but it was like someone else was speaking them. He wasn't going to pass the opportunity up – he was going to seize it. Phillip had brought it up, so he couldn't whip him, not for this. "Dad, why do we train? What is the purpose?"

James's jaw dropped open. Then he smiled, pulled out his Zippo, and began flicking it.

"Mr. Man!" his mother gasped. "You know better than—"

"Elaine, stop," Phillip said, holding up a hand. Then he did something weird. He made a face that Garrett almost mistook for a pained grimace, but then he realized... it was a smile. It was forced – not much more than a tight, joyless line – but a smile nonetheless. "You have many questions. You both do and you should. I ask only this. Wait until Wednesday, after you test. I will answer any questions you have then."

Lenny spoke quietly. "I am sworn to never speak of this outside my family, Mr. Turek. If my parents find—"

"I know, Lenny. Trust me, it will be fine. Come here Wednesday after your test. Tonight, you can stay here."

Lenny nodded. "Um, okay. If my parents are cool with it."

"Run home and grab your stuff. Say nothing of this to your parents, only say I asked for you to stay," Phillip said in an unusually soft voice.

Lenny stood up slowly. "Alright then, I'll go grab a change of clothes and my guitar."

Garrett looked at his mother and saw no smile. Instead, her eyes were glassy, her face still drained of blood, whiter than dead coral. She looked as though she would be sick.

"Garrett, the rules still apply. Speak to no one else about your training. Only Lenny."

"Yes, sir." Garrett nodded slowly. His mind raced. Did Phillip somehow know about his and Lenny's talk? No. That couldn't be possible. Besides, if he had, it wouldn't have made him want to be nice about it. No. If Phillip had known about the conversation, he would have been whipped. The phone call? He didn't think that was a wrong number. What was it Phillip had said to the caller? He'd looked Garrett right in the

The Secret Journal

eye and he'd said, *He has to be.* Has to be what? What did it mean?

Next to his throne, under the wall phone, leaned an old, crooked cane with an ivory handle. The warped shaft of the cane was a dark-stained wood, plain except for a few nicks. Garrett had never seen Phillip use the cane, no matter how bad his hip was bothering him. But each morning he carried the cane to the kitchen, and each evening he carried the cane back to the bedroom.

One day Garrett had decided to ask him why he had the old cane anyway. Phillip had glanced over at the cane, a melancholy expression washing over his face. "It was my father's, and there may come a day when I have to depend on it as my father did, so I keep it around in case that time comes."

Garrett looked at Phillip now and noticed that same sadness hanging heavy across his face like a soggy cloud hanging low in the sky. Phillip stood, picked up his father's old cane, and this time he didn't carry it – this time he leaned heavily on it as he made his way to bed.

Without a word, James snapped shut his Zippo, pushed his chair out, and carried his bowl across the kitchen, where Elaine was filling the sink with soapy water. "Thank you, James," she said quietly.

He nodded somberly and left the room.

"Mom? You okay?" Garrett asked.

Elaine turned and gave Garrett a weak smile, then she cupped his cheeks in her warm, wet hands. "Garrett, you are such a good boy. I am so proud of you." She squeezed his face. "I love you very, very much," she whispered, searching his eyes intensely with hers, searching for understanding – for confirmation – but as she searched, her eyes filled with tears that raced down her cheeks, betraying her charade.

"What is it, Mom? What's going on? I love you too,

please don't cry," Garrett said, his own eyes beginning to blur.

Elaine quickly pulled herself together, wiping her eyes with the apron. "Sorry, dear, don't mind me, it's just that you are so special and so loved." She did her best to smile as she sighed deeply, regaining her composure. "I am so, so proud of you." She leaned forward and kissed him gently on the forehead. "Now, listen to me, Garrett – this is very important. Wednesday, when you test, concentrate, clear your mind of everything, and *focus*, dear. You have to focus."

∼

"What's wrong with you?" Lenny said, smiling mischievously, as he bit his lower lip and walked his fingers across the frets from one end of the neck all the way down to the body of the guitar until both hands were almost touching. He paused there, fingering the strings magically before making his way back up the neck like a classical pianist effortlessly gliding across ivory keys.

"I just can't believe this," Garrett said. "You being here and now suddenly we can talk about our training with each other. Why now? And are other kids getting to talk to each other about their trainings? My dad said only you, Lenny, and that I can't talk to anyone else, but suddenly you're okay?"

"Who cares. I'm just glad we can talk to each other. It sucked keeping this secret from my best friend all this time. And your dad said he is going to tell us why after the test on Wednesday. We will finally know why we have been training all this time."

"Okay, but don't you think it is strange we have to wait until after the test? What's that got to do with anything? And

The Secret Journal

then there was that call and what my mom said while you were getting your stuff."

"The wrong number?" Lenny asked.

"Yeah, that was no wrong number."

"What did your mom say?" he asked.

"Something about focus – it was weird, that's all." Garrett shook his head.

Just then, James poked his head up from the stairwell leading to Garrett's room. "Hey, nice finger work, Lenny," he said, ascending the stairs the rest of the way. "Garrett, I heard you guys say you're testing for second-degree black belt this week?"

"Yeah, we're pretty stoked about it," Garrett replied, wondering why his brother would even come up into his room. He tried to stay ready. This could be a trap to catch him off guard. Any second, he might wrench either one of them into a knot, or worse.

"Garrett, come here for a second," he said, motioning Garrett towards the stairs.

Garrett looked at him with hesitation but followed cautiously.

"We'll be right back," James said, looking towards Lenny with a glare that dared Lenny to try and follow them.

Lenny shrugged and went back to playing his guitar.

Garrett watched James as he descended the stairs, flipping the lighter open and shut. How could someone so badly burned carry around a lighter without a care like that? From what Garrett understood, when the accident happened and James dropped the lighter, there was no putting out the cotton before it began to melt into his skin, burning his entire torso, arms, and even his cheeks. He'd required several surgeries to perform skin grafts. You would think something like that would have made him afraid of fire, but not James.

Once they were halfway down the stairs, James swiveled

to face him. Garrett stopped, unsure what to expect. Usually there were at least a few smart-mouthed comments exchanged between them before anything physical would happen.

"Are you ready for this test Wednesday?" James asked.

Whatever he had expected from James, that was not it. It took him aback, and he stuttered nothing intelligible.

"Well, are you ready?" he asked a second time.

Garrett narrowed his eyes, trying to read James's face but only seeing a quilt of stubbly blotches separated by random scars blanketing an emotionless cheek. "I don't know. Honestly, I didn't even think Mr. B would let me test anytime soon."

"Well, listen, best of luck to you. I truly hope you do well, Garrett." Then he reached out and slapped his brother on the shoulder, turned, and descended the stairs.

Garrett watched, stupefied, as he descended. Had he heard right? Did his brother just wish him good luck?

On the bottom step, James paused, turning back to face him. "Oh, hey… listen, little bro, one more thing."

"Yeah?" Garrett managed.

"It's all about *focus*. You remember that, and you'll crush this shit." He stood there for a moment longer, holding Garrett's gaze.

Garrett's eyes went wide. He searched James's eyes for an explanation that didn't come. Finally, unable to speak, he simply nodded.

James smiled tightly, gave a sharp nod, and vanished around the corner.

Garrett waited there for a moment, his mind spinning, trying to piece it out. First Phillip, then his mom, and now James. What weren't they telling him? He walked down the stairs, passing by his parents' bedroom door on his way to the kitchen, his throat suddenly all rust. After he sucked down a glass of water, he started back. This time he heard his parents' voices as he passed their room. He couldn't make out what they were saying, so he eased closer. He didn't dare risk hanging out outside his parents' bedroom door eavesdropping, but he couldn't help but pause briefly.

"He's not ready for this, Phillip."

"No. No one is."

Garrett pressed closer, but what followed was only silence. He waited and when no more sounds came, he became nervous, retreating back to the stairs, to Lenny and his guitar. He and Lenny stayed up far too late smiling, laughing, and sharing forbidden training knowledge. It felt good, like a weight lifted, to truly speak honest air with his best friend and know that at least with Lenny he had no more forced secrets.

Eventually, even the excitement of permission to break the rules wasn't enough to fight back the sandman, but it wasn't the soft sand sprinkled over Garrett's eyes bringing him magic dreams. No, it wasn't the sandman who came this night. Instead, Garrett found himself in a nightmare of hell as real as any fire he had ever felt. It burned everything and everywhere. A voice from the flames called, "All things will burn, whether flesh or bone, steel or stone, all things will burn." He saw someone and called out, and then the flames reached for him, grabbing hold with white-fire fingers. *Oh, God! God, no!*

Garrett jolted inside the tangle of sweat-soaked sheets as he opened his eyes and gasped. He rubbed his chest, then his face as he tried to recall the dream, but it was slipping further and further from the grasp of his mind, like water through his fingers.

"Hey, you okay? You were moaning in your sleep," Lenny asked, pushing himself into a sitting position from his nest on the futon.

Garrett didn't respond. The details were there somewhere, teasing at the edge of his mind. His eyes darted back and forth as he tried to grasp them, but it was no use. He could only recall the fire – *Jesus, the fire.*

"Must have been some bad dream. You were making all sorts of noises and talking in your sleep." Lenny gave Garrett a questioning look.

"Yeah, I guess so, but I can't remember much of it," he said, still trying to catch his breath. "What did I say?"

"I don't know. I couldn't make anything out, but it sounded like you were talking to someone."

The nightmare left Garrett feeling like there was something he was supposed to know or do. Kind of like the feeling he got when he knew he was forgetting something. The feeling hung with him all the next day, gnawing at the back of his mind like termites through rotting wood.

24

Fourteen Seconds to Adventure

Present day
Oak Island, Nova Scotia

"Bre, come join me, please," she heard through the camper wall. *That's odd,* she thought. *It should be time for his call with Sarah.* She was pretty sure tonight was a call night.

"What's going on, Dad?" she asked as she entered his camper.

"Sarah has big news – I want you to hear this," he said, motioning for her to sit.

"Bre! Hello! How are you?" Sarah asked. "I hope you are keeping your father in line." She laughed.

"Sarah! So good to hear you," Bre said. "I am good and, yes, trying to keep him in line. How is the weather in Mexico?"

"Hot as hell. Okay, you two! Let me get right into it. It has been one hell of a week. First of all, the cave is extraordinary!" Sarah's voice was animated as it burst through the static connection they had learned to ignore during their late-night phone chats.

"But I don't understand – I thought you would still be clearing it?" her father asked, shaking his head. "You mean you found some of it still intact?"

"Oh! Even better than that, Charles! The entire lower structure seems to be completely undisturbed, including the spiral staircase. It was only the upper portion of the cave that was destroyed – everything beyond the lintel was untouched!" she announced, with all the jolliness of a child who had just been told Christmas would come early this year and presents would be doubled.

Her father looked at her, speechless, before finding his voice. "The statue? And the skulls?"

"What about at the top of the stairs? The pottery and the lintel? Did any of it survive the collapse?" Bre asked.

"Slow down, you two," Sarah said with a laugh. "Yes to all your questions, as far as I can tell. Let's start with the archway. When we were finally able to widen the opening, clear the debris, and brace the cave, we discovered the lintel was cracked in half, but we were able to brace it too. The pottery didn't fare so well. All the pieces were damaged and some crushed completely, but one piece was left unharmed – it is beautiful!" she said.

Breanne could practically hear her smiling, even through the satellite phone.

"It was just as you described it. I want to get in there and investigate, but we're being extra cautious after what happened to you two."

"I just can't believe after that collapse the lower chamber is intact. I wasn't expecting that at all," Charles said in disbelief.

"You know, the lower chamber being intact really doesn't surprise me now that I understand what happened to you."

"What do you mean?" her father asked, elation giving way to curiosity.

"Well," she said with a sigh, "the day of the collapse, you were convinced you'd set off some sort of booby trap, but honestly, what you described, with the sinking tile and the click sound, was so unheard of that the more likely scenario, at least from the viewpoint of my team, was that the collapse was a natural occurrence. Further, the majority of my team's opinion was that the sound you heard preceding the collapse had a logical explanation."

Her father furrowed his brow. "So, what did your team think I heard?"

"Maybe the first stone falling as the cavern became unstable, but it doesn't matter, Charles. I believed you – and you were right."

"I was?" he asked in surprise.

"The whole ceiling in the upper chamber was designed to collapse. All those tons of stone were strategically placed on the ceiling of the cave. Then, through mechanical means, the ceiling was designed to fall should the switch be triggered." She paused, waiting for his response.

"That's impossible," he said. "I mean, I expected you to tell me you found something that caused the cave to collapse, but now you're telling me the entire ceiling was false? How in the world could they have possibly lifted the stones into place and held them there?"

Exhaling, Sarah said, "I know, right? It's amazing! I don't have all the answers yet, but we can see that the rocks did not break away from where they fell. Further, there is some kind of mechanism on the upper walls, near what would have been the false ceiling. Whatever you stepped on triggered the retraction of a cog, a sort of lynchpin that was keeping everything in place. Whatever it was, being pulled or broken created the chain reaction of the collapse. Imagine the entire ceiling was one giant Jenga puzzle, and when you stepped on the tile it triggered the pulling of that one single piece that brought the whole thing down."

They could hear Sarah rustling around as though she might be climbing into her cot.

"I can't imagine the difficulty someone went through to create such an elaborate trap," Breanne said.

"You both should have been killed, but lucky for you the creators didn't count on the shortcut out of that tunnel or what time might have done to slow the mechanism. If you had to follow the tunnel the other way, you would have been crushed for sure." She added, in a grave tone, "You were really lucky, guys."

Breanne and her father shared a knowing look.

"Please be careful in there, Sarah," he said. "I could never forgive myself if something happened to you."

"I will, and once I can get a closer look at the giant statue and the skulls, I can give you more information on which of the gods he represents, and hopefully we can figure out who our creators are."

"That sounds great. We look forward to it," he said.

"Charles, why don't you come here and join me? We can explore this together. I don't understand what you could be doing that's more important than this discovery. You should be here with—" She stopped short.

Breanne's eyebrows raised.

"I want to, Sarah... I really do, but you have to continue without me. And I promise, this is almost over, and then I'm on the first flight to you... I mean to the site. I'm on the first flight to the site," he said, slapping a hand to his face.

Breanne giggled. "Sarah, it was great to talk to you, and I can't wait to see you. Hopefully, on my first break from school, I will be able to come to Mexico and see what you guys have uncovered."

"Oh, Bre, I look forward to it!" Sarah said, as the rustle of her blankets filled the phone with static.

"Me too." She smiled.

"Okay, then, until tomorrow? Same time, same place?" he said.

"Same time, same place. Oh, and Charles?"

"Yes?"

"Whatever you guys are up to... please, be careful."

"Of course. Good night, Sarah."

∼

Once again, the Moores rose before the sun and began preparing for the day. However, on this particular morning, Breanne noticed her family seemed to be having as much trouble waking up as she was. They staggered around the camp like zombies, each of them looking just as exhausted as they had the night before. Maybe their sleep had been as restless as hers. Did they have nightmares? Or was their sleep only disturbed by fanciful dreams of treasure, priceless artifacts, and Templar secrets? To ask was to invite questions she had no interest in answering and, thus, she could only wish for such dreams, for to close her eyes was to slip into horror.

Last night she had been plagued yet again by the nightmares, tormented by a phantasmagoria of ash and ruin. What she remembered most was fire, cutting screams, a familiar voice from an old friend she did not know, and the bitter tang of things charred. She twisted her knuckles into her eyes, unsure she had actually slept at all. Something had to give and give soon. She needed off this island, away from this place, before... she didn't know. She just knew they had to get to the end.

Restless sleep or not, the mystery of the altar awaited, and it seemed the only way out was through. Breanne made her father a large mug of coffee to help him lift the fog of sleepiness.

"Thank you, baby girl. I didn't sleep well after our talk with Sarah. Too much excitement for an old man, I guess," he said, pulling a noisy slurp from the mug.

After breakfast, the family geared up and headed over to the pit site. For now, only Paul would be descending into the pit. The rest of the Moores would wait up top along with Jerry, who was now directed to stay on site and report any new developments as they were happening.

From what Breanne understood, Paul would be operating the crane remotely from below, taking position behind the excavated rock pile they had pulled from the tunnel. In theory it should give him a safe place to listen from in case the cable started to destroy the wood tunnel or rip the pulley from the bedrock.

Paul and Charles had done some quick calculations last night and concluded that they would need to pull the stone altar approximately seven feet to ensure they had completely moved it from its current location. However, they also didn't want to pull it across the entire space and end up blocking their entry. Paul was running the crane at a speed of six inches per second, so he should be able to move the stone the required seven feet in approximately fourteen seconds.

It was the moment of truth. With everyone in position, Edward radioed Paul. "All clear for go."

"Copy that," Paul said. "I'm in position behind the rock pile. Here we go." The cable tightened as a loud groan emanated from the tunnel.

Paul's voice crackled through the radio again as he began to count. "One one thousand, two one thousand, three one thousand…"

As the cable retracted, the sound of wood flexing evolved into sounds of splintering and fracturing. At first Breanne thought she was hearing the sound coming through the radio, but then, as the horrible noise got louder, she realized she was hearing it from the pit, a hundred and fifty feet below.

"Six one thousand, seven one thousand, eight one thousand…"

A loud screech resonated sharply above the noise of splintering wood, and for a moment the cable bounced violently, going slightly slack before tightening again. "Shit!" Paul cried, interrupting the count.

"Paul!" Edward called over the radio.

His voice came back. "Twelve one thousand! Thirteen one thousand! Fourteen one thousand!"

The cable stopped and everything fell silent.

Breanne was silent, too, the only sound her pounding heart and rapid breathing. After a moment the radio crackled, causing Breanne to jolt reflexively.

"Hooah!" Paul shouted.

"I take it you're okay down there?" Edward asked.

"Roger that – I'm okay. Let me check the structure. Stand by."

Her father grabbed the radio from Edward. "Do not, I repeat, do not go down in that tunnel until I am with you! We don't know what condition it's in now, or if it's structurally safe. It sounded like the whole damn place was coming apart, even all the way up here."

"Okay, Pops, chill out," Paul said. "We need to let the dust settle anyway. I will unhook the disconnect and attach the basket."

Twenty minutes later, the Moores were gathered in the pit. Paul entered first, followed by his father, then Edward. Despite her clear disagreement, Breanne was forced to wait outside the tunnel until the all clear was given. *This is such bullshit,* she thought. As she watched her family disappear into the floor of the pit, she considered throwing out that making her stay behind was completely sexist, but then decided not to push her luck. After all, she was in the pit and soon enough, once deemed safe, she would be at the altar. She positioned a piece of plywood next to the edge of the pit and sat down with her back leaning against the cool dirt wall. As exhaustion overcame her, she found herself thinking about the crazy nightmare that haunted her sleep last night. As she tried to pull something else from the shadows of her mind, she slipped into unconsciousness.

She woke somewhere else, surrounded by a raging fire – everything around her burned. After a moment, her surroundings came into focus… trees. *I'm in a forest fire?* There was only one direction she could go, but she was unable to see where it led. Now she heard something else, something besides the roar of burning forest. It was screaming. Someone was screaming. No, not someone – people… oh God! People were screaming! Burning! People were burning! She couldn't see them burning – but those guttural screams! *I'm in the nightmare. This is a nightmare and I am here, really here.*

She looked to her left as a crowd of people broke from the forest edge, all of them running, burning, falling, and dying. She pinched the skin on the back of her hand and it hurt. She pinched harder, digging her nail in, and it really hurt. She looked up ahead, in the only direction she could go, and someone came into view. She ran towards the person, but she couldn't close the gap. The silhouette suddenly stopped and turned. He was wearing a white robe with a red cross on the front. She knew then, not who he was, but what he was. He was the Templar Knight from the cavern, but he wasn't a skeleton – he was a man. As he gazed upon her with crystal-blue eyes, his smile was warm behind a thick carpet of grey beard. Then he turned his attention to the flames, and

The Secret Journal

his smile faded to a grave expression. He extended an arm, pointing at the flames.

Breanne tried to speak, but no sound came out. Her world roared as if a tornado was bearing down.

The knight's mouth moved, but his words were drowned beneath death screams and howling flames.

"I can't hear you!" she tried to shout, but the words were snatched from the air as soon as they left her mouth.

The knight pointed. She followed his gaze and could see someone else, but he was just a shadow. She thought he was a boy. Did she know him? She wasn't sure. She turned back to the knight, but now he was far away from her. She turned back to the shadowed boy, but the way she had come was closed off with fire and the shadowed boy was gone. She was trapped! Flames grew, springing up all around her. She felt the heat as the flames lashed out like a venomous snake striking her skin! She watched helplessly as the skin on her right arm and shoulder blistered. She screamed as the greedy flames laughed. *Oh, help – please, Daddy, help!* A deep voice spoke, but all she could hear was pain.

Then suddenly, she awoke.

Gasping, she jolted upright, pulling her shoulders off the wall as she grasped at her arm. Then she heard it – faintly. Someone spoke in her mind… *Or the world will burn!*

"Come on, Bre, let's go. Out here napping like you got all the time in the world to burn," Edward said, his head seeming to float just above the tunnel.

Her heart was pounding as she tried to recall the first part of the whisper in her mind… but it was no use. Her vision cleared, and she could see her brother's head wasn't floating at all, only poking up from the tunnel.

"Bre, it's all clear – let's go!" he repeated, grinning like a fool. "Adventure time!"

Breanne jumped to her feet and quickly realized the arm

that had been burned in her dream had fallen asleep and was now waking up with a pins and needles sensation. *Maybe that's all it was,* she thought. *My arm fell asleep, I had a bad dream, then I heard Edward calling to me in my dream.* That seemed very logical to Breanne, and Breanne liked logic, she trusted logic – as a highly intelligent young woman with a very analytical mind, she *needed* logic.

She grabbed her camera from atop the sawhorse and draped the strap over her head and jerked her helmet on over her braids.

"Bre," Edward said, his hand appearing from below to point a finger. "Why is your hand bleeding?"

She looked at her hand and the trickle of blood running down the back of it. Had she pinched herself for real during the nightmare and somehow not woken up? That was the only thing that made sense. But did it really? Maybe it was all the result of exhaustion? "I think I scraped it climbing into the basket when we came down – it's fine," she lied, wiping the back of her wrist on her pants. She sat down, preparing to enter the hole, and noticed the pins and needles from her other arm were gone. Now her arm felt like it had been really burned. As Breanne descended into the tunnel, she felt keenly aware she was losing her grip on logic. The fabric of reality seemed to be blurring, and for the first time since Mexico she was truly scared.

25

Dagrun

Present day
Petersburg, Illinois

"Lenny, you used that line on Tabitha and she *still* said yes? I'm surprised she didn't slap you in the face," Garrett said, stuffing his backpack into his locker and slamming it shut only to find Jack standing too close.

"So, what did you guys find out about the book?" he barked loudly, seeming not to have a care who heard.

"Jesus, Jack, keep it down. What, do you want the whole world to know?" Garrett said, his voice hushed.

Jack pulled a face. "Shut up and just tell me what you found out."

Obviously, expecting Jack to keep his mouth shut was a big negative. On to plan B, get rid of him. "Not much more really. The darn thing is just so dried out, and we're afraid we'll mess it up. Pete's working on it, though." Garrett feigned unconcern.

"Cut the shit, Garrett. I know you two figured out more

than that – you had plenty of time. Where is that geeky little nutsack anyway?"

"Haven't seen him."

"Well, you can bet your ass he's giving me that book today."

"Whatever, man," Garrett said. "I got to get to class."

Jack moved to stand in between Garrett and his locker. "Yeah, you do that, and let that little punk Pete know I'm looking for my book."

Ignoring Jack, Garrett sighed as he reached around the bully and gave his combo lock a spin.

Jack responded by grabbing Garrett's arm before he could pull it back.

For a split second, Garrett envisioned himself dropping his books, reaching over to Jack's hand, grasping it with his fingers around his thumb, while pressing his own thumb just under Jack's pinky knuckle, then twisting until he heard an audible crunch of bone and cartilage followed by a scream.

"Oh, and Garrett" – Jack placed his nose within an inch of Garrett's face as he gripped his arm – "I am getting real sick of your attitude, man. You walk around here like you're big shit. Well, I think it's about time we put your fake-ass karate bullshit to the test!"

Garrett did not back down, but God he wanted to. He wanted to run away, but he felt like his limbs were frozen with fear, and he wasn't sure he could get them to respond if he tried. And even if he could run, he would be laughed out of school for it. Jack's loud mouth had already drawn a crowd of kids, and Garrett could feel their eyes on him – even worse, he could feel Lenny's. He would never leave Lenny, no matter how scared he was. He would rather take the beating than abandon his friend.

"Yeah, that's right, Garrett. You just stand there and don't say shit," Jack said, as he poked Garrett in the chest. "Don't... say... shit."

Each poke to the chest stung, and still he stood, body locked up, eyes falling to the floor. He wanted to look Jack in the eye, but he didn't. Instead he turned inside to an old memory of his biological father. His sour vodka breath and slow-blinking eyes. He jabbed his finger, too, when Garrett did or didn't do something to his liking.

Lenny stepped forward, placing himself between Garrett and Jack. Garrett pushed the memory along with the rage deep inside, swallowing hard as if physically forcing it down into his stomach. Finally, Garrett spoke, "It's okay, Lenny, I got this."

"Yeah, boy! Know your place," Jack said, glaring at Lenny.

Something inside Garrett snapped. His limbs came loose, momentarily freed from their paralysis. He lunged forward past Lenny, finding a hold on Jack's throat with his right hand.

Lenny struggled to hold Garrett back as the crowd of students began to buzz with the excitement of violence to come.

Fight! Fight! Fight! they chanted.

Garrett's face twitched senselessly as rage boiled up.

Jack's eyes went wild as he slapped Garrett's hand from his throat. "That's it, Garrett! That's what I want to see! Let him go, Lenny. He ain't about shit. Oh, yeah. Oh, hell yeah! I'll be seeing you, Garrett!" Jack pointed. "I'll be seeing you."

Garrett had already known in his heart that Jack was racist. Lenny knew it too. They had talked about it. A black kid and his best friend in an all-white town learn how to read people. Lenny had told Garrett long ago, "I look for the little things, and there are dozens and dozens of tells. For instance, like how they shake your hand. Do they shake it like they really don't want to be touching you? When you enter a room, do they pull their purse close to them, like you might try and steal from them when they're not looking? When you enter a store, do they follow you around like you are going to shoplift?" Lenny dealt with all these issues and much more, on a regular basis.

But with Jack, he didn't need a tell. He'd said it all in four little words – and it was enough to make Garrett see red. *Know your place, boy.*

"Let it go, Garrett," Lenny said. "Not here, man."

Garrett eased back, the red rage fading with Lenny's words, taking with it the momentary bravery.

Lenny was calm, cool, and collected. "I tell you what, Jack. Why don't you poke me in the chest? I'll rip your finger off and shove it up your ass," he said evenly.

Jack glared at Lenny, then back to Garrett. "Tell Pete I want the book," he said, motioning the crowd to get out of his way with a wave of the hand.

The crowd of onlookers started to disperse, but as they melded back into the choked hallway of bodies reluctantly making their way to class like herded cattle to the slaughter-house, Garrett picked up on the looks some of the kids were shooting him. He even caught a few comments from some of the kids as they were absorbed back into the flowing throng.

"Garrett's a punk," one kid said to another.

"I thought that kid is supposed to be a black belt or something," another passerby said.

Then one kid, an older kid Garrett didn't even know, said, "Dude, you just got punked! How you going to let some kid get all up in your face like that?" The kid didn't wait for a response; he just shook his head and disappeared into the army of ants marching towards their classes.

"Goddammit," Lenny said, punching the locker. "I should have let you light him up right then and there!"

"Yeah, and then what, get kicked out of school? My parents would kill me," Garrett said, knowing it was a lame reason. "You saved me from getting expelled, Lenny."

"I don't know, but you're going to have to put him in his place. If you don't, I will. And Pete better stay low. If Jack catches up to him—"

The bell rang.

"Crap, catch you later," Garrett said, before hurrying down the hallway.

Later in the day, a rumor spread through the school like a wildfire on a dry day. Jack had caught up with Pete in the boy's bathroom during lunch hour and worked him over. Garrett didn't share a lunch period with Pete, nor did he have any afternoon classes with him. He didn't know how bad a beating Pete had taken, if Jack had taken the book, or if anyone was in trouble over the fight. Likely he wouldn't find out what happened until he got to the library after work.

Garrett's last period before leaving for work was physical education with Coach Dagrun, who also coached the cross-country team. It was known around school that Coach was a war hero who had received a Silver Star and a Purple Heart, but he never talked about it and no student dared ask him. He was open with his military service and proud to discuss his time in the Marines, but the events of that day were not something he cared to discuss.

However, Pete had uncovered an article about Lieutenant Dagrun and shared it with Garrett and Lenny. Not long after the start of the Iraq War, Dagrun's patrol convoy was struck by an IED, killing the soldiers in the lead vehicle and trapping the rest of the convoy. Dagrun had courageously maneuvered his own vehicle between the enemy and the trapped vehicles. Injured by the firepower focused on him and with his machine gun jammed, Dagrun had stepped fully into the open and finished off what remained of the enemy with his M4 carbine. The only attackers to live that day were the ones who had fled like cowards from their position of cover. Once the attack was over, Lieutenant Dagrun personally rallied his remaining forces, directed the security of the site, and ensured each of his injured men were cared for before he allowed his own wounds to be treated. After the boys read the article, they made a pact to respect Coach's privacy and keep their mouths shut.

If you were to ask Garrett to describe a leader, he would describe Coach Dagrun. There was something about the way his coach carried himself – a commanding confidence that made people want to follow him. His style, on the other hand, took a bit of getting used to, mostly because he still talked like a marine drill sergeant, especially when coaching or when offering wisdom, which turned out to be most of the time. The louder he became, the more the marine came out in his vocabulary. Sometimes, students would have no idea what he was talking about, but usually his unique combination of facial expressions and tone would help them understand what he expected even if they failed to comprehend his marine jargon.

On Garrett's first day on the junior high school cross-country team, Coach had looked at him and said, "*If* you're going to be on this team, you use your *dick skinner* for operating an ink stick, whereas you WILL be required to achieve a minimum of a C to run on my team. Do not use said *dick skinner* for stuffing your crumb catcher with the latest sensation from taco hell or the local choke-and-puke or you WILL find yourself duck-walking to the nearest shitter with a failing grade and a severe case of mud butt. Runners who eat poorly lack focus, get poor grades, crap poorly *and* frequently, and if you crap often, excessive use of moon floss WILL lead to a debilitating case of chap ass. Are we clear?"

The Secret Journal

All Garrett could do was stand there with his mouth hanging open and nod.

Coach Dagrun had looked at Garrett's long hair and muttered something that sounded like "goddamn hippie" before telling the entire team, "Now all you pukes line up for drills – nut to butt!"

Garrett learned quickly to respond, "Yes, sir," and figure out the rest later.

Near the end of phys ed class, the students were in a heated game of dodgeball and Garrett had just taken a hit to the shoulder while trying to spin away from an incoming ball.

"Turek!" Coach Dagrun shouted from across the gym. His brow was creased in angry horizontal lines that made his flattop, cut high and tight, look like it was standing at attention.

"Yeah, sir, Coach," Garrett answered as he sprinted over to him.

"Turek, I've noticed you running all over town, even seen you out running as far as New Salem. You know, cross-country practice doesn't even start until August – how many miles a week are you putting in?"

But before Garrett could answer, Coach turned back to the dodgeball game and began shouting at two boys who had apparently forgone all the rules, deciding instead to just chase each other in circles. "Mills, Watson, knock it off! What kind of goat rope you two trying to pull? How about you stop playing grab-ass and get back to your positions!"

Watson immediately ran back to his position, but Mills hesitated before slowly moving back to his side of the court – much too slowly for the coach's liking. "Dammit, Mills, are you a rock? Stop lollygagging and get your ass back to position most riki-tik!"

Mills froze, looking like a deer in headlights, then

regained his senses and quickly moved back to his side of the court.

"Not sure what's going on in that kid's grape." He shook his head disapprovingly as he turned back to Garrett.

"You're a freshman now, Turek, and with Johnston graduating, this team needs a new captain. I think *you're* that captain," Coach said, pointing decidedly at Garrett.

Had he just been complimented and promoted? Garrett was unsure because all Coach had ever done was yell orders at him. Hesitantly, he nodded. "Gee thanks, Coach, but I am not the fastest on the team. I think there are probably at least three that are—"

"Dammit, shitbrick, I didn't say you are the fastest, did I? I said you are a captain. Captains are leaders, and you're a leader. I need a captain who can rally his men to run drills, run miles, run in the heat, run when no one wants to, *dammit*. I don't need a captain who runs fast because he happens to have a natural gift for running and doesn't have to put in the work." Coach was shouting now, his hand raised in a tight fist. "I need a captain who is *willing* to put in the work, *willing* to lead his team *through* the work. Dammit, Turek, I need a captain who is *willing* to sweat! *Willing* to bleed! *Willing* to puke with his team!"

The sudden shouting caused Garrett to straighten into a civilian's version of attention.

Coach pulled a plastic bottle from the front pocket of his warm-up suit, removed the cap, and spit out a mouth full of brown juice collected from the wad of Copenhagen dip stuffed into the fleshy pocket between his cheek and gum. He eyeballed Garrett. "Well, brick?"

"Yes, sir! Thank you, sir," was all he managed. After all, what else was there to say? That speech was just another example of why Garrett would follow the man into combat if he asked him to.

"Alright, then," Coach said, poking at his tobacco wad with his tongue as he shook Garrett's hand. "Report to my office Wednesday after school, and we will go over the details. Be careful how much running you're putting in. I don't want you burnt-out when season kicks into high gear."

"Wait, um, Coach, I have another obligation on Wednesday. I'm testing for my second-degree black belt," he said, hoping this wouldn't trigger more yelling.

"Second degree, huh? Well, that sounds like a big deal. Maybe I will stop down and see you test," Coach said as the corners of his mouth turned slightly upward.

Garrett was almost sure the facial expression looked like a smile, or at least the makings of one. He couldn't believe his coach was actually offering to come down to the dojo to watch him test. It was just his luck that, of all the tests he had taken, this one happened to be closed.

"Actually, Coach," began Garrett, looking down at the polished wood slats of the basketball court, "this is a closed test, so unfortunately no one can watch this time. First time we've ever had a closed test."

Coach Dagrun met his eyes with a bleak stare as Garrett raised his gaze from the hardwood floor. Any hint of a smile on Coach's face had vanished. "Closed session? When did you find this out?"

"Just last evening. I'm really sorry, Coach. I'd sure love to have you there." Garrett shifted his weight to his other leg.

Coach lowered his voice and glanced over both shoulders. "He told you it was closed… to everyone? It's just you and Brockridge?" Coach asked uneasily.

"Well, no, Lenny too, but he is testing with me so he can be there. You know Mr. B?" Garrett asked in surprise.

Coach steeled his eyes as his lips contracted into a tight line. "Well, it's a small town."

"I guess," Garrett said, continuing to observe his coach look uncomfortable, a completely foreign sight to Garrett.

Leaning forward, Coach spoke quietly, as if he suspected someone might be trying to eavesdrop. "Listen to me, Garrett. When you test, it is imperative you focus with every bit of mental clarity you possess inside that brainpan of yours. Copy?"

Garrett nodded, scrambling to find words in his shock. "Coach, what does that mean? You're not the only person who has told me to focus. What does it mean, Coach?"

Coach looked flustered as he turned away from Garrett, but then glanced back over his shoulder. "You damn well know what focus means, and you'd better do it," he said, jutting a finger towards Garrett's face. Then with sudden speed he spun on his heels to face the class and yelled across the gym, "Rain locker… Now!"

Everyone raced off to the showers. But Garrett hesitated, unable to hear the sounds of squeaking sneakers on wood, dodgeballs bouncing across the floor, or the locker room door as it swung wide. His brain was stuck on a single word… *focus.*

26

Down and Up

Present day
Oak Island, Nova Scotia

Breanne stepped backwards off the slope into the lower chamber. She disconnected the carabiner from her rope and turned to find the altar several feet closer than it had been. She also noticed some chunks of stone, broken boards, and the pulley rigging lying twisted on the ground. "You sure it's safe?"

"It's safe. But we're lucky it didn't pull the whole damn ceiling down," Paul said, picking up a piece of the broken hardware.

Her father paid no attention, his eyes fixed beyond the altar, which was now sitting nearly ten feet closer to the archway than its previous position.

"Do you guys feel that?" Breanne asked, following her father around the stone altar.

"Feel what?" Paul asked.

"I don't know... something," she said uneasily.

"Look – I knew it!" her father said, as he pointed towards

where the altar had been. "There is a void where the stone was!"

They all approached the opening in the floor as if they were stalking prey and wanted to be careful not to spook it.

Her father quickly got down onto all fours to examine the opening, which was a few feet in diameter. "This hole is not natural – it has been excavated with some sort of tool, perhaps a pickaxe."

Breanne knelt down next to him to peer inside. As she prepared to click on her headlamp, she noticed something strange. "Do you see that?"

Her father flipped on his light.

"No wait, shut it off," she said.

He raised his eyebrows curiously, nodded, and flicked off the light.

A soft glow emanated from somewhere below.

Her brothers exchanged a glance.

"How... What in the hell?" her father said.

Suddenly all of the Moores found themselves lying on their bellies.

"This hole would have taken some serious time to excavate. It's several feet deep, but look, it opens up!" Breanne said.

"My God, Pops, there's another chamber below this!" Edward said, hanging his torso partially inside the opening.

"Dammit, Ed, be careful – I don't want you falling in. Can you see a way down or how far down it goes?" Charles asked as he shimmied part of the way into the opening, crowding Edward.

Breanne thought for sure her father's eagerness to see inside was going to result in him falling headfirst into the hole. She quickly dove forward, wrapping her arms around his ankles. "Careful, Dad."

"I got him," Paul said, grabbing ahold of her father's belt.

"Yeah, it looks like it is only about five feet to the water," Edward said.

"Water – that's not good," Paul said.

"Ed, I can't tell if the water is moving, can you? I am wondering if this is an underground river or something," said their father.

"No, I don't think so, but it's glowing."

"The water?" Breanne asked.

"Well, something in the water – algae maybe? Some kind of strange plankton? I mean, I'm not a marine biologist, but something in the water is glowing," Edward said.

"Daddy, get out of there – this isn't right. That shouldn't be possible," Breanne said. Something wasn't adding up. Something was wrong. Couldn't they feel it? Couldn't they feel the energy?

"I can rappel in and see what we have." Edward shimmied backwards, drawing his torso out of the hole.

With Paul straining, Charles also scooched and heaved his own bulky torso out of the opening. Then, rolling onto his side to push himself up, he said, "I don't think blindly rappelling into that water's a good plan, Ed. We don't know what that glow is or whether it's deep or there's an undercurrent."

"Just hook me to the winch and pull me out if I get in trouble," Paul suggested, as if rappelling into glowing underground rivers was as normal as a trip to the market for milk.

"Maybe, but first grab me one of the two-by-fours from the pit – the eight-footers."

Paul nodded, seemingly understanding where his father was going with this, and took off back to the slope, arriving only moments later with board in hand.

As Breanne watched, her father lowered the board down to the opening in the floor as if feeding a giant dipstick into an engine to check the oil. "Now, if this water is more than a few feet deep or so, I am going to lose this board." Suddenly, the board disappeared below the top of the opening. Now lying on his stomach once again, he extended his entire arm into the hole, giving his board an extra few feet of length.

Just then, at full extension, the board struck against something solid beneath the water. Their father pulled the board back up a few inches, then dropped it again, harder this time, *thunk!* He did it three more times, enjoying the sound of renewed hope, *thunk! thunk! thunk!*

"Paul, go back to the pit and bring down the extension ladder and rope – I'm going in!" He took hold of Edward's extended hand and pulled himself to his feet.

"You! Why you?" Breanne asked.

"I will make sure it is safe, explore around a bit, and then – if all is okay – you can all come down," he said decisively.

"But you said yourself we don't know what the glow in the water is. What if—"

"Baby girl, we can *what if* this to death, but the most likely explanation is algae. Now I am going in," he said with finality.

A few minutes later the extension ladder was in the hole. Charles tied the rope around his waist, turned, and started down the rungs.

"Pops, wait." Edward reached behind his back, producing a Sig Sauer handgun. He racked the slide. "Take this," he said, extending the handgun.

Charles frowned. "Ed, why in the world do you think I need that?"

"We don't know what's down there," Edward said flatly.

"Don't be ridiculous. Nothing is down there. We are over two hundred feet below ground," her father said.

"Pops, Ed's right. Listen, there's strange light coming from the water, which probably means some kind of life. If that's the case, what else could be down there?" Paul asked.

"Daddy, you shouldn't go down there. Let Ed or Paul go, if you insist, but you shouldn't go!" Breanne pleaded.

"Listen to me, you three. Something is making the conditions perfect for a type of marine algae to grow, that's all. But if it makes you all feel better, then I'll take the gun." He checked the safety and shoved the gun in his waistband.

She knew there was no changing his mind, knew he was beyond her reach now. His mind was set. He was so goddamned stubborn! But she had to try, she just had to. "I would feel better if you just didn't—"

"Bre, we're too close. We can't stop now. This is what we've been working for, and we're right there – we have to be. Now, I'm going. I will be right back." He smiled assuredly and descended the ladder.

Breanne chewed nervously at her lower lip as, bit by bit, the rope uncoiled like a thread of her reality unraveling, coiled loop by coiled loop.

Minutes went by. How many, she couldn't say. Her eyes were riveted to the chiseled hole with unflinching resolve as she willed her father to reappear. No one spoke until finally Paul shouted down the hole. "Pops! Everything okay?"

"You all have to get down here!" he shouted back.

Breanne felt physically sick and yet relieved he was okay all at the same time. She was uncharacteristically worried – even for her. *Stupid dreams messing with my head,* she thought as she filed in behind her brothers and descended the ladder. Her boots filled with frigid water. She took another step and her knees were submerged, then another, and she was down, soaked in the glowing water all the way to her mid-thighs.

The walls were sheer and bare. There were no stalagmites rising from the water, nor were there stalactites reaching down from the ceiling. There were no columns, no flowstones, no helictites, no soda straws. No cave formations whatsoever, which in itself was odd. They were in a large pool of glowing water. She moved her hand through the water and, as she did, the water glowed even brighter as if energized by an underwater moon. She suspected the beautiful light was some form of bioluminescent algae. The space was smaller than the one above them, maybe only ten feet in height, fifteen feet wide, and forty feet or so long. "I don't understand how they knew this was here," she said.

Edward and Paul began tying a long length of rope around their waists. The rope would tether them all together to ensure no one inadvertently stepped into an unseen void, potentially spelling disaster.

"I think it's becoming obvious," her father said. "Logic be dammed, I can't help but think the people who created this place must have been guided here by God."

Breanne blinked in the soft moonlike light. She had no words to respond with. This was not like her father at all. He was a scientist first and foremost, and he always worked to find the logic.

No one spoke; the only sound was Paul's teeth as they chattered uncontrollably.

They stood still, heads on swivels as their headlamps darted around the room. "So, what now?" Edward asked.

As if in response, the water before them brightened, creating a trail about two feet wide that snaked along, seemingly leading them to the far wall.

"Um, how do you explain that, Pops?" Paul pointed at the soft-blue trail.

Her father pulled off his fedora. "Dear God, this has to be God guiding us." He made the sign of the cross on his chest and waded forward. "See there," he said, pointing. "That shadowed area on the far wall. Quick, let's check it out. I'm afraid we've a real chance of hyperthermia if we stay here

The Secret Journal

long. We're not dressed right for this." His voice was urgent as it reverberated in the eerie chamber.

They fanned out and made their way slowly across the forty-foot span towards the shadow on the far wall, the water becoming nearly waist-deep.

Edward grunted through clenched teeth. "Sorry, boys," he said, glancing towards his testicles as they came into contact with the frigid water.

Paul chuckled. "No shit, my balls just shriveled to the size of two peas."

"Your balls were already the size of peas," Edward said, smiling through a pained grimace.

Breanne shook her head and rolled her eyes as the cold water hit her waist, racking her body with shivers.

When they approached the shadowed wall, they realized the shadow wasn't a shadow at all, but a crevice. "This is the way," her father said, and without hesitation they entered single file, eager to get out of the frigid water.

Breanne's breathing became shallow and rapid as she stepped inside. The crevasse wasn't like Mexico, but it was still dark and narrow, and she didn't like it. She didn't like any of this. They weren't being cautious. They were rushing. *Please… please don't lose it, girl. Dad needs you to keep it together.*

Paul took her hand. "It's okay, Bre. I'm right here. Just take a deep breath."

She pulled in a deep breath, then another. "Thanks, Paul." She gave him a tight smile.

The narrow crevice sloped upward quickly and steeply, allowing them to get out of the water. As Breanne cast her headlamp beam back and forth, she focused on the formation of the crevasse to keep her mind off her fear. It seemed pretty much natural except that the floor had a few places where rough steps had been gouged out, but only in the steepest parts of the slope. Also, tooling marks could be seen on the walls in places where the crevice was perhaps too narrow and needed to be opened up to allow access. Then she noticed something else. Her head began to ache dully.

"Do you feel that?" Paul whispered to his brother from over his shoulder.

"What?"

"I don't know. Bre, remember when you said you felt something earlier?" he asked.

"Yes, I feel it too – stronger now," she said.

"What are you talking about?" their father asked, glancing back over his shoulder.

"Do you feel that, Pops, what Bre was talking about?" Paul asked.

"I only feel that we are very close," Charles said excitedly.

"Hey? Is it getting warmer in here?" Edward asked.

"Maybe it just seems warmer because we are out of that freezing-ass water," Paul replied.

"This is fascinating," her father said. "Do you realize we have climbed higher than the original chamber?"

"What do you think that means, Pops?" Edward asked.

Before his father could answer, the slope leveled off and they stood looking at another rough-cut opening, this one completely closed off by a strange foliage in an interweaving, cross-thatched pattern.

The thick vines had large, leathery, cream-colored leaves unlike any leaf she had ever seen. Even stranger were the multi-colored tubular spirals, several inches long and as big around as a garden hose. She wasn't sure if they were some kind of seedpod or flower bud. The vines covered every inch of the opening.

Her father's brows furrowed as his eyes danced side to side, searching for a logical explanation. He muttered, "Perhaps some seed washed through the tunnel from the swamp… yes, and they ended up here. Some conditions were met and they grew."

"Pops, there are no plants on the island like this. Jesus, I've never seen plants anywhere in the world like this." Paul reached to touch a spiral pod but then stopped, unsure.

"Shit, we are going to have to push past this to enter." Her father reached forward, and his arm sank deep into the foliage. The plant pods began to pulse with colors that radiated down the spirals. He yanked his hand back. "Holy shit!"

Breanne's headache worsened. She swallowed. "Please, Dad, I don't think we should."

"It's okay, Bre." Her father reached for the vines again, but before he could touch them they began to move.

Bre watched in disbelief as the vines slowly untangled themselves until they were draped on either side of the opening, like a curtain drawing back before a play. She tried to logic it out. Perhaps they were having a group hallucination? The headache? Maybe the plants were releasing a chemical causing them to all see the same things?

Her father smiled, made the sign of the cross again, and waved them forward. "Come on!"

One by one, they passed cautiously through the opening.

Once inside she could see this chamber was even smaller than the last, roughly eight feet by eight feet, with scarcely room to stand upright. The strange foliage covered the walls and the ceiling. Something in the center of the room glinted, catching her eye.

Breanne gasped.

In that moment, she forgot the glowing water, the strange vines, and even her headache.

In the center of the room she beheld a small chest. This chest did not sit on an altar and was not protected by a Templar Knight. This chest just sat, unceremoniously canted to one side, on the dirt floor of the small chamber. As the light from their headlamps struck the chest, it mirrored brightly, casting golden rods of light all around the small chamber like the sun's reflection shimmering off still water on a bright day. Magnificent golden molding adorned the edges of the chest, and two cherubs sat atop the lid, facing each other with wings extended in front of them. Long gold rods fit through golden rings, securing the lid, and extended beyond the chest to double as handles. The strange foliage was wrapped around one end of a rod and stretched tight, as if trying to pull the rod loose.

For a long moment they didn't speak.

Finally her father whispered, tears filling his eyes, "We have found the Ark of the Covenant!" He staggered forward, then dropped to his knees in front of the chest. "I never believed it was real," he said in a choked voice.

She and her brothers exchanged looks of wonder.

"You did it, Pops! You found it!"

"No, son... we found it."

Let's open it up!" Paul said.

Breanne forced her eyes to break free of the Ark's spell. She spun in a slow circle and considered the location and design of the place the Templars had chosen for the Ark. They had taken something so incredibly important to the world and placed it here, like this, obviously never meant to be recovered. If the swamp had not been drained, the other two chambers would have been full of water, and dive equipment would not have even existed back then. She couldn't imagine getting to this place if the first two chambers were underwater. This Ark was never meant to be recovered – ever. But why?

"This is genius – they placed the Ark up here where it would remain dry, sealed, and preserved for all time," her father whispered.

In the dimness of the headlamp-lit chamber, Breanne

lifted the dangling camera looped around her neck like an oversized necklace and clicked the shutter-release button. The camera flashed and the vines pulled tight to the wall and shuddered violently. For a long second after, the spirals glowed with a faint light that slowly faded.

"What was that?" she said. She raised the camera again and snapped another photo of the Ark, and again the foliage shook and the spirals glowed briefly.

"Did you see that?" Edward asked.

"Yeah, sis, let's not take any more photos," Paul said nervously. "These plants are somehow reacting to the light, and I can't tell if that's good or bad."

"Wild, and creepy as hell," Edward said.

Breanne nodded uneasily and lowered her camera, returning her focus to the Ark. Suspicion tugged at her mind. She wanted to push it away, but it held on, nagging her. She wanted to ignore it because more than anything she wanted this moment to be true. It wasn't true. She knew it now. Logic intruded, and the pure adrenaline clouding her mind cleared like smoke on a windy day.

She looked at her father and she waited. After a moment, she watched logic slap him unapologetically in the face. He met her gaze as deep furrows fractured like fault lines across his forehead.

Slowly he began to speak. "According to the Book of Exodus, which gives a detailed description of the Ark, including measurements, I'm afraid something is amiss here."

"What? What do you mean?" Paul asked.

"First of all," he continued, "it's only about *half* the size it should be. Exodus calls for the Ark to be approximately two and a half cubits in length, one and a half in breadth, and one and a half in height, which translates to fifty-two by thirty-one by thirty-one inches. This is definitely much smaller. Second of all, look at the engravings etched into the center of the lid and all around the box. They appear Egyptian in style, but I don't recognize them. Okay, third, and most strange, the two golden cherubs on the lid – well, those aren't cherubs at all. They're dragons."

Thank God, Breanne thought. He was finally seeing logic and questioning—

"But history seldom gets these sorts of things right."

He's not seeing it. "Dad?" she urged. "Can we get out of here? My head is really starting to hurt. Something is wrong – very wrong."

"I'm not feeling so good either," Edward said.

"My head is aching too," Paul said. "Let's open this thing, see what's inside, and get the hell out of here."

27

The Culvert

Present day
Petersburg, Illinois

Since Lenny and Pete had no plans to meet after school, Garrett couldn't find either boy before leaving for work. Reluctantly, Garrett climbed onto his bike and started to pedal hard for New Salem. Then, when he got to Sixth Street he turned left when he should have turned right. He didn't know when he made the decision exactly – perhaps when he couldn't find his friends, or perhaps when he pulled on the handlebars. It didn't really matter when; the decision was made. He wasn't going to work – something he'd never in a million years thought he'd ever do. He was going to find Lenny and check on Pete. He didn't know what kind of trouble he would get from Phillip, and he just plain didn't care. He would deal with the razor strap later, but right now he knew where he needed to be.

A few short minutes later, he squeezed the brake handle and locked up his wheel, sliding the bike sideways in the gravel before slapping one foot to the pavement. "'Sup, fellas!" he shouted towards Lenny and David.

"Awesome! I thought you had to work?" Lenny asked, hands pointing up.

"Yeah, well, whatever. I didn't want to miss this. Besides, I wanted to check on Pete. Did you hear what happened?

"Really, whatever? You're skipping work? Are you sick or something? I have never seen you miss work. Your stepdad's going to kill you, bro!" Lenny said, shocked.

"I'll deal with it." Garrett said.

"'Sup, Garrett," David said. "I saw Pete last period. He is fucked up, bro – got a black eye and shit."

"David! Language," Lenny said in a mock scold. "You kiss your momma with that mouth?"

"No, but I kiss your mom with this mouth," David said with a snort.

Garrett lifted his bike over the tracks and stashed it in the woods. "Let's do this – I want to get to the library and check on Pete. The tunnel should be right here." He pointed over the side of the ravine.

Lenny leaned out over the side. "I see it," he said as he started backing away from the edge.

Garrett nodded. "It's really steep. Our best bet is to ease down—"

"I'll go first!" Lenny ran past the two boys and leapt over the side.

"Holy shit!" David shouted.

Both Garrett and David ran forward to watch Lenny as he slid recklessly down the steep embankment towards the large concrete culvert protruding a dozen feet above the silty water of the Sangamon River. When Lenny reached the smooth concrete of the culvert, he spun around so he was facing back towards Garrett and David. He shot them a wry smile just as gravity yanked him off the edge of the culvert and downward towards the river. But as he dropped, he grabbed the edge of the culvert and swung his body inward, allowing his momentum to carry him effortlessly into the mouth of the tunnel. He landed softly, as if he had performed the stunt hundreds of times before.

"Dude! You're crazier than a shithouse rat!" David said.

Garrett jumped over next. The bank was so steep he was able to slide while staying up on both feet, as if riding a surfboard. Just before he got to the top of the culvert, he sat down and rolled to his stomach as he slid. Going over the culvert's edge, he caught the lip with his hands and swung inside.

"Crazy sons a' bitches!" David shouted, choosing a far more conservative approach to the culvert. One that required sliding from sapling to sapling on his bottom. "You guys know that's probably the worst part of the Sangamon, right? If you had lost your footing or tripped, you'd be floating down river." He scrambled for a handhold on a thick vine. "You'd be fighting like hell to get out before going over the old busted dam or getting stuck under a brush pile."

"Get in here, man," Lenny said, laughing.

Still sitting on his bottom, David carefully slid out to the edge of the culvert, allowing his legs to dangle over the side before turning over onto his stomach and chest. Finally, he gently slid his torso over the concrete edge, and for a moment that lasted far too long, he just hung there, unable to go back up, but not able to drop into the opening for fear of falling.

"You're like a foot from the bottom, man – just drop," Lenny said.

"Lenny, man, I'm way shorter than you. Are you sure it's only a foot? You better not let me fall in!" he said.

Garrett laughed. "We got you – just drop."

David dropped to his feet, landing on the edge of the

culvert opening. His heels hung over the culvert's edge, forcing him to balance on the balls of his feet. He teetered there on the brink for a frightful second, wide-eyed, his oddly thick adolescent mustache twitching and arms flailing, before finally losing his balance completely and tipping backwards towards the river.

Garrett quickly lunged forward and snatched David by the collar of his shirt, pulling him forward into the tunnel. "Gotcha," he said, smiling.

David steadied himself, placing his hands on his knees as he puffed out a relieved breath. "Whew! Dude... my asshole puckered! I thought I was going over for sure," he said, peering uneasily over the edge.

"Nah, bro, I wasn't going to let you fall," Garrett said easily.

Lenny smirked at his friend. "I got a question. Why you think God let a chickenshit kid like you grow facial hair this early in life? You should probably go ahead and shave that off till you grow some balls to go along with it. I mean talk about putting the cart befo—"

"Piss off, Lenny! Sorry I don't want to end up in the drink, but you ain't got to hate on my 'stache just because you can't grow one."

"That's what I like about you, man – you give it just as good as you take it."

Clicking on his flashlight, David began to peer down the tunnel. "So, Garrett, during lunch, Lenny brought me up to speed on all this crazy shit you guys got yourself into. What are we looking for exactly?"

"First, we need to find this archway made of old bricks," Lenny said.

"Come on, it's right back here." Garrett moved quickly down the large pipe.

"Man, I'd love to get my skateboard in here! I forgot how huge this culvert is," David said.

"Well, here we are, check it out," Garrett said as they reached the end of the pipe. The walls on both sides were not round like the culvert but perfectly vertical until near the top, where they began to make their slow arch. In the newer concrete culvert, they could stretch up and touch the top of the pipe, but at the transition to the archway it extended upward a good three feet further. The culvert they stood in now was like a round peg mating into a much larger square hole. The difference in the two sizes had been made up for by adding modern bricks to fill the gap between the two sections.

"Wow, it's so much bigger than I thought it would be," Lenny said.

"Yeah, it's big alright, but watch for bats… and rats," David said uneasily as they began moving further into the tunnel. "Remember when Jack whacked that bat back here, Garrett?"

Garrett frowned absently. "Yeah, I remember." He was focused on the ceiling and wondering how he would be able to inspect the upper portion of the arch without a ladder.

"Rats?" Lenny said, looking down the archway tunnel.

The culvert dropped a couple feet into a pool of stagnant water. The distance across seemed to be maybe twenty feet before it stepped back up into a smaller tunnel.

"Sometimes, and those suckers can swim too," Garrett said.

"They don't call them river rats for nothing," David said.

"Well, this is going to suck," Garrett said, as he took his first tentative step. The water was colder, fouler, and deeper than he had hoped, reaching mid-shin. This meant he could not see the bottom; hell, he couldn't even see his feet.

Lenny stepped into the water behind him. "Bro... Nasty."

"Garrett, man, if I get in that water with these shoes my dad will kill me. If I had known yesterday, I could have brought my crap ones, but these are my good shoes," David said apologetically.

"Look, David, it's cool," Garrett said. "I'm wearing my junker work shoes. Just keep an eye out for rats."

"I freaking hate rats," Lenny said, taking another cautious step.

David nodded, sweeping his flashlight back and forth across the top of the water. "Yeah, no doubt."

Moving quickly, Garrett walked to the opposite end of the tunnel. "Lenny, start down there and I will work my way towards you. We can meet in the middle."

"Cool."

Garrett inspected all the bricks from the water to as far above his head as he could reach. Even though he couldn't see the bricks above with much detail, he cast his light up the arch of each staggered row anyway, just in case there was something obvious.

Lenny worked from the opposite end back towards Garrett.

All the bricks looked pretty much the same with only slight variations. Some were different in color, some had chips missing out of them, but as far as shape, size, and texture they were pretty much the same. Garrett didn't even know what he was looking for other than finding a brick that somehow was not like the others, and this made him feel like he was hunting for a needle in a haystack.

Then he found it... a brick that didn't look like the others.

Instantly his adrenaline surged, giving him renewed focus. "We got something, guys!" he said excitedly.

The Secret Journal

"What is it? What have you got?" David asked, leaning out over the water, one arm on the wall and the other extended outward with the flashlight beam pointing.

Lenny waded over.

Garrett had been three-quarters of the way down the south wall and about two bricks above the water line when he had noticed something carved into the brick. "Initials! We have initials here," he said in amazement.

"Abraham Lincoln's initials?" Lenny asked.

The initials were carved carefully into the upper right-hand corner of the brick. They were small and could have easily been overlooked. At first Garrett thought he had indeed found Lincoln's initials but quickly realized he was looking at A.R., not A.L.

"Well, no… but this has to mean something," he said, feeling less sure of his find.

"Hold on a second," Lenny said, pulling a folded notebook from his pants pocket.

"What's that for?"

"So we can find these again." Lenny said as he started counting the number of bricks from the arch down towards the water. He tallied a total of thirteen rows to reach the initialed brick. Next, he determined the left-to-right location on the wall by counting the number of bricks from the closer side, which happened to be the far side from the entrance, back to the initialed brick. However, as he was counting across, he found another brick with initials. "Check it out, Garrett. This brick has the letters B.G. carved into the upper right-hand corner, and in the exact size and style of the A.R. brick."

"What do you think means?" Garrett asked.

They continued to search in the general area, and Garrett found a third brick. "Got another! This one is marked J.C. in the same size, style, and position as the other two."

Lenny noted the location.

They searched for a while longer and, just when he was ready to call it quits, Lenny found one more brick with two small initials in the upper right-hand corner just like the previous three.

"We got it – we freaking got it! A.L., baby!"

Garrett splashed over. "Hell, yeah!"

"You shitting me?" David asked excitedly.

"Nope! Check it out, Garrett!" Lenny laughed, marking the location in his notepad.

"That's A.L. alright. Okay, let's get out of here and show the gang what we've found."

"Agreed, this place smells like shit," David said. Just as the words left his mouth, they heard a noise from the entry of the tunnel.

"Did you hear that?" Lenny asked in a whisper.

"Yeah," David whispered back.

Garrett nodded silently.

They were only about twenty yards from the entrance and they could clearly see no one was in the tunnel, yet they all had heard it. They slowly began making their way towards the tunnel entrance when dirt and rock spilled over from above the culvert, as if someone was hurrying away from the entrance and scrambling to get up the embankment outside. Or worse, about to come over the side and enter the tunnel.

Had Jack followed them? They froze, unsure what to do. *The last thing we need is Jack finding out our best clue – if that happened there'd be no keeping this from him,* Garrett thought, giving the other boys a look of warning as he held a finger to his lips.

The boys waited apprehensively for feet to appear over the side of the culvert, but after a long moment, when no feet came into view, David whispered, "I think whoever was there is gone."

The Secret Journal

"I don't know, but there's only one way to be sure," Garrett said, stepping to the mouth of the tunnel. He turned and faced them, then jumped up, grabbed the top of the tunnel, and pulled his head above the upper edge, hoping he didn't get a mouth full of shoe for his curiosity. "Nothing," he grunted, dropping back down into the tunnel. "But if someone was up there, they might have overheard everything."

"I'm freaking out." David shook his head. "That's the second time in the last hour my asshole puckered. Can we please get out of here before there's a third?"

"Yeah, I agree. Let's get to the library, but do me a favor," Lenny said.

"What's that?"

"When you get home tonight, please shave that 'stache, pussy."

"Whatever, Lenny. I would but I would hate to disappoint your mom!" David grinned, somehow making the 'stache waggle like a caterpillar on the move.

Garrett laughed.

"Eww, no. Don't ever do that! Never! Ever! What are you, a seventies porn star?" Lenny shook out his shoulders in disgust. "Creepy bastard. You look like someone parents should keep their kids away from."

28

Tentacles

Present day
Oak Island, Nova Scotia

"Pops... can we please open it now, see what's inside, and get out of here?" Paul asked.

Bre drew in a breath as she rubbed her temples, trying to loosen the grip of her headache.

"No, not here, let's get it topside where we can all see it. I want Jerry to be there too." Charles looked around at the plants. "Plus, I don't think we should open it in this place," he said nervously.

"Right," Edward said. "But it looks really heavy – hopefully Paul and I can carry it."

Paul sighed, clearly disappointed. "Well, let's go then. My head is hurting worse, and I'm starting to sweat in here."

With all the excitement upon entering the room, no one had noticed how warm it was, but now all of them took notice. They noticed something else, too – their clothes were no longer wet from the trek through the icy water; they were completely dry.

The Secret Journal

"Let's go," Edward said, reaching for the Ark.

"Wait! Do not touch it! I will touch it first," Charles said, waving the brothers off as if it were suddenly about to burst into flames.

"What the hell?" Edward said, startled at his father's sudden outburst.

"I'm sorry, Ed. Just let me be the first to touch it, okay?"

Edward shrugged.

"Daddy, no. Don't touch it!" Breanne shouted. She reached out to intercept his arm, but she was too late.

Her father clenched his teeth and pressed his eyes closed tight as he slapped a hand on top of the lid, only to quickly snatch it away again. Nothing happened. He sighed, relief plain on his face.

"Dammit, Dad!" Breanne scolded.

"Bre, what's the big deal?" Paul asked.

"Don't you remember what Dad said about the Ark? In the biblical accounts, only the high priest was allowed to touch the Ark. In one account a man was even killed when he reached out to steady the tipping Ark as it was being transported."

"Look, I never put much faith in any of the Old Testament stuff, but I had to be sure before I let you guys touch it, that's all. Now come here, all of you. Lay your hands on it and feel this!"

Each placed a hand atop the lid between the golden dragons.

"It... it feels so otherworldly," Edward said. "Like an energy or power. A warmth – no, something more... something moving, no, pulsing through the lid, through me!"

"I feel it tingling all the way down into my toes," Paul said.

Her father looked at them as though he were about to cry. "This must be of God!"

Breanne pulled her hand away, unsure of what she felt.

"Okay, let's go," her father said, standing and dusting himself off. He grabbed hold of the vines and pulled them loose, clearing them away from the Ark. They radiated light at his touch but they yielded, offering no resistance.

"This is even creepier than the altar," Paul said. "This whole pace is full of this electric... I don't know... energy, and it's all coming from this thing!"

"It's the Ark, my boy, and it's wonderful, absolutely wonderful," her father said.

"Let's just get it topside. On the count of three, lift," Edward said. "One, two, three, lift!"

Her brothers lifted with an abrupt jerk, expecting it to take a colossal effort to raise the Ark, but in fact it did not. The men stumbled, nearly falling, as the Ark came up off the floor, stopping just short of slamming into the ceiling of the low chamber. It was as if they had placed all their strength into lifting a pillow.

"What the hell?" Paul said, his eyes widened in wonder.

"How can it be this light, Pops? It feels like it is made of Styrofoam!" Edward said.

"I don't know, Ed. This thing is supposed to contain a pot of manna, Aaron's rod, and two stone tablets – the Ten Commandments. And there is all the gold in the trim and in the dragons on the lid. Seems as though it should be heavy, but who knows what power any one of the items inside could hold?"

They turned to the doorway. The vines once again covered every inch, twisted like intricate braids made of foliage. Her father stepped forward and pushed against the living wall. The vines danced with illumination from his touch, but they did not move.

"Why aren't they moving?" Edward asked.

"I don't know." Her father gripped the thick vines in each

hand and tried to pull them apart, but they held fast. "Open, damn you!" he shouted, his pull becoming a desperate yank.

Her brothers gingerly placed the Ark on the ground and stood on each side of the door, gripping fistfuls of the thick vines. They gave each other a silent nod and began straining against the vines, but the vines didn't move.

"What in God's name is this? Do you have knives?" Charles asked.

Paul knelt and pulled a boot knife as Edward unsheathed a scuba knife from his hip.

"Wait, Daddy, I don't think this is a good idea."

But her brothers didn't wait – they started hacking at the vines. For every vine they managed to cut through, another grew in its place. The foliage on the walls of the room began to shake violently. "Stop. You're pissing it off!" Breanne screamed.

Her brothers stopped, seeing little good anyway. "We'll never cut through this, Pops!" Edward said. "It's no use."

"Why in the hell won't it let us out?" her father demanded.

"Can't you feel the hate? It hates us," Breanne said.

"What do you mean it hates us? It practically welcomed us in, dammit!" Her father grabbed the vines and pulled again.

She wiped the sweat from her face. "I think I know what it wants. It wants us to open it." She gestured at the gleaming chest. "That's it, it won't let us leave until we open it."

In the back of the room, three spirals dropped from the vines to the ground. They began to spin into the earth like a corkscrew into a cork. When only the very tip remained above ground, the spirals fractured with a loud crack.

Breanne began to breathe too hard, too fast. They were shut in, and this damn plant wasn't going to let them go. Somewhere from deep in her damaged memories, a song played. A song she hated with all her heart. A Christmas song.

Dark green-black tentacles burst from the fractured spirals. Up into the air, they stretched one foot, then two feet. Deep-blue thorns grew from the strange appendages. Three feet, then four feet, up and up they squirmed. The thorns stretched long, thick, and deadly sharp.

Paul grabbed her hard by the shoulders. "Breathe, Bre. Don't you go away! Don't you leave!"

She felt herself shake hard as her brother's thumbs pressed deep into her shoulders. "Stay with us, sis." Her eyes rolled back into her head. "No! Look here. Look at me! We need you, Bre! We need you to figure this out!"

A violent explosion of sound. Gunshots! *Crack!... Crack... crack, crack!*

29

Abraham's Secret

Present day
Petersburg, Illinois

Bursting into the library elicited a frown from the librarian. The boys slowed to a walk as they skirted the front desk and quickly descended the stairs into the basement. There they found Pete and Janis huddled closely together, poring over one of many books they had stacked on the big round table.

"Pete! You live!" Lenny shouted way too loudly from across the room.

"Shh! Easy, man!" Pete said, ducking down like Lenny had thrown something at him.

Lenny looked around and shrugged. Besides Pete and Janis, no one else was even in the lower level of the library, so he didn't see what the big deal was.

"It's all over school that Jack caught up to you at lunch," Lenny said before turning to Janis. "Hey, Janis."

"Hey, fellas," she said.

"Pete, man, I heard about the fight, are you okay?"

Garrett asked, looking Pete up and down as if expecting to see he was missing a limb or at least had one in a cast.

"I'm okay... my ribs hurt and I got a black eye, but I'll live." Pete removed his glasses and pointed at his eye. "Jerkwad almost broke my glasses too. I wouldn't call it a fight, though – it was more Jack throwing punches and me getting hit by them," he said sourly.

Lenny flipped a chair around backwards and flopped down facing Pete. "Dang, bro! How many hits did you take? What are you going to tell your mom? How will that go over with Jack's dad dating your mom? Did you turn him in to a teacher? Crap, did he get the book?"

Pete waved off the questions, unconcerned. "I'll just tell her I took an elbow in PE class playing dodgeball."

"Ugh, I hate that guy – he is such a loser!" Janis said, balling her fist. "Someone needs to teach that jerk a lesson."

Everyone looked at Garrett.

Garrett looked at the floor. "I'm really sorry, Pete, I feel horrible. I never should've let you hold that book – I should have taken it with me." Then he raised his head and locked eyes with Pete. "At least then it would have been me he was after and not you."

"It's not your fault, Garrett," Pete said.

But Garrett knew in his heart it was his fault. "I assume he took the book then. Did you at least get it all transferred?"

"It's not that easy – the book's in bad shape, and unless I disassemble it at the binding, my only option is to rely on my humidity chamber to moisten it. It is like starting over every time I turn a page. There was no way to give it the time needed in one evening."

"So we're screwed," Garrett said, pacing to and fro in front of the table.

Pete sat back, crossed his arms, and smirked.

"What are you smiling about? It's only a matter of time

The Secret Journal

before Jack either figures out where the tunnel is or sells the book to someone who will."

Pete continued to smirk.

"Pete! What's with the shit-eating grin? You fart or something?" Garrett asked.

Pete's grin twisted to a frown and his cheeks flushed cherry red as he glanced towards Janis. "No, I didn't fart or something! Look, I never said Jack took the book."

"What?"

"I'll tell you, but sit down, man. You're doing that thing where you pace, and you're making me nervous," Pete said, smiling wide.

"Alright, alright, but get on with it already," Garrett said anxiously. He could tell Pete was thoroughly enjoying the suspense.

"Last night after you guys went to class, Janis and I searched and couldn't find a single thing on the Keepers of the Light, so we decided to research something else." Pete shot Janis a knowing look that elicited a giggle.

Garrett sighed.

"Alright, alright. Anyway, we researched how to age paper, then when I got home, I made a replica of the book. I copied some random text onto some blank paper that I cut down to the correct size. I burned the edges, then I rubbed off the burns to make the paper look chewed or rotted. Then I brewed some of my mom's tea and soaked the paper in it. I already had an old book with a similar cover, so I just took the old book apart and inserted the fake pages using glue, matching it as closely as I could. It wasn't easy, but using our space heater I was able dry the paper and leather out. I almost caught the whole thing on fire with that space heater. Anyway, by the time I finished, I'd created a decent enough fake to fool that idiot Jack."

The prideful smile on Pete's face and the way he placed

both hands behind his head, interlocking his fingers as he leaned back, said it all, but Lenny went ahead and confirmed it for everyone anyway. "Dude's a freaking genius!"

"Okay, Pete, well done, but what happens when he opens it and tries to read it? Or when he takes it to one of the antique stores? He's going to figure it out pretty quick, right?" Garrett asked.

"Well, sure. Listen, I didn't say how long it would fool the idiot. If he even tries to open it, it *will* fall apart. The purpose of the fake was to get me out of the situation I knew I would be in when Jack caught up to me. The fake already did what I hoped it would do… save my ass and buy us another day."

"Screw Jack! I would love to be there when he tries to sell it to an antique store and they laugh in his face," Janis said.

Pete shrugged. "Well, if he's smart enough to at least open it he may already know it's a fake." Pete looked at Janis and gave her an ornery smile. "Plus, I left some surprises inside the book for him."

"What surprises?" Janis asked, wide-eyed.

"Just a few choice words for Jack," Pete said, raising his eyebrows up and down deviously.

"Oh no, Pete! What did you do?" Garrett said.

Lenny laughed.

"This isn't funny, Lenny – he's going to get himself beat to a pulp!" Garrett said.

"Well, whatever you do, don't let him kick you, man – he kicks like a mule," David said. "I should know. I'm the only one out of us who's fought him."

"Yeah, David, and when we were yelling, 'Kick him back, David. Kick him back!' you should have listened," Lenny said.

"I had hiking boots on. I wasn't going to cheat and kick him with my boots on."

The Secret Journal

"He was kicking the shit out of you, bro. There is no 'fair' in that situation, there is only survival," Lenny said.

"Maybe, but I have my morals."

"No, what you had was three broken ribs and a busted lip," Lenny said.

Garrett started in again. "I don't know what you were thinking, Pete! This is cra—"

"I don't care, Garrett! I'm sick of the way he treats people, I'm sick of watching him bully people, I'm sick of the way he makes fun of... my speech." His eyes started to glisten with moisture. "I'm sick of... sick of him! I don't *care* what he does, I'm not scared of him." He slammed his hand palm down on the table with the loud *whack!* of flesh slapping wood. "I'm not taking his shit anymore! I'm just not."

The room fell uncomfortably silent.

Garrett had never felt so ashamed of himself. He swallowed hard, pulling his eyes from the floor until he found Pete's, then he found his voice – but it was a new voice, quiet and determined. "Listen to me, Pete. If he opens or tries to sell that book today, he is going to find you tomorrow, and when he does, you need to tell him the whole fake was my idea."

Everyone at the table stared, wordless.

"Whatever messages you left for him in that book, you tell him I made you write them. You tell him I have the book. You tell him if he wants it to come and get it. You send him to me, Pete. You send him to me, and tell him... I'll be waiting."

"Hell, yeah! That's what I'm talking about!" Lenny said, jumping up from the table.

Pete held Garrett's gaze, unable to say anything. The silence stretched out, pregnant with emotions that needed no words. More than simple acknowledgement, Pete's eyes were grateful.

"Alright!" Lenny said, breaking the stillness. "Now that we have that out of the way, let me tell you guys what we found in the tunnel." He drew in a deep breath. "Okay, here goes. We found a total of four bricks on the south wall of the arch, with each brick containing a different set of initials, and best of all... the last brick had the initials A.L. on it!" He slapped the table, beaming with pride.

"Perfect!" Pete said, shifting in his chair.

"Perfect what?" Garrett asked.

Pete pursed his lips in thought. "This is a major find, and further, I think I have already figured out who most of those initials belong to."

"What? When?" Lenny asked in surprise.

"I just figured it out as we were sitting here," Pete said.

"Of course you did," Janis said, smiling.

Garrett shook his head, unsurprised.

"Come on, Lenny. It's fairly obvious. We have the initials A.R., B.G., J.C., and A.L. Anyone want to take a stab at who these guys are?" Pete looked around the table.

They all looked at one another.

"No. Just tell us!" Lenny said, giving Pete's chair a kick.

"Very well. A.L. is Abraham Lincoln, of course. J.C. is John Calhoun, a close friend of Lincoln's from his days in New Salem, and last but not least, B.G. Last chance... anyone? Bueller? Bueller? Bueller?" asked Pete.

"Biscuits and Gravy," David said, laughing.

"Bubble Guts," Lenny said, glancing over to David. "That's what happens every time I eat biscuits and gravy."

"Nice, Lenny," Janis said, pulling a face.

"You guys disappoint me," Pete said, shaking his head disapprovingly. "B.G. is Bowling Green, Lincoln's friend, also mentioned in the *journal*. Come on, guys." He threw his hands up in the air. "As for A.R., I'm still working on that one."

The Secret Journal

Lenny cocked an eyebrow at Pete. "I am convinced someone dropped you on your head as a child but instead of it damaging your brain like it did for poor David here" – he shook his head sadly at David – "it somehow made you into a freak genius."

David threw up his middle finger.

"Okay, so what's our next move?" Garrett asked.

Pete opened his notebook containing his transcriptions from the journal. "Well, the journal says, *Once inside, look for the archway, which holds a **xxx xxx xxx**. When you find **xxx xxx** remove **xxx** beloved **xxx** and, once removed, reach inside and pull the lever. This will allow the way to open, showing you the path.*"

Janis reached over and pulled Pete's notebook close, studying the entry. "So now we can assume the part that says 'when you find xxx xxx' means when you find the 'initialed bricks' or 'the initials,' but what does 'xxx beloved xxx' mean? Remove beloved brick?"

Pete shook his head. "No, that can't be right."

"Pete, are you sure you transferred this correctly?" she asked.

"Yeah, I'm sure, but we're obviously missing something. The names I have given you guys were all people Lincoln would have cared about."

Lenny rapped his fingers on the table in thought, then stopped abruptly. "I think we just need to go back in and start pulling bricks one by one, starting with the one that's initialed A.L. As long as we have a hammer and screwdriver, it won't take long to chip the mortar out and pull the bricks. If there is a lever behind one, we will find it easy enough."

"Right, and by then we can just try and figure out the next step of the journal," Janis said.

Garrett nodded, addressing the group. "Okay, well, I'm working for Eugene tomorrow to try and get the first half of the book. Pete, you're supposed to go with me, Lenny is teaching class, and that leaves David and Janis to pull bricks in the tunnel."

"Wait, there is something else," Lenny said uneasily. "We weren't alone at the tunnel today."

"What do you mean?" Pete asked.

"Someone was outside while we were inside," Garrett said uneasily. "They came all the way down the embankment and were right outside the tunnel. I think they were listening to us. We did get pretty loud when we found the bricks."

"Are you sure?" Pete asked.

"He's sure alright. We were whooping and hollering plenty loud," David said.

"No, I mean that someone was there, dumbass," Pete said.

"Oh. In that case, piss off, Pete," David said. "And yes, to answer your questions, he's sure. I heard it, too, and it was definitely a person. When they heard us talking about leaving, they scrambled back up the bank, knocking down dirt and rocks, obviously in a hurry not to let us see them," David said.

"Who could that be... Jack?" Janis said.

"I don't think he would have been secretive if he knew we were there. He would have just come in," Lenny said.

"Yeah, I agree. It had to be someone else," Pete said.

"So, yeah, no offense, guys, but I'm not going back in the tunnel unless we all go. Besides, we should all be there when we find the lever thingy," David said.

"I agree," Garrett said, nodding. "Alright, well, we all have a pretty busy week. Let's just plan on Saturday morning, and by then we'll hopefully have the second half of the book and understand what we're dealing with." Turning to Pete, Garrett asked, "Do you think you can decipher the rest of the journal over the next couple days?"

The Secret Journal

Pete pulled at his lower lip in consideration, then nodded slowly. "Maybe. I'll sure try."

"Alright, then, it's Eugene's for Pete and me tomorrow, then Lenny and I test on Wednesday, so let's regroup back here on Thursday to review what we have," Garrett said.

Everyone agreed.

"Janis, I'll walk you home," Pete said, picking up her backpack.

"Thanks, Pete."

The sun sank low behind the old slate roofs of the Victorians dotting the hillsides of Petersburg as the teens made their way out of the library. Soon the streetlights would be on. They paused briefly in front of the library and said their goodbyes. Garrett could feel his friends' excitement for the possibilities held by the secret they shared, and he felt it too. They were part of something important, some historic mystery – Lincoln's secret.

To Garrett's surprise, Phillip had informed Lenny's parents he would be spending the night for a second school night in a row. For Phillip's next mind-blowing feat, he told them there was no need to train or to do chores. Instead, his father recommended he and Lenny practice for their test, then hit the sack. Garrett asked no questions. He only nodded.

It was apparent to him now that there was a secret, a conspiracy – something the adults knew that he simply wasn't in on. What he didn't know and couldn't know was whether this deception was foul. He only knew he didn't like the feeling and he didn't trust what was happening. Because when it came down to it, he simply couldn't fathom why. Was this another test? Was it really just part of his training? A trick by Phillip to give him hope, then take it away? Was there a lesson in this? Something he should be figuring out? Would Phillip really tell him everything if he just waited? All he could do was play the game and find out. But two days felt like an eternity.

By some point late in the night or early in the morning, all the speculations about the day's adventures were vetted and the talk was tired. Eyelids hung heavy as all the excitement flushed out, leaving both boys exhausted. Still, sleep didn't come easy for Garrett, a boy heavy in thought. When finally it did come, it wasn't real. It wasn't rest. It was horror, raw and vivid. He couldn't escape the great fire that consumed everything it touched.

Garrett's night offered no repose as he tossed and turned, fighting with nightmares of dragon's breath.

30

This Must Be What It Feels Like to Die

Present day
Oak Island, Nova Scotia

Breanne blinked wildly, throwing her hands over her ears.

"That's it, stay here! Stay with me!" Paul shouted, but the gunshots were deafening in the small space. She could only see his lips moving now. What were they shooting at anyway? She broke her gaze from Paul to see her father shooting at thorny octopus tentacles coming from the floor. But they weren't octopus at all, they were covered in thorns. *Crack... Crack!* He shot again and again. She flinched away, then finally, after many shots, she couldn't say how many, the gun went quiet.

She drew a deep breath and another, steadier now. Hesitantly, she looked back at the tentacles. They were almost reaching the ceiling, whipping wildly, stretching to reach her, her brothers, her father. She looked back to the doorway, where Edward had squatted down, chopping wildly at the vines near the floor.

"Maybe I can hack them off near the roots!" he shouted.

More spirals dropped around them, twisting into the earth, cracking and writhing.

"I'm going to just open the damn Ark!" her father announced. "Do you hear me, damn you? I will just open it."

The room quieted as the foliaged walls stopped shaking and the writhing tentacles slowed their erratic advance.

Edward turned and stopped chopping.

Paul looked at her. "This is a mistake, isn't it?" he asked, his lips a tight line as he searched her eyes. "You said it hates us? This is a mistake?" Then his look became hopeful. "Bre, can you see any other way out of this?"

She shook her head. How was she supposed to help? They had a gun and knives. She had nothing. All she had was a camera. All she could do was take pictures. All she could do was take… pictures? Pictures! Her eyes flung wide.

She pushed Paul out of the way and stepped directly in front of the doorway. "Don't open it, Dad! Get ready to run!"

God, please work. Oh, please work.

She raised her camera. She pointed it at the foliaged doorway and clicked the shutter. The camera flashed bright. The foliage shivered, recoiled, and glowed. She clicked it again and again. The vines started untwisting, trying to recoil, trying to get away from the bright flash.

"It's working," her father shouted.

Paul and Edward snatched the Ark from the floor.

The shutter clicked and flashed, clicked and flashed.

More tentacles burst from the floor between flashes, only to freeze up again and again.

Finally, with only a few vines blocking their way, her father threw himself against the remaining tendrils as Breanne captured photo after photo of her father's desperate attempt to break free of the room.

The Secret Journal

Her father burst through the doorway and tumbled to the ground as Paul and Edward ran forward with the Ark.

"Go, Bre!" Paul shouted, the tentacled thorns catching on his shirt sleeve, vying for purchase. He ripped his arm free, pressing for the door.

Click, flash! Click, flash! She fingered the switch again and again until she was free of the room.

"Keep moving!" her father said as he scrambled to his feet and led them back down the crevasse.

They reached the water to find the soft glow of algae was gone, replaced by an angry swirl of yellow, orange, and red. The water didn't boil but steam rose, creating a thickening fog that hung like smoke on a calm day.

"Shit!" her father said as he bent to touch the water. "It's hot, but I think manageable." He stepped into the water where the color swirled orange. "Ahh. Dammit. I don't think we can cross this!" Then the color swirling around his feet turned a bright red. "Gahh!" he shouted, jumping back out. "Nope, if the water turns red when we are submerged, we are screwed."

"We are not going to open the Ark!" Breanne shouted as loud as she could. "Do you hear me? Not here! We won't do it here! And if you kill us, it will never be opened! Let us pass, and we will open it when we get out!"

They stood there at the water's edge for a long moment, watching the swirls of color.

"I don't think it is intelligent, baby girl. That would be absurd. It must be reacting to us trying to take what gives it life. This is something primal... something instinctual—"

"Don't call me absurd!" she shouted.

"I didn't mean—"

"Absurd is thinking this is God. This isn't God, Dad! This is... I... I don't know what. But it isn't God. God wouldn't hate us like this," she said, her face contorted in confusion. "Whatever happens, we can't open it here!"

Charles nodded. "Okay, Bre. Okay," he said softly. He turned and called out over the strange water, "You heard her! We won't open it unless we are free to leave!" He shouted the words with no belief behind them.

Paul said, "I think we are going to have to try and cross as quick as we can and just hope..." He stopped, caught by strange movement in the water.

Breanne followed his gaze. The red water swirled away to the walls, leaving only orange and yellow swirling together but then apart. The orange moved next to the red on both sides of the chamber, leaving only a trail of yellow leading to the ladder.

"For the record, Pops, I don't think this is some instinctual reaction from an unintelligent lifeform," Edward said quietly.

"Then what on earth is going on here, Ed?" his father asked.

"I think it's time to go," Paul said, stepping into the path of yellow water. "It's warm but manageable."

They moved swiftly. Her brothers hoisted the Ark above their heads while making sure to stay only in the yellow water. Soon they all reached the ladder and were up and out as quickly as they could climb.

Once through the chiseled hole, they sat catching their breath for a long moment.

Finally, it was Breanne who was first to speak. "Sorry I snapped at you. I... I just want to get topside."

"It's alright, baby girl," her father said, smiling weakly. "Let's get the Ark to the pit. Bre, can you radio Jerry and tell him we have what we are very confident is the Ark of the Covenant, and we're bringing it up?"

The Secret Journal

"Okay," she said, snatching the radio from her gear. She turned on the radio, but before she could depress the button, the radio crackled to life. Static exploded, but nothing audible could be heard.

"It must be the bedrock interfering with the signal. Let's just get to the pit," her father said.

They all nodded.

Breanne ran ahead, climbed the slope, then made her way through the tunnel and finally up into the pit. Once on the pit floor, the radio crackled again, and this time she could hear Jerry's voice.

"Come in, Charles, Breanne, can you hear me? Over."

"I can hear you, Jerry. Over," Breanne said, shouting into the radio. She looked up and waved her arm wildly.

Jerry's silhouette appeared far above. He leaned out over the railing and waved back. "Have you recovered the Ark? Over."

The question took Breanne completely off guard. *What? Wait… why would he ask that… how would he know?*

Before she could respond, Jerry's voice came back over the radio again. "Listen to me, Breanne. Tell your father not to open it until he brings it up here. Over."

The bad feeling suddenly came surging back—not your common *I don't like the looks of this* bad feeling, but a very bad feeling, sinking and sick, from somewhere deep within her.

"Breanne, do you hear me? Over."

She did not answer.

"Breanne! Come in, Breanne! Over!"

She turned off the radio.

Jerry's voice echoed down the pit walls. "Breanne!"

Now she was certain something was wrong.

She turned to find her brothers and father climbing up

into the pit with the Ark. Paul picked up the remote as Edward and Charles prepared to place the Ark in the basket.

"What did Jerry say?" her father asked.

"He said not to open it until you bring it topside," she said.

"Well, I don't plan to. We should all be there when we open it."

Breanne took a deep breath. "Daddy, he told me to tell you not to open the Ark before I even told him we found it."

Everyone stopped cold, turning their attention to Breanne.

"Well, he knew we hoped to find it. Maybe he is just being optimistic," Paul said.

She shook her head. "No. You don't get it. It was the way he said it, like he was sure we found it. How could he know?"

"What? How is that possible?" her father asked.

"It isn't," she said.

"We're talking about Jerry here," he said.

"I don't know, but Dad, something is wrong – something is so wrong, I can feel it in my heart!" Breanne said, almost frantically.

Her father reached for her and hugged her tight. "Now, baby girl, I'm sure there's a logical explanation." He tried to keep his voice steady, but he couldn't mask the confusion underneath, betraying his calm.

Paul and Edward shot each other a look that said, *Logical, my ass.*

Reaching over to Breanne's hip, her father unhooked the radio, turned it on, and depressed the button. "Jerry? We have found something here, and we are ready to come up. Over."

Jerry's voice crackled back through the radio. "Don't

open the Ark, Charles. Just load it in the basket and send it topside. Over."

Charles bit his lip in thought.

"What do we do, Pops?" Paul asked.

"Well, let's head up and see Jerry," he said uneasily.

Then another voice cracked over the radio. "Dr. Moore?"

The voice was Jerry's boss. *He was here?*

"Place the Ark in basket and send it up." It wasn't a request. It was an order.

Her father placed a hand on his brow and peered up towards the top of the opening.

Breanne followed his gaze to the silhouetted man standing next to Jerry. She hadn't known he was going to be here, and from the look on her father's face, she guessed he hadn't known either.

Her father moved over to the center of the pit, waved his arm, and depressed the button on the radio. "We are ready to bring the Ark of the Covenant up. It's light, so it shouldn't be a problem for all of us to come up in one trip. We are loading it now."

The voice returned from the radio in a crystal-clear high-pitched cackle. "The Ark of the Covenant. Is that what you think you've found?" The laughter stopped as the voice changed to anger, as if someone had flipped a switch that controlled the man's emotions. He spat harshly into the radio. "Listen carefully, Dr. Moore. Do not open it! I've waited an incredibly long time for this!" The voice quieted to a whisper. "Incredibly long." There was a pause of dead space before the voice spoke again. "Now, place the artifact in the basket and stand clear. We are patiently waiting, Dr. Moore – do hurry."

The boys had set the Ark down on the floor of the pit, turning to their father for direction.

Breanne's hackles raised at the tone in the man's voice.

"Dad, this feels wrong – all wrong," she said, her eyes pleading for her father to feel the same. In a moment of clarity she realized this wasn't what it appeared to be, none of it was. She looked into her father's eyes and could see the wheels turning. She could see him sorting it out, making a plan, and she didn't like it.

"How does he know it isn't the Ark of the Covenant before he's even laid eyes on it?" Edward asked, his face contorted in a combination of skepticism and confusion. "I agree, Pops, this is all wrong."

"They know way too much. Way too damn much," Paul added.

"Daddy, listen to me. That thing, whatever it is, it isn't the Ark of the Covenant. It isn't. It can't be. I know you want it to be and I do too, but it's not." Breanne pressed her lips into a determined line. "Let's just send it up. Let that man open it."

Charles's eyes darted around the pit as if trying to find some way to gain control of the situation. The man standing over a hundred feet above had them at a disadvantage. Giving up on whatever train of thought he was pursuing, he chewed his lower lip before finally setting his jaw in determination. His face steeled, and Breanne knew he was about to take control. As soon as her father spoke her heart dropped like a heavy stone in deep water.

"Stand back – I'm opening it!" He pushed the radio into Breanne's hands as he rushed forward and dropped to his knees in front of the Ark.

"Right on!" Edward said.

Paul nodded and smiled in agreement. "Do it!"

"Wait, Dad!" Breanne said, running forward to her father's side. "Please! Don't open it! Just get it topside first… please!" Her eyes were beginning to well with tears.

In her heart, she knew it didn't matter where the Ark was

opened – she still would not want her father to open it. Let the psycho up top open the damn thing. For God's sake, let Jerry open it, but not her father

"Baby girl," he said, smiling, "I love you. Now, trust me. We've worked too hard to risk something going wrong up there, and I just don't trust that man." He pointed towards the top of the pit. "Now stand back."

"Dr. Moore! Do not open it!" shouted the angry voice.

Two golden rings were attached to the chest and two to the lid. Long rods were fixed through each of the four rings, securing the lid in place. He grabbed hold of one of the long golden rods and twisted it back and forth as if working the throttle of a motorcycle. The centuries-old rod slowly worked loose from its motionless state. He gently pulled, sliding the first golden rod through the rings, freeing it from the Ark.

No one in the pit breathed.

"One down, one to go."

Tears began to run down Breanne's face as the feeling of dread overwhelmed her. After exhaling heavily, she drew in another deep breath and held it.

Her brothers watched on in anticipation.

Her father removed the other rod and sat it gently on the ground.

The radio crackled to life, causing Breanne to jump. Jerry's boss whispered, "Have it your way, Dr. Moore."

Breanne's eyes went wide. "Please, Daddy. I beg you, don't!" she cried.

"Here goes," her father said, and with that simple statement he lifted the lid.

Instantly, the world changed and would never be the same.

Breanne felt something in her mind fracture as her vision filled with white-hot light. The pain was instant and intense, as if a red-hot poker struck her brain – not from the outside but from the inside, from the very center of her mind. In the split second before she lost consciousness, she was sure her brain matter was being forced through her ears, eyes, and nose.

This must be what it feels like to die.

31

Prime Focus

Present day
Petersburg, Illinois

Garrett made his way down Snake Hollow at an easy run, heading towards Eugene's place, the old Victorian. As he listened to the hypnotic rhythm of his feet softly thudding against the cobblestone, he contemplated the past several days. He needed this run. He needed to figure it all out, and the best way to come up with something that made sense was to run. Running allowed him to go inside himself to an inner place, his sanctuary. Best of all, getting there was easy. All he needed was his old, ratty pair of sneakers, the great outdoors, and a little time. This was the place where he formed his best ideas, found courage, and even solved what, to a young man, seemed like huge problems. But not today. No, not today. Today's problem seemed to have no answer except to wait and see.

He replayed the last week over and over, finally coming to two possible conclusions. One, he was becoming paranoid and losing his mind. Two, he was being lied to by at least his family and who knows who else. The latter worried him the most. *God, I would rather be insane,* he thought. Everyone was acting so bizarrely that maybe there was a third option. Space aliens had taken his family and those around him, then sent clones to replace them. He vaguely remembered a movie where this happened. This ridiculous thought retreated quickly, and he settled back on the more likely scenario. He was losing his shit.

To top it all off, he had experienced the crazy forest fire dream again last night, and this time it seemed less like a dream and more… real. He shuddered now as he recalled the screams and the smell of burning meat and hair. He frowned, pressing his mind to remember as the blood pushed fast through his heart. In the dream he could feel the heat washing over him, choking his breath. Someone was there with him, he was sure. He couldn't see the face, but he'd called out, hadn't he? Someone familiar, he thought.

Damn it all, he thought, sick of holding it all shut up inside himself. He needed to tell Lenny what was up, confide in him as he always had. Mr. B's ring, the crazy dreams, and all this strange behavior from the adults. His only hesitation was his best friend might think he was crazy. Was he? Was all this in his head?

More than anything else, this was the conclusion he needed to draw out of this run. Explain all this to Lenny and risk him thinking he had gone crazy or just keep it to himself. Approaching the driveway to the old Victorian, he had decided. They would test for second degree tomorrow, and afterward Phillip had promised to explain about the training. So he would wait then, till after the test. Then he would spill it to Lenny. He breathed deep but didn't feel much better.

Pinching his lower lip, Garrett waited for Pete at the foot of the driveway, pacing and contemplating. So much on his mind. The least of it wasn't what they were about to do. He didn't feel good about tricking Eugene, but they needed the other half of that book. A few minutes later Pete showed up.

"'Sup Garrett," he said.

Somehow, seeing his friend's bespectacled face calmed him, and he felt some of his anxiety slip away. "Pete, you ready for this?" he asked.

"Yeah, let's do it."

They ascended the stairs to a vast wraparound porch and knocked on the large ornate door of the old Victorian. Seconds later, Lilith promptly answered. "Well, hello, boys," she said, smiling.

"Hello, Mrs. Lilith, is Eugene home? I'm supposed to do some work in the basement for him today," Garrett said.

"Oh yes, dear, he's already down there," Lilith said as she ushered the boys across the threshold of the mammoth entryway.

The boys shot each other a concerned look.

"Peter, I wasn't aware you were joining in the project today. It's so nice to see you."

"Actually, Pete just came by to see Eugene. I've been bragging about his awesome collection of Native American artifacts. Pete's hoping Eugene might show them to him."

"Well, that's sweet. Why don't you go on down in the basement and ask him? I am sure he will be happy to show off one of his collections. That man has more collections of odd things than a junkyard has junk," she said, smiling softy.

"Thanks, Mrs. Lilith," Garrett said.

They crossed the kitchen and made their way around the corner to the basement entry. As they descended the old, creaky stairs, they heard grunting and scuffling from somewhere far off in the distant bowels of the basement. Once at the bottom, they could see faint light emanating from a hallway opening.

"Here we go," Garrett said, navigating the narrow corridor toward the lit room.

Pete nodded.

Garrett entered the small room to find Eugene attempting to manhandle a large piece of broken drywall out of the scrap pile. His eyes darted across the room, quickly finding the entry to the crawl space.

"Garrett! Am I glad to see you! This drywall business is darn hard work," Eugene said as he wiped the sleeve of his flannel shirt across his brow.

Garrett thought the flannel looked funny on the man. It looked new and unworn. Eugene the accountant was better suited to a heavy, starched button-down collared shirt and tie.

"Let me get that," Garrett said, quickly moving forward and taking the piece of drywall from the clearly exhausted man.

"Well, boy, oh boy, it's probably a good thing you brought your pal Peter with you," Eugene said, slowly bringing his breath under control.

"Actually, if it's just the same, I can handle this pile of drywall. Pete here was hoping you might show him your Native American artifact collection."

Eugene's eyes lit up like a child's. "Yes, well, I have quite a collection, Peter, and you betcha, I'd love to show you. I keep the whole collection boxed up in a spare bedroom on the third floor," he said, but then his eyes narrowed and he rubbed a hand on his bald head. "Hmm, maybe we can make arrangements for this Sunday after Sunday school?"

Both the boys wore a look of unexpected disappointment.

"Oh, dear, I am sorry, boys. I just hate to leave you to all this work, Garrett. That doesn't hardly seem right. Tell you what, if we all work together, maybe we'll have time after we finish up."

This wasn't going how Garrett had hoped. He needed a solution and fast. He looked at Pete searchingly, but his gaze found nothing to answer it. Garrett kept staring at Pete. *Come on, Garrett, think!* Then a thought registered. "Eugene, Pete isn't dressed for work and if he ruins his good school clothes, well, he'll be in for it, won't you, Pete?" he asked hopefully.

"Oh, uh... yeah, sure will," Pete said.

Eugene pursed his lips in thought but before he could come up with a solution, Garrett went on, "I don't think this will take me that long anyway. I'll carry all the pieces to the bottom of the stairs, then once I have them all stacked up, I can start carrying them up. Maybe by that time if you really want to help, we can just make a chain on the stairs with me at the bottom, Pete on the stairs, and you at the top?"

"Well, I am not sure how that keeps Pete from ruining his school clothes, but..." Then his face brightened as he snapped his fingers. "Okay, well of course, I have another old flannel shirt you can wear, Peter! That ought to keep you clean."

The two boys nodded with excitement.

Eugene looked to Garrett, then to the pile of drywall and wood backer strips, then back to Garrett. "Now, you be careful – some of those boards have nails sticking out of them. There are a few different pairs of work gloves on the bench, so make sure you find a pair and wear them to protect your hands."

Finally, Eugene turned to leave, then paused, turning back to Garrett again. "You're sure you don't mind?"

"Not at all, you hired me to do this. It won't be a problem," he said. *Come on, don't change your mind now, just give me five minutes* – just *five minutes.*

"Well, alright then, Garrett. Just remember this – the greater the difficulty, the more the glory in surmounting it!" He turned back to Pete. "Do either of you know who said that?"

Garrett shrugged and looked to Pete.

Pete shrugged back.

"Epicurus!" Eugene said, in a proud matter-of-fact tone. "I don't agree with the man on much, but on this, we can agree. Now, follow me, Peter, if you wish to behold the most amazing Native American artifact collection you have ever, well… beheld!" The two were off and on their way up the stairs.

Garrett quickly grabbed a pair of gloves, picked up a piece of drywall, and carried it to the foot of the stairs, ensuring they were all the way up and gone before making his move. He could hear them as they climbed up to the main floor.

"You know, Peter, I found a fair amount of this collection myself walking corn fields in southern Illinois as a child, but the rest I bartered for. When we get up there, I'll show you which is which. I have this one piece…" As they reached the upper landing, Eugene's voice faded, stifled by the century-old wood floor.

Garrett waited a moment longer until he couldn't hear them at all. *They must be up the second set of stairs by now,* he thought. He raced back to the room, pulled the small flashlight from his pocket, and set it on the ledge of the opening. Without missing a beat, he leapt up and grabbed the opening to the crawl space, pulling himself up and inside, onto his stomach. As he shimmied around to face back towards the opening, he knocked the flashlight off the ledge, sending it clattering across the concrete floor. *Crap!* There was no time to retrieve it now, if it even still worked. He eyeballed the gap between the dirt underneath him and the back side of the old wall with trepidation. The place was dark and super creepy. The thought of reaching down between the wall and the dirt was freaking him out. Just being in the crawl space made him feel like something was going to grab him and pull him into the shadows.

One thing was sure. Pete had some serious balls, blindly fishing down into the gap. Well, he had no choice now. He sucked in a deep breath, then plunged his arm into the pitch-black hole. Even wearing thin gloves, he hated it and had to fight with every ounce of his soul not to immediately yank his arm back out. He was certain something was either going to grab it or bite it. Driven by fear, he wildly swept his arm back and forth, dragging his thinly gloved fingertips along the bottom of the gap. He felt something once – a tin can, maybe – but no journal.

He shuffled further and further along, pushing through cobwebs thick enough to blot out the sun – not that there was any sun in this ungodly dungeon of a crawl space. Realizing the cobwebs must have been years in the making, he turned back in the other direction, knowing Pete couldn't have ventured this far. Shimmy, stretch, reach, and shimmy again. The gap deepened. Shimmy, stretch, reach, and shimmy some more. He could barely get his fingertips to skim the bottom.

Forcing his shoulder down into the void, he stretched to full extension. A scream welled up inside him, but he held it in. Finally, his fingers hastily brushed across something that felt, yes, like paper. He passed his fingertips over it again and confirmed it… it was the journal! It had to be! He strained desperately now, his pulse quickening. *Oh dear God!*

He strained, the side of his face pressed to the dirt as he shoved his shoulder in, trying to force it to go. He managed to get his index and middle finger over the binding of the book.

Gently he pulled, hoping not to drop it even deeper in.

He carefully lifted the book up over the edge of the crevasse. Once it was safely out, he let the book fall to the dirt floor, but he would feel no relief until he, too, was out of the crawl space.

Scrambling over to the opening, he climbed back through and dropped onto the basement floor. He had made sure to wear a baggy shirt for the sole purpose of concealing the book. So, like Pete had done with the first half, he stuffed the book down the back of his pants, allowing his shirt to overhang his jeans. Once his hands were free, he quickly brushed himself off as best he could.

Per their plan, Garrett was counting on Pete to try and stall Eugene for as long as possible by asking a ton of questions about the Native American artifacts. Still, he needed to hurry – his time in the crawl space felt as though it had taken forever. He quickly went to work, dragging drywall and wood scraps as fast as he could to the base of the stairs. As he worked, he thought about their plan and wished they had determined a time frame, then synchronized watches like in the spy movies. At least then they would know what target they were shooting for. He noted for future reference that the next time they planned a covert operation that required infiltrations, distractions, and a heist, they should synchronize watches.

Garrett made six trips before he heard voices returning from above. He raced back to the room, scrambling for a seventh. He wished he had more of the pile moved. Suddenly, he became very paranoid at the sound of Eugene's voice as they descended the stairs. He took a deep breath and tried to control his nerves. *Play it cool, Garrett. Just play it cool,* he thought.

"Right, well, that one is called hematite – it's an iron ore. The interesting thing about that one is its shape. Did you take notice of the shape, Peter? You see, the Native Americans would have used that as a weight for a fishing net."

They reached the bottom of the stairs, and Eugene immediately began to survey Garrett's work. Pete was now wearing what Eugene would refer to as an "old flannel shirt" and though it might indeed be old, Garrett doubted it had ever been worn.

"Well, you've been busy," Eugene said, still assessing the pile.

"Yeah, the stuff is a little heavier than I thought, and I had to be extra careful with all the nails but, yeah, it's a good start," he said, looking over to Pete and nodding, careful not to let Eugene see him. "I only have a few trips left before we can make a chain up the stairs?"

"Alrighty, that sounds like a fine plan," Eugene said.

For the next thirty minutes, the three worked side by side, making the chain on the stairs and passing the material up the steps piece by piece. The conversation stayed on Native American artifacts as Eugene spoke passionately about the history of his collection and how he came upon each piece. Garrett and Pete enjoyed the light conversation, and the work passed quickly.

"Whew, all in a day's work," Eugene said, as the boys tossed the last of the scraps into the pile outside the old Victorian.

Eugene settled up with Garrett and even gave him a bonus to share with Pete. The extra money didn't do anything for Garrett's guilt at deceiving Eugene, but he was glad the ordeal was over with. Thanking Eugene, the boys started off down the driveway. But then, just as they reached the bottom of the driveway, they heard Eugene yelling for Garrett to come back.

"Crap, you think he knows? What do I do?" Garrett asked.

"Give me the book, and I'll stay here," Pete said, motioning frantically for Garrett to hand it over.

"Garrett! Can you come here, please," Eugene's voice called again.

"No way, he might be able to see us. Just wait for me," he said, turning to run back up the driveway.

When he reached the top of the drive, Eugene was waiting for him. The thin, balding man didn't say anything right away. Instead, he just stood there seemingly lost in thought or struggling to begin. "Garrett, I need to ask you something," he said slowly.

I'm dead, I'm dead, I'm dead. The words repeated over and over in his mind like some kind of twisted mantra. "Oh… okay, Eugene," he said, trying hard to play it cool.

Eugene sighed. "Is there something you want to tell me?"

Oh man, oh Jesus, shit… He knows? He knows… Dammit!

Silence hung there like a foul fart that refused to clear and no one would claim. The awkward standoff between them left Garrett with a decision. Come clean or take a chance on a lie that could make everything even worse.

Garrett tried to play the middle. "I'm n-not sure what you mean, Eugene," he said, unable to control the quavering in his voice.

Eugene stared down intently as if trying to read his mind.

Garrett could only stand there uneasily, trying to maintain eye contact as he waited for Eugene to accuse him of theft. Already racked with guilt, he knew when the time came, he would confess to stealing the journal because he simply did not have it in his heart to lie to the man outright.

Garrett braced himself.

"Listen, I know something is going on with you. Now, you don't have to tell me what it is, but I want you to know

The Secret Journal

you can. I am here for you, *whatever* it is," he said, extending a hand and placing it on the boy's shoulder.

"What?" Garrett said, his fear turning to confusion.

"Listen, I'm a pretty good judge of people, and I can tell something is wrong. Now, I know you have your big test tomorrow, and you're probably worried about performing well, but I sense something else is bothering you. I am offering you a chance to unburden yourself of whatever it is. Sometimes just getting it all off your chest is the best thing you can do."

"I... I'm okay, Eugene," he said, still in shock at the sudden turn of events. He felt dizzy, realizing he had been holding his breath. Letting out a long exhalation, he pulled in deep.

"You can trust me, Garrett. You know that, right? Whatever is happening, you can trust me."

"Really, Eugene, I'm fine."

Garrett felt he really could trust him, with almost anything... almost. Not this, not the journal, not the weirdness with his family, Coach, and Mr. B.

He studied the man's concern for a moment. It was so genuine. Then the thought struck him – perhaps he could confide in him. It would be nice to tell someone, especially someone he trusted. Now that he thought about it, Eugene was probably the only adult he *could* trust with something like this. He might even help them get to Lincoln's temple and decipher the rest of the clues. After all, he was into old stuff like this.

"Alright, Garrett, but listen carefully to me now. Proverbs 12:22 says, 'Lying lips are an abomination to the Lord: but they that deal truly *are* his delight.' Let me in, trust me, and I can help you. I'm sure I can... whatever it is," Eugene said, his brow creased with concern.

Garrett swallowed hard, taking a long moment to decide.

He would tell Eugene the truth. Finding the courage to speak, he started to open his mouth.

Eugene shrugged in resignation. "Alright then, Garrett. I'm here if you change your mind. Now, I guess you better run along home and get some rest for your big test tomorrow." He checked carefully over his shoulder and bent forward to bring his eyes even with Garrett's. His voice was low and guarded. "Most of all, you'll want to be sure your mind is in *prime focus* for the journey ahead." He tapped his finger against his head.

Garrett's heart leapt into his throat as he recoiled. Eugene's strange words dashed all hope of unloading the guilt he felt and the burden he carried. Just like that, gone – slipped away like a slimy fish from the hands. The words *prime focus* echoed in his mind.

Eugene held Garrett's eyes for what seemed like an eternity. Garrett could do nothing but stare back, heart banging against his chest. The moment stretched between them, lasting long enough to forever change Garrett's perception of the man he thought childlike, trusting, and innocent. He was one of them now – a stranger, a clone, a big fat question in a sea of questions. Or maybe he was just crazy after all, seeing something that wasn't there.

Eugene straightened, turned, and began walking back to the old Victorian. He reached the back door and placed his hand on the doorknob, but before turning it he paused and looked back over his shoulder, his face stony and serious. "You're not good at lying, young man," he said, his tone matter-of-fact. "Not even when you wear a baggy shirt…"

Garrett gasped.

"Good luck tomorrow," he said, the warm smile having returned to his face. He turned the knob and went inside.

Garrett bolted back down the driveway and found Pete pacing back and forth, still waiting on his return.

The Secret Journal

"Jesus, bro, what happened? What did he want?"

"He knows, Pete! He knows we took it. Dammit… he freaking knows," he said, pushing Pete away from the old Victorian.

"Easy, man, calm down."

They began hurriedly walking.

"How could he? What did he say!" Pete asked.

"He mentioned my baggy shirt, Pete! The only reason I wore it today was to make sure it covered the journal."

"What do you mean, he mentioned it? That doesn't mean anything," Pete said.

"You weren't there, man. I'm telling you he knows… *he knows.*"

"What?" Pete asked.

They were far enough away from Eugene's that Garrett felt confident they wouldn't be seen. He pulled the journal from behind his back and pushed it into Pete's hands. "Listen to me, take it home and transfer all of it tonight. We have to know what it says. Something is wrong, Pete. We're running out of time."

"You want me to destroy it? Take it apart at the binding and destroy it?" Pete asked in disbelief.

"Take it apart at the binding and transfer it!" Garrett said desperately.

"But why? Why hurry… because of Eugene noticing your shirt?"

"Not just that, man. I have a feeling we are running out of time."

"Is this about Jack? You heard about today and now you're freaking out? Is that it?" he asked, as they turned into the church parking lot to cut through to the alley.

"What are you talking about? What about today?"

"Jack cornered me again. I guess we should have known he would open it despite the damage it probably caused. He read the choice words I wrote into it. Man, was he pissed. I swear he was going to pound my face in until I did exactly like you said."

Garrett felt his heart begin to pound even harder as if it were the target of a blacksmith's hammer. *Thump! Thump! Thump!* "What did you say?"

"I blamed the whole thing on you... just like you said." A proud smile formed on Pete's face. "I said the whole thing was your idea. I even told him if he had a problem with it, *you* said he was to see *you* about it."

Garrett didn't say anything.

"Man, I thought his head was going to explode, but it worked – he let me go. He said he would be seeing you, though, then he went on to describe what he was going to do to you," Pete said, grinning mischievously. "Of course, I then proceeded to tell *him* how everyone was sick of his shit and how *you* were going to put him in his place once and for all. Then he almost decided to beat my face in anyway... but, yeah, next thing I know, he lets me go."

Garrett sighed. Jack was a problem that would have to wait. "Listen, man, just please get it all transferred tonight. I have a bad feeling, don't ask me why, I just do... I really need you to get this done, Pete."

"Okay, already, I'll get it done. Don't you even want to know what I found in the other part?" Pete asked.

In all the craziness, he had forgotten to even ask about the progress with the first half. "What! You finished it? Of course I want to know!" Garrett said, giving his friend a shove. Pete staggered sideways before quickly regaining his balance.

"Alright, listen," he said. "Without going word for word, Lincoln basically says we have to get inside, and once we are in, it's basically a natural cave system that leads south about a mile or mile and a half. Then, according to old honest Abe, we should reach the temple entrance. If my calculations are right, though, we are going to end up near New Salem and pass in front of, or somehow under, Lake Petersburg!"

Garrett shook his head. "So, this temple? You think it could be under Lake Petersburg?"

"I think so, and it kind of makes you wonder when the lake was created if someone was trying to make sure the temple was never found."

The boys were standing in the alley now, at the point where they needed to go their separate ways. "What did he say about traps?" Garrett asked.

"Well, most of it was undecipherable old stains and smudges. I made out one part that talked about a hidden spiked pit, and then a part about animal traps, but that's it."

"Any idea how we're supposed to get past them?"

"No, not yet."

"Will you be at the library after school tomorrow?"

"Yeah, Janis and I are meeting there. I want to do some research on Lake Petersburg. I know it's man-made, and if the temple really is under it, that seems like a pretty big coincidence."

"Well, good for you, man. It's about time," Garrett said.

"What's that supposed to mean?" Pete asked.

"You and Janis. Just happy for you, buddy."

Pete smiled shyly, face flushed.

"Look, Pete, I know I sound crazy but something more is going on and, I don't know, I feel like this whole thing is coming to a head. Can you please see what you can get figured out? Lenny and I will try and swing by after we test, but it will have to be fast."

Pete frowned, not understanding. An expectant moment passed, and when Garrett didn't respond his friend simply nodded. "Okay, I will transfer this tonight and see you at the library tomorrow then."

"Hey, you want me to walk you home in case Jack jumps you on the way? I would hate to lose this thing after all the work we put into getting it." Garrett motioned at the journal.

"No need – Jack doesn't know about this half, and he thinks you have the other half. Besides, after today he's saving it all up for you – I'll be fine," Pete said, grinning again.

"Later, Pete."

"Later."

The boys parted, each going their separate ways. Neither knew, nor could know, their world was about to change forever.

~

Garrett arrived home to find his mom just starting the prep work for dinner and his father taking a nap. He found his brother working on a puzzle in his room and decided to poke his head in. "Hey, James?"

"What's up?" he asked.

"I want to cut my hair. Can you help me?"

"Why don't you ask Dad? He was the barber, not me," he said, snapping a puzzle piece into the border.

That was true – once upon a time his father had been a barber in the military. This was almost assuredly where he obtained his beloved razor strap. "No way! Two reasons that isn't going to happen. First, I will end up with a crew cut or flattop – not happening! Second, he's been telling me to cut my hair for years, and there's not a chance I'm giving him the satisfaction of being the one to cut it."

His brother looked up and to Garrett's surprise… he grinned.

Garrett took the grin as permission to enter his brother's room whether it was meant to be or not. He moved from the

The Secret Journal

doorway toward the folding table his brother sat at working on the puzzle.

"Why do you want to cut it anyway?" James asked.

"I don't know. I can't really explain it. I just feel like… like something's coming. Change, I guess," he said.

James nodded. "And you want me to do it? You realize I can't style your hair, right?"

"Yeah, I know."

"So, what do you have in mind?"

"Well, I thought about just cutting it short and leaving the bangs longer so they hang in my eyes… just to piss off Dad," he said with a smirk.

"Ha, I would love to be there when he sees you've cut the parts he doesn't even care about and left the *only* part that sets him off, but like I said, I can't style your hair."

"Right, so just cut it all off… I mean I don't want to look like a monk, but cut it short, really short – short enough no one could grab ahold of it," Garrett said.

James stared at his little brother for a moment. Garrett waited for the questions but none came. Finally, his brother just nodded. "Alright then."

A few minutes later Garrett stood in front of the bathroom mirror and James stood behind him, a pair of scissors in his hand. "You're sure?" he asked.

"Yeah, do it," Garrett said decisively.

James went to work hacking long locks of hair chunk by chunk from Garrett's head. His hair hung down to the middle of his back, but James showed no hesitation in shearing off what had taken years to grow. Once he had removed the hair down to a manageable length, he went to the bathroom cupboard and removed his father's clippers, put on a number-one guard, and buzzed Garrett's head.

Once finished James removed the guard and lined up his neck, then stood back to admire his work. "Well, no one will be grabbing you by the hair now," he said approvingly.

Garrett almost didn't recognize himself. He looked older somehow, and his remaining hair was a sandy brown, a major change from the sun-bleached blond locks now filling the bottom of the sink.

"Thanks, James," he said, rubbing a hand over his head, realizing this was the most time he had spent with his brother without them ripping on each other since, well, since he could remember.

"See you at dinner," James said.

Garrett showered, dressed, and entered the kitchen, finding his seat at the table. When his parents noticed him enter, they froze in place and stared while James busied himself segregating his food, making sure none of it touched.

"My God, Garrett, your hair... what have you done?" his mother asked.

He just shrugged and sat down.

Elaine darted her eyes to Phillip. "It's about goddamn time," he said approvingly.

"You want me to go out back and time myself at fire-starting, or study primitive structure building? Oh, or I could work on my sword forms?" he asked. As the words slipped from his lips, he questioned himself as to why in the world he would want to do his training. He didn't. What he wanted was for things to be normal. But things weren't normal.

Phillip lifted a glass of iced tea from the table and paused before taking a sip. "No, not tonight. Just feed and water the rabbits. Lenny will be here in a few minutes to spend the night. You should try and get plenty of rest. Tomorrow is test day."

Lenny gets to stay over again, no chores, no training. None of this made sense. Phillip didn't make sense. Leaning across the table, Garrett stared at Phillip's eyes. His eyes were familiar, yet stranger deeper in. Closer still he bent, squinting his eyes to peer in past the familiar, all the way to the hidden secrets.

"What the hell is wrong with you?" Phillip asked, his tone unusually patient. "Why are you squinting at me like that?"

Dinner passed without further conversation. Yet thick were the thoughts no one shared, each lost in their own. Each gathering in their own enigmas, keeping them all shut up and covered, hidden from him. Garrett chewed slowly and deliberately, studying them as one might study strangers. For who were these people if not strangers with their secrets?

∾

Pete sat down at his desk and tried to open the journal, but instantly the page began to crack. He sighed, hating what he was about to do. Carefully, but quite easily, he pulled loose the binding and laid each page out on his desk one by one. Next, he went to work transcribing Lincoln's entries the best he could. When he was done, he sat back in his chair, all the blood draining from his face.

This can't be real… It's not possible!

32

The Birthplace of Fire

Wednesday, April 6th, 9:00 a.m.
Day One
Oak Island, Nova Scotia

As the pain subsided, a now familiar roar of flames and screams filled Breanne's ears. When her eyes cleared and her surroundings came into focus, she fully expected to see the forest burning around her, but she did not. She was in a familiar city – *New York,* she thought. Breanne had never been to New York, but Times Square was familiar even to those who had never seen it in person. Only now, Times Square was on fire. Buildings were burning, steel structures were melting and twisting, concrete blazed as if made of wood, things that should not burn were consumed in flame. But worst of all, she could see the source of the screams, the people... oh, the people! The ones that were not burning were running, but they couldn't get away, and as she watched, dozens, maybe hundreds, of people, whole crowds of people, burst into flames, falling to the ground, screaming in agony as they burned.

The Secret Journal

Breanne wanted to look away, wanted so badly not to watch the horrible scene playing out before her, but it did not matter where she turned – the fire was everywhere, the burning bodies were everywhere, and even slamming her eyelids down tightly as she clutched her hands over her ears would not allow her to hide from the horror of the screams nor the smell of burning flesh. She didn't need to pinch herself to know this was real. How could she be smelling something in her dreams she had never smelled in life… so sharp, so pungent? The stench made her want to vomit. Heat hit her in a wave that sucked the air out from her mouth, leaving her gasping, sweat-soaked. As she stood there in the middle of Times Square, she screamed and gasped, but she couldn't hear herself over all the screaming people and roaring flames and she couldn't catch her breath. She feared the fabric of her sanity was beginning to tear away when suddenly…

The sound stopped, the air cooled, and the burning stench faded away.

She opened her eyes, no longer able to hear the screams or the roaring flames. The Knight Templar stood in front of her, his white robe billowing as hot wind gusted across it. Though she no longer heard anything, she could still see the chaos as Times Square and all it held descended into fiery chaos. She tried to keep her focus on the Templar and not the burning people, some young, some old, and some children.

Then he spoke. "Child."

She realized then she was sobbing and could only nod.

He knelt down, placing his hand lightly on her shoulder. Breanne searched deep into his piercing, crystal-blue eyes and she could see goodness there, but it was overlaid with profound sorrow.

"The Ark has been found – thus, the prophecy has

begun. He has come to take the God Stones," the Templar said, his sorrow deepening as he swept his hand across the fiery scene. "Soon all will burn."

Breanne's mind reeled as she found her voice. "Is it... Satan?" she asked, immediately feeling the question was ridiculous, but then again, she was talking to a dead Templar in a nightmare of fire.

"His name is Apep, and he will stop at nothing to see this world in ruins and humanity destroyed. Child, you must stop at nothing to get the God Stones... before it is too late," he said, pointing at her. "You must go and find the boy named Garrett in the land of Lincoln." He turned his attention towards a young man approaching from across the street.

She didn't understand how she knew it, but this was the shadowed figure from her last dream in the forest. The boy appeared to be around her age and was lean and muscular, with his hair clipped very short. She felt like she knew him, like she had always known him. He looked terrified as he ran towards her.

She turned to look back at the Templar but he was walking away, towards the flames. "Wait, please! Don't leave. Please tell me, who are you?"

He turned back to her and smiled. "I've many names, child, but my last was Hugues."

"You're Hugues de Payens, founder of the Knights Templar?"

He nodded once, fixing her with his crystal eyes as they burned with dancing blue fire.

She had done her research on the Knights and knew that Hugues was born in approximately 1070 AD and allegedly died in 1136 AD, but from her research she also knew that there were no records as to where the man came from. The circumstances surrounding his death were just as mysterious, as no records existed chronicling any details of his death. "What happened to you?" she asked.

"Happened? Child, what was is and is will be. Death mortal begets life eternal."

Hugues turned away from her, paused, and turned back again. "You must leave your father's side and find Garrett. He needs you now." Then, motioning towards the approaching boy, the Templar said, "Heed these words, child. You can't help your father without first helping Garrett."

Help my father? she thought, glancing back over her shoulder. She watched the boy as he stepped up onto the sidewalk and approached her, then she looked back to the Templar Knight. "Wait!" she shouted. But it was too late… he was gone.

As the young man approached, she could see he must be around her age.

"Do you know what's happening?" he asked, the sound of the screams and flames increasing as if being controlled with the volume knob on a radio.

The boy was obviously just as scared as she was and just as confused, maybe more.

"I don't know!" she shouted, having to strain to be heard. "He said I have to find you! You're Garrett, right?"

The boy's eyes widened in surprise at the mention of his name.

"Yes, but who said?" he asked.

"Hugues," she said, pointing in the direction the Templar had gone. "Didn't you see him?"

Garrett held out his hands and shook his head.

"The Templar Knight! He was standing right here a second ago!" Breanne shouted, but the boy's expression told her he had not seen the Templar.

That god-awful noise, the smell of burning flesh, and now even the temperature were increasing, quickly becoming unbearable. Breanne tried to push down her rising nausea. "How am I supposed to find you, Garrett?" she managed.

"I'm in Petersburg!" he shouted, stepping closer to her.

The smells and sounds increased as the flames closed in around them. They could both feel the heat and neither knew what to do – there was no place to run.

"What's your name?" he yelled.

"What?"

"Your name! What's your name?"

"Breanne!" she shouted.

The flames crept ever closer. The concrete sidewalk around them ignited, then it too burst into unnatural flames.

"It's burning me!" she screamed as the flames lapped at her back.

Garrett grabbed her by her shoulders and spun her while pulling her to his chest. He moved his body to position himself between her and the flames, wrapping his arms around her. She buried her hands and face in his chest. Chunks of sidewalk exploded from the heat as bits of concrete popped into embers. The boy shielding her screamed in pain as he was showered with the burning cinders. Still he held her. Even as he burned, he held on, pulling her hard into him. Another explosion of sidewalk. He screamed again. Even with her ear pressed to his chest, she struggled to hear, didn't want to hear.

The flames continued to press in as both squeezed their eyes closed, clutching each other as tight as they could. The roar became so loud it threatened to burst eardrums. The ground began to shake beneath them. Then they heard it. A piercing scream that cut through the roar of flames past their ears to penetrate deep into their very souls. The scream was inhuman. What followed the scream was fire, pure and absolute.

In that instant Breanne learned the birthplace of fire.

Just as Garrett's back burst into flames, he shouted in her ear, "Find me, Breanne! Find me in Petersburg!"

33

That's Going to Leave a Mark

Wednesday, April 6th, 7:00 a.m.
Day One
Petersburg, Illinois

"Breanne!" Garrett shouted, tearing free from the tangle of sheets coiled around him like a giant snake. Panting, he lurched upright to a sitting position. Both he and his bedding were soaked with sweat. As he moved, his entire body felt sore, as if he had just finished a twenty-mile run.

Breanne? he thought, catching his breath as he tried to clear the morning fuzz from his mind. The nightmare had been so real. *The flames – oh God, the fire… Everything was burning, the buildings, even the sidewalk burned.* He recognized Times Square in New York as the place where he had watched the ball drop to mark the new year, at least the few times he could stay awake. In his nightmare, there had been no ball, only fire, and the only thing that wasn't burning was the girl… *Breanne.*

Garrett sat there in his bed for a long moment, afraid to

get up, afraid he would lose the memory, as horrible as it was. He wanted to understand, and he knew this wasn't the first time he had dreamt of the fire, but it was the first time it was so… *clear*, so real. He tried not to focus on the nightmarish surroundings or think about the smell of burning people. He tried to push away the roar and screams that still echoed his mind, tried not to think of the intense, burning pain he had felt on his back – still felt on his back – as he had taken Breanne into his arms and pulled her close to his chest. Instead he tried to focus on just the girl. She was beautiful – even scared, she was stunningly beautiful. He felt as though he knew her somehow. But it wasn't as if he could have somehow forgotten her. She was black, and he could count on one hand the black kids he had met in his life, Lenny included. Yet he was sure he knew her, that this wasn't the first time they had met. *Have I dreamt of her before?* She had spoken to him. *What did she say?*

Garrett rubbed his face. His back still felt as though it was burning, not like in the dream, but enough he could still feel it.

Suddenly what the girl had said came back to him in a rush. *"He said I have to find you!"*

"Who said?" he had asked.

"The Templar Knight Hugues!"

Then he had told her told her how: *"Find me in Petersburg."* Why had he said that?

This didn't feel like a dream to him at all, more like a memory of a real event. Unsure what to make of it, he pulled himself from his damp bed and descended the stairs to the bathroom for a shower. After washing he went to the bathroom sink and began brushing his teeth, still in deep thought over the nightmare. *What kind of messed-up dream includes a hot girl, hellish flames, and burning people?* Thinking about it made his back burn. No, it wasn't thinking about it that made his back burn – his back had never stopped feeling like it had been burned. He turned away from the mirror, then looked back over his shoulder. He dropped the toothbrush in the sink and gawked in shock at his back. His back was covered in tiny red marks – red burns. Some were even starting to blister. *The exploding concrete from the sidewalk, the small red-hot pieces... how the hell?* There was something else. Some kind of strange sound. When his back was burning, there was a sound... a scream. It sounded unlike anything he had ever heard. He didn't know what the hell last night was, but one thing was for sure – this was no normal nightmare.

School dragged on and on. All he could think about was the nightmare, the sickening scream echoing in his mind, and the girl – Breanne. He found himself worrying about her. He was struck with a feeling that she was in danger. He told himself this made absolutely no sense; after all, she was just a dream... wasn't she? The burns on his back were real enough.

He knew he should be focusing on his second-degree black belt test so he tried, but that only led to more worry. Finally, the whistle blew and Garrett made his way through the masses to the front of the school to meet up with Lenny. On his way, he ran into Coach Dagrun. "Hey Coach," he said as he walked by.

Coach grabbed his arm and pulled him off to the side, away from the throng. At first, he thought he had done something wrong, but then Coach said in low tone, "Testing today, right?"

"Yeah, Coach, actually heading there now."

"That why you cut your hair? For the test?"

"I... I don't know."

The Secret Journal

Coach stared at him for a long, awkward moment. "It's about goddamn time, brick," he said grimly.

"Thanks?" Garrett said, unsure.

"Listen, that place you go when you run..." Coach paused to look around, like he had the other day in the gym – like they were being watched.

"New Salem?" Garrett asked, his head tilting to the side.

"No!" Coach said in an urgent whisper, tapping his head with a finger. "The place in your head."

Garrett just stared at the man. *How could he know? Because he is a runner too?* He didn't think so. "But what—"

"You *know* the place. Find it today – you will have to find it when you *aren't* running, Garrett. That's your door. That's the way to your *focus*."

Garrett blinked and tried not to show how confused he was by the man's strange behavior. "I got to go, Coach. I... I don't want to be late." Only now did he notice that Coach's eyes were wild, and he didn't look himself as he stood there, continuing to tap his head.

Garrett pulled away, backing into the mass of eagerly exiting students.

"That's your door, Garrett!" Coach shouted after him as he made his way through the double doors. "That's your door!"

Once outside, Garrett stood off to the side of the main entry, near a bike rack and a couple of benches. A few minutes passed before he saw Lenny come through the doors with his backpack slung over one shoulder. He noticed Garrett and nodded excitedly, a big smile stretching across his face. *Well, someone is excited about the test at least,* he thought. But then Lenny's smile changed as his eyes tripled in size. Lines of confusion barely had time to form between Garrett's eyebrows before he felt the sharp pain of a fist connecting with his face.

Garrett fell hard. Lying facedown on the ground, he turned his head and squinted up at the source of the sucker punch through one eye.

Jack stood over him, seething with rage. "So you think you can make me look stupid and get away with it, Garrett? Send me into an antique store with a fake?" he yelled as he raised his foot high and stomped down at Garrett's ribs.

Garrett rolled, trying to dodge the stomp, but he was too late. He felt his ribs give as Jack's foot found his side. Struggling for breath and with his heart beating in his eye, he grunted up at Jack. "Not sure… I can… make you look… any more stupid than—"

"Get up, you little bitch! I've been waiting for this!" Jack motioned.

A crowd formed as Garrett struggled to get to his hands and knees.

Lenny rushed into the circle, throwing himself in between the two of them. "Not here, man!"

"You know, Lenny, my problem isn't with you, but it can be if you don't step off!" Jack said, poking Lenny hard in the chest.

"Look, man, he'll fight you, but not here and not now!" Lenny nodded back towards the school, motioning towards Coach Dagrún, who was just exiting the double doors with an expression of pure irritation. "Come on, Garrett, we got to go!"

"When and where? Name the place!" Jack said.

"Around five – behind the arcade," Lenny said, hauling Garrett up by the arm. "Now, come on, Garrett. There is no way we can afford to be held after school today." Lenny snatched up Garrett's backpack and pushed him away from the crowd and away from Jack. "Come on, let's go before Dagrun tries to hold us for questioning."

Somehow, he didn't think Dagrun would be a problem,

The Secret Journal

but Lenny was right. If they missed their test, no excuse would be good enough. They would be forced to wait until Mr. B decided to give them another opportunity, and who knew when that would be.

"You better show, Garrett, or everyone's going to know you're a coward!" Jack shouted, driving a fist into an open palm.

"You okay, man?" Lenny asked, keeping stride with Garrett.

"Yeah, dickhead sucker punched me."

"Dude, you went down like a sack of potatoes!"

"Thanks a lot, *friend*!"

"Sorry, man, but *damn*, talk about a haymaker – the whole school saw that coming! Well, almost the whole school."

"Well, I was looking at you, so if I had so much time to get out of the way you should've had time to warn me!" The words stretched his jaw, causing him to rub his eye reflexively.

"Yeah, I'd say that's going to leave a mark."

"And what's with you volunteering me to fight him after our test tonight? I'm going to be completely wiped out and now I got to go fight Jack? Seriously?" Garrett asked.

"Hey, man, I was just trying to think on my feet. We couldn't be getting held after – not today. You should be thanking me. I saved your ass."

He knew his friend was right, but his head was throbbing, his side hurt, he had to worry about his test, and now he had to worry about a fight with Jack on top of it. "Don't you remember my dad said after we test to come straight back home and he would answer all our questions about why we have to train?"

"Yeah, well, you will just have to make short work of Jack then. Easy enough," Lenny said simply.

The backpack straps rubbed against his blistered back as they ran, stinging as if he had a harsh sunburn. He tried unsuccessfully to adjust them as he pressed his fingers into his bruised side and winced. *Yeah, that's it, Lenny… easy enough*, he thought. Except nothing about this day felt like it was going to be easy.

34

The Corner of Her Eye

Wednesday April 6th, 9:00 a.m.
Day One
Oak Island, Nova Scotia

Breanne woke with a jerk. *It's burning me!* Her mind screamed the words, but they wouldn't form on her lips. Her jaw was clenched tight. Her teeth were mashed together, fixed so tight they might break. Every muscle seized, and she went rigid as a washboard. Her body shook uncontrollably. Her head bounced, thumping against cold dirt. White light flickered bright between glimpses of blue sky as if a paparazzo held a camera to her face, flashing it over and over. What was happening? She couldn't breathe. She gasped. She shook. She tried to cry out again. Waves of pain racked her taut muscles until finally the shaking slowed, then stopped altogether. Her muscles unclenched. She sagged back, lifeless.

The pain in her head faded. Her eyes cleared. Struggling to gain her bearings, she looked around in confusion, unsure for a moment where she was. *I'm... I'm in the pit,* she realized as she lay sprawled awkwardly in the cold dirt. The last moments before the dream came rushing back to her. Her father – he had opened the Ark, then there was pain in her head, horrible pain. Then she was in the dream. She reached, dragging her fingertips across her forehead, expecting to find blood. Nothing. She looked around, picking herself up slowly. She could see her brothers and father scattered against the walls of the pit, discarded like used towels. They were still unconscious, except Paul.

Paul moaned.

She pulled herself up, dizzy, and heaved dryly. Straightening, she staggered over to him, dropping to her knees, and shook him. "Paul! Please, Paul, wake up!" she pleaded.

Paul struggled to open his eyes, blinking several times. "Bre? Are... Are you okay?" he asked finally.

"I think so, but I feel... different."

Paul sat up slowly, holding his head in his hands.

A voice boomed from above them, from the top of the pit. "Hello, below!" It was the voice of Jerry's boss. "To whomever opened the chest, I thank you. I knew I could count on you! You should count yourself blessed. Not many humans survive their first exposure to the God Stones. Typically, your weak minds just pop like too-ripe tomatoes. Fun to watch, but oh, so messy."

Breanne looked at the chest. The lid sat ajar. Her father lay across the pit, still unconscious. She could see no visible injuries, no blood, thank God. Edward lay sprawled across the pile of stones excavated from the tunnel and was starting to stir. His right leg was twisted in an unnatural position. Oh no, Edward. Her heart began to race.

Cautiously, she eased close to the chest, just close enough to see inside. Her breath caught. Seven separate items were lying in the chest, each one oddly shaped, about the size of her hand and just as thick. They didn't look like stones to

The Secret Journal

her, at least not like any stones she had ever seen. They weren't glowing or pulsing, yet they were. They were both translucent and opaque, yet they were neither. The cloudiness inside them seemed to move through the stones, changing from one color to another, then back. Strangely, the stones changed colors until they flashed a color she had never seen nor could comprehend. When this color flashed, it pained her eyes, like looking into the sun, forcing her to squint and shield her eyes. But, oh, how she wanted to see it, the color never seen.

Breanne longed to reach in and pick up one of the stones, to hold it, to feel it in her hands, but forced herself instead to look away. Placing her hand against her forehead, she craned her head back, trying to see the source of the voice.

"Paul, do you see the radio?" she asked.

Paul frantically scanned the pit, locating the radio near their unconscious father.

Edward's eyes opened, and he groaned.

Paul handed Breanne the radio and she depressed the button, but the indicator light failed to come on – the radio was dead. She threw it to the ground and yelled towards the top of the pit. "Help us, my dad is unconscious! Ed is hurt! We need help! Jerry, can you hear me?"

Jerry appeared on the platform, leaning out over the railing. "Yes, I hear you, Breanne! What the hell was that? My God! Are you alright?"

"No! Ed is hurt! We need help! My dad is unconscious! Please!" she pleaded. "Get us out!"

Jerry turned and began speaking to the cloaked man in a tone barely lower than a shout and still audible in his panic. "I don't know who in the bloody hell you think you are or what the hell is going on here, but I know you know damn well more than you let on," Jerry said, wagging a finger towards the cloaked man. "Right now, my friends are in that pit, and we need to get them out!"

Breanne listened intently from the floor of the pit. She squinted up. Jerry's boss stood next to him in a black duster with a large hood, revealing only shadowed facial features.

"We need to help them and I've been trained on the crane, we can get them out!"

"Stay put, Gerald," the cloaked man said, turning to face Jerry. "Your crane won't work now."

Jerry shouted back down into the pit. "Not to worry, Bre! We will figure out how to get you out. I'll find rope... we *will* get you out!"

The cloaked man shook his head. "No, Gerald, we won't be using ropes either."

"Well, what then?" Jerry shouted.

Breanne could hear his panic, causing her own to well up.

The man ignored him, turning back to the pit. "I have longed for this day, Gerald! The day I would claim what is rightfully mine! Long ago, far away from this wretched planet of yours, my own father robbed me of my heritage, my future. He made my undeserving brother his heir and banished me from the kingdom – my kingdom!

"Oh, but I'd had a plan, Gerald! And it had been brilliant – simple. Use the God Stones to come to this world, create an unstoppable army, return to Karelia, and overthrow my father and brother. Take back what is mine!"

"What are you talking about? We have to—"

"Humans, Gerald! It was humans who ruined it all! It was they who cost me precious time. You know, they imprisoned me in Egypt? Me! They took the God Stones and squirreled them away. So afraid of power. So pathetic! Ah well, unfortunate mistakes of a time long past. You see, this world once made the perfect place to build an army

The Secret Journal

away from the watchful eye of my father, and I *will* do so again."

Breanne couldn't understand what the hell this guy was going on about, but she could feel something... something awful!

"I spent thousands of years imprisoned in sleep before I finally broke free! Then for centuries I searched tirelessly to find the God Stones, Gerald! Hundreds of years of relentless determination, all for this day and the days that will follow. I lived among the rodents of this world. Disguised myself as one of the scourges. I watched your race fail to evolve, fail to learn from your pathetic past. Instead, I watched your kind make the same absurd mistakes over and over. You're nothing more than a defective race of amnesiacs who can't remember their past and are too stupid to see their future. Poisoned to the core, Gerald – poisoned to the core. That's why you and your god were banished from our world long ago. But never fear, for I will *cleanse* it all away! I will unleash fire upon this planet, the likes of which have never been seen!"

Breanne gasped. *Fire?* The man in the cloak, Jerry's boss, was the man the Templar had warned of... Apep!"

"He tried, Gerald! Oho! He tried to make sure I would never get them! But here we are! The beginning of the end before the new! Oh, yes! *Yes!*" the cloaked man shouted gleefully. "I promise you this – *here* and *now* – I will watch this world burn in chaos and from the ashes will rise the greatest army ever seen! With this army, I shall rule anew!" He raised his arms out from his sides above the pit.

Apep's hood fell back. His human features twisted and fell away to something else. He stretched tall. She thought she glimpsed the color of his skin change to a blue or grey blue. His ears seemed longer somehow, pointed maybe. She wasn't sure, but he changed from incredible and dreadful into something terrible.

"Barmy hell! You're some kind of... You're a... Can't be..." Jerry sputtered, unable to say the word.

"No need to hide from you. Not now, not in this moment," Apep said without concern.

What is he? Say it, Jerry. But Jerry didn't say it. Breanne could only see the shadowed figure of the man and his outstretched arms. Then her attention was drawn from the top of the pit back to the Ark as it began to rattle and shake violently. The lid, which had been sitting only partially on the top of the Ark, fell away to the pit floor, and the God Stones began to rise from the Ark, one by one. Breanne watched helplessly as the stones floated or levitated impossibly, all the way into the silhouetted hands of Apep. Their only bargaining chip out of the pit had just floated away like a puff of smoke.

Apep cupped his hands as the God Stones settled softly in them, one after the other. His voice echoed off the pit walls, seemingly coming from everywhere all at once. "I have suffered centuries of longing, but I never gave up. I kept my faith that one day the wrong done to me would be made right, and I would be made whole. I *will* unleash hell upon this world. I *will* build my army. And by the gods, I *will* return to my world and have the vengeance on my father I am due."

Jerry stood next to Apep, his face washed in terror.

Paul yelled up from the pit below. "You can't leave us here! For Christ's sake, Jerry, my dad needs you. Ed is hurt! *We* need you – get us out!"

Jerry found his courage and looked to Apep. "You... Whatever you are. You can't leave them down there alone. At least two of them are injured. We have to help them. Dammit, this is madness! We have to help them now!" Jerry turned away from Apep. "I will find a rope my goddammed self."

The Secret Journal

Apep reached out and grabbed Jerry by the arm. "You're right, of course, Gerald. We can't leave them down there alone."

Breanne looked up towards the top of the pit and in a fleeting moment her mind flashed an image… only glimpsing it from the corner of her eye. She screamed out, "Jerry!"

Jerry nodded uneasily. "Well… alright, help me find a bloody rope."

"No, Gerald, I mean you should join them," Apep said, as he reached out and grasped the smartly dressed man by the throat, lifting him up off his feet. He turned with a sudden jerk, forcing the back of Jerry's legs to drag across the guard rail. He dangled out over the pit as Apep held him there with incredible strength.

Jerry struggled, kicking and trying to gasp a breath as his face turned from a horrible shade of red to purple. He flailed wildly, hammering his fist down upon the arm holding him with the steely grasp.

Breanne watched in horror as the British man's eyes bulged from his head as if about to burst from his face like a cork from a champagne bottle. She watched as Jerry dangled over the pit, clawing at his own chest, and she knew his heart was failing. She had seen it play out in the span of a second from the tiny flash in the corner of her eye. The panic racing through Jerry was enough to put him into cardiac arrest. Even if Apep was to stop, to somehow realize the horror of what he was doing, it was already too late – Jerry's heart was failing.

But Apep wasn't stopping. There would be no change of heart. She looked through Jerry's eyes and into Apep's, and they were not human. They were yellow embers of hate relishing the fear… and they smiled. Oh, how horribly they smiled. The eyes smiled back at him and through him to her.

She pressed her own eyes tightly closed, not wanting to see – but still she saw.

"Thank you, Gerald, but I no longer require your services," he said as he released the man's throat from his grasp, carelessly discarding him into the pit like some useless piece of trash.

Breanne covered her face and screamed.

Jerry sucked in a gasp, deep enough to release a terrified screech, only to be cut short as he collided with the golden Ark at the bottom of the pit. His body came apart upon impact in a horrifying explosion of twisted flesh and bone.

Muffled screams rang out in the pit as Breanne continued to scream through her hands. But hiding behind her hands hadn't stopped the splatter of blood and flesh from finding her, as it hurled in all directions around the pit.

As her scream faded to sobs, she heard Apep's laughter from atop the pit.

"When I get out of this pit, I will end you! Do you hear me up there?" Paul shouted. "So help me God – I will end you!"

Apep continued to laugh before finally settling down enough to address the young Moore. "It's just that today's, well, it's just such a damn fine day after so many bad ones. Today is a day of joy, a day of promise, and, yes indeed, a day of laughter."

"You're insane. I'm going to kill you for what you have done!" Paul shouted.

"Oh my, I don't think so. As fun as this has been, I think it's time I bid you adieu. I've much work ahead of me, much preparation. Now, admittedly, I am a little rusty, having gone so long without the power of the Sentheye, but what the hell, let's give it a try, shall we? I imagine it's like riding a bike."

Breanne wiped the blood and bits from her face, and for the second time in minutes her stomach wretched and she

The Secret Journal

heaved. She felt herself slipping back to another time and place. *No! Don't! Not now! Not the car!* Then something else. Her mind flashed a picture, a frozen frame of time still to pass. Only a glimpse of a particular moment to come. "Paul, we need to move now – get Daddy!" she yelled, running towards Edward.

Edward was awake, but his injuries appeared severe. "Ed, can you move? You have to move!" she begged.

"My leg is broken, maybe my ribs too, but yeah – I can move," he said, taking her hand.

She heaved, pulling him to his feet. "We have to get to the tunnel now!"

She looked back to find Paul dragging her unconscious father towards the tunnel, pulling him along with one hand like he weighed nothing. She frowned, not understanding. Adrenaline or fear? Perhaps a combination of both.

Apep stood next to the pit, one arm extended towards the giant crane. His hand was splayed open, palm facing the sky. He mumbled ancient words, and as he did, he drew on the power inside the stones. He drew on the Sentheye. As he moved his hand toward the pit, the crane followed, but the tracks were not moving. The crane wasn't even turned on. It was as if the crane was being dragged toward the pit by an invisible tow truck, but there was no tow truck… there was only Apep. The crane's giant bulk dug into the earth, trying to make a stand against whatever force pulled it. Like a young child stubbornly trying to refuse being pulled along, the crane stood no chance against Apep's power. Slowly, the crane was dragged through the soil, dirt mounding in front of the giant steel beast.

Apep laughed. "Indeed, I do remember how to ride a bike!"

Breanne and Edward scrambled towards the tunnel. She glanced back up towards the top of the pit and was instantly halted in stark terror. The frozen frame she had glimpsed came to pass as dirt rained down over the side of the pit and the giant crane blotted out the morning sun. Her hesitation lasted only a split second before she pushed Edward down into the hole of the tunnel. She threw herself into the tunnel behind her brother. She landed hard on top of Edward, causing him to grunt in pain, but there was no time for apologies or forgiveness as they both scrambled like combat soldiers under fire, belly crawling for safety, Breanne on her hands and knees and Edward dragging himself as he pushed frantically with his one good leg. They made it only a few feet away from the opening before the crane crashed into the floor of the pit in an earth-shaking crunch of steel. The braced ceiling creaked and flexed, threatening to collapse on them, and if the crane had hit the tunnel full-on, it surely would have.

Paul grabbed hold of the wrists of both his brother and sister and began pulling, simultaneously dragging them both. If Breanne didn't know better, she would swear she was being dragged by a horse. Once Paul had his momentum, he didn't stop until he reached the slope to the lower chamber, where he had left their father.

They sat there, gasping.

For a moment, everything was quiet. The only sounds were their heavy breathing and Edward's grunts of pain. Breanne wanted to start crying again, but she did not, would not – not now.

"I don't understand why Pops isn't waking up," Paul said. Then, shifting his attention to Edward, he began assessing his wounded leg. Paul removed his Ka-Bar tactical knife, the single piece of military equipment he never left home without. He flicked open the knife with an easy snap of the wrist and quickly began cutting the leg of Edward's cargo pants all the way up to the knee.

The Secret Journal

"How... bad... is it?" Edward asked.

"Pretty goddamn bad, bro, but from what I can tell, you'll live. Good news is you're not coughing up blood and your breathing sounds okay, so I don't think you punctured a lung. Your leg's broken, but the break is clean and somehow the bone hasn't come through... yet."

"Sucks... to be... me," Edward grunted.

Paul smiled. "Well yeah, I mean, you're ugly as shit. Whatever happened back there didn't fix your face, but you'll live."

"Dick."

"Agreed. But like I said, that's the good news. The bad news is this – I need to set that leg before we can even think about how we're going to get you out of here."

Edward grimaced at the notion.

"Bre, grab me some small pieces of wood." Paul began cutting the lower portion of Edward's pant leg into strips.

Breanne searched the area, finding a few pieces of wood around the same size that had splintered from the support structure when they had moved the altar earlier in the day. She handed the wood pieces to Paul. "What now?" she asked.

Paul pressed his lips into a tight line. "Now you hold his shoulders down."

Breanne swallowed and nodded.

"Ed, this is going to hurt like hell," Paul said, positioning himself to set the leg.

Edward didn't say a word – he just nodded and closed his eyes.

"One, two, three!" Paul flexed his hands, forcing Edward's leg bone into alignment with a fierce thrust.

Edward lurched and reared, screaming out in agony as he was flooded with pain. "Fuck me!"

Breanne held fast to her brother's shoulders as tears streamed down her face. She leaned in with all her weight, trying desperately to hold him still as his body bucked. Just as she thought she wouldn't be able to hold her big brother down, he suddenly went lax, slipping into unconsciousness. It pained her to see him in agony, and when he passed out she was almost relieved – almost.

Paul went to work right away, positioning the splint and tying the strips of cloth around the wood slats to hold them firmly in place. Once he was satisfied with his work, he searched the tunnel, scavenging another piece of wood. He found a long piece of two-by-four that could serve as a makeshift crutch.

Meanwhile, Breanne knelt at her father's side. This was all her fault. Why couldn't she stop him from opening the Ark? Why wouldn't he listen? She hadn't insisted enough. She hadn't stopped him. Now he wouldn't wake up. His breathing seemed normal, but he still wasn't waking up. It was like he was in a deep sleep or the other word for deep sleep. The one playing at the edge of her mind, and one she dared not say, not even think. *Please wake up, Daddy. Please!* she pleaded silently. She gently shook him, hoping somehow it might rouse him from unconsciousness, but if dragging him down into this tunnel didn't stir him, gentle nudging wasn't going to either.

"I'm going to look outside the tunnel and see if that psycho is gone. If he is, I'll see what we need to do to get out," Paul said.

Before Breanne could answer, it happened again. She saw something flash from the edge of her vision – something that shouldn't be there. "Paul, wake up Ed," she said.

"Maybe we should just let him rest for a bit while I try to figure out a plan to get us out of this pit."

"We don't have time, Paul! We have to get out of this tunnel right now!" she said, scrambling to her feet.

Paul's eyes widened. "Why, Bre? What's going to happen?" he asked.

She looked at him in surprise – *he knew she could see it.* "Apep is going to flood the swamp!"

"Bre, if he floods the swamp, this tunnel will flood!"

"We're going to drown, Paul!"

35

Do You Accept?

Wednesday, April 6th, 4:05 p.m.
Day One
Petersburg, Illinois

Garrett turned the knob and shouldered open the dojo door as he had a thousand times. The familiar smell of sweat and lemon cleaner hung in the air. Despite their run-in with Jack, the boys had arrived at the dojo directly after school as instructed.

Mr. B was standing in the middle of the mat, waiting, already dressed in his black dobok. He gave Garrett a long, hard, assessing look. "You cut your hair," he said flatly.

Garrett nodded. It was all the talk at school – some liked it, some hated it. When Lenny had seen it, he had pulled back, eyes wide. "I'm going to need some time to process what you have done to your head, bro." But for all the opinions, Garrett simply didn't care. He knew it was just hair, but somehow he felt different – as if cutting it marked the end of one thing and the beginning of something else.

"Change quickly and let's get started," Mr. B said evenly.

The Secret Journal

The boys removed their shoes and hustled to the locker room. They changed into their white doboks as quickly as possible and returned to the dojo. As they changed, Mr. B had set up two folding tables, each with three rectangular concrete patio blocks standing up on end, like giant dominos.

Garrett felt his apprehension rise, the scene reminding him of his test for black belt. He had passed each stage with ease, demonstrating perfect technique in his forms, his sparring, and even the required written essay on the history of taekwondo.

Everything had been going perfectly until they came to the part of the test where he was required to demonstrate power in the form of an open-hand palm strike through a concrete patio block. He had never attempted to break concrete before. He had broken plenty of wooden pine boards, even as many as five at one time, but never concrete. The concrete patio block sat only about a foot off the ground, spanning two cinder blocks.

"Look beyond the concrete, past it, then go there," Mr. B had said.

Garrett had positioned himself over the concrete patio block, careful to make sure his technique was perfect, his left foot out, his right foot back, his shoulders squared. He took in a deep breath, then leapt into the air, mustering all his strength into the force of the strike as he drove down with the full weight of his body. But when his hand struck the concrete, it did not break – and it hurt like hell.

He'd tried two more times to break the patio block, but his hand was deeply bruised and hurt so bad there was no way he could continue striking the concrete. Lenny crushed his block on his first attempt and passed the test, while Garrett would have to continue to wear the half-red, half-black probationary black belt. He never told anyone – not

Lenny, not even his mom – but he cried himself to sleep that night, so disappointed in himself for failing the break.

From that moment on, every time Garrett came to class there was a concrete patio block set up just for him, and every day Mr. B would say, *Look beyond the concrete, past it, and go there.* And every day he would look at that brick like he hated it, get into position, and strike it, but the damn thing just *would not* break.

This went on for a few weeks, but then one day he came into class and noticed something different about the patio block. It was there, just like always, set up the same way, but this time it was wet. Then he remembered that somewhere he had heard if you soak concrete in water it becomes softer. That's when he realized Mr. B must have soaked the block in water to make it easier for him to break! *This must be a trick to build my confidence or something,* he thought.

Mr. B pointed at the block and said the same thing he always said. "Look beyond the concrete, past it, and go there."

Garrett got into position and prepared for the umpteenth time to strike the block, though this time his confidence was high because the block had obviously been soaked in water. As he assumed the position to strike, Mr. B repeated the words, "Look beyond the concrete, past it, and go there."

Garrett looked over the edge of the block and focused on the floor. He leapt into the air and launched his hand downward with the same open-hand strike that had failed to break the concrete time and time again, but this time the concrete yielded – shattering into pieces. Garrett's hand continued downward until it struck the floor.

Lenny was there, of course, and cheered audibly for his friend. "I knew you could do it!"

Even Mr. B smiled approvingly as he handed him his black belt and bowed. "Well done."

The Secret Journal

Garrett looked down at the floor, ashamed.

"What is wrong, Garrett?" Mr. B asked.

"I didn't really break the block," he said sadly.

Mr. B frowned. "Leave us for a moment, Lenny."

Lenny crossed the dojo and began to do his warm-up routine on the heavy bag.

"What do you mean, you didn't really break it?" Mr. B asked.

"You soaked it in water to make it softer, easier for me to break." Tears began filling his eyes. "I can't take my black belt, not like this," Garrett said, handing his belt back to Mr. B.

Mr. B smiled. "Garrett, are you aware that it rained today?"

Garrett crinkled his brow and nodded.

"And are you aware I store the patio blocks out back?"

Again, Garrett nodded.

"Come here, let me show you something." They stepped over to the broken pieces of block now littering the floor. Mr. B reached down and picked up a piece of the broken block. "Garrett, I want you to look at this." He held out the broken piece of concrete.

Garrett looked but failed to understand right away. It wasn't until he turned the piece of stone over in his hand that he could see only the very outside of the stone was wet. "You mean you didn't soak it in water?" he asked, hope filling his voice.

"No, Garrett, it simply rained." He handed the belt back to his student. "Besides, who on earth told you soaking concrete in water made it softer? That is ridiculous," he said, smiling.

From that point forward, Garrett's confidence never waned and he had never again failed to break a patio block, whether it be for practice or for demonstration. But what he saw before him now shattered that confidence. Three blocks? And they were freestanding. They would have to hit the blocks so fast and hard they shattered before falling over. They had seen Mr. B do it, but they had never attempted a break like that. Garrett swallowed hard, unable to help the worry that played at the back of his mind. What if he couldn't do it and Lenny could? He didn't want to go through that again.

Over the next hour, they went through what felt like a pretty normal test, minus the fact that it was just Mr. B and the two boys. When it was time to be evaluated on forms, Lenny went first, executing his forms with flawless precision. Garrett went next, and all in all he thought his forms were good. Not as good as Lenny's, but his technique felt tight and movements crisp.

After forms, he and Lenny sparred with each other, and this part Garrett actually felt good about, that is until Mr. B yelled for them to stop.

Approaching Garrett, he said, "Where is your focus?"

"What?" Garrett asked uneasily.

"Your focus – find it."

Garrett frowned, that word again… *focus*.

Mr. B yelled, "Break!" and the two began sparring again.

But Garrett was off his game now more than ever, and if anything, the odd comment made him *less* focused.

A few minutes passed, Garrett trying to find his rhythm, before Mr. B motioned them to stop again. The boys were allowed a quick drink but told not to speak. They hustled to the water fountain, then back again, never saying a word. Mr. B explained the next part of the test would be the final part – the break. Again, Lenny was to go first, performing a knife-hand strike through the three concrete patio blocks. The blocks stood like a miniature row of ominous headstones, each spaced a few inches apart. Garrett knew this break was incredibly difficult and would take perfect form and perfect technique to execute.

Lenny bowed, stepped into position, and took a deep breath, exhaling very slowly. Pausing for a moment, he closed his eyes. Garrett knew he was clearing his mind and visualizing the break just as they had been taught. Then, falling into a comfortable fighting stance, he chambered his right fist. With a loud *kiup!* Lenny thrust his fist forward and opened it to a knife-hand strike. His rigid hand passed through the first brick, resulting in a chain reaction that broke the next brick and the next. They didn't explode like when Mr. B performed the strike in the alley so long ago, back when the boys first met him, but they broke nonetheless.

"Yes!" Garrett shouted as he threw a fist into the air for his friend. Mr. B shot him a disapproving look, but he couldn't help himself. Now it was Garrett's turn to break. Ready to take his position next to the table, he stepped forward and bowed to Mr. B, but his master did not bow back.

"No," Mr. B said evenly.

Garrett's eyebrows quirked. No? Had he heard that right?

"Lenny, come here." Mr. B beckoned, grabbing ahold of Garrett's table. He nodded for Lenny to do the same. Lenny obeyed and together they carefully placed it atop the other table – the table Lenny's blocks had sat upon. The blocks Garrett were to break now stood over eight feet in the air.

"Now, find your focus and break the blocks. Use any strike you like, but I would suggest a roundhouse kick as your best tool in this situation."

Mr. B bowed and stepped back.

Slack-jawed, Lenny looked at him with eyes wide.

"But, sir, that's more than two feet over my head. I can't reach it, and even if I could I wouldn't get there with the power to complete a three-block break," Garrett said, hoping this was some kind of joke, but finding no humor in it.

"You can't! You wouldn't! You fill my ears with excuses! You lack focus! You lack belief in yourself! Find it now or you fail the test! Now *complete* the break!"

Garrett didn't understand why this was happening. He didn't understand why his teacher was so angry with him. Why couldn't he just perform the break as Lenny had? At least then he had a chance. He considered pushing the table over and watching the blocks fall to the floor. There was a small chance they would break when they struck the mat, but he knew that was not what Mr. B wanted. *Then what?* he thought. He couldn't really expect him to perform a roundhouse kick eight feet off the ground

"Complete the break!" Mr. B snapped again.

"Master, focus isn't going to get my foot eight feet in the air with enough power to break those blocks," he said, pointing up at the patio blocks. And with that he felt his eyes beginning to blur with confused anger.

Lenny stepped forward. "Mr. B, I couldn't make that break in a hundred tries. Why can't he just do it the way I did? He could do it the way I did – I know he could!" Lenny's voice pleaded.

"Stop! I am not asking him to make the break you did, Lenny." He looked hard back to Garrett. "I am ordering you to make this break."

Garrett took a deep breath, trying not to let his emotions take over.

"Fine, I will give you another option," the master said. "You will spar with me. I will give you as much time as you want to score three strikes on me, but if you quit, can't go on, or give up in any way, the test is over and you fail. If you fail... never come back here again," he said, showing zero emotion.

What the hell did I do to deserve this? Then the answer came to him as suddenly as the question. The cigar box. *Could Mr. B have found out I looked inside?* Suddenly he felt sick. If he knew Garrett had looked inside the box, then it was also possible he knew he had seen the ring.

"Do you accept?" he asked.

"Yes… I accept," he said heavily, his shoulders slouching as he surrendered to whatever fate Mr. B had destined him for. He needn't throw a single strike to know he'd already lost. He had sparred with the master many times over the years but never, not one time, had he landed a strike on the man. He was untouchable, like sparring with a ghost. On rare occasions, he and Lenny had even gone doubles against him, neither landing a strike. But what other choice did he have? An eight-foot, three-block break was physically impossible.

Mr. B turned and walked to the center of the dojo. "Lenny, you have not passed the test yet. When Garrett and I are finished, I will tell you if you pass."

Lenny bit back his protest, bowed, and sat down, but he made no effort to hide the confusion creasing his face.

Garrett strained to control his inner turmoil as he wiped the tears away with the sleeve of his dobok. He met Mr. B in the middle of the dojo where, following tradition, they bowed first to Lenny, then to each other. Next, they shook hands, but before letting go of Garrett's hand, Mr. B pulled him close.

"Focus your mind, Garrett. It really is that simple."

Garrett assumed a fighting stance, sliding his right leg back and holding his left arm up, bent at the elbow. He held his right fist chambered next to his ribcage, ready to launch on command. Mr. B fell effortlessly into a similar position, and the two began to circle.

Garrett launched the first attack, throwing a combination

roundhouse kick, front snap kick, followed by a front knuckle punch.

Mr. B moved with subtle motions that were small, purposeful, and impossibly quick.

Garrett's opening attack not only failed, but Mr. B did not block a single strike as Garrett's assault simply found air. However, the flurry did leave Garrett's side exposed.

Mr. B fired a single palm strike into Garrett's right ribcage.

Garrett exhaled sharply with a loud *Oomph!*

The force sent him scrambling backward as he tried desperately to maintain his footing and not end up on his ass. The strike to his ribs made Jack's earlier stomp feel like a love pat.

Lenny flinched.

Garrett regained his composure, pulled a sharp breath, and launched into another attack, throwing combination punches and kicks, all easily blocked by Mr. B. The attack ended again with a single open-palm strike, this time to the solar plexus. Garrett gasped, straining to suck in the air stolen by the vicious strike.

For several minutes this continued as Garrett launched attack after attack, all ending in a single strike from Mr. B. The strikes became progressively harder and landed in more sensitive areas.

Garrett launched the next attack with everything he had, using his entire arsenal, from helicopter kicks to roundhouse kicks – even a jump spinning back kick, just for good measure. Not only was he unable to land a strike, Mr. B didn't even bother to block the assault. Instead, as before, he simply moved out of the way of every single attempt.

The irritation on Mr. B's face was evident as he stepped forward with a ridge-hand strike to Garrett's throat, causing the boy's feet to be lifted into the air until they were horizontal with his head. He landed hard on his back, all the air evacuating from his chest in a guttural *oomph*. For the second time, he gasped helplessly for air that he could not find.

Lenny stood. "That's enough!" he shouted.

"Lenny, sit down," Mr. B ordered.

"No, I don't think so. He's *had* enough," Lenny said, even louder.

The rotund man turned to Lenny and squeezed both hands into fists. His knuckles cracked, like popcorn popping. "What are you going to do, Lennard? You can stand next to your friend and fight me, but win or lose you *fail* the second-degree black belt test. By fail I mean you are never to return here again. Ever. Or you can select the better choice – you can *sit down*." He pointed to the spot Lenny had stood from.

"Master, I don't know what's going on here. I don't know why you are doing this, but I don't think there is any choice at all." Lenny walked over to Garrett, who still lay on the floor.

Trying not to vomit, trying to push the pain away, not wanting to get up, Garrett lay there, holding his throat, trying to find breath. As many times as they had sparred over the years, he had never been hit like this, never with so much force. In his heart, he knew this was not a winnable fight. His time here at the school was over – he had failed. But he could not let Lenny throw away his martial arts training, and he would not let him get kicked out of the school. Not for him. Not for something he had done.

Lenny knelt down next to his friend. "I'm here, man, I'm here."

Dragging himself to his hands and knees, Garrett reached up and grabbed Lenny's collar, pulling him close. "Lenny, thank you, man. Now… please… go sit down," Garrett said, trying to ignore the fire in his throat dominating all the other pain.

"But Garrett, you can't win this alone – let me help you," Lenny said, as he searched Garrett's eyes for understanding.

"You… can't, Lenny… it has to be me." He collapsed back down onto his stomach.

"But Gar—"

"Go sit down," Garrett croaked.

Lenny hesitated a moment longer, then reluctantly returned to his seated position at the edge of the dojo.

Garrett lay there, bile creeping up the back of his throat, trying to piece it together. Why was everyone telling him to focus? Wasn't that what he had been doing? He had tried everything he knew, thrown every attack he could think of. *What have I missed?* Then Coach Dagrun's paranoid whisper returned to him. *You know the place. Find it today – you will have to find it when you aren't running, Garrett – that's your door. That's the way to your focus.* Was the answer there, in Coach's words? Something told him it was, but how?

"Do you yield, Garrett?" Mr. B asked.

He rolled to his side and looked at Lenny, now sitting on his knees with his hands on his lap. He figured he must look pretty beaten because Lenny's eyes begged him to stay down. He gave Lenny a weak smile and crawled to his hands and knees again.

"No… I don't yield," he said, looking up at the hulking man.

"Very well then, rise," Mr. B said, motioning for the student to come to him as he settled back into his fighting stance.

Garrett pushed himself up. Blood, thick and coppery, filled his mouth – the result of a tooth puncturing his inner lip. Respect wouldn't allow him to spit on the floor but he couldn't swallow it either for fear of puking, so he spit it into the elbow of his dobok sleeve.

Lenny winced.

He sucked in a breath and felt the sharp pain from his ribs. He looked Mr. B in the eyes and let all his fear go from his mind. "I want… you to know that… that I know who you are! I know what you are!" he said, pointing at Mr. B.

Mr. B's eyebrow rose. "Do you?" he asked, deadpan.

"You're a Keeper of the Light! Your people killed Abraham Lincoln! You know I have his journal! You *know* I know about the temple, and that's why you're doing this to me!" Garrett said in an *aha* tone, like he had just announced Colonel Mustard did it in the Conservatory with the candlestick.

Lenny slapped his palm to his forehead, looking as if he might faint right there on the edge of the dojo mat.

Garrett exhaled a long breath and felt a massive weight somehow lift off his shoulders, a soul-crushing, unseen monstrosity he had been carrying around for over a week, *gone* with the few words he had spoken.

Mr. B's eyes widened in surprise, but when he opened his mouth to speak, Garrett let out a guttural war cry and launched himself at Mr. B in a dead run.

36

The Flood

Wednesday, April 6th, 9:30 a.m.
Day One
Oak Island, Nova Scotia

Paul dragged his unconscious father toward the opening to the pit. There was no time to waste; they needed out of the tunnel and fast. "When is it going to flood, Bre?" Paul asked in a panic.

"I don't know!" she shouted, doing her best to support Edward as they followed closely behind.

"Well, what do you see?" Paul asked, looking up at the hole and realizing the entire opening above him was blocked by the crane boom.

"I… I don't see anything now! It was like a flash. Apep was standing near the dam and water was gushing into the swamp – filling the tunnel!"

"How… do you know… his name, Bre?" Edward asked through gritted teeth as he collapsed onto the floor of the tunnel.

"I heard it in a dream," she said, knowing the explanation sounded crazy. But to her surprise, Edward only nodded.

"Bad news – we're trapped in this tunnel," Paul said, still assessing the obstruction.

Breanne's face contorted in terror. "What! No. We can't be – we'll drown!" She positioned herself under the opening next to her brother and began pushing on the crane boom, trying hopelessly to get it to move.

"You can't move it, Bre! That boom weighs tons, we're trapped. We need another way out!" Paul said.

They heard it before they felt it – water! It was rushing towards them from the rock-filled portion of the tunnel leading back to the swamp. A moment later, cold ocean water rushed over their feet, like a small wave lapping onto shore, except this wave didn't recede – it just kept coming.

Breanne screamed. She felt trapped. She was trapped. Just like in the car. God! She was trapped like in the car.

"Listen to me, Bre, we have some time. Stay calm. You are okay. We are okay. We just need to think of a way out of this. In the meantime, I need you to breathe and think. Focus on the problem," Paul said with a glassy calm. If there was one thing his military training and time in the field had taught him, it was the ability to stay calm.

Edward struggled to push himself to a seated position.

Breanne blinked numbly and reached for Edward, helping him out of the water. Then she and Paul heaved their father up, and he sagged back against the wall of the tunnel. They needed her. Her father needed her. She couldn't let herself go there. She couldn't. She wouldn't. *Dammit, breathe. Just breathe.*

The water rose.

Edward leaned back heavily. "The water is rising… Listen… The lower chamber… leads to the Ark room… remember what Pops said? … The ark room never got wet. It was… high enough to… to stay dry even when the chamber was flooded," he grunted.

"That's not an option, Ed. Or did you forget the plants that tried to kill us?" Paul said.

"If it is a choice between high ground or drowning, it may be the only choice."

"Then what? What do we do when we get there? We'll be trapped and probably killed!" Breanne argued.

"Maybe, the plants died… when we took the Ark… took their power?" Edward said.

"There is no way I'm going back there!" Breanne said.

"What choice do we have, Bre? If we stay here, we'll drown!" Paul said.

Edward shivered as the cold water flowed over his legs. Because he was unable to position himself into a squat like his siblings, half his body was quickly becoming submerged. "He's right, Bre. If we go… we have a… chance to figure something out, but if we stay… we'll drown for sure."

Breanne shot Edward a worried look. He was losing color in his face and looked as though he may pass out or go into shock any minute. "You can't make it through the chambers and up that climb, Edward," she said sadly. "And how would we get Daddy there without drowning him?"

"But we're going to drown anyway if we don't move now!" Paul shouted, his calm slipping. "We have no other choice!"

"We do have a choice!" she shouted back.

"What? Tell me, Bre, because I don't see it! All I see is us dying if we don't move now!"

The water was moving swiftly, getting deeper by the second, almost up to their knees now. Breanne struggled to hold on to her father to keep him from washing down the tunnel. She knew the sudden increase in water flow must mean the swamp was filling faster than the tunnel could take it in, increasing the pressure through the tunnel.

"Paul, move the crane!" Bre ordered.

"What? I told you, that thing weighs a couple tons – we can't move it! Not even if we all push together! Now goddammit we're out of time. We *have* to move – now!" Paul grabbed ahold of his father, preparing to drag him.

Breanne grabbed her brother by the arm. "Paul, listen to me. Not us – you're right. We can't move it. But you can!"

Paul locked eyes with her. "What are you talking about?"

"You can move it, the same way you dragged Daddy and Ed when the crane fell!"

"That's the stupidest thing I've ever heard. We have to move now before it's too—"

"It's already too late! Look at the water. The lower chamber will be filled by now! How are we supposed to get Daddy through – he isn't going to hold his breath, is he? I know you can do this. Can't you feel it in your mind?" she asked.

"Feel what?" he asked.

"Feel… different," she said, her eyes pleading for him to feel what she felt. "Listen to me. Whatever was in that Ark, it did something to us – it changed us. I *know* you can feel it! For God's sake, Paul, you dragged Daddy and Ed at the same time. That's nearly five hundred pounds!"

The tunnel was over half full now. The water rushed past them, vanishing over the slope into a finality – icy, dark, and awful. When the bottom chambers finished filling, their fate would rapidly rise to meet them.

Paul turned away from her and peered desperately back towards the slope leading to the lower chambers.

Breanne began crying, holding her father close, trying frantically not to let him slip away from her grasp in the ever-pressing gush. Edward held on to a board with one of his massive arms as he tried to help hold their father with the other. But in his condition, he was little help. Breanne watched helplessly as Edward's eyes rolled back, then forward, then back again. He was going into shock. His consciousness was slipping away along with his grip and, any second, he would be washed away from her, gone from her life… just like her mother.

Paul chewed his lower lip.

"Please, Paul!" she begged.

Paul made his decision and pushed himself into a squatting position under the opening to the pit floor. He looked back at her. Reaching above his head, he grabbed ahold of the twisted steel of the crane boom with both hands and pushed. He strained with every ounce of his strength, pushing and pushing and pushing and then… nothing. It didn't budge, not even a little.

"Dammit, this is stupid! It's impossible!" he shouted, looking at Breanne.

Breanne calmed herself as best she could. "Listen to me, Paul. You can move it, but you have to stop thinking."

"Stop what! What are you even talking about, Bre? We're going to drown!" Paul pleaded, losing whatever remained of his characteristic calm. "Edward is about pass out! Pops won't wake up, and now I don't even think I could get us to the dry chamber even if I wanted!" he said, his own eyes beginning to well with frustration. "What the hell is 'stop thinking' supposed to mean?" he shouted.

The water was three-quarters of the way to the top of the small tunnel, leaving them only about a foot of space. She pushed her father's head up, and he slipped off the wall. She gasped, grabbed his collar, and wedged her foot across the tunnel. "Paul! We are not going to die here, okay?"

"But we are, Bre! Jesus, don't you get it! We *are!*"

"I have already seen you move it. I know you will. But

you have to forget the water, forget us, and just focus on the crane." She shoved her shoulder against her father's chest as she pressed her feet into the opposite wall of the tunnel.

He stared at her for a long beat, confusion pasted across his face. "You've seen it?"

"Yes. I've seen it."

"You're sure?" he asked, a hint of hope in his voice.

"Yes, now please, I can't hold Daddy here forever. Move the crane!"

He positioned himself again, took a deep breath, and pushed and pushed and pushed.

Breanne could see nothing was happening. "Stop thinking about the water, just think about the crane. See it moving. Visualize it moving in your mind."

Closing his eyes, he tried to do as she said.

Edward's eyes fluttered closed and he slumped over.

With the collar of her father's shirt balled into her fist, she reached out with her other hand, snatching ahold of the cuff of Edward's pants. "Forget all about the water and us. Just focus on the crane and pushing it out of the way. Push with your muscles and mind at the same time. Picture it moving, Paul."

He shook out his hands, reached up, and pushed.

The crane began to creak.

Suddenly, he dropped down several inches through the wooden floor of the tunnel, the sheer weight pressing him down. He relaxed a little more as he pushed again, his feet sinking even deeper as the crane groaned louder.

"That's it, Paul, you're doing it!" Breanne gasped. The water was up to her neck now, with less than a foot between the water and the ceiling of the tunnel. She was afraid to move – afraid the slightest twitch would lift her away and send the three of them plummeting down the tunnel.

Slowly, the crane started to yield to him. Its giant boom

inched ever so slowly across the opening as he extended his arms and forced it to shift until an opening appeared. It was small, but it was enough.

Collapsing, Paul slumped back against the wall of the tunnel.

"Paul, help me!" Breanne begged. Pushing himself back up, he tore his feet from the floor of the tunnel and grabbed his unconscious father from Breanne's white-knuckled grasp. After heaving the large man through the hole, he pulled Edward up and out, followed by Breanne. Once they were all free of the tunnel, Edward slipped into full-on unconsciousness.

Breanne checked her father's pulse and assessed his breathing. "Daddy's barely breathing and his pulse... I can't find it! Why won't he wake up? Why?" she shouted. "Is it because he was closer to the stones than we were?"

"I don't know." Paul knelt at her side to try and find a pulse. "There! He has a pulse. It's weak, but it's there. His breathing is shallow. We need to get him out of this pit, and we need to get him help."

Her head buzzed with questions. Maybe it was because he was older and maybe not as physically capable of taking the strain? Or her worst fear, he hit his head so hard when he was thrown into the wall of the pit that he suffered brain damage and was now in a... coma. *God, please don't let him be in a coma. Please wake him up, God! Please!*

"Breanne," Paul said, pulling her back to the moment.

She turned to face him.

"You knew? You knew I could move it? You said you saw me doing it. You can see the future?" he asked in wonder.

Her hands shook uncontrollably as she turned to assess Edward. "No. I mean, yes. Sorta... yes," she said, her forehead creased with worry.

He grabbed her hands in his. "It's going to be alright,

Bre. We will get out of this. Tell me, how did you know, please?"

"I knew you could do it because I saw the way you pulled Ed and Dad down the tunnel at the same time. I knew something happened to me when the Ark was opened. After watching you move them so easily, I knew something happened to you too."

"So, you didn't see me doing it before I actually did it?"

"No… I didn't. I'm sorry I lied to you but—"

"Breanne! Look!" Paul interrupted, pointing at the hole they had just climbed through. Water burst from the hole in a turbulent gush that covered the pit floor within seconds.

"The lower chambers must be full! What do we do?" she asked, holding her father's head up to keep him from breathing in the water while Edward leaned against the crane, safe from downing for the moment.

"It's filling fast! Really fast! God, we can't get a break!" Paul said, wading in the already knee-deep water around to the opposite side of the crane, beyond Breanne's sight.

"Wait! Help me, Paul, it's getting too deep – I won't be able to keep both their heads above the water!" She pulled her now-floating father closer to her brother.

A few seconds later, Paul returned with a coil of rope slung over his shoulder, pushing several four-by fours through the water. "Give me a few more seconds," he said as he lashed the boards together.

"Please hurry!"

"Here," he said, pushing the makeshift raft close to her. The water had reached her waist and already consumed Edward's shoulders in his seated position. "Hold the raft still for me," Paul said.

Breanne held the raft in place as she watched her brother pick up their father and sling him onto the raft, positioning his torso on the boards while allowing his legs to hang off.

Then he positioned his head to the side so he wouldn't suck in any water. Quickly he repeated the process with Edward, placing him chest down over the boards and turning his head to protect him from inhaling water.

After only two minutes, the water level had climbed to over five feet. Both Breanne and Paul held tight to the ends of the raft.

"Is this your plan – we just float to the top?" Breanne asked, already shivering from her time in the cold water.

"It's all I got," he said, peering at her from around the edge of the raft. "It will be okay – at this rate, we should be at the top in less than an hour," he smiled assuredly.

"It's a good plan, but there's a problem," Breanne said, teeth chattering.

Paul's teeth began to chatter too.

"It's not going to fill all the way up. It's going to stop about thirty feet short of the top."

"Crap! Did you see that or something?" he asked.

"No, I just know the history of this place, and I know that in the past, attempts to dig out the Money Pit always ended up the same. The hole doesn't fill to the top. It stops about thirty feet short."

Breanne gazed up to the sky far above the pit. A sea hawk circled silently and patiently against a backdrop of blue. Waiting, she knew. Waiting for the inevitable. Waiting for them to die. Breanne's whole body shuddered uncontrollable. "We… need… another plan… Paul."

37

Focus

Wednesday, April 6th, 5:05 p.m.
Day One
Petersburg, Illinois

Garrett fired a volley of kicks and strikes with perfect technique. This was no longer sparring. This was an all-out assault on Mr. B at a level Garrett never imagined himself capable of. He held nothing back. Every kick and punch was meant to cause real damage. Still, he couldn't hit the master. Mostly, he was only hitting air, which he actually preferred to Mr. B blocking his strikes. His wrists and ankles were bruised and stinging from the forceful blocks.

He knew Lenny's mind must have been struggling to process his accusations towards their longtime teacher. He only wished he had told him before this happened. Lenny had to know the Mr. B they knew would not act like this, would not treat them like this, would not hurt them like this, didn't he? He had to know their Mr. B would never threaten to ban them from the dojo, *their second home*. Lenny had to know something was wrong. Seriously wrong. He wanted so bad to glance towards Lenny, but to take his eyes off Mr. B during an assault was to ask to be kicked in the face.

By the end of Garrett's volley, not a single strike had landed. Once again, he had failed to hit Mr. B, and once again Mr. B had waited for his attack to finish before counterattacking with a single strike.

Mr. B stepped in with his right leg and went into a spin.

Garrett knew what would come next, and he simply couldn't stop it. Pain. His body went tense. The universe expanded a little more, as inevitable as the passing of the moment itself.

Then something happened to Garrett. He let go.

In that moment he surrendered to himself and accepted it all. He closed his eyes and drew in a single breath. Then he smelled it… the forest floor, damp leaves, crisp air.

He frowned. He opened his eyes. Mr. B's foot slowly pivoted, his knee bending slightly. Everything around Garrett suddenly slowed. Somehow, the moment itself slowed. He watched Mr. B's foot sliding into place.

A bird sang and leaves crunched under his feet. He was no longer in the dojo. He was out on the trails at New Salem. He was bombing down his favorite section, a devilish piece of single-track trail. He could feel the cool spring air on his face and smell the forest all around him as dirt churned under his feet. The uneven terrain, tree roots, and large rocks jutted out everywhere, refusing to be called anything less than perilous. He was running as hard as he could, his mind instinctively processing everything around him. Foot placement wasn't even a thought, but rather an involuntary action, like breathing or blinking, and he didn't need to watch for low-hanging branches, he just dodged them impulsively. This feeling was more than familiar—it was home. He had been here before, on this very stretch of trail, shredding it, owning it, everything happening instinctually.

Was this the focus?

Garrett pulled himself back from the trail and wondered, *how long was I there?* It felt like a long time to be distracted – too long. But he knew this was more than a distraction. He felt as though he had physically gone there.

Yet, as his vision refocused, Mr. B's foot had only now completed its pivot motion, locking into place. He must have run the whole stretch of trail in his mind in a nanosecond. He read Mr. B's foot placement and body position like a seasoned defensive lineman. *He's going to spin into a back fist and strike me in the face.* He waited, easily, patiently, as everything around him continued to slow. Time still stretched on, like a long piece of taffy being slowly pulled.

Mr. B completed the slow-motion spin before striking out with the back fist. *Why was he moving so slowly?* Finally, the fist reached him. Garrett ducked, slipping easily under the strike. Then, unbelievably, Mr. B made a gross error, the first Garrett had ever seen him make. Mr. B tried to recover the miss by slapping his open palm into the back of Garrett's head in an attempt to grab for his ponytail, but there was no ponytail to grab. *He's human after all. He can make a mistake!* Smiling, he ducked again, easily, then he countered with a knuckle punch to the back of Mr. B's upper arm. His own movements were at normal speed. The strike forced the sensei off-balance and placed Garrett slightly behind him. For a split second his master's back was exposed. It might as well have been an eternity as Garrett struck again, fast and hard. But this time he aimed his fistful of knuckles at Mr. B's right kidney.

Mr. B yelped in pain, spinning around to meet Garrett at normal speed.

Lenny blinked disbelievingly. "Hooolllyyy shit!"

"That's one!" Garrett said, holding up a finger triumphantly.

Mr. B nodded, the tight line of his lips curling into a devious smile. Then, for the first time, Mr. B hurled himself forward into an offensive attack.

Lenny leapt to his feet.

With overwhelming force, Mr. B. threw strike after strike in forward combinations of complex movements.

Garrett half ran, half stumbled backward across the dojo with Mr. B's assault ending in a sidekick that he somehow managed to block, for whatever good it did. The force of the kick sent him bouncing off the mirrored wall, fracturing the glass panel with a loud *Pop!* of splintering glass. Shards of mirror fell from the webbed fractures, raining down on Garrett from above, as he slowly got to his feet. This time he managed to keep his breath.

Lenny stepped onto the mat, but Garrett waved him off.

Garrett attacked again, and again failed to make contact. Desperately he tried to focus his mind, trying to find his way back to the trails, trying to slow the moment. The harder he tried, the more it seemed to elude him. *Stop trying,* he told himself.

He drew in a deep breath, and smells of the forest filled his lungs.

Mr. B countered with a front snap kick, but before the kick extended Garrett matched it, blocking the kick with his own, then, instead of setting the foot back down, he kicked upward and struck Mr. B in the face.

Garrett gasped.

Mr. B wiped his fingers across his mouth and looked at the blood, rubbing it between his fingers. Glancing back up at Garrett, he wiped the blood on his dobok, smiled, and nodded.

"That's two!" Lenny shouted with excitement. "One more, Garrett! One more!"

With incredible speed, impossible for a man his size, Mr.

The Secret Journal

B attacked again. Though Garrett managed to block most of the assault, he could not match the speed of the determined master, as the last three strikes found purchase. Two punches to the gut and a jarring open-palm strike to the right ear, followed by a wrist throw that ended in Garrett landing hard on his back. The pain was disorienting, blurring his mind, filling it with a fuzzy spinning sensation. He scrambled again for the trail of his mind, but it was lost to him. He closed his eyes and took in a breath, but he could not smell the forest or see the trees. Instead, his mind filled with the color of agony.

Mr. B did not wait for him recover. Before Garrett could find his bearings, Mr. B flung his foot high above his own head, only to drive it back down, heel first. This was a kick of absolute destruction, used to break blocks… or bones. The kick was known as the axe kick, and both boys had seen Mr. B use the devastating kick to crush stacked slabs of concrete with ease.

Garrett never saw the axe kick coming.

Lenny did.

As Mr. B's foot extended upward, Lenny leapt from his sitting position, hurling himself towards his teacher. "No! You'll kill him!" Lenny screamed as Mr. B's powerful leg drove the heel of his foot downward like the head of a sledgehammer. Lenny dove at Mr. B's opposite leg, knocking it out from underneath him.

The large man landed hard on his back.

With almost supernatural fluidity, Mr. B rolled onto the palms of his hands and launched himself back to his feet.

Garrett also rose to his feet, but there was nothing fluid or magical about it. The world still spun slightly as he fought back the nausea.

"You have made your choice, Lenny. You understood the

consequences and still you chose to disobey me." Facing the two boys, he bowed. "We are finished here."

"No!" Lenny shouted. The word escaped his mouth more forcefully than he meant it to. He turned to his friend. "We're not finished here."

"No, we… sure aren't," Garrett said, smiling through the pain. He didn't have to force the smile. Lenny brought it out of him. His best friend in the world would not let him down. They would not let each other down. Not ever.

"There is no need to continue the test. You have both failed. Garrett, my hopes were high and I thought… I thought you were ready," Mr. B said, clearly disappointed.

But it was too late, an unseen signal had been given. Perhaps a look or maybe a hand gesture. Or perhaps no signal at all. Maybe the two friends just knew each other that well. Whatever the catalyst, they were not about to let it end like this. This wasn't about the test, not anymore.

Both boys stepped back comfortably into attack positions.

Mr. B straightened, raised an eyebrow, and bowed. "Have it your way."

They leapt at Mr. B in unison, attacking from both his right and left.

Mr. B didn't respond the same as he had one-on-one with Garrett. He spun in and out of their attacks, utilizing hapkido joint manipulation to toss the boys to and fro. He would grab one by the wrist, pulling him close, using him as a shield, causing the other to hesitate for fear of striking the wrong person. In a few instances, one of the boys did actually strike the other. Their confusion and hesitation led to swift and vicious counter attacks, and in that cool evening hour, both boys learned of pain.

Garrett noticed Mr. B turning most of his attention to Lenny. Seemingly, the teacher felt the need to help the boy catch up on all the beating he had missed out on while sitting lineside. The combination executed on the disobeying student was almost spiteful. The final kick combination ended in a powerful spinning back kick to the center of Lenny's chest, lifting him off his feet, sending him airborne, slamming him into the wall of the dojo. Upon impact, every ounce of air evacuated from Lenny's chest. The young man's body shattered a section of mirrored glass, just as Garrett's had, but with much more force. His body was driven so hard into the wall, the drywall itself collapsed under the force, leaving a large impression. Lenny crumpled to the floor. His eyes were wide with panic as he strained to breathe.

Garrett's ribs, back, and head throbbed painfully and, thanks to the ridge-hand strike to the throat, it hurt to swallow. Even through the pain and intense moments of battle, he searched his mind for the trail, the door to his focus, but it had been out of reach. Now Lenny, his best friend in the world, lay on the floor unable to get up, gasping for air. He had been crushed into a heap after coming to his aid, all while knowing he would lose not only this fight but his future at the school.

Suddenly, Garrett knew exactly what to do.

On his feet once again, Garrett backed away from Mr. B to the opposite end of the dojo. There, the two tables still stood, stacked one on top of the other. Upon the upper table stood the three stones, mocking him, like stars in the night sky… hopelessly untouchable.

"I choose the break," Garrett said hoarsely, his right hand covering his bruised ribs as he stared back at Mr. B.

Mr. B pressed his lips into a tight line, narrowing his eyes at Garrett.

Lenny lifted his head. Deep lines creased his brow in a combination of confusion and pain as he managed to wheeze out a whisper of words through sharp gasps of air. "But… that break's… not possi—"

"I *choose* the break." It was an exhausted plea.

Mr. B searched Garrett's eyes. He looked as though he might say something, but no words came. Instead, he slowly nodded, then, taking two steps back, he nodded and bowed.

38

Trust and Protect

Wednesday, April 6th, 9:45 a.m.
Day One
Oak Island, Nova Scotia

Pushing off from the raft, Paul swam over to a barely visible piece of the crane. It was part of the telescoping boom that had broken off, but was now wedged against the wall of the pit. The boom was constructed of latticed steel rods. Paul grabbed onto the section above the water and heaved a leg over it.

"What… are you… doing?" Breanne asked as she clung to the raft. The cold water was becoming unbearable and threatened to send her into hypothermia.

"I'm… trying to pull… this steel framework… apart." He grunted, pulling on the steel with everything he had, but nothing happened.

Breanne thought about the way the crane hadn't moved until he was truly afraid they were going to drown. "Paul… concentrate… please. We're going to freeze in this water. Whatever… you're trying… to do… please… hurry."

He looked back towards Bre, Edward, and his unconscious father. "You're right. We have to get out," he said, pulling so hard his body shook. He looked desperately at his sister.

Breanne nodded weakly. "Just... relax." Her whole body jackhammered as she shook uncontrollably, her body attempting to generate heat that the frigid water pulled away from her with relentless cruelty.

She watched on as her brother shook out his hands and closed his eyes. With a deep breath, his body appeared to go slack. *That's it, Paul. You can do this,* she thought. Slowly the steel boom groaned like a mighty oak being forced into an unnatural bend. With a final, wrenching jolt, a foot-long section of steel broke free from the boom.

Paul reached up and stuck the piece of metal into the dirt wall of the pit for safekeeping before grabbing another section. Once more, he strained with all he had to break the piece of steel loose from the structure. Again, it was only when he relaxed and concentrated that the steel broke free from the latticed framework.

Taking the piece of steel already protruding from the wall in his left hand, he pulled himself up. Next, he plunged the steel held in his right hand into the wall as high as he could reach. Pulling the rod in his left hand free, he again pulled himself up. Then in a giant arc he swung his left arm up as high as he could reach and thrust the rod into the dirt.

Now it became clear to Breanne what her brother was doing. He was going to scale the pit wall using the two pieces of steel as spikes. *My God!* she thought. *This might actually work!*

It did work. In only a few short moments, Paul had ascended the wall and disappeared over the top of the pit. *What if Apep is up there? What if he came back? Wait,* she told herself. *Calm down, Bre.* In her heart, she was somehow sure he had gone. She no longer felt his presence on the island, but then again, she wasn't certain she would. She was freezing and all she could concentrate on was how cold she was. This strange new... *Ability? Sixth sense?* Whatever it was, it might not even be working now. Maybe she wouldn't know he was there at all. Maybe the ability could come and go. Maybe when the stones were away from here, their abilities would be gone too? Maybe when the stones were far enough away her father would wake up? Her heart caught in her throat. *Daddy.* She needed out.

Abruptly, her concentration broke when a length of rope connected to a safety harness nearly struck her in the face.

"Bre, can you put the harness on Pops?" Paul shouted from topside, the silhouette of his head and shoulders poking out over the side of the pit.

"I'll try," she shouted back between chattering teeth. It was still a good distance to the top, probably seventy-five feet or so. But just as she had thought, the water had stopped rising.

"You have to get it secure. We don't want to risk him falling out."

She was trying, but her fingers were going numb from the cold water, and even if she could feel her fingers, trying to maneuver her large father around while unconscious and slung across a raft was not going to be easy. She was afraid if she knocked him off the raft, she might not be able to keep him above water long enough to get the harness on. Carefully, she worked the harness around him, first one side, then the other. Finally, when she was satisfied she had it secured, she signaled for Paul to begin pulling. She heard an engine and realized Paul must be using his truck to pull her father up.

Her father's slumped form rose from the water and slid

lifelessly up the sheer side of the pit. Once he vanished over the top, she let out a long sigh of relief.

Moments later, the harness and rope came hurling towards her again from the top of the pit. This time she was paying attention, quickly retrieving the harness and going to work on Edward. Floating in and out of consciousness, Edward moaned as Breanne tried to get the harness on him. Suddenly his eyes opened weakly, finding his baby sister.

"You okay?" he asked in barely a whisper.

"I'm... okay. Just... cold," she said, giving him a faint smile. "Can you lift your arm?"

"Well, I can't feel my leg. So, I guess—" Edward's eyes rolled back in his head and he shut off like a light switch, slipping once more into unconsciousness.

Struggling, Breanne somehow managed to secure Edward's harness and signaled to Paul with a wave.

Paul fired up the truck and began pulling Edward up the wall of the pit, but about halfway up Breanne noticed Edward's harness slipping over his head.

Breanne gasped.

The harness pulled completely free just as Edward's eyes popped open.

Breanne flinched away, bracing herself for the inevitable splash to come. But the splash didn't come. Edward didn't fall. Instead, he looked up at the harness as it slowly moved away from him, then he looked down at the water below, frowning. Just before the harness was out of reach, he stretched his arm up and grabbed a fistful.

A second later, Edward was being pulled over the lip of the pit.

What? But how? Breanne thought. She shook her head back and forth. She was sure she had seen the harness pulling away. Was she sure? Maybe the cold water was getting to her?

The harness came back over the pit, and two minutes later she was being pulled over the side.

Safe and free of the underground death trap, Breanne found herself with no time to celebrate. Her father and Edward were lying prone a few feet from the pit. "We have to go!" she said as she frantically unclipped the harness.

"I know. We have to get them to a hospital," Paul said, running back toward the truck.

"Paul! Wait!" Breanne yelled after him.

Paul slid to a stop and turned around. "What?" he asked.

"How far is the hospital? Should we call an ambulance?"

"Too far. I have a better idea. We have a helicopter, and I can sure as hell fly it."

"Okay, but we have to hurry. We have to get the stones back. We have to find Apep and get the stones." She knew in her heart it was the only way to save her father and if she failed – oh dear God, if she failed it would be her fault. It would be her fault just like with her mom. No, she could not let that happen.

"How? We have no idea where that… that thing took them!"

"Petersburg," she said matter-of-factly. "We have to go to Petersburg, to the land of Lincoln – to find Garrett." There, she said it. *That didn't sound quite as ridiculous as I thought it would sound.*

Paul stared blankly at her for a long moment. "Where in the hell is that?"

"Well, I'm not exactly sure yet," she said.

"Bre?"

"Yeah?"

"How do you know all this? How?" Paul asked.

It all came out in a hurried scramble of words flowing from her mouth like a fire hydrant being purged in the street. "I had a dream. A horrible dream of fire, and the Templar was there, and he told me we need to go to Petersburg to find this kid, Garrett, and he was in the dream too, and… my God, Paul, people were burning, and the Templar spoke, and he said it's the only chance to help Daddy, and—"

"Okay, okay… alright, Breanne," he said finally.

"Okay?" she asked in surprise.

"Yeah, okay. I believe you," he said.

Breanne threw her arms around her brother and squeezed him tightly. "Thank you, Paul. I honestly didn't think you'd believe me."

Paul smiled weakly. "I have no choice but to believe you."

Relinquishing her embrace, she pulled back to meet his gaze. "What's that mean?"

"I had a dream too. A dream of fire and burning people," Paul said, swallowing hard as he squeezed his eyes together, as if trying to force the horrible memory away.

"And you saw the Templar?"

He nodded. "Yes, I saw him and he spoke to me."

Breanne brightened as his words confirmed she wasn't delusional. "And he told you about Petersburg? About Garrett?" she asked.

"No… not exactly."

Breanne's eyebrows knitted in surprise as she searched his eyes. "Then what?"

"He told me to trust you. Trust you and protect you."

Breanne blinked.

"So, baby sis – how do we get to Petersburg?"

39

Feathers

Wednesday, April 6th, 5:20 p.m.
Day One
Petersburg, Illinois

Jumping up to reach the stones was not an option and Garrett knew it. There was simply no way to get to that height with the power he needed. The key to this had to be the focus. Garrett closed his eyes as he settled back into a fighting stance, facing the tables head-on. He drew in a long slow breath, exhaled, and drew in another. His pain subsided. The sound of leaves rustling through trees filled his ears and a cool breeze hit his face. *Stay with me... Please... Stay with me.* He opened his eyes and thrust his right leg outward, curling his toes backward as the simple, but powerful, front snap kick struck the underneath of the lower table with a loud *crack*. The two tables lifted into the air, causing the patio blocks to launch skyward towards the ceiling.

Lenny gasped.

The trail rushed back to Garrett, filling all his senses. The faint smell of sweet crab apple mixed with the fresh scent of pine. He could practically taste it. A rod of light pierced the forest canopy, bathing him in the warmth of the sun. He squinted into it as he ran. Up ahead he could see a creek crossing. Water crashed around him, so real he could feel the coolness against his skin, the splashing over his feet, water kicking up onto his thighs, as the trail led him bounding through the shallow creek. Everything around him slowed as the vision cleared from his mind like a daydream.

The three stones slowly rose, each at different heights, surging skyward through space. The stones stretched up and up until gravity finally took hold, then they paused for an abnormally long second, maybe two, suspended perfectly. Garrett watched as each stone slowly made its way down towards the ground. Not like a stone falling, but like a feather drifting lightly, gliding downward on unseen currents. When the first stone came within reach, Garrett jumped, kicking upward with the same front snap kick he used to kick the table, but the jump allowed him to get much higher. Instantly, he realized he was not moving at the same speed as the world around him. As he watched the stone slowly rotating, his foot extended out above his head, connecting dead center on the spinning concrete block.

The patio block exploded in real time – a burst of fragmenting concrete.

Before his feet found the mat of the dojo, his eyes locked on another concrete block. This one was closer to him, already at shoulder height. Sliding his left foot forward as he landed, he chambered his right fist next to his ribcage. Without hesitation, he stepped forward with his right foot, set to launch a front knuckle punch through the stone. But it was too close. With only inches between himself and the stone, if he tried to punch there was no way he would have the power to break it. In this fraction of a second, he changed fluidly from the front knuckle strike to an elbow strike, as

The Secret Journal

easily as changing from a long step to a shorter step when measuring space between roots and rocks on the trail.

He connected with the patio block dead center and, like the first block, it exploded in real time into a burst of concrete scattering across the mat.

The third and final stone had fallen to waist height directly off his left side. It was spinning awkwardly in the air, not like the first two. He had been able to front snap kick the first block from underneath as it tumbled horizontally in the air. The second block had spun vertically, allowing him to take it head on, pushing his power through it as he stepped forward. But this block was tumbling catawampus, neither vertically nor horizontally, and it was too low to take from below or beside. He would have to strike it from above. Garrett watched the block summersault askew, mentally measuring every rotation as if he had all the time in the world. He turned into a left spin while drawing his right fist deep into his ribs as if he were trying to get his fist into his armpit. Too afraid he might just push the block down into the floor, he couldn't risk an open-hand strike. He would have to punch through the block with a closed fist if he were to have any hope at all. Squeezing the tips of his fingers tightly to his palm, he curled his thumb firmly over his index finger and formed a fist he hoped would be tight enough to shatter concrete. With the block to his right side, his left spin took him away and forced him to lose sight of the block for a split second, but he needed both the space and momentum.

Garrett not only had to find the block after the spin, he had to find, strike, and break a block that was falling downward with a downward strike from above. He had never seen anyone, not even Mr. B, break a block that was falling downward while utilizing a downward strike, but Garrett didn't have time to think about any of that. In fact, only one thought ran through his mind in this fleeting moment. A special mantra, taught to him by a grand master. Despite the beating Mr. B had just given him, it was the wisdom he had shared so long ago when Garrett struggled to break his first block that played over and over in his mind as he watched the block tumble downward.

Look beyond the concrete, past it, and go there.

Garrett completed the spin while at the same time sliding into position for the break. The stone was at knee level but not in the position he needed it to be in.

He sucked in a short breath.

The block fell to shin height as he found the center. He imagined what the mat would feel like against his knuckles and punched downward, releasing a guttural *kiup!*

His fist connected with the block.

The block burst into pieces as Garrett's fist passed through the concrete and sank into the mat. Chunks of stone bounced before settling around his fist and feet. Kneeling on one knee, he left his fist in place, afraid to move, unable to comprehend what he had just done.

Lenny struggled to his feet, rubbing his eyes, not trusting what they had just shown him. "I don't... understand. The blocks slowed down. You saw them slow down, right? You were moving normally, but the blocks... the blocks... I don't understand? Garrett, how could they slow down?"

Mr. B bowed. "Very good. I should have known sooner to use Lenny to trigger your focus."

"What? What do you mean use *Lenny*?" Garrett shouted before standing to run to Lenny's side. "Are you okay? Anything broken?" Garrett asked, his face ashen with worry.

"I don't think... my ribs... they aren't broken, but Mr. B packs... a hell of a kick," Lenny said, sucking short gasps between his teeth. "Why did you... call him a... Keeper of the Light? Garrett, what's going on?"

"Boys, come here and sit down," Mr. B said, wiping his

brow with the sleeve of his black dobok before seating himself cross-legged in the center of the dojo.

Garrett eyed the man apprehensively. His master, teacher, the most trusted in his life, a Keeper of the Light. "I don't think so," Garrett said, turning his back on the man as he helped Lenny to his feet.

Lenny glanced to Mr. B, hurt and tears filling his eyes. "We passed… your test," he said bitterly.

"You're right, Lenny, you both passed the test, and I'm sorry it had to be like this."

"Let's just go, Lenny," Garrett said, pulling at Lenny's dobok. Something told him he didn't want to hear what was coming.

Lenny shrugged Garrett off and took an unsteady step towards Mr. B. "Why did Garrett call you that? Why did he call you a Keeper of the Light?"

"Because you see, Garrett is right, Lenny. I am a Keeper of the Light, just as you are."

Lenny stepped back, confused.

Garrett looked at Lenny. "What? What does he mean, Lenny?" Garrett asked uncertainly.

"Don't look at me like that! I have no idea what he's talking about."

"Come, sit down," Mr. B said, beckoning with his hands. "You have both passed your test. You weren't testing for a second-degree black belt in a taekwondo academy. No indeed. You were testing for so, so much more. Now, come and sit, and I will make you a promise."

Garrett turned back to see a warm smile stretching across Mr. B's face. His arms were outstretched with his fingers splayed open, as if to show he had nothing to hide. But Garrett knew better. Mr. B had been hiding plenty. "You can make your promise while I am standing right here," Garrett said, making no effort to hide his anger.

Garrett glanced over to Lenny, who stood, arms crossed, in a defiant stance that contrasted with his look of utter confusion.

Mr. B lowered his arms with a defeated sigh. "I understand, you're confused, you're sore, you have a lot of questions. Sit down and I'll try to answer all your questions about the Keepers of the Light and the journal you and your friends have found."

Garrett blinked.

"Ah, yes, Garrett, I know about the journal. I know about everything. I even know about the strange behavior from your family and friends. Sit with me," he said, patting the mat. "I'll tell you who you can trust and who you cannot trust. I'll tell you of the past and of the present. And most important... I'll tell you of your destiny. But be warned – time is not on our side, and we must begin now."

No one spoke for a time as all three just stared at one another.

"Did I mention time is of the essence?" Mr. B asked.

Lenny leaned in close to Garrett's ear, laying a hand on his shoulder. "Garrett, I don't like this. Something is wrong with him. We should go."

Garrett hesitated. He could leave now with Lenny and never come back. Could he really walk away from a chance to understand? Of course, on one hand, it could all be a trick of some kind. On the other, he needed answers – wanted answers. Then Mr. B made his decision for him.

"Garrett," Mr. B called. "Don't you want to know why you're having the dreams of fire?"

A chill ran up Garrett's back as his arms broke out in goose bumps. *How could he know? How on God's earth could he know?*

"Time is fleeting. All your chosen will be here soon, now please come."

Garrett frowned. *All my chosen? Chosen what?*

"Garrett, are you sure about this?" Lenny asked.

"No, Lenny, but he knows about my dreams," Garrett said, approaching Mr. B cautiously, as if approaching a poisonous snake. Keeping his distance and remaining out of reach from the seated Grand Master, Garrett sat down across from him, taking on the same cross-legged position. He glanced back at Lenny with a pleading look.

Lenny was already off the mat, but hesitantly he stepped back on and took a seat next to Garrett.

"Good. Now allow me to explain—"

A frantic pounding erupted from the front door, rattling the blinds and causing both boys to jump.

40

Petersburg

Wednesday April 6th, 10:45 a.m.
Day One
Oak Island, Nova Scotia

Breanne came bursting out of the camper with a backpack containing her laptop slung over her shoulder.

Paul had just finished loading Edward and Charles into the chopper and was impatiently waiting for his sister. "The chopper is ready – we need to get to the hospital. Did you figure out where we're going?" Paul asked, taking his sister's hand and helping her climb aboard the helicopter.

"Yes, we're going to Illinois. Petersburg, Illinois," Breanne said, strapping herself into the copilot's seat. "Will they be okay?" she asked with concern. She craned her neck, assessing the position of her father and brother, both strapped into the rear seats.

"They're secure. Let's get them to the hospital. I already called ahead to the QEII Health Sciences Centre and they know we're coming," he said as he flipped a series of switches on the helicopter's console.

"Jesus, what did you tell them?"

"Only that there'd been an accident, and we were coming in with one unconscious due to unknown injuries and one with a compound fracture," he said as he turned to look at her. He paused, pressing his lips together in a tight line.

"What?" she asked.

"That's not the hard part, Bre. The hard part will be unloading them and then leaving. I don't know how we will explain that. They're going to want to detain us for questioning."

She didn't try to respond with a solution. They would just have to cross that bridge when they got to it. "I booked us a flight to Peoria, Illinois. It leaves from Halifax Stanfield International Airport at 12:00 p.m. We need to hurry."

The helicopter lifted off the ground as Paul navigated towards the hospital. "ETA fifteen minutes," he said.

Just as Paul hoped, hospital staff were waiting there on the helipad to meet them, stretchers at the ready. The siblings helped the staff unload their father and brother. Breanne began crying as she felt the grave reality of the situation weigh on her. A member of the staff, an orderly, or perhaps she was a nurse, began consoling her. She knew the woman couldn't possibly understand why she was so upset. She was about to leave her brother, her father – and for what? To chase an imagined boy from a dream because a long-dead knight told her she had to. No, she knew it was much more than that, but it didn't make leaving them any easier.

"There now, child, it will be okay," the kind woman said, wrapping an arm around her. "You're in the right place now. Come with me. We'll take care of you." The woman was so kind and gentle as she attempted to guide Breanne off the helipad.

"Please can I wait for my brother?" Breanne asked.

"Of course, dear," the woman said.

Breanne watched Paul assist with getting his father and brother loaded onto stretchers. A tall older woman in a nurse's uniform asked him what happened. She also had a warm, caring smile. A plastic badge hanging from a red lanyard identified the nurse as Doris. Carefully he explained, leaving out the parts about Oak Island, the secret dig, the God Stones, and Apep. "Doris, there's been a collapse on an archeological dig. The collapse caused the site to flood, and both my father and brother were injured. I set my brother's leg the best I could to get him out, but my father... he may have been shocked. There was a power source that became submerged in the flood – it must have shorted out through the water."

Breanne knew it was important for Paul to get as close to the truth as possible so that her father could get proper care, and an electrical shock seemed as good a way as any to describe the insane event with the God Stones.

"We will take great care of your family. Now please come with me – I'm sure the doctor will have questions, and you both look just awful. We need to get you checked out," Doris said, securing the buckles on the stretcher as she motioned for Paul to follow.

"Yes... of course, let me secure everything here, and I will be right in," Paul said, turning back to the helicopter.

Meanwhile, Breanne caught the look from Paul and pulled away from the kind woman consoling her. "I need to grab my backpack," she said.

They both boarded the helicopter as her father and brother were wheeled inside. Paul leapt into the pilot's seat and began readying for takeoff. The kind woman waiting patiently for Breanne was the only staff member still on the helipad.

Breanne made a show of trying to find her backpack, stalling to give Paul time to get ready.

"Okay. Sit down, Bre, here we go," he said, as he fired the ignition.

Breanne couldn't hear the woman, but she could read her lips well enough to get the gist of what she was saying.

"Wait!" the woman screamed, as she ducked instinctively and squatted to the ground. "What are you doing? Where are you going?"

The helicopter defied gravity as it broke free from the helipad. Within minutes they would be at the airport, and with any luck boarding a plane to Peoria.

"They *will* call the police, Bre," Paul said.

"What do we do?"

"We get to the airport, get on that plane, and we hope to hell they stay confused long enough for us to get out of here," he said, slipping on a radio headset.

They landed moments later at Stanfield International Airport. It was already 11:30 a.m. and they still needed to get through security, but with the added perk of Paul being a military pilot they were able to cut through some of the red tape. As Paul hoped, there was no sign that the police were looking for them, at least not at the airport – not yet anyway. Soon they were safely aboard the plane bound for Peoria.

Once in the air, the siblings were faced with a three-hour flight. Finally, they had some time to think, talk, and allow the reality of the situation to sink in.

"When we land, I want to call Sarah – she'll be worried if she doesn't hear from Daddy."

"We'll need a car," Paul said.

"I took care of that too."

Paul raised an eyebrow. "Wow, sis. How did you have time?"

"I did it before we left, when I was trying to find Petersburg and book our plane. I knew we'd need a car," she said, giving her brother a shaky smile. She was trying not to cry, but everything was hitting her all at once. She'd left her father and her brother behind. Edward would be fine, but leaving her father at the hospital might have been the hardest thing she ever had to do. The Templar's words kept playing through her mind: *Heed these words, child... You can't help your father without first helping Garrett.*

Both sat in silence as the jet left the ground, soon humming southward above the clouds. Neither wanted to say what was really on their minds, though both couldn't help but think of it –of him. But it would do them no good to talk about their father now. There was nothing they could do that they weren't already doing. They had to find this Garrett kid.

As the long flight wore on, the silence was broken as the two spoke in quiet whispers of the God Stones, Apep, and the dreams. Once they'd exhausted their recounting of the day's events, they tried to formulate a plan, knowing any plan they could conjure was thin at best.

"What will we do when we get to Petersburg?" Paul asked.

"We have to find Garrett," she said, confused.

"I know, Bre, but how? How big is this Petersburg anyway?"

"Not big, just over two thousand people," she said, rubbing her eyes.

"How will we find him?"

"I don't know, but we have to – we just have to." Her voice was shaky. The truth was, she had no idea. Thankfully he didn't press.

As the plane descended into Peoria International Airport, the Moores' anxiety rose. They half expected to find the police waiting for them, ready to take them into custody for fleeing the hospital. But there were no police. Neither had working cell phones, so Breanne tried to reach Sarah by payphone. No luck there either. Not reaching Sarah really wasn't a surprise to Breanne, given she was on a remote dig site.

By 4:00 p.m. they had picked up their rental car and were on the road. One hour and fifteen minutes later they descended the Highway 123 bridge over the Sangamon River. Coming across the bridge, Breanne could see the entire river valley stretched out before her. On the opposite side of the valley, the bluffs climbed steeply, speckled from bottom to top with Victorian-era homes, some as large as mansions, with their slate roofs peeking out from trees. It was picturesque – almost as if this little town had stopped aging over a century ago. They had finally arrived in the historic town of Petersburg.

The beauty was lost on Breanne, her mind fixed solely on one thing – finding Garrett. "This is it. The land of Lincoln."

They hadn't a clue where to start searching for this boy and were trusting in the faith of a dream as their only clue.

"What now? We've made three laps through town, Bre, and we're no closer to finding this kid. Are you just hoping we happen across him?" Paul asked.

Actually, that was exactly what she was doing. She knew what the kid looked like and she knew his name, but that was all she had. "Wait… did you see that? Go back!" Breanne said.

"See what? Back where?" Paul asked.

"The alley behind the arcade. You didn't see that group of kids?"

"Was he there?" Paul asked hopefully.

"No, but it's a small town. One of them probably knows him," she said.

Paul sagged, then shook his head. "Alright, we can ask,

but I don't like the idea of stopping to talk to large groups of white kids."

They went around the block, then stopped in the mouth of the alley. Breanne didn't get out – instead she just shouted toward the group of kids, maybe twenty or more. "Hey, excuse me, any of you know a kid named Garrett?"

Everyone froze and stared expressionless at Breanne, like they had never seen a black girl before. *Great,* she thought. She had already started to understand that there weren't many black people around here when they had stopped at a gas station in a small town on their way from Peoria. She went inside to grab some water and a map. An elderly white woman had looked in her direction, eyes wide. She quickly approached Breanne and grabbed ahold of her braids.

"Oh, wow. How long did that take you to braid your hair into those tiny braids? There must be hundreds of them!" the lady had said. Breanne knew it wasn't malicious, more curious, but it felt invasive and gross – she didn't know where that lady's hands had been. She had learned through countless encounters like this that the fastest way out of the situation was to just agree politely and move on. Smiling at the woman patiently, she said, "It sure did take a long time." In fact, the tiny braids were not themselves hand-braided, nor were they even her real hair for that matter. But she wasn't going to take the time to explain the workings of black hair to a stranger whose hands, with untold amounts of grossness on them, were invading her hair.

There was a different vibe coming from this group, though, and it wasn't curiosity. Suddenly a very angry, very scrappy-looking kid stepped forward from the center of the crowd. "Why you askin'? You know Garrett or something?"

"We're looking for him. Have you seen him?" Breanne repeated.

The Secret Journal

"You family of Lenny's or something?" the angry kid asked.

"No, I don't know a Lenny," Breanne said, crinkling her eyebrows in annoyance at the boy.

"Well, listen, you tell that little bitch Garrett I'll catch up to his ass, and when I do, I'm going to beat the shit out of him in front of the whole school," the angry kid said, smiling and punching his fist into his palm.

The whole crowd laughed except for one kid who rolled his eyes. Breanne caught the look and took note of the eye roller.

"Test or no test, he was supposed to be here twenty-five minutes ago. So, if you find him, you tell him Jack's waiting!"

The crowd laughed again – except for the eye roller.

Breanne rolled up her window. "Let's get out of here before this gets ugly."

As they started to pull away, Breanne noticed the eye roller and two other kids slip discreetly away from the crowd. The eye roller, a geeky-looking kid with glasses, was holding hands with a cute nerdy-looking girl, followed close behind by a shorter stocky kid. They hurried down the street past the arcade and around the corner. In the center of the town stood a giant historic courthouse with streets on all four sides forming a town square. Each adjacent street was lined with connecting businesses facing toward the courthouse. The three kids began making their way around the town square.

"Hey, follow those kids," Breanne said curiously.

"I can't – the street is one way and they're heading the opposite direction. I'm not trying to get pulled over in this place."

"Well, pull across into the courthouse parking lot. Over there," she said, pointing to the empty lot.

They pulled in and drove across the lot towards the end, then parked facing the kids, who were now on the opposite side of the street walking towards them. Before reaching the end of the square, the three kids stopped and approached the door to the Taekwondo Academy. The eye roller twisted the door handle, evidently with no luck, then began pounding frantically on the door. *Why the urgency?* she wondered.

"Look!" Breanne said, pointing. The door opened and a round man in a black martial arts uniform opened the door, ushering the three kids inside. Then just before closing the door, he did something strange. Something that prickled Breanne's skin into instant goose bumps. He looked up, directly towards them. Then, even stranger, he began waving as if he were waving them to come over.

"What the hell? He couldn't possibly be waving at us?" Paul asked.

"He couldn't know we're here. He shouldn't even be able to tell we are in the car from this far away," Breanne said skeptically. But she knew she was wrong. He was looking right at them.

"Then who is he waving at?" Paul asked.

She placed her hand on the door handle and pulled. "I don't know, but grab your gear – we're going to find out."

41

Answers

Wednesday, April 6th, 5:30 p.m.
Day One
Petersburg, Illinois

A frantic pounding continued to rattle the door of the dojo.

"Well," Mr. B said, "I had hoped to be further along than this by the time everyone arrived, but maybe it's for the best. Boys, please excuse me." He rose quickly to his feet and hurried to the door.

Garrett and Lenny stood too, craning their necks to see who had come in.

"Ah, welcome," Mr. B said. "Please, come to the mat, remove your shoes, and sit with us. We're about to begin." He motioned Pete, David, and Janis towards the mat as he turned back to the door.

Garrett observed Mr. B as he peered out, as if looking for someone else, and then motioned with a hand signal. He paused there briefly, perhaps even expectantly, but no one came and he closed the door.

Garrett and Lenny shared a sideways glance.

"What are you guys doing here?" Garrett asked, turning his attention to Pete.

Pete's face was ashen. "I tried to catch you after school but missed you. Then I heard you were fighting Jack behind the arcade around five, so I thought I'd catch you there."

Great, he had forgotten all about the fight with Jack. It was way after five, and he had failed to show. This was bad.

"I waited along with half the school," Pete said. "But you guys didn't show. Then the girl showed up looking for you and—" He paused, glancing nervously at Mr. B, who was seating himself cross-legged in the center of the room. He quickly stepped in close to Garrett, continuing in an urgent whisper. "Look, I transferred the rest of the journal – it's unbelievable—"

"Wait. What girl?"

"Boys, please sit down," Mr. B said. "We are almost ready to start."

"You will have to tell me after," Garrett said, still holding his ribs as he lowered himself onto the mat with a wince.

Pete's eyebrows knitted tight as he looked at Garrett holding his ribs. His eyes rose to Garrett's face and he frowned. Then he glanced around the dojo, taking in the back wall of broken mirrored panels and the flipped tables and busted concrete. "Christ, Garrett. What the hell happened here? Is this all from your test?" he asked in an urgent whisper.

"Tell you later."

Another knock at the door, but this time softer – less sure.

"Ah, this should be everyone!" Mr. B said as he stood and hurried back to the door.

Garrett noticed two silhouettes step inside. His eyes went wide as he instantly recognized one of the silhouettes. "Breanne!" He jumped to his feet and ran over to her. She was with someone else, an older, muscular black man, maybe in his twenties. When he approached her, he hesitated only for a second before grabbing her and hugging her like a long-lost friend he hadn't seen in years. But in fact, he had never seen her – not in person anyway.

Breanne hugged him back tightly, as if she had known him forever. "It's you. It's really you!"

Ignoring the pain from his ribs, he held her tight, not wanting the embrace to end. "Oh my God, you're... you're real! And you remember the dreams?" he asked.

"Of course," she said. Releasing her embrace, she let the canvas backpack drop from her shoulders. "That's how I found you, but for the record, you could have given me a bit more to go on – a last name, an address, something."

"Well, the world was sort of on fire," Garrett said, smiling thinly.

Lenny looked from Breanne to Garrett, back to Breanne, then to the older guy, then back to Garrett again. "What the *hell* is going on around here?" he asked. His look was accusing, as if to say, *You bastard! You've been keeping the biggest secret of your life from your best friend!* "Do I even know you?" he asked, his face turning from shocked perplexity to betrayal.

Pete, Janis, and David looked at each other in shared confusion.

Breanne pointed to her muscular companion. "This is my brother, Paul."

"Glad to finally meet you, Garrett," Paul said with a tight smile and a sharp nod. He pulled off his own pack, stowing it next to his sister's near the edge of the dojo. "It has been quite the journey trying to find you."

"Somebody please tell me what the hell is going on here?" Lenny asked.

"Thank you all," Mr. B said. "I know this is confusing, but please, everyone sit down, and I will try and clear up as many of your questions as I can." Then he looked to Lenny and Garrett. "I know you do not understand why the test was so rigorous, but I assure you it was necessary."

"Test? You call beating the crap out of us a test?" Garrett said.

Paul raised an eyebrow towards Mr. B.

"Yes," he said, his expression calm, unreadable. "It was in fact a test. I had to help you find your focus, Garrett. I had to ensure you were ready. You are capable of so much you can't even begin to understand." Mr. B turned his head slowly, looking at each of them in turn as they fidgeted uncomfortably on the mat, gathered around him in a half circle. Sucking in a deep breath, he let out a long sigh and began. "I want you to imagine everything you ever heard about magic was actually true – well, true enough."

"But it's not – and that's sort of ridiculous," Pete said. "No disrespect, um, Master B.

"You can just call me Mr. B, Peter."

"Okay, Mr. B. But come on, magic isn't real."

Mr. B smiled. "I am only asking you to imagine it is," he said carefully. "Now imagine a time long ago when the magic that existed could also move through any creature or object that contained it, effectively altering anything – perhaps everything."

"I don't follow," Lenny said.

"What, like wizards, fairies, and unicorns?" Garrett asked.

"Yes! Sort of like that," he said, pointing a finger at Garrett. "Maybe not as your modern-day stories go, but yes. Imagine those many things of legend were in fact true. After all, legends start from something. Imagine walking trees, powerful mages, dragons, giants, elves, gnomes, even fairies.

The Secret Journal

Other species you never heard of that do not exist today but that existed in the past." Mr. B spread his arms wide.

"One word. Awesome!" David said.

Mr. B looked from one to the next as he spoke, giving everyone seated the feeling he was speaking directly to each of them. "These things are not mere myth but are indeed real. Many years ago, in fact thousands and thousands of years ago, magic *did* exist. It existed because of a very special set of stones. These stones went by many names. For example, when Plato wrote of Atlantis, he called them the Sound Eye. For our purposes, we will call them God Stones."

Breanne gasped. "I have seen these stones! They are real. There are seven of them, and they have some kind of... of power. We found them and now they are..." She glanced at Paul, unsure.

Garrett caught the look. Whatever she was going to say, she stopped herself.

Everyone's eyes widened as they turned to stare at her.

"I've seen them too," Paul said, nodding seriously.

"Yes, I believe you have," Mr. B said. "Even now their energy pulses powerfully through you, Breanne" – he shifted his eyes to Paul – "and you as well." Then, addressing everyone, he said, "The stones' energy will soon pulse powerfully inside all of you too."

They all shifted uncomfortably, glancing at one another with questioning eyes. Except for David, who grinned widely.

Mr. B pressed his lips tight. "Listen carefully now. The freeing of the God Stones from deep within the earth will change the energy in everything – specifically, inside the brains of all of us, as well as those of earth's animals that possess a gland called the pineal gland. You have heard of this gland?" he asked.

The group nodded simultaneously. Garrett understood the basic components of the brain from health class.

"Good," Mr. B said. "Many cultures consider the pineal gland the third eye. What you need to know is that this gland can tap into the energy of the God Stones. A person with an awakened third eye can sense and even manipulate the energy around them, allowing them to become a powerful mage or warrior. A rare few even became oracles said to be capable of seeing the future. However, the God Stones' energy does not give everyone magic ability – the vast majority will become nothing more than what they already are."

"So, some people don't get any power from these stones?" David asked in what almost sounded to Garrett like disappointment.

Mr. B nodded. "The stones don't affect everyone, and those who are affected are never affected the same way. Think of the gland as a muscle that must be exercised. Sometimes a muscle never used atrophies beyond repair. Especially as you get older. This is why I train your focus and your mind," he said, looking to Garrett and Lenny. "Some humans won't even survive their first exposure to the God Stones. Their pineal gland won't be able to handle the exposure and will just burst, resulting in instant death. To my knowledge, no human has survived touching the stones with their bare skin. Do this and the pineal gland will explode, most certainly."

Garrett hadn't been able to take his eyes off Breanne since she arrived, and now he saw panic cross her face.

"When my dad opened the chest, he... he passed out. And he never woke up. Is... is that what happened to him? Oh my God, did his pineal gland burst?" Breanne asked shakily.

"Did he touch the stones?" Mr. B asked seriously.

"No. He never touched them – only the Ark," Paul said. "He is alive, but he is in a coma in the hospital."

Mr. B shook his head. "I don't think his gland burst. The good news is he didn't touch the stones and he didn't die instantly. However, I'm afraid his gland may have been damaged, or at least overloaded. I just can't say what this means for him – I am sorry, Breanne."

Breanne looked away and pressed the collar of her shirt to her eyes.

Garrett wanted to say something to comfort her, but what could he say? He reached for her, putting his hand on her back lightly, unsure.

She turned towards him and buried her face in his dobok, wrapping her arms around him.

Garrett hugged her back.

She pulled back, as if remembering suddenly he was a stranger, and smiled weakly. "Thanks."

"Now, the God Stones affect other living things besides humans and animals."

Pete spoke up. "But trees don't have pineal glands – or brains, for that matter."

"Being affected by their power and being able to manipulate their power are two different things, Peter," he said. "Take your example of trees, for instance. Trees don't have physical brains in the sense that you or I do, but they are alive and they feel – make no mistake about it, they feel. Their life force may be different but they, like all living things, will change as the energy of the God Stones begins to flow through them. To what degree change occurs is anyone's guess. The easiest way to effect or manipulate the power of the God Stones is to command it with the language of the gods. The first language. Understand?"

Garrett's brow knitted together, trying to process what the hell he was hearing.

Mr. B paused. "That's a two-thousand-foot view of what they are, but you might be wondering how they came to be here."

Garrett looked around and noticed that while Pete and Janis looked skeptical, and Lenny and the others shrugged or gave half nods, Breanne leaned in with intensity.

"A long time ago, some thirteen thousand years, eight beings came through a portal to this planet. The portal was a violent thing that tore open the fabric of space and caused a great cataclysmic event that nearly destroyed our planet. But humans are survivors by nature and though many died, an equal number endured. The God Stones were the key to opening this portal and the catalyst for our near extinction.

"The result was a mini ice age that funneled humans into the Middle East. The ones who brought the God Stones to earth sought out the densest population, presented themselves as gods, and began sharing their knowledge of language, astrology, math, and agriculture. From this the five cities were born. These beings are responsible for our transitioning from hunter gatherers into an agriculture-based society." Mr. B said.

"Are you saying these *beings* were responsible for the Neolithic Revolution? And that these cities, they were all located in the Fertile Crescent?" Breanne asked.

Garrett traded a confused glance with Lenny, then they both looked to Pete.

"It's a stretch of land that runs along Mediterranean Sea with several countries bordering it. It's where the first societies sprang from," Pete said.

Mr. B waved a dismissive hand. "Indeed, but what's important to know is that they didn't teach us for our benefit. They did it for themselves. All along they only cared about what they wanted."

"And what was it they wanted?" Paul asked.

The Secret Journal

"An army." Mr. B's forehead furrowed as he said the word. "They thought by bringing dragons here from their world, they could control them and breed them. And worse, they wanted to breed with us to create something else – super soldiers for their army. They needed us to be intelligent enough to work together. It was all part of a sick plan to create an army in secret that they could then take home, to their world, and use to overthrow the ruling powers there."

"Wait," Lenny interrupted, "I have sat here with my mouth shut listening to this, Mr. B, but I can't... I just can't sit here any longer in silence." He turned to Garrett and then the others. "Are you hearing this?" He didn't wait for a response. "I'm sorry, Mr. B, but you want us to believe there is, or was, or whatever, *magic* that *aliens* brought here? Let me say that part again. Magic aliens! Oh, and let's not forget dragons! And magic... creatures! I don't get it." He threw his hands up. "I don't get it, and I don't know what you are trying to pull. But I know you're a Keeper of the Light – you said so yourself."

That comment drew a look from Pete. "He's a Keeper of the Light?"

Lenny rose to leave. "We have a journal that Abraham Lincoln wrote basically saying he didn't trust your kind. I don't know why you think telling us this crazy story is somehow going to justify you kicking the crap out us?"

"Sit, Lenny," Mr. B said.

"I trusted you, Mr. B, and you told me I failed!" Lenny said, hurt saturating his voice. "You told me I was no longer welcome here. Now you tell me this... this crap." He looked to Garrett. "Let's go, man. I've heard enough."

Garrett looked at Breanne, then to Mr. B, and finally back to Lenny. He couldn't leave. Not now. There was too much he didn't know, too much he had to know. "Wait, Lenny, just a minute more." Garrett knew it wasn't the story that made Lenny want to walk away. It was the betrayal. He felt it, too, but Lenny hadn't seen what he had – hadn't felt what he felt. He had to stay.

Lenny shot Garrett a look of disbelief. He paused. Everyone stared at him. He looked to David, then Pete.

Pete shrugged. "I'm not leaving until this guy explains everything, especially the part about the Keepers of the Light!"

Breanne looked at Lenny. "Please stay – this is really important. My dad… his life depends on this."

"Lenny, please, man, something is going on. I… I don't know why, but we have to hear this," Garrett pleaded.

Lenny shook his head and settled back onto the mat. "Fine, I'll stay, for now," he said with a sigh.

"Lenny," Mr. B said, shaking out his hands nervously, "this wasn't what I wanted. It wasn't how I planned it, but things moved quicker than even I expected." He looked around the circle, pausing to catch Pete's eye. "I know this is hard for some of you to believe."

Heads nodded and a small chatter broke out.

Mr. B said something, but Garrett didn't hear him over the sudden talking. Then Mr. B closed his eyes.

Was Mr. B… meditating? Garrett recognized the technique as Mr. B chanted a soft mantra under his breath. Then he saw something impossible. Very slowly, very evenly, the large body of Mr. B began to lift, featherlight, off the mat, as if he were a flower petal gently elevated by a sudden breeze.

Janis gasped and pointed, drawing all their attention. The group silenced and stared, jaws slack.

Garrett gaped as Mr. B opened his eyes, hovering in a spot several feet above. The master was still seated crosslegged, with the backs of his hands resting gently on his knees.

Seemingly satisfied he had their attention, he continued,

"The old ones, who brought the God Stones here, were ultimately defeated." He paused and this time no one interrupted. "After that, it was decided that because of the unnatural effects the God Stones have on the world, they were to be sealed inside a lead chest crowned with gold and hidden deep in the earth. With the stones sealed away, their effect on the world faded."

Garrett watched, bewildered but amused, as Pete bent down and then leaned back, peering below and above the floating man, looking for some logic to explain what he was seeing.

"You won't find that I am using tricks, Peter." Mr. B began to move in a circle around them. His body moved up and down slightly as if he were riding an invisible magic carpet or cloud.

No one took their eyes off of him, and no one spoke.

Finding nothing obvious to explain the levitation, Pete retrieved his jaw from the floor, closed his mouth, and gulped.

"Okay," Garrett said, speaking softly, as if afraid of interrupting the impossibility he was witnessing, "if what you have told us is true, what does any of this have to do with Breanne, with focus, with the Keepers of the Light, with all the weird stuff going on around here?" His voice rose with each question as he struggled to contain his emotion. "Dammit, Mr. B! What does any of this have to do with me?"

Mr. B settled gently down to the floor. He smiled weakly at Garrett, as if he were a doctor about to share bad news about a family member.

"Oh, my dear boy. I'm sorry to say it has everything to do with you."

42

The Past

Wednesday, April 6th, 5:55 p.m.
Day One
Petersburg, Illinois

The decades-old building housing the dojo drew a draft from its many cracks and crevices. Outside, a cool April wind blew swirls of leaves mixed with cigarette butts and gum wrappers into a miniature cyclone. It was the wrong time of year for a dust devil, but nevertheless it spun and raced across the nearly vacant parking lot, swirling around Bre and Paul's rental car, before dissipating into the wall of a nearby storefront. There, as if out of nowhere, a figure appeared.

Inside the dojo, Breanne, along with the others, listened intently to the incredible story the floating teacher guy was telling. These other kids were obviously having a hard time with this. How could she blame them? She wouldn't believe any of this if she hadn't seen it for herself? Apep, what he did – it was horrible, unthinkable, and impossible all at the same time.

She felt the sudden chill of a draft as it blew gently across her arms, raising goosebumps. She glanced around at the others. She wasn't the only one who felt the cold. The cute geeky girl was hugging herself, vigorously rubbing the backs of her arms to try and shake off the shiver. The equally geeky kid with the oversized glasses – *what was his name? Pete,* she thought – he noticed the cute geeky girl hugging herself and removed his jacket. Without saying a word, he gently draped it over the shivering girl's shoulders. She threw him a shy smile. Then she noticed Breanne watching her.

The geeky girl narrowed her eyes and scooched over next to Breanne, then leaned in close.

"It's getting cold. Feels like a storm is coming," Janis said evenly.

Breanne nodded.

The geeky girl refocused on the teacher guy, who was about to tell Garrett his part in this whole crazy story.

But before he could get to that, Pete interrupted. "Wait a minute, sir. I don't understand. If this were all true, where did these space aliens go, and why is there no evidence of any of this in the history we've been taught? I just feel like if there were a race of aliens breeding with humans, and if earth were a breeding ground for dragons, wouldn't there be some evidence?"

Breanne couldn't argue with this kid's logic. But while the others questioned the truth of the karate guy's story, she did not – could not. Her skeptical mind clashed with what she had seen and felt over the last twenty-four hours, and while part of her instinctively wanted to mount a logical and scientific argument for this nonsense, the other part of her mind swam with questions of her own.

Mr. B nodded his understanding. "After their arrival, it took them twelve hundred years to build their army of half-breeds and dragons. This part they had done in secret, in another part of the world. Remember when I said they needed humans to be intelligent and work together? In order to go home, the old ones needed to reopen the gate from this side. To do that, they needed manpower to construct a great monolithic structure. This structure would be used to harness the energy from the God Stones in the way necessary for the gate to open. They fooled the humans of the five cities into aiding in their construction. But something else was happening – as the centuries passed, some humans were beginning to learn how to tap into the power themselves. This must have felt like a true bonus to the old ones at first as they raced to construct megalithic structures. Some of the most powerful human mages could levitate stones weighing several hundred tons. Others could superheat stones and actually shape them somehow."

"Like at Sacsayhuaman in Peru?" Breanne asked.

"Oh! Right," Janis said. "Scientists have debated about how the structures were truly created."

"There is no way they could have superheated stones and manipulated their shapes – no one then or even now possessed that kind of technology," Breanne said.

"Exactly," Mr. B said. "The limestones at Machu Picchu and Sacsayhuaman were superheated until pliable, then placed using magic, without the need to physically touch the impossibly hot stone."

Breanne found herself nodding slowly at the absurdity of it, but unable to find in her mind a more logical explanation.

"After more than twelve hundred years of work, they were ready to open the gate and lead the army through the portal and back to their own world. Once again, they ripped open the fabric of space That's when things went horribly wrong. Once again, the portal wreaked havoc on the world, but this time the change in temperatures was catastrophic, resulting in the instant incineration of the ice caps. This rapid melt resulted in a flood unlike anything the world had ever seen."

"Oh my God!" Janis exclaimed. "The great flood! It's been written about by practically every culture of the ancient world!"

"Like the story of Noah's Ark?" Lenny asked.

"Precisely!" Mr. B said. "But that's just one of many stories of a great flood. Look in the history of any culture or religion, and you will find stories of a great flood. The flood was so great, in fact, that it wiped out the five cities and all the massive monoliths were lost. Thus, without the monoliths to harness the energy of the God Stones, the portal closed."

The fluorescent lights of the dojo flickered.

Mr. B blinked, glancing up towards the lights with sharp eyes.

Everyone followed his gaze.

"What is it?" Lenny asked.

Mr. B pressed his lips together. "Time, Lenny. I fear we don't have much left. Let us press on."

The group exchanged uneasy glances.

"Most of the humans from the five cities were lost in the flood, but some survived, as did the old ones," Mr. B continued. "But with their portal destroyed, along with most of their army, the old ones were forced to start over. Only now, what humans from the five cities survived no longer trusted them."

"I wouldn't trust them either after the last time," David offered.

Mr. B nodded. "Right, so, with the humans no longer trusting them, the old ones sought out new humans in a different part of the world to trick into building their portal, and they found them – in Egypt. Once in Egypt they started over by building the Sphinx and using it as an offering to the first king of Egypt."

"Wait, you're saying these old ones built the Sphinx?" Peter asked.

"In Egypt? Oh, yes," Mr. B said, "and that's just for starters. Over the next thousand years, many humans flocked to Egypt after hearing of the gods who could build great structures. So, the humans came, and they worshiped, and they helped construct new monoliths – great structures that in time would allow the old ones to once again open the portal."

"Oh no! They were going to do it all over!" David said.

Mr. B nodded. "Yes, that was their plan. However, as I was saying, from the original five cities' flood survivors, seven were special. These seven were known as the Seven Sages. They were the most powerful human magicians on earth. They suspected other humans had survived the flood and that they would be hunting and gathering and breeding. They began to travel and teach others they found their knowledge of the stars, their math, and their language. Unlike the old ones, their purpose was true. They wished to rebuild society and create new cities."

"Seven Sages," Breanne whispered to no one.

"I'm not surprised you have heard of them, Breanne. The Seven Sages are written about on the walls of Mayan temples, in Sumerian tablets, and in Egyptian hieroglyphs, and as I am sure you know, on Easter Island there are even seven massive statues facing out to sea. What you wouldn't know is that these statues represent the sages themselves." Mr. B waved a hand. "The sages traveled all over teaching, and soon they learned the old ones were at it again."

"In Egypt?" Janis guessed.

"Yes." Mr. B nodded.

"Sorry, but you started this story thirteen thousand years

ago, and now we are talking early Egypt, which must have been thousands of years later. How many years have gone by?" Breanne asked. "If the old ones are aliens, they aren't subject to human biology, but how long do humans live in this story? Your Seven Sages from the original cities have to be really old by now, right?"

Her question elicited curious nods from the others.

"Ah, good question, Bre. You're paying attention," he said. "Under the power of the God Stones, in humans with a fully opened third eye, aging slows drastically."

"How drastically we talking here?" Paul asked.

"For a human, I don't know. Near as I can tell, it could have slowed as much as one hundred years to every one year. Give or take. It's different for everyone."

"Practically immortal!" Pete exclaimed.

Suddenly Mr. B looked very sad. "No, Peter, death is still possible, especially when life is stolen."

"What? But wouldn't that mean these sages could still be alive now?" Garrett asked.

They all stared, confused, waiting for him to elaborate – but he did not.

Drawing in a breath, Mr. B shook off whatever unwelcome thought had invaded his mind and continued. "Once the Seven Sages arrived in Egypt, a great battle ensued. When the old ones realized they couldn't win, they escaped with the God Stones. This time, however, the seven old ones split up, each taking one of the seven God Stones. Each old one fled to a different part of the world, where they would build new kingdoms with new pyramids. They planned to reunite when their forces were strong."

Paul frowned. "It is good they were stopped again, I guess, but those old ones needed to be put down – permanently. Also, you said in the beginning that eight space aliens, old ones or whatever, came here with the God Stones, but you just said seven old ones escaped with seven stones. What happened to the eighth?"

Mr. B nodded and continued. "When the old ones fled with the God Stones, one of the seven sages turned on the others, attacking them. When he failed, he tried to flee with the old ones. It turned out this sage had been keeping a very dark secret. He was covertly working with the old ones. In fact, he was leading them. He had only been posing as a human, a traitor in their midst. The ultimate betrayal."

"So, this traitor, he was actually one of the old ones?" Lenny asked.

"The eighth alien guy," Paul said.

"He was indeed, but a different breed," Mr. B said.

Garrett shook his head, struggling to take it all in. "I still don't understand what any of this has to do with me."

"Context, Garrett. I will get to you, but to understand you need the full context." Mr. B looked back to Lenny. "Simply put, he came from the same world as the old ones. He was leading them, but he was not the same species of… well, of alien as the other seven were. Unlike the old ones, he was able to use magic to disguise himself as a human. You could be looking right at him and never know he was anything but human."

Lenny raised a brow. "So, they were different races of aliens."

"Here, think of it this way. I come to your world and I bring seven grizzly bears with me. You see what I mean? I look a whole lot different than a grizzly bear, but we're both aliens," Mr. B said.

Lenny nodded.

"Ever notice that all the good stories throughout history have a traitor?" Janis asked.

Pete smiled and nodded. "Judas, Benedict Arnold…"

"And Brutus! Et tu, Brute?" Janis added.

The Secret Journal

Mr. B waved a hand dismissively. "The great king of Egypt wanted to have the traitorous sage killed, but the leader of the Seven Sages convinced him to only imprison the false sage."

"I would have executed him on the spot," Paul said.

Nodding his agreement, Mr. B looked down at the floor again. "In hindsight, I wish he had been killed. But faith played a part, Paul. The king of Egypt was convinced because one of the sages, we'll call him the leader, told the king of a great prophecy still to come, and the king listened, and he believed. So it was that the false sage was cast away into a prison of darkness deep beneath the sands of Egypt, where he could never escape."

Breanne listened intently, chewing the nail on her thumb.

"The six remaining sages spent hundreds of years tracking down each old one, seven in total, and each time they defeated one, they took his God Stone," Mr. B said. "Each time they found an old one, they discovered them building new pyramids, superconductors, to harness the power of the God Stones. They were preparing for the day they could reunite and open the gate back home. But worse, the great deceivers were breeding with humans, as well as enslaving them. One by one, the six sages sought out each old one and rallied whatever native humans they could find to join with them and overthrow the old ones and their armies. The battles raged viciously, and by the time the last old one was defeated only the leader of the six sages remained. The other five had been killed in the horrific battles.

"Finally, with all seven old ones defeated, and all seven God Stones collected, the only sage left alive returned to Egypt. The sage shared with the king his tales of battles – the great armies he had defeated, and the heroic deaths of the other five sages. The last remaining sage explained how he ordered the old ones to be imprisoned on each continent. How each were placed into a deep underground chamber, hidden and guarded, buried and forgotten. The king asked, why not killed? The wise sage reminded the king of the prophecy still to come, and why it was so important that the old ones not die, but be cast into a dark slumber until the time the prophecy would be fulfilled."

The lights in the dojo flickered again.

Mr. B paused, shifting nervously. "The question became what to do with the God Stones. To the surprise of the sage, the king decreed the God Stones too powerful for this world and their magic too great for any one man to possess. Thus, it was decided that for the world to be as it once was, the God Stones must be sealed and hidden until it was time for the prophecy to be fulfilled."

Breanne swallowed. *Could her family have initiated some eons-old prophecy when they opened the Ark?*

"And so the king of Egypt decreed that it would be the last sage, keeper of the prophecy, who would be given the burden of hiding the stones, keeping them safe until the time the prophecy would come to pass."

"Wow! That's crazy," Paul said.

"So, teacher guy, what about the traitor sage?" Janis asked. "They just locked him up forever in darkness? Did he just die or is he still in a pit somewhere? I mean, doesn't it seem kind of harsh?"

"No! It wasn't harsh. He is a soulless creature void of anything good. If anything resembling a soul ever existed in him, which I am sure it did not, it has long since been replaced by a black abyss of evil!" Mr. B said, his voice uncharacteristically venomous.

A heavy awkwardness hung in the quiet moment that followed.

Mr. B closed his eyes and drew in a deep breath, followed

The Secret Journal

by a slow, calming exhale. Then he opened his eyes, his sense of calm seemingly returned. "His imprisonment under the sand ended a thousand years ago. Now, as foretold by the last sage, he has returned and obtained the God Stones. He will stop at nothing to finish what he began so long ago."

Breanne flashed back to her dream with the Knight Templar Hugues and what he had told her. *His name is Apep, and he will stop at nothing to get the stones.* She shuddered as her mind stitched together what this man was telling her with what she had seen and heard from the bottom of the pit.

"Please tell me this sage who escaped wasn't... wasn't Apep?" Bre's voice was shaky. She knew the answer already, but she clung to the last moment of silence before she heard it.

Mr. B nodded sadly, gazing at her as if he could read her emotions. "Indeed, he was."

Breanne bowed her head to her chest.

"So, you're saying this guy – the false sage – is... is still alive?" Garrett asked.

"He is." Mr. B said. "Breanne has met him."

Breanne took a deep breath and raised her head. Everyone in the circle was watching her, waiting for her answer.

Breanne looked from one to the other. "Well, remember how I said that my father had opened the Ark containing the stones and then passed out? Well, after that, Apep took the God Stones – they just levitated out of the Ark and into his hands – and then he tried to kill us!" With all eyes locked on her, she launched into a summary of the Oak Island story and what had happened there. The part about Jerry dying right in front of her elicited a gasp, and Bre had to fight off tears. What was important was to tell them what she knew about Apep, to convince them that he was real – and dangerous. "I can't tell you what he is, but he isn't human – he... he had kind of blueish skin, and pointed ears I think, and his body seemed to, like, I don't know, grow or something." She shook her head. "I know this sounds crazy, but it's true."

"One hundred percent," Paul said.

The room was silent. The teacher guy believed her, but what about the others? What about Garrett?

Garrett reached over to her, took her hand in his, and squeezed. His eyes met hers consolingly. He didn't say anything, but she felt his reassurance and for the briefest moment she knew that everything would somehow be okay.

Paul looked suspiciously at Mr. B. "Excuse me, Mr.... B, is it? We tell you this Apep guy killed our friend and tried to kill us, and you don't seem surprised by any of it. It's like you already knew? Why don't you tell us how *you* fit into this and how you know so damn much about us?"

"Of course, Paul, please forgive me," Mr. B said, as if responding to a longtime friend.

Paul's scowl deepened.

"Apep could not stand the thought of losing the power of the God Stones, or the thought of being stuck on earth with no way back. Before the deep pit was sealed, he promised the last sage that, no matter how long it took, he would find the stones and, when he did, he would watch this world burn before returning to rule his."

"Let me guess. The other sage is you, isn't it?" Paul asked.

Everyone in the room sucked a breath in and held it, weighty and expectant.

Mr. B's face twitched, and he looked at Paul and then at Breanne. "No, but I believe you both have met not only Apep but my dear friend... the last sage?"

Heads swiveled to look at them in bewildered surprise.

"What do mean, met him?" Paul said defensively, as if

being accused of some sort of criminal activity. "What the hell are you talking about? We've met no sage!"

"Wait, Paul!" Breanne said. "We have! Don't you see? It's Hugues from the nightmares."

"The Templar guy you mentioned earlier?" Pete asked, looking to Breanne.

"Right!" Breanne said.

Paul's face changed from confusion to comprehension like a switch being thrown. "Right," he said slowly.

Breanne's mind spun, trying to fit this newest bit of information into the puzzle. "Wait a minute. This doesn't make sense. I've done my research on Hugues, which wasn't really all that hard considering he is the founder of the Knights Templar. You said, 'your dear friend.' Hugues is dead and must have been dead for hundreds of years. His skeleton was in the first chamber we found, but supposedly he died in Palestine in 1136. Even if he didn't die until much later, he has been at the bottom of Oak Island a minimum of some five hundred years. How could he be your friend?" Breanne asked.

"Mr. B, I think it's time you tell us how it is you know so much about the past," Paul said.

Mr. B folded his hands together and nodded slowly. "Indeed. It is time." He stood and began to pace before them. "I met Hugues when I was but a young man, maybe around your age, Paul. But this was in a much later time, after the old ones had been put down – long after the battle in Egypt. He had already taken on the persona of Hugues de Payens when I came to know him. Soon he became like a father to me. I learned from him the story of Apep and the God Stones."

Breanne began to count years off in her head as the impossible revelation was washing through the group like a wave through water.

"Hugues formed the Knights Templar out of a need to protect the stones' location from Apep after his escape," Mr. B said. "Despite whatever else history has taught you, the protection of the God Stones was always the driving force behind the Knights. If you know the history of the Templars, you know we were established to protect visitors to the Holy Land and specifically the Temple Mount. You may also know that the Temple Mount was built on top of the Temple of Solomon. This temple was where Hugues had hidden the God Stones in a much earlier time when he was posing as someone else. After he learned of Apep's escape, Hugues formed and grew the Templars into a powerful army. After his escape, Apep tried numerous attacks against the Templars, but without the God Stones or the old ones, we were able to thwart his attempts easily."

Mr. B is one of the original Knights Templar! Breanne thought, squeezing Garrett's hand even tighter.

The heavy man's feet pressed deep into the mat as he paced, the skin of his bare feet emitting soft squeaks each time he turned to pace in the opposite direction. "After a couple hundred years of failed attacks on the Knights, Apep decided on a new strategy. By bending King Phillip's ear, he successfully orchestrated the arrest of the Templars. For this part, as it is written in history, so it was. On Friday, the thirteenth of October, 1307, the Templars were arrested. Many of my dear brethren were killed. I escaped along with several others and Hugues, who had faked his own death years before and taken on the persona of yet another—"

"Mr. B, you're saying you're over nine hundred years old!" Lenny blurted.

"I am nine hundred and twenty-five-years old, Lenny," Mr. B proclaimed without a hint of humor.

Breanne observed as everyone stared at the man in the

black dobok anew, as if seeing a miracle come to life before them.

Lenny swallowed. "But you said the God Stones were sealed away by order of the King of Egypt and that once they were sealed the world would return to normal. You said the power would fade away or whatever. How can you, Apep, and Hugues all live so long if the stones were sealed?" he asked, any hint of disbelief having fallen away and been replaced by wonder.

Mr. B paused his pacing and smiled. "You have always been very keen at noticing the details." Then he cocked his head to the side. "I want you to know, Lenny, earlier when I said what I said – it was because I had to. I needed to see if you would come to Garrett's aid despite my orders. That was your *true* test, Lenny – and you passed. You are incredibly important to the success of what's to come."

Lenny blinked and gave his master a slow nod.

Resuming his pacing, Mr. B clasped his hands behind his back. "Now to answer your question. Once the third eye is open, it does not close simply because the stones are gone. The human mind is capable of great things if only we could really tap into it. If we could use one hundred percent rather than ten percent, the possibilities may be endless. Also, the power to harness the energy of the stones and work the magic was not simply… gone. The stones were sealed, true. Also true, the trees took root and were unable to walk, and other unnatural creatures, once dead and gone, did not rebirth, ultimately ceasing to be. But even sealed in the lead box, the energy found its way through in small amounts and if you were close you would feel it."

"That's why you buried it so deep in the ground," Breanne said in new understanding. "Not just to hide it but to isolate it. The lead box wasn't enough." She thought about when she first put her hands on the altar. She remembered the feeling of power coursing through the stone. Her body shivered involuntarily as she recalled the plants and the glowing water.

Mr. B nodded. "I spent many years under Hugues's teachings and *he* was able to help me open my mind. But yes, I also spent much time near the stones, even though they were sealed. I helped to transport them and guard them. Their power was around me, flowing through me, for years."

"So, even without the stones, you can float and live forever?" Garrett asked.

"Not forever, and like it was for the rest of the world, the power of the stones was lost to me while they lay buried on Oak Island. Now, I can feel the stones are close, feel their magic inside me. Just as Breanne and Paul can."

Breanne nodded in agreement and looked at Paul, remembering the sight of him moving the crane boom.

"The rest of you can also feel it – will feel it – when you're ready or when the stones become close to you. And for each of you it will be different, but it will happen. This is your destiny." Mr. B paused for a moment, to let those words hang in the air. "As for the rest of the world and the creatures in it, well, I just can't say how fast it will change, perhaps very fast. Who and what will be affected is anyone's guess."

"You're not sure?" Pete asked.

"When it comes to effects, Peter, I can only theorize. Unlike Paul and Breanne, I have never seen the God Stones outside the lead-lined box. I can feel them now, though, and I fear they are close."

A chill crawled up Breanne's spine, forcing a shiver. *If the stones are close, so is Apep.*

"I'm sorry. Where was I? Ah yes, the horrible day of October thirteenth. As my Templar brethren were being tortured and burned at the stake, a small few of us escaped with the sealed chest. We made our voyage here – to America – just as I promised Hugues."

"Wait, Hugues wasn't with you? But then how did he end up in the pit on Oak Island?" Janis asked.

Mr. B's face darkened sorrowfully. He knelt down, bringing his eyes level with the sitting group. The room suddenly felt different somehow. Mr. B changed too. He looked much older, as if dark shadows had descended over his face. Finally, he found his voice again and, in not much more than a whisper, he choked out the words. "Hugues was with us but… he didn't survive the final attack before our escape."

The words hung there.

Finally, Mr. B's face hardened with determination. "Hugues told me of the perfect place to hide the stones, even providing me with instructions for how to access the underground chambers. To this day I've no idea how he knew the chambers would be there, right where he said they would be. Following a rough map, we found the place he spoke of – the place known now as Oak Island. I personally met with the indigenous people and, once again following Hugues's direction, I reminded them of the old ones, the stealing of their women by the army of ruthless killers. I told them if they didn't help us hide the stones, the old ones would return and kill us all. The stories of the old ones were alive and well, and they remembered, through stories passed down, the horrors they had caused. I only needed speak one word – Apkallu – to gain their support. This was the word known to them to signify sages. I told them the Apkallu needed their support. They agreed without question and together we worked to create a place that could never be discovered—"

"And then you killed them!" Breanne said accusingly, as the weight of what Mr. B said dropped on her like a piano. "Killed them and buried them under the swamp! I spent a whole summer sorting the bones of those poor dead people!" She gripped Garret's hand tighter, balling her other into a fist as her face flushed with fury.

Everyone jolted at her sudden outburst, but she didn't care.

"Breanne, is that what your heart says? You think I killed all those people?" Mr. B asked, opening his hands to reveal empty palms.

Breanne studied him for a moment. Some of the anger drained from her face. "Well, no... but..."

He lowered his hands to his thighs and narrowed his eyes. His voice shook as he spoke. "Each of them sacrificed their own life to ensure the God Stones were never discovered, to ensure none of them ever spoke of their location. By the time construction was complete on Oak Island, I knew all one hundred seventy-eight natives by name and considered *each* of them my friend. It was both the most moving and saddest thing I have ever witnessed – to watch each of them enter that swamp and take their own life. But understand this, Breanne, no one made them do it – they chose to. It forever changed my life. I'll carry the weight of all one hundred seventy-eight of them in my heart forever."

Breanne suddenly felt strangely guilty. Maybe it was her assumption or maybe it was the reality that she and her family had cracked the mystery and found the stones. She knew she shouldn't feel guilty. They had no idea what they were digging up. Yet she couldn't help it.

As if reading her mind, Mr. B spoke softly to her. "Oh no, Breanne, don't feel as though any of this is your or your family's fault. Before Hugues was killed, he prophesized that one day the stones would be found and that Apep would try to use them to create another army and open the gate."

Breanne smiled weakly, thanking him with her eyes, but the knot in her gut didn't fade.

"Mr. B, please tell me what this has to do with me?" Garrett asked again, his voice devoid of all venom. His anger had drained away over the course of hearing the surreal story.

Once more Mr. B stood and began to nervously pace back and forth in front of the group. He stopped in front of Garrett and turned to face him. "In the later years of Hugues's life, he married and bore a child. Not only did he prophesize his own death at the hands of Apep, but Hugues assured me that one day his descendant would battle Apep for the stones and for all of humanity. He asked me to promise him I would protect his bloodline until the time came and his descendant was ready. I tried to tell him this was madness and that he would not be killed by Apep. I still remember, as if it were yesterday, the way he looked at me that day. I could see it in his eyes, his sadness at my denial, and so, though I hated the thought with every ounce of my being, I promised him then and there that I would *always* protect his bloodline – until my dying breath – and that I would ensure the stones were hidden until the time foretold."

She felt Garrett fidget, flexing his fingers in hers, but he didn't let go.

The old master's face became very heavy, and his ancient eyes filled with tears. "Soon after he told me of this prophecy, many of our Templars were arrested while the rest of us made our escape. But Apep was expecting some of us would flee with the stones and he set an ambush. We battled fiercely but with so many arrested our numbers were too low. I was separated from Hugues," he said, swallowing hard in an attempt to push the emotions down deep into his large chest.

Breanne flashed back to the Hugues of her dreams, his kind voice and caring smile. She pressed her eyes tight, her heart sinking deep into her stomach.

Mr. B's voice came in a whisper. "I tried to get to him, to help him, but I could not. I had to protect his wife and daughter, as I promised I would." Tears fell down his face as he wiped the cuff of his dobok across his face. "There was a fire – it burned all around us. I could see him through the flames, but I couldn't get to him without abandoning them. Two other Templars made it to him and stood with him, battling Apep, but neither were powerful enough to stop him. By the end of the battle both were severely wounded and would surely have been killed if it were not for Hugues sacrificing himself. Somehow… to this day I still don't understand, but I… I know what I saw. I watched it all through the flames. Apep was losing the battle but then, just as Hugues was set to deliver the final strike, Apep cast a spell, a spell that should not have been possible with the God Stones sealed. Yet… he did it. I don't know, maybe there was enough power leaking through the lead ark or maybe it had something to do with him not being human at all…" He trailed off, then shook the thought away.

"The spell forced Hugues to the ground. He raised his shield, but it was no match for the power of Apep's spell… and he died. Frozen in that horrible position for all time. Forced to kneel forever." His voice lowered even further, barely even audible. Then as if looking at each of them and none of them all at once, he lay bare his soul. "My master, my best friend, he died right there. My God, he… he died right before my eyes."

Breanne thought of the way they had found the Templar Knight crouched on the altar, his shield raised. Everything this man said aligned with what she had seen.

Tears fell onto the blue mat of the dojo as the group tried to fight them back.

Pulling in a shaky breath, Mr. B's shoulders slumped as he exhaled. Then, picking up his head, he smiled weakly. "After freeing his wife and child from the flames, I arrived only in time to pull the two Templars out before they were killed. One of the Templars had been nearly burned to death and the other was partially crushed by a collapsing beam trying to save Hugues. Next, I managed to pull Hugues's frozen body out before the fire consumed him… but he was already gone."

"And Apep?" Lenny managed.

"I… I don't know. He was gone."

"And the God Stones?" Pete asked.

"Safe." Mr. B gave a snort void of humor. "Apep was never even close to getting to them."

Again, silence.

Mr. B pulled himself back to the present and looked directly down at the young man sitting before him. "You ask what this has to do with you, Garrett, and I will tell you now. But be warned – this will not be easy for you to hear."

Garrett raised his eyes to meet Mr. B's.

"Hugues had another name… his true name. That name was Turek."

Garrett stared up at him, then rubbed a hand over his recently cut hair in confusion. "But I don't understand – that's my last name?"

"It is." Mr. B nodded.

"But I'm adopted… that's my *stepfather's* name," Garrett said.

The ancient man knelt down before Garrett and placed his hands atop his shoulders. "No, your adopted name *is* your true name, and what you thought was your real birth name was a fake, given to you to protect you from Apep until the time was right. You see, the bloodline of Turek runs through your mother's side, not your father. What happened to him, became of him, well, it's of no matter. You are the one Turek prophesied. It is you who will lead the new sages into battle."

For a silent moment, no one even dared to breathe as all eyes were on Garrett.

The large man in the worn black dobok stood regarding him with a solemn expression. It was obvious to Breanne he had just unloaded a burden he had carried for so long.

Breanne realized she was still holding Garrett's hand in hers. She squeezed.

Garrett blinked in disbelief, unable to speak. He felt his hand being squeezed, looked down, and realized Breanne's hand was in his. He blinked again and swallowed hard. What did he mean, that it didn't matter what had happened to his father? He knew what had become of his father. The bastard drank himself to death. His mind reeled with questions, but he couldn't think about that now. There was too much else to process. *Leading sages into... did he say into battle?* His emotions spun wildly as he tried to digest the words. For some reason, he felt embarrassment, like he had done something wrong, but as quickly as the embarrassment came it passed – into anger.

That's when he noticed everyone was looking at him. His face flushed and that made him feel even more pissed. He had to do something. He let go of Breanne's hand and leapt to his feet, finally finding his words.

"You're insane!" he shouted and, not knowing what to do next, he abruptly turned to leave. "This isn't real. None of this is real! How could it be? It doesn't even make any sense! I'm out."

His instincts told him to go, run away, get away from this craziness that couldn't be happening. He needed to go. He spun on his heels and faced Mr. B. "This is some Keepers of the Light trick. Maybe the way you tricked Lincoln before killing him for whatever's in that temple. Why don't you admit that's what this is really all about. You just want to trick us to get the journal and get inside that temple!"

Garrett huffed. He knew that didn't feel... right, but he was committed now. He didn't want to go, but you can't get pissed, make a scene, and then just change your mind. He spun again, showing Mr. B his back as he took a reluctant step towards the locker room.

Lenny stood, confused but ready to follow his friend.

"You're right, Garrett," Mr. B admitted, spreading his hands open before him. "I'm a Keeper of the Light. You wanted to know what this has to do with you – now you know. No more secrets. Isn't that what you wanted? To know?"

"Wait," Lenny said, raising a hand, "you're saying Garrett is the descendant of this sage guy. The most powerful wizard ever to walk the planet?"

"Sage," David corrected.

"Wizard, sage – whatever," Lenny said.

"Yes," Mr. B said. "Garrett is the descendant of Turek, who was, I guess you could say, the most powerful *human* wizard to ever walk the planet."

Everyone stared at Garrett in awe, as if they expected him to perform an illusion or something. This wasn't right. It wasn't real – it couldn't be. Even if it was it couldn't be him. If he were this... this great wizard guy's descendent he wouldn't feel so... so afraid. Would he? He was just a kid. Just a kid from a little town. It had to be a mistake.

"So, since you just admitted you're a Keeper of the Light, you want to tell us why you killed Lincoln?" Pete asked. "He was our sixteenth president and he freed the slaves, you dick!"

Mouths hung agape. Garrett turned to Pete who shrugged, seemingly surprised himself at what had come out of his mouth.

"No, Peter. That's not what happened," Mr. B said solemnly. "Lincoln knew something Apep didn't. He knew the location of the temple. Apep got to him somehow, probably disguised as a friend. He must have fooled him into believing the Keepers were an affiliate of the Masons. Lincoln planned to give that journal to Apep, but then for some reason didn't. The next thing you know Lincoln was assassinated."

Pete pondered this a moment. "So, what you're saying is that Lincoln was actually unknowingly writing the journal for Apep, but when the plan failed Apep just had him killed?"

"Yes," he said. "That's precisely what I'm saying. We think Lincoln discovered Apep was trying to fool him into showing him the location of the temple, but Lincoln figured it out and planned to tell the world instead. You must remember Apep hadn't discovered where the stones were, and he couldn't risk the world finding out about the temple before he was ready, so he cut his losses and had Lincoln killed."

Pete nodded slowly.

"Why does Apep need to get into the temple?" Breanne asked.

"Yeah, tell them what's in there, Mr. B," Pete said knowingly.

Mr. B nodded. "I told you there were seven old ones and that Turek and his sages put them down one at a time, casting them into a deep sleep and imprisoning them beneath the ground."

"Our temple is a prison for one of the old ones," Pete said.

"And that's what Lincoln saw in that temple – what he was going to tell the world about – one of these old ones?" David asked, his tone more of an announcement than a question.

"But you are a Keeper of the Light," Janis said accusingly. "You just said so yourself."

The Secret Journal

Garrett turned back to face Mr. B, crossed his arms, and waited for the explanation.

Mr. B looked at them and nodded. "I am a Keeper of the Light just as all of you are Keepers of the Light."

They looked at each other in confusion.

Then Mr. B turned to Garrett. "But not you," he pointed. "Not you."

"Then what... what am I?" Garrett asked, terrified to hear the answer.

"You *are* the Light."

"What's that supposed to mean?" Garrett demanded.

"I founded the Keepers after the death of Hugues, though now we can call him by his true name, Turek. The Keepers were tasked with protecting the Light—"

"What you're saying makes no sense," Garrett interrupted. "Why in the world would my stepdad adopt me and give me my supposedly true name? Wouldn't that allow this Apep guy to find me? It doesn't make sense!"

"It does, Garrett. You see, we decided back when Keeper Phillip adopted you that there would be no more hiding who you are. We believe in Turek's prophecy – therefore, we know not to fear you having his name. As cliché as this sounds, you are the chosen one and despite all of our past efforts Apep has the God Stones. The prophecy is unfolding just as Turek said it would. So, you see, we decided what will be will be, because we believe prophecy is prophecy."

No. No way. He didn't want to believe it. *My family... is in on this?* He had to know. He had to know for sure. He had to hear it. "We? You're saying my parents are in on this? My... my mother?"

"Yes," Mr. B said. "All the late-night training, Garrett. The bug-outs, the primitive survival training, geography, astrology – it was all to prepare you."

"Wait. That's why you asked me about chores, Garrett?" Pete asked.

"This can't be happening," Garrett said.

"It is happening," Mr. B said. "Your whole life has been about this moment and the moments to come."

Garrett's knees felt weak, and suddenly he felt sick. "And what in the hell are you even talking about? We can't fight some magic guy. I can't even fight some bully from school!" he shouted.

Lenny's head drew back as his eyes widened.

"Listen to me," Mr. B said. "You and Lenny have been training for this your whole childhood. The whole reason I am here is to protect you, teach you, train you, prepare you. And not only me but other Keepers too. So many Garrett. So many are committed to this cause. You are the Light we protect. You are the one who will lead the new world against Apep."

The old master pointed towards the group, gazing at each one of them in turn. "You have chosen your six sages to begin the journey, Apep has the stones, and *you are ready!*"

"And *you are crazy!*" Garrett responded, flailing his arms wildly. "No one is going to follow me to fight some magic guy trying to burn down the earth. The only thing this will do is get a bunch of kids killed! Now you're telling me my whole life has been a lie? Even my parents are in on it? I'm just supposed to buy in, huh? And all these guys are just supposed to... to what? Just go along with it and..."

As Garrett ranted, the craziest thing he could have expected to happen, happened. One by one, each of the six stood. Lenny was the first to stand and approach his friend. He took up position next to Garrett and placed a hand on his shoulder.

"...and I'll tell you something else too. If you think—" Garrett stopped. His eyes knitted together as he looked at

Lenny's hand, then slowly raised his gaze to his friend's eyes.

"I would follow you into fire, bro – any day of the week," Lenny said, giving his shoulder a reassuring squeeze.

Garrett stared blankly at him, dumbfounded. Then he turned back to Mr. B. "If you think—" But then he stopped again. Breanne had stood, too, taking up position on his other side.

She took his hand in hers. "I have been in the fire with you, Garrett, and you have already shielded me from flames. I know this is where I am supposed to be, and I'll follow you into the fire again and again if that's what it takes to make this right and save my dad."

Paul stood next, walked over to Garrett, and gave him a sharp nod. "I am here to protect my sister and find a way to help our pops. Sounds to me like you're the key to this, kid." He turned and faced Mr. B, taking a place next to his sister.

Pete stood next.

Garrett swallowed. "No, come on. This can't..." His voice was weak, barely a whisper.

"I've followed you since I was a little kid," Pete said. "Besides, you need me or you'll just get yourself into a mess." He smiled and took up position by Lenny.

Tears threatened to spill down Garrett's face as he fought to blink them back.

Janis stood and approached. She smiled shyly. "Listen, Garrett, you trusted me and you trusted Pete to bring me in. I don't much like fire, but I trust you – I'm totally in."

"You've all gone mad!" he choked out.

Finally, David stood. He stepped over to Garrett and looked up at him, pursing his lips as he rubbed thoughtfully at his scruffy face. "I haven't said much through this... well, whatever this was. Mostly I've just been trying to figure out if what I was seeing and hearing was real. We've been friends a long time, and I have always looked to you as a leader, but Garrett, I can tell you want to run away right now. I don't blame you because it sounds like shit's about to get very real very fast. I'll follow you, man, even into fire or whatever, and I'll do it because I believe you will lead us out the other side. Also, this is just plain cool as shit! But for this to work you need to believe in yourself, man, and well, to do that you need to believe, well, in all of it. Mostly, though, you need to believe in us."

Garrett just stood there for a long moment, unable to speak – afraid his emotions would betray him if he dared try. When he finally could muster some words, he looked at them and said, "And you guys believe this?"

They all nodded in unison.

Garrett shook his head. "You're all crazy, you know that?" He turned to Mr. B and rubbed both palms down his face, drawing in a deep breath. "Okay, Mr. B. What happens now?"

Epilogue: Jack

Wednesday, April 6th, 6:22 p.m.
Day One
Petersburg, Illinois

If Garrett thinks he's gonna get away with weaseling out of our fight, he's wrong... dead wrong. Ain't no way he's gonna get away with giving me a fake book either, Jack thought, rounding the corner of the arcade. He had looked like a damned idiot when he tried to sell that thing at the Petersburg Antique Mall. They even threatened to call the police.

He paused. Down the street he noticed Pete frantically pounding on the door to the karate place. David and that new girl were with him. *What was her name?* He watched as the fat karate guy opened the door. Then he noticed those two blacks crossing the street, the ones who had been looking for Garrett earlier.

The way he figured it, they had to come out sometime and when they did, he would be waiting. He made his way to the empty parking lot across the street where the blacks had parked their car. He sat down on the hood of the rental and watched. As the minutes passed, the sun sank low in the sky. Jack leaned forward as a shadowed figure approached from down the street. A dark duster flapped behind him. The figure's face was completely cloaked with a hood.

Most of the stores were closed by now, and only one car was parked on the street. Mr. Douglas came out of Double D's Dollar Store just as the figure was passing. He turned his back to the figure, slid a key into the deadbolt, and locked the door.

The dark figure stopped.

Mr. Douglas turned around and looked at the cloaked man. He froze. Even from across the street, Jack could see his eyes go wide in terror.

The figure stepped towards him and pointed.

What the fuck? It looked like smoke or... something... something thick and grey was coming from the figure's hand. The smoke wrapped around Mr. Douglas's head, and he started clawing at his face. Jack leapt to his feet but he stayed put. A second later Mr. Douglas fell forward and landed face-first on the sidewalk. He didn't move.

The cloaked figure continued to move down the street, stopping at the karate place. *What the hell is going on?* The figure tried the door handle, tried again, and when that didn't work, a blue glow began to radiate from in front of him. Jack stepped forward cautiously.

The figure had his back to Jack and whatever was causing the weird glow was hidden. The door began to push in. No, not push exactly, but stretch? Jack rubbed his eyes, not believing what he was seeing. The door flexed further and further, beyond possibility. The light became brighter and brighter until he could no longer see the door at all.

Jack eased forward to the edge of the street.

The door exploded inward with an echoing boom that

cracked across the evening sky, taking the doorframe and a chunk of the wall in with it! Jack ducked down, pulling his arms up. The cloaked man stepped through the opening and vanished inside. Lowering his arms, Jack looked to the right and then to the left. Mr. Douglas still lay sprawled on the sidewalk. A dark pool was forming under him.

Jack swallowed hard and walked to the edge of the street, hesitant to cross. Peering beyond the street and through the hole where the door once stood, he could still see the strange light, but it was different somehow. Jack stepped off the sidewalk and into the street. Suddenly, his head began to ache. He took another step and the ache became a pain. He stopped. The pain was unbearable. He threw his hands over his ears and worked his jaw back and forth until, without warning, he puked right there in the street. Staggering backward, Jack tripped over the curb and landed hard on his ass. He opened his eyes, realizing he had passed out. The pain slowly subsided as the nausea passed. *What was that?* Jack thought, gasping for air. *What the hell was that?*

Jack looked back through the jagged opening and blinked twice. Flames, strange and wrong, poured out of the opening.

Acknowledgments

First and foremost, I want to thank my wife for her patience and honesty. I want to thank her for asking questions and for helping me find the answers to mine. Mostly I want to thank her for allowing me to read her the same chapter over, and over, and over. And every time you truly listened. Thank you, my love.

I want to thank my editing team. Specifically, Kristen Tate at the Blue Garret. She made the editing process fun, and I learned so much that I can carry forward. This is my first novel, and I would not be exaggerating to say stepping into this world felt like stepping into a bottomless abyss. Kristen was more than an editor – she was a guide, patiently answering all my questions, not just about editing, but about the process of publishing in its entirety. Thank you for the thousand answered questions, Kristen.

Lastly, a special thanks to my friends who read the early drafts, for the conversations on long Saturday trail runs and over lunch at work. Thank you for getting excited with me.

Otto Schafer, October 2019

About the Author

Otto Schafer grew up exploring the small historic town in central Illinois featured in his first work of fiction, *The Secret Journal*. If you visit Petersburg, Illinois you may find locations familiar from the book. You may even discover, as Otto did, that history has left behind cleverly hidden traces of magic, whispered secrets, and untold treasures.

Like many of you, Otto Schafer always wanted to write though, occupied with raising a family and building a successful career, he struggled to find the time. But the stories refused to rest, springing into his mind as he ran the forested trails of Illinois and invading his dreams at night, until finally he began writing them down.

Otto is currently working on the second book in the *God Stones* series. He and his loving wife reside in a quiet log cabin tucked away in the woods. You can often find him sitting out back by the koi pond, whittling words into stories for his readers.

Sign Up to Read More

Garrett and Breanne are just beginning their adventure. If you want to see what happens next please sign up here and I will be sure and keep you abreast on how the next book is progressing as well as other projects I am working on. Just click here to sign up or go to my website: www.ottoschafer.com.

If you enjoyed this book, I'd love to hear from you and hope that you could take some time to post a review on Amazon. Your feedback and support will help this author continue to create future works for your enjoyment. I want you, the reader, to know that your review is very important and so, if you'd like to leave a review, just go to my author page on Amazon. I wish you all the best and thanks again.

Check out my website and blog here: www.ottoschafer.com

Connect with me on social:

Instagram – www.instagram.com/ottoschaferwriter

Facebook – www.facebook.com/ottoschaferauthor